Poison

A NOVEL

BETSY BRANNON GREEN

Covenant Communications, Inc.

Cover photograph by Mark Andersen © 2005 Rubberball Productions/Getty Images, Inc.
Cover design by Jessica A. Warner, copyrighted 2005 by Covenant Communications, Inc.

Published by Covenant Communications, Inc.
American Fork, Utah

Printed in United States of America
First Printing: October 2005

11 10 09 08 07 06 05   10 9 8 7 6 5 4 3 2 1

ISBN 1-59811-037-3

For Emily—
my precious angel

Acknowledgments

My name is the only one that appears on the front cover, but this book is not a reflection of my efforts alone. I am particularly grateful to my editor, Peter Jasinski. He always goes the second mile (and often the third and fourth) in my behalf. I'm also thankful for my association with Shauna Humphreys, who until recently was Covenant's managing editor and who will forever be my friend. She is proof positive that you can do a thousand things at once and do them all well. I'm really going to miss them both. I'm grateful to the many talented people at Covenant—a company that provides authors like me with the opportunity to write and LDS readers with a wide variety of quality fiction to read.

The greatest blessing in my life is my husband and the beautiful children who were entrusted to our care. They love and sustain and support and encourage me not only in my efforts to write, but also throughout the trials of life. They are the finest people I know, and I'm honored that I've been given the privilege to work out my salvation with them.

And finally thanks to all the folks who buy my books and read them and tell others about them. You make the sleepless nights and sore fingers worthwhile!

CHAPTER 1

Mila Edwards made a final notation in the case file she had been working on for the past hour, then put it in the drawer of her desk at the Alapai district station of the Honolulu Police Department. She stood and smoothed her skirt automatically and checked her watch. Her long-awaited vacation was about to start. With a smile, she fished her cell phone out of her two-year-old Prada handbag and called her fiancé, Quin, at the surfboard store he owned and operated.

"Surf Shop," he answered after two rings.

"Hey," she greeted. "I'm about finished here and thought I might bring you lunch at the shop."

"Lunch sounds great," he responded. "But I'm headed to the bungalow to finish painting so could you bring it there?"

Mila smiled in anticipation. "I'll see you soon."

She was closing her phone when her partner, Jerry Hirasuna, a native of the island, poked his head around the opening between partitions that served as a door to her cubicle. "Bad news, Mila," he informed her with a smile. It was impossible to determine the seriousness of any situation from Jerry's demeanor because he was always cheerful.

"How bad?"

"A wino has been found dead in an alley near Kuhio Avenue and they want us to take a look at the crime scene."

Mila didn't even try to hide her irritation. "Since when does a wino in an alley qualify as an actual *crime scene*? And why do they need a pair of detectives? Can't the uniforms assigned to the beat ask all the necessary questions?"

Jerry shrugged. "The chief said one of the victim's friends is claiming that the guy was murdered. He figures if he sends us in it will appease the guy, and it won't take more than a few minutes."

"My vacation starts in one hour," she reminded him.

He gave her a grin. "We'll be done in half that time."

Ten minutes later Mila was standing in an alley behind an Indonesian restaurant, trying to breathe through her mouth. She wasn't sure which was contributing most to the stench: the body on the ground, the overflowing dumpster to her left, or the dead man's friend who was earnestly trying to convince them that the deceased did not die of natural causes.

"He was as healthy as any of us," the scrawny young man with bright yellow hair and terrible acne proclaimed. "And he's got rights just like the rich folks. You got to investigate."

Mila opened her mouth to dispute this, but Jerry spoke first—employing his limitless Hawaiian patience. "We will certainly investigate this situation, but we don't have much to go on, and you fellows are going to have to help us out."

"Of course we'll help you," the boy said. "We're law-abiding citizens." He waved his hand to include two other derelicts standing a few feet behind him.

Law-abiding citizens, Mila thought to herself. She'd be willing to bet that each of them had a rap sheet as long as her arm.

Jerry, however, seemed to accept the boy's claim of civic responsibility. "Okay, for starters, what's this guy's name?" Jerry gestured toward the corpse.

"We all call him the Gent," the blond youngster provided, obviously anxious to show his willingness to cooperate. "Because of the fancy way he talked and his nice manners."

"In order to identify him we'll need his *real* name," Mila said.

The boy scratched his scalp, and Mila took a step back. "Don't know that. We all just go by street names. Mine's Spike."

The boy had an assortment of cowlicks that caused his hair to stick out from his head at odd angles, and Mila guessed that this was the inspiration for his nickname.

"This is Wiregrass." Spike pointed to each of the men behind him in turn. "And this is Tarzan."

Mila studied the others for a few seconds but couldn't determine the reasons for their names and finally decided that she probably didn't want to know. "Without a name, we can't open an investigation," she told them.

"When they do the autopsy they can take his fingerprints and identify him that way," Spike said. "They do it all the time on *CSI*."

"Well, this isn't television, and we don't do an autopsy on every body that turns up," Jerry informed him. This wasn't exactly a lie, but close. All bodies found dead in alleys definitely qualified for an autopsy. However, Mila didn't contradict her partner. "Autopsies are expensive," Jerry was continuing. "We have to have some kind of reason to believe that the Gent died under less than natural circumstances in order to justify the cost."

Spike looked at his comrades, and after a silent consultation, he nodded. "Okay." He walked over to the dumpster and returned with an empty wine bottle. He handed it to Jerry and said, "We found that in the dumpster this morning. It wasn't there last night."

Mila was about to ask how they could possibly know that the bottle was a recent deposit, but then she realized that they probably checked the dumpster and its contents regularly.

Spike pointed at the wine bottle. "And that ain't the Gent's regular brand neither."

Mila didn't know anything about wine, so she looked to Jerry.

"It's pretty fancy stuff," he told her softly. "Expensive."

Mila frowned. "Rare enough to trace?"

"Maybe." Jerry addressed Spike. "What kind of wine did the Gent normally drink?"

"The Gent was partial to Two-Buck Chuck—he said it was cheap and potent," Spike said. "I never seen him drinking this stuff before. And he never would have put the bottle in the dumpster, even if he was able after he drank the whole thing."

"Why not?" Mila asked.

The boy looked at her like she was crazy. "A bottle like this could get you ten bucks if you take it to the right place!"

Reluctantly, Mila took out her notebook and started writing down information. "So you think someone else gave him the wine?"

Spike nodded his head vigorously. "And it must have had poison in it. They got him to drink it. Then they threw the bottle in the dumpster because they didn't need the ten bucks."

Mila felt a grudging respect for the boy. He wasn't dumb, and he obviously cared for the dead man. She had no reason to believe him, but she did. "If what you say is true, it would have been smarter for the murderer to take the bottle with them."

"If they got caught with that bottle it could put them in the slammer!" Spike pointed out. "The best thing is to put it in this dumpster. Chances are nobody was even going to find it, but as long as they didn't leave no prints on the bottle—they'd be in the clear either way." The boy looked down at the man on the ground. "With the Gent here dead as can be."

"That's a pretty weak theory," Jerry said. "Give me something else."

Spike made a face, and Mila wondered how much he was holding out on them. "This isn't where the Gent is supposed to be."

"What do you mean?" Jerry asked.

"The Gent wouldn't never have come into this alley of his own free will."

Mila looked up from her notebook. "Why not?"

"We're organized into kind of territories," Spike explained. "This here is Tarzan's alley."

Mila glanced back at the thin man who didn't resemble the king of the jungle in any way. "Where was the Gent's territory?"

"He liked to work the business district uptown," Spike explained. "Don't know why. Poor people are more generous." He looked up at Mila with a puzzled expression. "Ain't that crazy?"

Mila didn't have an explanation, so she just stared back.

Finally Jerry said, "So, the Gent panhandled to support his addiction to alcohol, and the area he preferred to work in was north of here?"

"Not preferred," Spike corrected. "He wouldn't work nowhere else."

"Because anywhere else would have been in another person's territory," Mila guessed, and Spike rewarded her with a crooked-toothed smile.

"Right."

"Maybe he made an exception last night and worked here," Jerry suggested.

Spike shook his head. "No way. The Gent was too polite, and besides, if he'd been working here, Tarzan would have seen him."

Mila felt a headache beginning to form and rubbed her temples. "So what is your explanation for the Gent's presence here in Tarzan's alley?"

The boy waved for them to follow him around to the dead man's feet. "I've seen a lot of folks fall asleep after they've had too much to drink, but I ain't never seen nobody do it like that."

Mila looked at the position of the Gent's body. He was lying on his back with both arms flung out. "A curled up, near-fetal position would be more logical," she murmured to Jerry, and he nodded.

"And look at the backs of his shoes," Spike continued. "He didn't have those scratches before last night."

Mila watched as Jerry squatted down to examine the shoes.

"The body was dragged across this gravel for a couple of feet." Jerry stood up and asked Spike, "Why would anyone want the Gent to die?"

Spike hung his head in dejection. "I ain't figured that out yet."

Mila and Jerry exchanged a glance, then he said, "We'll order an autopsy and see what it turns up. If the tests show any signs of poison, then we'll get you to show us the area where the Gent usually worked. How can we reach you?"

The boy shrugged. "I ain't got no phone number. Give me your card, and I'll call you." Mila watched Jerry produce a business card and decided to give Spike one of hers as well. The boy took them both, then he turned and walked away, followed closely by his companions.

"So, what do you make of that?" Jerry asked once they were alone.

"I think the dead man was given the wine in the location where he normally panhandles and then brought here, just like Spike suggested."

"Do you believe that the wine was poisoned?"

"Probably," Mila confirmed. "And he was either already dead or unconscious by the time they arrived here, so the murderer had to drag him into the alley."

"And the murderer didn't realize that this territory belonged to Tarzan," Jerry added with a smile.

"Exactly," Mila agreed. "Of course, under normal circumstances it wouldn't have mattered because none of the other winos would have risked talking to the police."

"So the Gent was special."

Mila nodded. "To Spike anyway."

"It's going to be very hard to prove any of this," Jerry warned.

Mila sighed. "Great. Why couldn't this just be a simple case of death by self-neglect?"

Jerry smiled. "We won't jump to any more conclusions until we get the autopsy report."

"I won't be jumping to any conclusions ever," Mila told him as a team from the Medical Examiner's office entered the alley. "I'm going on vacation."

"Then why did you give the kid your card?"

Mila shrugged. "A moment of weakness." She turned and headed for the street. "I'll leave the car at the station. I'm sure these guys won't mind taking you back to the station once you're all finished here."

Jerry made a face at the prospect of riding in the coroner's van, and Mila was laughing as she climbed into their unmarked car.

After a quick stop at the station to change cars and an even quicker stop at Subway to get Quin a sandwich, she rolled down her window and headed toward Makai, the estate where she and Quin would soon be living as husband and wife. Mila propped an elbow on the open window and thought about how perfect her life was at the moment. She was living in the most beautiful place on earth, preparing to marry the world's most wonderful man. She was taking night classes—working toward a degree in social work—and in the meantime, she had a good job at the Honolulu Police Department. Quin's surfboard business was doing well, and one of his best customers had offered them a bungalow on his estate for a rent so low Mila almost felt guilty about accepting. Almost.

Mila took a deep breath of flower-scented air and savored the feel of the warm wind against her cheeks. It just didn't get better than this. She slowed her car as she reached the entrance to Makai and drove carefully through the open gate. Following the narrow, winding driveway, she passed the huge mansion house to the last of three identical bungalows. Then she parked her car beside Quin's old Nissan truck and hurried toward her future home.

Mila walked into the bungalow and found Quin in what would soon be their bedroom. Intent on his task, he didn't hear her approach.

He was wearing a paint-splattered T-shirt, and the muscles in his well-tanned arms flexed as he pushed the roller up the wall. She leaned against the doorframe and indulged herself by watching him work. After a few seconds, Quin seemed to sense her presence. He turned, and when he saw her a big smile spread across his face. He put the paint roller down and crossed the room to kiss her—careful not to get any paint on her suit.

"You look beautiful," he said.

Before Quin came into her life, Mila would have been suspicious of such an extravagant compliment, but she knew that he was completely sincere. Even though her auburn hair was windblown and her clothes wrinkled, to him she really was beautiful. She tousled his short, dark hair. "You don't look too bad yourself."

He used a finger to tilt her chin upward then he kissed her again. When he finally pulled away she felt breathless and a little disoriented.

"Didn't you say you were bringing lunch?" he asked.

"Lunch?" she repeated, still staring at him. Then she shook her head to clear it. "Oh, yes, I brought you a sandwich." She held up the Subway bag.

"You're not hungry?"

She grimaced. "Not anymore. Jerry and I just got finished conducting an interview near a dumpster full of putrid food."

He laughed as he took the bag from her hand. "I can see how that might affect your appetite." He extracted the sandwich and took a big bite. "I hate to waste time that I could be painting," he said around a mouthful of turkey on wheat bread, "but I'm starving."

She studied the walls that were half garish turquoise and half soothing French vanilla. "Maybe we could leave it like this and call it modern art-deco."

He took a swig from a bottle of water on the nightstand then leaned down and touched her nose with his. "Or maybe I could just finish painting."

Overwhelmed with feelings of tenderness toward him, she wrapped her arms tightly around his neck, oblivious of any potential damage to her clothing. "I love you," she whispered intensely. Then they heard a knock on the open front door.

"Quin? Mila?" The voice of their landlady, Raquel Simon, floated toward them.

Mila let her arms fall to her side, and Quin gave her a regretful smile before calling, "We're back here."

A moment later, Raquel stepped into the small room wearing a gorgeous Albert Nipon suit with a bias-cut aqua skirt and a waist-length white cardigan. The detailing around the sweater was understated yet feminine and the buttons were made in the shape of little flowers . . . Realizing that she was staring, Mila forced herself to look away from the suit that she knew was well out of her price range.

Raquel had been a television actress during the 80s and now hosted the cooking segment on a local morning show. Judging from the expensive suit and heavy makeup Raquel was wearing, Mila guessed the woman had come straight from work.

"I hope I'm not interrupting anything," Raquel said as she glanced around.

"Not a thing," said Mila.

Quin walked over and picked up the paint roller. "I'm just finishing up the painting, and Mila brought me lunch."

Raquel smiled. "I'm sure you'd rather be alone so I won't stay long, but I know your family and friends begin arriving today." She gestured toward the window with one of her manicured hands. "The other two bungalows are available, and we have plenty of empty guestrooms in the house so there's no need for anyone to stay at a hotel."

Mila was surprised by this very generous offer. Although her relationship with Raquel was friendly, they were not close. In fact, they had only met a couple of months before when she and Quin were searching for an affordable place to live once they were married. Raquel's husband, Cade, overheard them discussing their bleak options and offered them one of the bungalows on the estate he shared with Raquel.

Quin cleared his throat, and Mila realized that Raquel was waiting for a response. "Oh, I'm sorry," Mila apologized. "The wedding has me a little distracted."

"Brides are entitled to a few distracted moments," Raquel said graciously.

When Mila didn't accept on behalf of their family and friends, Quin stepped forward and said, "Thank you very much. I'm sure our guests will accept your offer." He glanced at Mila. "It will be more convenient to have the entire wedding party in one location."

Mila smiled. "Yes, much easier to coordinate activities."

"I'm glad to help." Raquel extended a key ring toward Mila. "These are for the bungalows, and when you're ready to put someone in the guest rooms, just bring them to the house. If I'm not there, Mrs. Rose will get them settled."

Mila accepted the keys. "Thanks."

"And now—the most important reason for my visit." Raquel paused dramatically then continued. "This evening I'm having a little get-together at the main house, and you're all invited—you, your guests, everyone."

"Tonight?" Quin and Mila asked in unison. The schedule for the next few days was carefully coordinated, and any deviation would require tiresome juggling.

"Don't thank me!" Raquel twisted a finger in one of her artfully arranged blonde curls. "It was the least an old married woman could do to help you entertain your wedding guests."

Mila recognized the blatant plea for a compliment but ignored it. Quin had better manners. "You are certainly not old," he told Raquel.

She batted her eyelashes at him. "You're just saying that."

Mila decided to step in before the conversation became nauseating. "We appreciate your offer of dinner, but we already have plans for tonight. We're taking our guests to Aloha Sushi."

Raquel wrinkled her nose in distaste. "You can do that anytime, but tonight might be your only chance to meet several influential local businessmen." Her expression became shrewd. "And you know that having the right contacts can really help a business take off."

Mila sighed. An opportunity to promote the Surf Shop was something they could not afford to refuse. She nodded grimly. "I guess we'll see you tonight then."

Raquel gave Mila's arm a friendly squeeze. "Wonderful. Come about seven o'clock." She took a step toward the door, then paused and added, "Since we're trying to promote Quin's business—dress to impress!"

Mila waited until she was sure Raquel was gone before she said, "That woman thinks the entire world revolves around her."

Quin laughed. "Yes, I guess she does. But looking nice tonight won't be a problem for you."

Mila narrowed her eyes at him. "So, now you're resorting to flattery."

He laughed again. "I'm not above flattery, but it's true. You have all kinds of impressive outfits."

Mila couldn't argue with his statement. Investment in the Surf Shop had required her to curb her clothes-buying habits, but she had an extensive wardrobe from her earlier, less responsible days. "I'm sure I can find something appropriate to wear," she told him. "What concerns me is Raquel's lack of respect for our privacy. If she feels free to intrude on our lives continually, this place might not turn out to be such a bargain . . ."

"It's a bargain," Quin disagreed. "If Cade hadn't offered us this bungalow, we'd probably be living in the storage room behind the Surf Shop," he reminded her. "And since there's no kitchen there, we'd have to eat peanut butter and jelly sandwiches for every meal. And since there's only the little employee rest room, we'd have to take spit baths. And since . . ."

Mila held up a hand. "I get it. This place is more than a bargain—it's a miracle."

"And Raquel just invited us to her party to be helpful."

Mila shrugged. "If she really wanted to be helpful, then why didn't she consult us about the date of the party and give us more than a few hours notice?" Mila asked, knowing she sounded petty. "I'd be willing to bet she has an ulterior motive."

"That's your police training talking." Quin crumpled his sandwich paper and tossed it into the garbage can. Then he dipped his roller into the tray of paint. "We'll put in an appearance at Raquel's party, and then we can go on to Aloha Sushi." Quin pushed his roller up the wall. "How are we going to divide our guests in the free accommodations that Raquel is providing?"

Mila considered this. "We can save the first bungalow for your parents when they get here on Friday. The Iversons will need extra room because of their children, so they can have the middle bungalow. When my mother and Terry arrive, they can stay here with me."

"What about Miss Eugenia and her friends?" Quin asked.

"They can use the guestrooms at the main house."

Quin gave her a quizzical look. "Is that a subtle form of revenge against Raquel?"

Mila laughed. "A week with Miss Eugenia will do Raquel a world of good."

"Remind me never to get on your bad side."

She wrapped her arms around him. "Impossible," she whispered into his ear.

"At this rate I'm never going to get this room painted."

Mila stepped back reluctantly. "Since Raquel killed the romance, I guess I might as well go."

Quin shook his head. "Nothing could kill the romance," he told her with sweet sincerity. "But we need to keep it on the back burner for a few more days."

Mila smiled. "I'll try." She glanced at her watch. "I really do need to head to the airport. The folks from Haggerty will be arriving in less than an hour."

"Drive carefully," he requested.

"I will if you'll let me have one more kiss."

He grinned. "It's a deal."

* * *

The landing at the Honolulu Airport was smooth, much to Eugenia's relief. But she and her companions from Haggerty were the last to leave the plane, since Polly insisted on getting the recipe for clam chowder from the woman in the seat beside her. Polly was helping to compile a cookbook that the Haggerty Baptist Church would use as a fund raiser to buy Bibles for the people of India.

"For heaven's sake, Polly," Eugenia said irritably when they were all off the plane. "What was so special about that woman's clam chowder recipe?"

"She is from *Ohio,*" Polly explained as she tucked the recipe card safely inside her purse.

"What makes you think a woman from Ohio knows anything about making clam chowder?" Eugenia asked.

"The title we've chosen for our cookbook is *Dishes from Sea to Shining Sea*," Polly explained. "So, we're hoping to get at least one recipe from each state in the nation. Martha Nell says that will give us broad-based appeal and possibly a niche in the national market."

"And where did Martha Nell come up with that?" Eugenia wanted to know.

"She read it on the Internet," Polly replied.

"It sounds like a good idea to me," Annabelle said. "I bet you'll sell lots of the new cookbooks."

"Oh, I really hope so." Polly paused as her eyes filled with tears. "Because the more profitable the cookbook is—the more Bibles we can buy!"

"I think that's a wonderful goal," Annabelle said.

"Well, from now on, just try to do your statewide collecting on your own time," Eugenia requested.

"Eugenia!" Annabelle's tone was scandalized. "We don't mind waiting a few minutes while Polly collects recipes for the Lord!"

"You might not mind, but you have younger bones," Eugenia replied. Then she turned as the Iversons approached. Mark was carrying two-year-old Charles, and Kate's arms were full of their carry-on luggage. Emily, who was about to turn four, was standing beside Kate. "Do you need me to hold Emily's hand?" Eugenia asked.

Kate shook her head. "No. Emily is big enough to walk by herself."

"Humph," Eugenia said to let them know she disapproved.

"When are we going to go swimming?" Emily asked.

"Soon," Kate promised, but before she could say more, George Ann Simmons stepped between them.

"Thank goodness we're finally on land again!" she proclaimed.

Kate gave George Ann a polite smile. "Did you enjoy your first airplane flight?"

"Not really," George Ann replied with predictable pessimism. "The food was just awful and the magazine selection very limited. I didn't have nearly enough leg room and the pillow was much too small."

"Thank goodness you didn't *pay* for your ticket, or you'd be demanding a refund," Eugenia muttered.

George Ann went on as if Eugenia hadn't spoken. "And I can't believe the travel agent reserved me a seat so far away from the rest of you. I spoke with the stewardess about it, and she said that on our return flight I can request a seating change."

"I wouldn't do that if I were you," Eugenia warned. "They arrange people carefully to be sure the plane is balanced. If you change your seating assignment, the plane could tilt and make us crash."

Mark Iverson raised an eyebrow but didn't comment.

"Oh dear," Polly said, taking a lace handkerchief from the bosom of her muumuu and pressing it to her lips.

Annabelle gave her sister a stern look. "One person changing their seat will not make the plane crash."

"I think you'd better sit where you were assigned, just the same," Eugenia replied. "Now, let's collect our luggage and find Mila. Then we can rent our car and get to the hotel."

"Then are we going to go swimming?" Emily asked again.

"We'll go swimming as soon as we get to the hotel," Kate promised.

"This way to the baggage claim area," Mark said after studying the airport signs.

"I need to use the bathroom," Emily announced.

"Me too," Charles echoed.

"The rest of you go on," Mark suggested. "We'll take the kids to the bathroom and meet you at the baggage claim area."

Eugenia wasn't pleased about separating from the Iversons. "Do you want me to stay and help?" she asked.

"No, we can handle it," Mark replied.

Eugenia took a reluctant step down the hall. "Well, don't take too long. Mila will be waiting for us."

Mark nodded before leading his family toward the rest rooms.

Once the Iversons were gone, Eugenia joined Polly, and they fell into step behind Annabelle and George Ann. "Are we going to get something to eat?" Polly asked. "I'm starving."

"We'll see what Mila has planned and go from there." Eugenia stifled a yawn.

"Are you tired?" Polly inquired.

Eugenia nodded. "I dozed off during the flight, and I can't seem to wake up."

Annabelle smiled. "You *dozed off* before the plane left the runway in Atlanta, and you slept during the entire flight."

Eugenia wanted to dispute this, but as she searched her memory she realized that she didn't remember anything about the flight. "I did?"

"You did," Annabelle confirmed. "But don't worry. I kept the slobber wiped off your chin."

"Slobber, the very idea," Eugenia responded, hoping that Annabelle was kidding.

"I didn't sleep a wink!" George Ann contributed. "I was awake during the entire miserable flight."

"Maybe it was those motion sickness pills you took, Eugenia," Polly said. "The warning label on the box said they can make you drowsy."

"Well, I'll never take them again, I can tell you that!" Eugenia assured them. "Drowsy is one thing, but sleeping for hours sitting upright on a plane in the middle of the day is something else altogether!"

Annabelle laughed. "At least you should be well rested."

Eugenia shook her head. "It wasn't a very restful sleep. In fact, I had a nightmare."

"What was your nightmare about?" Polly asked.

Eugenia frowned trying to remember. "I dreamed that I was about to blow out the candles on my birthday cake."

"It's not your birthday," George Ann informed her.

"I know when my birthday is," Eugenia said, struggling to keep the annoyance from her voice.

"And it's been years since you've let us put candles on your birthday cakes," Annabelle added.

Eugenia shot her sister a stern look. "It was a *dream*. It's not supposed to be accurate."

"What kind of cake was it?" Polly, a food connoisseur, wanted to know.

Eugenia was irritated by the constant interruptions but tried to sound patient when she replied. "It looked like one of those you buy at the deli at the Piggly Wiggly." Then she continued her story. "Anyway, I leaned down to blow out my candles, and maggots started coming out of the cake."

"Maggots!" Polly cried. "How horrible!"

Eugenia nodded. "It was horrible. They were crawling around in the icing, messing up my name and *Happy Birthday*." Eugenia shuddered. "The whole thing was very disturbing, I can tell you."

"I wonder if it means something," Polly mused. "Like a prediction for the future."

Annabelle smiled. "Maybe it means that the kitchen facilities at the Piggly Wiggly are less than sanitary."

"I think it means that you need to watch your diet more carefully," George Ann proposed.

"Are you calling me fat?" Eugenia demanded.

George Ann lifted her chin, exposing her long neck. "No, of course not. I'm just saying that sweets, like cakes from the Piggly Wiggly, are not good for you."

"I'd rather be fat and happy than thin and crabby," Eugenia replied, thinking that George Ann could benefit from some sweetness to balance out all her sourness.

"Maybe it just means that you're getting old," Annabelle suggested.

Eugenia rolled her eyes. "I don't need a dream to tell me that."

Annabelle was warming to the topic. "The cake might represent age, and the maggots mean death."

"Oh, please, let's talk about something else," Polly requested. Then she pointed at a door that led out into a garden area. "Can we go that way?"

Annabelle checked the signs. "It's probably not the fastest route, but it's definitely the most beautiful."

"This way it is," Eugenia said, pushing open the door and stepping into the garden. For a few seconds she was too overcome by the beauty to speak. Finally, she managed to say, "There are flowers here I've never seen before."

Her sister smiled. "You'll see plenty of unusual plant life in Hawaii."

Polly reached out to touch a profusion of red flowers with yellow sprouts in the center. "I just love these."

"They are called Tropical Anthuriums," Annabelle provided knowledgeably.

Eugenia frowned at the display. "I don't particularly care for them. They look like they're sticking their tongue out at me."

Annabelle shook her head. "For heaven's sake."

"Aren't these little huts just precious." Polly said.

"They're miniature pagodas," Annabelle informed them. "You will notice many oriental influences while on the island."

"Can we hurry?" George Ann complained, using her boarding pass as a fan. "It's hot and my feet hurt."

Eugenia scowled in her direction. "Goodness knows we wouldn't want to waste time enjoying the scenery while we're here in Hawaii."

George Ann spotted a door that led back inside and headed that way with determination. "You can enjoy the scenery after we've changed out of our travel clothes."

Eugenia watched George Ann disappear through the door. "If we don't follow her, maybe she'll get lost and we won't have to share our vacation with her."

Annabelle leaned closer to her sister and spoke in hushed tones. "I still can't believe you let George Ann muscle in on this trip."

Eugenia had no defense. "I can't believe it either." George Ann had always been a worthy opponent, but Eugenia was usually able to stay a step ahead. This time George Ann had outmaneuvered her. "I arranged for George Ann to be seated away from the rest of us on the plane. Now if I can just figure out a way to make her sleep in the rental car instead of the hotel room."

Annabelle laughed. "Good luck on that one."

Eugenia squared her shoulders. "I'm determined not to let George Ann spoil things for us. We're in Hawaii and it's beautiful and we are going to have a wonderful time!"

Annabelle looked around the little garden and sighed. "It is beautiful," Annabelle agreed. "Unfortunately it reminds me of Derrick."

Derrick was Annabelle's recipe-collecting, flower-growing, soap-opera-watching husband. They had been to Hawaii twice already during their brief marriage and did almost everything together in a near-sickening display of marital bliss. Derrick had been asked to go on a men-only deep-sea fishing trip, and Annabelle was still mad at him for accepting. Personally Eugenia felt that several days of intense testosterone exposure would do wonders for Derrick. And as an added bonus, his weeklong absence freed Annabelle for the trip to Hawaii.

"It's natural for you to miss Derrick," Eugenia said, hoping that a quick, if insincere, expression of sympathy would forestall further sentimental reminiscences. "But you know they say distance makes the heart grow fonder."

"I don't believe I *could* love Derrick more than I do now."

Eugenia resisted the urge to roll her eyes again. "Miracles happen every day." After taking a deep breath, she motioned for Polly to leave the pagoda she was examining and said to Annabelle, "I guess we'd better catch up with George Ann. Turning her loose on Hawaii would be like unleashing the black plague."

* * *

By the time the ladies arrived at the baggage carousels, the Iversons were already there waiting. "We were starting to get worried about you," Kate said with obvious concern.

"We took the long way," Eugenia explained briefly. "Is our luggage here?"

"Not yet," Mark answered as he transferred Charles from his left arm to his right.

"Well, grab mine when you see it," Eugenia said and sat on a vinyl chair. She searched the large canvas beach bag she was using as a purse several times and finally dumped everything out on an adjacent bench and meticulously sifted through the contents.

"What on earth are you looking for, Eugenia?" Annabelle demanded.

"The travel agent gave me a coupon for a ten percent discount on our rental car, but I can't find it." Eugenia squinted at the baggage carousel as it began its first sluggish rotation. "Maybe I put it in one of my suitcases."

Annabelle shook her head. "You are not going to unpack your luggage in the middle of the Honolulu International Airport just to find a coupon. Go rent the car and I'll pay the 10 percent difference."

Eugenia frowned at her sister. "Why are you always looking for an excuse to throw money away?"

"I don't want to throw money away," Annabelle returned. "But I do want to keep you from making more of a spectacle of yourself than absolutely necessary!"

Before Eugenia could think of a reply, George Ann pointed at a large suitcase and screeched, "That's one of mine! Could someone get it for me?"

Annabelle hurried to the carousel and grabbed the suitcase. Then she hauled it over to the bench where George Ann was sitting with her feet propped up.

"There's another one!" George Ann cried again.

Polly spotted her luggage. "And here's mine!"

Mark put Charles down beside Eugenia and walked to the carousel to collect the luggage. Soon the group was surrounded by suitcases in various shapes and sizes.

Mark retrieved Charles as George Ann asked, "How are we going to get all this to the rental car?"

"I'll handle the luggage," Mark offered.

"It will take forever if we let Mark take them a few at a time," George Ann said, the whine in her voice more pronounced than usual.

"We could each take our own," Annabelle suggested. "Then it wouldn't take long at all."

"I can't carry my own luggage!" George Ann was aghast. "The doctor advised me against lifting anything over ten pounds."

"Don't worry," Eugenia said. "Since Annabelle has money to burn, I'm sure she's planning to hire each one of us a personal valet."

"And what was your plan, Eugenia?" Annabelle wanted to know. "To pile whatever Mark can't carry on my back?"

Polly twisted her handkerchief, looking anxious. "Oh dear," she said. "Maybe Mila will bring her fiancé to help us."

"There's Mila!" George Ann informed them, pointing into the crowd. "And there's no one with her."

Eugenia turned and saw Mila approaching. Impeccable as always, the bride-to-be was wearing a tailored gray linen suit with a black silk blouse. Her auburn hair was a little longer than Eugenia remembered, and she now boasted a tawny tan, but the bright green eyes were the same. Mila's arms were full of flowers, and she looked very happy.

"Welcome!" Mila said. "I've brought each of you a lei."

"What's a lei?" Emily asked.

"It's kind of a flower necklace," Mila explained as she looped one of the smaller leis over the little girl's head. "The Hawaiians give them to guests to make them feel welcome."

Eugenia abandoned her coupon search in order to hug Mila and receive her lei. "Thank you so much." Eugenia ducked her head to smell the sweet fragrance of the flowers.

"I hope I'm not allergic," George Ann said with a worried look.

"I've never worn a necklace before," Mark said as Mila draped a lei around his neck.

"There's a first time for everything," Kate told him with a smile.

"The correct Hawaiian way to present a lei is to give the recipient a kiss," Annabelle said.

Mila laughed. "I'll let Kate finish welcoming her husband."

Kate accepted her own lei and gave Mila a hug. Then she winked at Mark and said, "We'll take care of that later."

As a blush stained Mark's cheeks, Mila changed the subject. "I can't tell you how much I appreciate you coming for the wedding."

"It was our pleasure," Eugenia assured her.

"We wouldn't miss it for the world!" Polly added.

"Eugenia is paying for everything with her reward money for finding a missing woman," George Ann chimed in, earning herself a cross look from Eugenia.

"Yes, well some of us were planning to come even before I solved that case for the state attorney general's office."

Annabelle stepped forward and extended her hand to Mila. "You probably don't remember me, but I'm Eugenia's sister, Annabelle."

Mila shook her head. "I'm sorry. I don't. Didn't someone tell me that you used to work at a bank in Albany?"

"I did," Annabelle confirmed. "I was mostly responsible for new accounts and . . ."

"As much as we'd all like to hear about Annabelle's long and illustrious career handing out car loans," Eugenia interrupted, "I think we need to get to our hotel."

Annabelle shot Eugenia a venomous look, and Mila laughed. "Well, I have some good news for you on that subject. Our landlords have offered everyone free accommodations."

Eugenia raised her eyebrows. "Free?"

"Free," Mila confirmed.

Mark didn't look completely pleased by this prospect. "We don't want to inconvenience anyone," he said. "And we already have reservations at a hotel."

Mila smiled. "There's no inconvenience. Miss Eugenia and the other Haggerty ladies will stay in the guestrooms at the main house, but you and your family will have a separate bungalow right on the beach."

Kate's eyes started to glow at this announcement. "It sounds perfect," she said, forestalling any further objections that Mark may have had.

"The bungalows aren't luxurious," Mila warned. "But they are nice enough, and it will be easier to coordinate activities if everyone stays in the same location."

"I just have ten minutes to cancel the hotel reservations before I get charged for the night," Eugenia said. "Annabelle, do you have that number?"

Annabelle pulled out her cell phone. "I'll take care of it."

As Annabelle walked over to a relatively quiet corner to make her call, Polly patted Mila's arm. "I know you must be so excited about getting married."

"Yes, I am," Mila replied.

"Quin seems to be a wonderful man," Kate added.

"He is," Mila confirmed.

"Speaking of Quin, where is he?" Eugenia asked.

Mila checked her watch. "He should be back at the Surf Shop by now, but our landlady is hosting a dinner party tonight, and we're all invited so you'll see him there."

Kate and Mark exchanged a look. Then she said, "The children have had a long day, and I promised them that we'd go swimming."

Mila nodded. "I understand completely. You take the kids swimming and then put them to bed while we attend the party. If you'd like we can fix you a plate of food and bring it by afterward."

Kate smiled. "We would appreciate that."

"It's very nice of your landlady to invite us to her party," Polly remarked.

"I hope I brought something appropriate to wear," George Ann said. "I wasn't expecting to be invited to a dinner party."

"Since the hostess didn't give us much notice, she can't be too particular about what we wear," Mila replied. "Anything will be fine."

"Is your mother here yet?" Eugenia asked.

Mila shook her head. "No, Quin's parents and my mother and her husband don't arrive until Friday."

Eugenia smiled. "Good. We get you and Quin all to ourselves for a few days."

"Hotel rooms are cancelled," Annabelle informed them as she returned.

"Can we go soon?" George Ann whined. "My feet are throbbing."

While returning the contents of her purse to their proper place, Eugenia came across the coupon. "Found it!" she declared triumphantly. "Now I can get the rental car."

"I'll go with you," Mila volunteered. "We can drive it around to this side door so Mark won't have to carry your luggage very far."

"I'm coming with you," Mark said as he handed Charles to Annabelle. "I've decided to rent a car too."

"That's completely unnecessary," Eugenia told him. "I'll get a van so we can all ride together."

"I appreciate that," Mark said, his tone gentle yet firm. "But with the kids, Kate and I need the flexibility that separate transportation provides."

"So that if we're taking a tour and the kids get tired, everyone won't have to leave," Kate elaborated.

Eugenia was disappointed. "I wanted us to visit the sights together."

"We'll still go to the same places you go," Kate reassured Eugenia. "We'll just be in a separate car."

Eugenia wasn't happy, but she decided that arguing wouldn't help the situation. "Okay. If that's the way you want it."

Kate nodded. "It is."

"Thank goodness that's settled," George Ann said. "Now, please hurry and get that car. I can't be standing on these throbbing feet all day."

* * *

After the payment arrangements had been taken care of at the Hertz counter, Mila stood with Eugenia and Mark on the sidewalk, waiting for the rental cars to be brought around.

"Is the weather always this nice?" Mark asked conversationally.

"Most of the time," Mila confirmed.

"Hawaii is almost as beautiful as Georgia," Eugenia said. Then she added, "And that's the highest compliment I can give."

Mila nodded. "We love it here." She spoke to Mark. "So, how will the FBI manage without you for a whole week?"

Mark smiled. "I'm sure they'll manage very well."

"Based on the amount of time he spends at his office and away from his family—I'd say that the whole organization will probably fall apart in his absence," Eugenia countered.

Mark ignored this. "So, Miss Eugenia tells us that your surfboard shop is doing well?"

"Business is a little slow," Mila admitted. "But we expected that for the first year or so."

"And you're a detective with the Honolulu Police?" Mark confirmed.

"Yes."

"I thought you wanted to get away from police work," Eugenia said.

"I do," Mila replied. "But until I get my degree in social work I need an income, not to mention insurance benefits. I was lucky to get the job here."

"I'm sure that Chief Monahan in Albany gave you a glowing reference," Eugenia predicted.

"Actually, I think he did," Mila said with a smile. "But mostly just to get rid of me."

Eugenia chuckled at this. "It sounds like you were also lucky to get very nice landlords, since they're letting us stay in their house."

Mila laughed. "The Simons are nice, but *house* is an understatement. Makai is a hundred-year-old estate, and the main residence is a *mansion*." She turned to include Mark. "The original owner entertained on a large scale, and the bungalow you and your family will be staying in is one of three he built for his frequent guests."

Eugenia raised an eyebrow. "So, I gather that the Simons are rich in addition to being nice?"

Mila considered this. "They must be to maintain that huge estate."

"Old money or new?" Eugenia asked.

"I don't know," Mila replied. "Raquel was in a television drama during the 80s called *Class Act,* about a woman who ran a modeling agency. I guess she made some money with that."

Eugenia nodded. "I remember that program. Do you think she'll give me her autograph?"

"Oh, I'm sure she will," Mila said with confidence. "Now she does the cooking segment on the Channel One morning show."

Eugenia frowned. "She must have made her fortune during her younger days since I doubt there's much money in local television."

"No," Mila agreed. "She also does commercials and speaking engagements, but you're right—she can't be making enough to support Makai that way."

"What does the husband do?" Eugenia asked.

Mark looked uncomfortable with the discussion. "That's not any of our business."

Mila smiled. "It's not a secret. Cade has an income tax preparation firm."

Eugenia considered this. "That could be fairly lucrative."

"It could be," Mila agreed, "if he worked at it, but Quin says Cade spends most of his time surfing."

"Maybe he's able to take a lot of time off because his business is doing well," Mark suggested impatiently.

Mila shrugged. "I guess that could be the case."

"Is he a good surfer?" Eugenia asked.

This seemed to amuse Mila. "Quin says no, but he spends a lot of money at the Surf Shop."

Eugenia lifted a shoulder. "Then it doesn't matter."

Mila laughed as a sporty red convertible rounded the corner and came to a stop at the curb in front of them. It was followed closely by a sensible silver Taurus. Mila looked between Mark and Eugenia. "Which one belongs to who?"

Eugenia smiled. "The sports car is mine. Since we won't be needing a van, I figured it was time to live a little."

CHAPTER 2

It took almost thirty minutes for them to find parking spots in front of the airport, collect the other travelers, load their luggage, and retrieve Mila's car from the short-term parking lot. When they finally left the airport, Annabelle offered to ride with Mila to keep her from being alone. "I really don't mind solitude," Mila said as they climbed into her sedan.

"But I really mind being with George Ann," Annabelle responded. "Riding with you will provide me with a much-needed break."

Mila smiled as she led the small caravan out of the parking lot. Miss Eugenia was right behind her in the red sports car, with the Iversons bringing up the rear. After merging onto the Kamehameha Highway, Mila turned to Annabelle and said, "I hope everything won't be this much of a production."

Annabelle smiled. "Then you're a hopeless optimist."

When they reached Makai, Mila circled the property once to give her guests a glimpse of the gorgeous estate. Then she parked in front of the bungalow that the Iversons would be using during their stay. After giving Mark the key, they left the little family to settle in and drove back around to the main house.

"This is incredible!" Annabelle exclaimed when Mila and all the Haggerty ladies were gathered at the bottom of the front steps. "I wish my husband, Derrick, could see it. He loves old houses."

"It is beautiful," Mila agreed as she reached into the trunk of Miss Eugenia's rental car and extracted two suitcases. "Now, let's go inside and get you settled."

Everyone except Miss George Ann picked up a suitcase and followed Mila up the steps. Mila's knock was answered by Mrs. Rose, the housekeeper. She was a plump woman in her late fifties who always looked like she had just received bad news.

"Hello," she greeted without a hint of a smile. "It's Mila, I believe?"

Mila nodded. "Yes, ma'am. Raquel invited some of my guests to stay here in the main house . . ."

"She told me to expect you." Mrs. Rose pulled the door open wide and stepped back to admit them.

"Oh, my," Miss Polly whispered as she took in the real parquet floors, high ceiling and the huge, Victorian-style staircase.

"It's unbelievable," Miss Eugenia added, rubbing a newel post with reverence.

Annabelle was staring at the crystal chandelier that provided light for the room. "It looks just like Manderly from the movie *Rebecca*."

Miss Eugenia turned to Mrs. Rose. "Do you suppose that's what the original owners intended?"

Mrs. Rose did try to smile at the remark, although it looked more like a grimace. "The original owners did their decorating well before any movies were made. But Raquel completely remodeled the place when she moved in, and I think there's a good chance that it was her intention to turn Makai into a Hollywood set."

"Makai," Miss Polly repeated. "Is that a Hawaiian word?"

Mrs. Rose nodded. "Yes. It means 'toward the ocean.' Mr. Solomon, the man who built the place, liked the name and thought it was appropriate since the property has a long stretch of beach."

"We could see the water when we drove up," Miss Eugenia said. "It was like a painting."

"What an incredible luxury to have so much private beach," Annabelle added.

"Yes," Mrs. Rose agreed without enthusiasm. "Now, if you'll follow me, I'll introduce you to your hostess."

Mila was surprised by this. "Raquel is home already?"

Mrs. Rose nodded. "She's in her office."

On their way, they passed a dining room that could probably seat fifty and a parlor crammed with antiques. Mila enjoyed watching the expressions on the faces of the visitors as they saw each new amazing sight. Finally, Mrs. Rose stopped in front of a door, rapped on it twice, then pushed it open. "Your guests are here."

Raquel was sitting behind a dainty writing desk, and she waved them inside. "Thank you, Mrs. Rose," Raquel said in dismissal. "I'll call if we need you."

Mrs. Rose acknowledged this with the smallest nod before exiting the room.

Raquel waited until the housekeeper was gone, then stood and spread her arms wide. "Welcome to Hawaii!"

Mila introduced her guests, and Raquel asked if they'd had a pleasant flight.

"I thought it was fine," Miss Eugenia responded. "But don't ask George Ann's opinion. She always finds something to complain about."

"Well, I never!" Miss George Ann said in obvious annoyance.

Miss Eugenia ignored her friend's reaction and told Raquel, "It's so nice of you to let us stay at your estate."

Raquel waved this aside. "I'm glad to help."

"And I remember you from your days on *Class Act*," Miss Eugenia continued. "In fact, I was hoping I could get your autograph."

"I have some autographed pictures of myself dressed as Lisa Spain, my character on *Class Act,* and I'd be glad to give each of you one," Raquel offered.

"Oh, thank you," Miss Polly breathed. "I've never had the signature of a famous person before."

Raquel smiled tolerantly, but Mila could tell she was pleased. "You are very welcome."

Mila cleared her throat to regain Raquel's attention. "I put the Iversons in the middle bungalow and thought I'd save the first one for Quin's parents. That means that these ladies will be using your guest rooms."

"Whatever is most convenient for you," Raquel replied.

"We sure are lucky that your bungalows weren't rented out," Miss Eugenia commented. "With all that beautiful beach, I'll bet they are in constant demand."

"We've never rented the bungalows," Raquel said, then smiled at Mila. "Until my husband came up with the idea to rent to Quin and Mila."

"Really?" Annabelle seemed surprised.

Raquel shrugged. "We didn't want to sacrifice the privacy, but Cade assured me that if we were careful about whom we rent to, the inconvenience would be minimal."

"Well, I'm glad you made an exception for Mila and Quin," Miss Eugenia said. "I've heard that finding decent and affordable housing on the island is nearly impossible."

"We were desperate," Mila confided. "I had a dorm room at the school, but Quin's sleeping on a friend's couch, and neither situation would work after we get married."

"It must have been divine intervention," Annabelle said with a smile.

"Cade is divine, all right!" Raquel agreed. "Just wait until you meet him."

"Oh my, doesn't this look delicious?" Miss Polly said, pointing at a box on the corner of Raquel's desk. "A chocolate chip cheesecake!"

"From The Cheesecake Company," Miss Eugenia read the label. "A gift from an admirer?"

Raquel laughed. "I guess."

"You don't know who it's from?" Miss Eugenia sounded mildly intrigued.

Raquel shook her blonde curls. "No."

Miss Eugenia lifted the box and examined it carefully. "There's no card."

"I'm constantly receiving little gifts from viewers, and they are often sent anonymously," Raquel told them.

Annabelle fingered the sturdy, red foil-embossed box. "I'll bet this cheesecake cost a fortune."

"I'm sure it did," Mila agreed. "I've seen their stores around the island. They have the look of a Rodeo Drive boutique."

Miss George Ann nodded. "Even just the ingredients for a chocolate chip cheesecake cost a fortune. I have a delicious recipe but I rarely make it because the expense is prohibitive."

"I declare, George Ann," Miss Eugenia said with a look of disgust. "You can easily afford a few packages of cream cheese and some chocolate chips."

Before Miss George Ann could defend herself, Miss Polly stepped forward, licking her lips. "Would it be too rude for me to ask if we can have a piece?"

"Polly!" Annabelle and Miss Eugenia cried in scandalized unison.

"I'm sorry," Polly was instantly contrite. "But we haven't had anything to eat since that little bag of pretzels they gave us just before the plane landed."

"Don't apologize," Raquel said with a smile. "I understand completely, and it does look good, but we wouldn't want to ruin your appetite by giving you a piece now. However, I'll arrange for the caterer to serve the cake at the dinner party this evening."

Miss Polly was obviously disappointed, and Mila heard Miss Eugenia murmur, "Nothing could spoil Polly's appetite for dinner."

Mila was searching for a safe subject when they heard a knock at the door. All heads turned to find Cade Simon standing in the doorway. Considerably younger than his wife, Cade was indeed divine. With dark, curling hair and dreamy, brown eyes, he was almost too beautiful to be true. Since he was wearing swim trunks, the ladies got a close look at his excellent physique, and Mila suppressed a laugh when she heard one of her guests sigh.

He crossed the room and tucked an orchid behind his wife's ear. "I'll put it on the left side so everyone will know you're already taken," he told her in a seductive voice. Then he kissed Raquel passionately, and Mila was afraid the old women were going to need oxygen. Cade was a truly gorgeous male specimen.

Finally, Cade released his wife and turned to Mila. "Are you going to introduce your friends?"

Mila cleared her throat then pointed out each woman in turn. "Cade, this is Miss Eugenia, Miss George Ann, Miss Polly, and Miss Annabelle. They've all come for the wedding. Ladies, meet Cade Simon."

Cade gave them a heart-stopping smile. "Well, aloha!"

Annabelle was the first to recover from the spell that Cade had cast on them all. She turned to her traveling companions and said, "That can mean either hello or good-bye."

Miss Eugenia frowned. "So, now we just have to figure out which way Mr. Simon meant it."

Cade rewarded Miss Eugenia with his undivided attention. "Please, call me Cade, and my *aloha* was definitely a greeting."

"These ladies are staying in our guest rooms," Raquel told him. "And I gave Mila the keys to the extra bungalows for their other visitors."

This was obviously news to Cade, but he didn't seem bothered by the prospect of houseguests. "Well, then, I'll be seeing more of you ladies." He leaned down and gave his wife another kiss. "But now I've got to get into the water for a swim."

"Make it a quick one," Raquel requested. "Our dinner party starts in an hour."

Cade nodded and moved toward the door. "I'll be there."

"Don't be late," Raquel added, almost as if she couldn't help herself.

He winked at his wife then waved to the other ladies. "Aloha! And this time I do mean good-bye!"

* * *

When Cade left the room, Eugenia felt as if he had taken the sunshine with him. Glancing at Raquel, she could tell that Cade's departure had affected her negatively as well. Raquel looked suddenly tired and much older than before. Raquel called Mrs. Rose and asked the housekeeper to show the ladies to their rooms. "I'll see you at the party," she said with a professional smile that didn't reach her eyes. "If you need anything before then, just let Mrs. Rose know."

As the others turned to leave, Eugenia watched Raquel walk to the window and wondered if she were trying to get a glimpse of her husband.

Mila led them all into the hallway then said, "I need to check in with my partner about a new case we just got today, so if it's okay, I'll leave you with Mrs. Rose."

"You go ahead and handle your new case," Miss Eugenia encouraged. "We'll be fine."

Mila seemed reluctant about deserting them. "Do you still have my cell number?"

Annabelle nodded. "I already entered it in my phone, so we can call you if we need you."

"I guess I'll see you at the party," Mila said as she walked off.

After saying good-bye to Mila, the others followed Mrs. Rose upstairs. On the way, the housekeeper said, "Raquel didn't give me much notice about your arrival. I was able to get fresh sheets on the beds and towels in the bathrooms, but the rooms may be dusty."

The sisters exchanged a quick glance, then Eugenia said, "I hope our staying here isn't an inconvenience."

"Because we can certainly go to a hotel," Annabelle added.

"Oh, no," Mrs. Rose replied. "Raquel wouldn't hear of it."

Eugenia noted that Mrs. Rose did not include herself in the emphatic invitation. "We're very pleased about staying here," Eugenia said in what she hoped was a conciliatory tone. "And we'll try not to be any trouble."

"It's my job to see to the needs of houseguests," Mrs. Rose said as they reached the landing on the second floor. "The guest rooms are here and then the more public rooms on the ground floor. Raquel converted the entire third floor into a suite of rooms for herself and Cade."

It seemed like a sensible arrangement to Eugenia, but she could tell Mrs. Rose didn't approve of the changes Raquel had made. "How long have you worked here?" she asked.

"For almost twenty years," Mrs. Rose said grimly, confirming Eugenia's suspicion that the housekeeper's occupancy at Makai had preceded Raquel's. Before Eugenia could question the woman further, they stopped in front of a door. "Here is the first guest room. There are three more, two on each side of the hallway. Help yourselves and let me know if you need anything." Then without further comment, Mrs. Rose turned and descended the stairs.

Polly walked into the first guestroom. "This one faces the ocean. Isn't it beautiful?"

Eugenia crossed to the window and looked down at the beach where Cade Simon was standing. The incoming tide was bubbling around his knees, and he had a surfboard tucked under his left arm. "Breathtaking," she agreed.

George Ann crossed her arms over her thin chest and raised her long neck. "Well, if Polly's taking this room, I want the one next door so I can see the ocean too."

Annabelle shrugged. "That's fine with me. I'm sure the view from the other side of the house is equally gorgeous."

Eugenia smiled. "As long as Cade is allowed to roam freely, I'm sure you're right."

Annabelle and Eugenia followed George Ann back into the hallway, then they separated into their individual rooms. Eugenia's room was very nice and did not seem particularly dusty. She opened the drapes and confirmed that her view was lovely, even if Cade was nowhere in sight. She unpacked her clothes and had just changed into a new outfit when there was a knock on her door. "Come in," she called.

The knob turned, and Annabelle pushed into the room. "I came to see if your room is nicer than mine."

Eugenia had to laugh. "Well, even if you think it is, I'm not trading."

"I see you're ready for the dinner party," Annabelle remarked. "I love that color on you."

Eugenia glanced in the mirror. She had given up trying to look good years before, but the cut of the pantsuit was flattering and the bright pink color did reflect nicely in her cheeks. "I certainly hope you like it, since you picked it out," she told her sister.

Annabelle sat on the end of Eugenia's bed. "Wasn't it generous of Raquel to invite us to stay here?"

"Incredibly generous," Eugenia agreed.

"And Cade is so . . . handsome and romantic." Annabelle sighed. "He reminds me of Derrick."

Eugenia hooted with laughter. "The only thing Derrick and Cade have in common is a Y chromosome."

"I didn't mean their looks," Annabelle replied primly. "I meant how Cade is so sweet and thoughtful. Didn't you just love the way he tucked that flower behind Raquel's ear?"

Eugenia frowned. "Actually that seemed a little odd to me."

"Odd how?"

"Well, like you said, it was a very romantic gesture. So, why did he do it in front of a room full of strangers rather than wait until he and Raquel were alone?"

"Maybe he was afraid the flower would wilt."

Eugenia glanced out the window. "There are plenty more where that one came from. And there *is* a significant age difference between them."

"And that means they can't possibly love each other?" Annabelle snapped.

Eugenia regretted her words. Annabelle was several years older than her own husband and was touchy about the subject. But rather than point out that the difference between sixty and seventy was less significant than the difference between thirty and fifty, she just said, "A man who looks like Cade is bound to attract a lot of female attention, and that would be hard for any wife, but it must be especially difficult for a wife who is several years older."

"Maybe that's why he goes to such lengths to reassure her," Annabelle suggested. "Like with the flower behind the ear in front of company."

"Maybe," Eugenia said, but she didn't agree. "I wonder how Raquel got this house."

Annabelle frowned. "Well, I guess she bought it."

Eugenia shook her head. "No, I don't think so. Mrs. Rose said Raquel changed things when she 'moved in,' which I thought was a strange choice of words. And when you buy a house you don't ordinarily get the housekeeper as part of the deal. I'd be willing to bet that Raquel got this house under something other than conventional means."

"You think she stole it?"

"No. Of course not."

"She won it in a poker game?" Annabelle's tone was dubious.

Eugenia gave her sister an impatient look. "That only happens in the movies. Maybe it was a gift."

"Who gives gifts like this?" Annabelle waved around the room to emphasize her point.

"Maybe the previous owner was elderly," Eugenia proposed—her mind racing. "Raquel befriended him and when he died, he left the property to her."

Annabelle shook her head. "Ridiculous."

"Okay, maybe the previous owner was Raquel's first husband, and she inherited the estate."

Eugenia *expected* Annabelle to disagree. Arguing had been their basic form of communication since childhood. But she was surprised by Annabelle's vehemence when she stood and demanded, "Why can't you just leave it alone!"

"Leave what alone?" Eugenia asked, taken slightly aback.

"Raquel, Cade, this fabulous house," Annabelle itemized. "We're here on *vacation*."

"I know that, but I can't help it if my inquisitive tendencies cause me to notice things and then bring me to certain conclusions . . ."

"You don't have inquisitive tendencies!" Annabelle interrupted. "You're just nosy!"

Eugenia stood a little straighter. "I am employed by Kelsey Pearce, owner of For Your Information, to investigate various situations . . ."

"You've made two phone calls for Kelsey," Annabelle broke in again. "That does *not* qualify you as a private investigator."

"I don't know why you're getting so snippy," Eugenia said. "But in the future, I will keep my observations to myself."

"I'd appreciate that." There was a brief pause, then Annabelle held out her cell phone and asked, "Do you want to call Whit and check on Lady?"

Eugenia really hated cell phones, but her concern for her little dog, Lady, was stronger, so she extended her hand. "Thank you."

She called Whit's office number and after several rings, she murmured to Annabelle, "If Whit had any sense, he'd fire Idella. She's the poorest excuse for a receptionist I've ever seen."

Annabelle stifled a yawn. "That may be true, but you can't blame her for not answering the phone at Whit's office now. It's almost midnight in Haggerty, so Idella has been off duty for hours."

Eugenia disconnected her call, feeling foolish. She had forgotten about the time difference. "No wonder Whit didn't answer at the office!" Eugenia dialed Whit's home number and let it ring twenty times before giving up.

"No answer at home either?" Annabelle asked when Eugenia returned the phone.

Eugenia shook her head. "Where in the world could he be at this time of night?"

"Maybe he's asleep."

"He stays up late." Eugenia frowned in concentration. "Besides, he'd hear the phone and answer it even if he was already in bed. He's a lawyer, after all, and is used to getting important phone calls at all times of the day and night."

"Maybe he's on a hot date," Annabelle said slyly.

"Humph! He's welcome to any hot date that will have him," Eugenia replied, although she didn't really mean it. "I just hope nothing is wrong with Lady."

"If there were a problem with your dog, I'm sure Whit would call us. Now let's go down to the party and eat before Polly starves to death."

* * *

Mila dialed Jerry Hirasuna's cell number as she walked inside her bungalow. She had almost given up when he finally answered.

"So, any autopsy results yet?" she asked.

"I thought you were on vacation," he returned.

"I am." Mila walked into the bathroom and turned on the shower. "I'm just curious."

"You know what curiosity did to the cat," Jerry hedged.

"Come on," Mila pleaded as she adjusted the hot and cold water until she had the perfect combination. "Some day you might need a favor from me."

"It's not even a case, Mila," Jerry reminded her. "It's more of an incident. And like you said at the first—one dead wino isn't breaking anybody's heart."

Mila winced at Jerry's version of her insensitive remark. "Humor me," she requested.

She heard Jerry sigh heavily. "Okay, the autopsy results show signs of malnutrition, an enlarged liver, and stomach ulcers consistent with chronic alcohol abuse. The victim had also aspirated a fair amount of his own vomit, and all of the above, plus a bottle of wine, contributed to his death."

"Did the medical examiner think he had been drugged or poisoned?"

"He couldn't rule it out, so he took some samples. It'll be a few days before he gets the toxicology report back."

"You could try to rush it up," Mila said.

"Yeah, but why should I?"

Mila didn't have an answer, so instead she asked, "What about the fingerprints?"

"They're being run through the computer tonight. We'll have a name in the morning."

"What about Spike?"

"My guess is that he's a runaway from foster care," Jerry hypothesized. "But without prints I can't be sure. We could drag him in and find out."

"I'd rather not alienate him at this stage," Mila said. "I have a feeling about him. I think he's telling us the truth."

"Mila, don't kid yourself. I will guarantee you that Spike is no Boy Scout, and if he's a minor, we have a responsibility to get him to DHR. They can identify him."

"I'll get his prints another way and *if* he's a minor, we'll call in DHR." Mila kicked off her shoes. "You'll let me know as soon as you hear something?"

"I will," Jerry promised. "But I have to say, you have a weird way of going on vacation."

"Good night, Jerry," Mila said, then disconnected the call.

After a quick shower, Mila pulled on a black dress that was elegant enough for a dinner party but comfortable enough for a trip to Aloha Sushi afterward. She dried her hair, brushed her teeth, and had just finished applying her makeup when Quin knocked on the bedroom door.

"Are you decent?" he asked.

"That depends on your definition of *decent,*" Mila replied as she stepped out into the small hallway.

Quin's eyes widened in appreciation when he saw her. "You are more than decent," he assured her. "You're beautiful!"

Mila smiled. "You always say that."

"Only because it's always true." He took her hand and pulled her gently toward the front door.

"Remind me again why we have to go to this party," she requested.

"Because I like to eat, and if we don't sell surfboards, we can't buy groceries."

Mila sighed. "Oh yeah."

"Come on. It won't be that bad."

She gave him a sidelong glance. "That depends on your definition of *bad.*"

As they walked toward the house, Mila noticed that cars were parked along both sides of the driveway. "Didn't Raquel say she was hosting this dinner party for a few local businessmen?"

Quin nodded. "That's what she said."

"Well, it looks like she's invited half of Oahu."

"I guess her definition of *few* is different from ours."

"This is going to be worse than I imagined," Mila muttered.

Quin wrapped an encouraging arm around her. "Look on the bright side. Lots of people will make it easier for us to slip out early."

Mila squared her shoulders as they reached the front steps. "I'll cling to that thought. Now, let's get this over with."

The main doors of the house were flung open wide, and Cade and Raquel were in the entryway, receiving guests. When Raquel saw Mila and Quin she waved them forward and introduced the man standing beside her. "Quin, Mila, this is Hubert Lehman. Hubert, this is the couple that rents one of our bungalows." After everyone shook hands, Raquel continued. "Hubert owns a lot of property on the islands—including a chain of luxury hotels. I told him about the Surf Shop and he wants to talk to you about putting some of your surfboards in his hotel gift shops."

"Sounds interesting," Quin replied.

"Space is at a premium in my gift shops," Hubert Lehman warned. "So, I'd only be able to display a few boards in each location."

Quin frowned. "Surfing isn't a sport for amateurs. I wouldn't want anyone to try and use a board and get hurt."

Mr. Lehman shrugged. "The boards you sell to my guests will end up in the corner of their garage at home or nailed to the wall in their game room—a reminder of their trip to paradise."

"A surfboard is a pretty expensive souvenir," Quin remarked.

"As long as my guests are happy, and you're selling boards—what do we care?"

Before Quin could reply, Raquel reached over and hooked an arm through one of Mila's. "Come on, let's leave the men to this business talk and get ourselves something to eat."

"You'll join us soon?" Mila asked Quin over her shoulder as Raquel pulled her away. He nodded before turning his attention back to Mr. Lehman.

"Let Quin get to know Hubert," Raquel advised. "He's a financial genius and with his support, the Surf Shop will become a huge success."

Mila wanted the Surf Shop to make enough profit to support them, but she knew that Quin was interested in making boards for serious surfers. He approached board making as a science and tried to incorporate technical improvements in each new design. She couldn't see him being satisfied making boards that would end up being expensive souvenirs. But Quin was capable of handling himself, so she allowed Raquel to pull her away.

As they walked through the crowd, Raquel introduced Mila to several people, including her boss at Channel One, her dentist, and her hairdresser.

"I wasn't expecting so many people to be here," Mila whispered between introductions.

"Neither was the caterer," Raquel confided with a wicked little smile. "She's complained all night long! I guess I shouldn't have invited everyone from the television station. I hope you don't mind, since the party is sort of in your honor."

"Oh, no," Mila replied automatically.

"Then I saw some other colleagues at a luncheon and invited them as well," Raquel continued. "They say you can expect half of those you invite to actually attend, but I guess I've proved that statistic wrong."

Mila looked around. "I guess you have." Realizing that this might sound rude, Mila added, "We appreciate your help publicizing the Surf Shop."

This comment seemed to please Raquel. "You're very welcome."

"Excuse me," a voice said from behind them. Mila turned to see Mrs. Rose sidling up to Raquel. "I'm sorry to bother you, but we have a problem in the kitchen that requires your personal attention."

Raquel leveled a withering look at the housekeeper. "Surely you don't expect me to leave my guests to come and help you do your job?" she asked, a little louder than absolutely necessary.

Mrs. Rose held her ground. "I wouldn't bother you if it were something I could handle myself. If you'll just come with me for a minute . . ."

"What is it?" Raquel demanded, her eyes glittering with rage. "Tell me this instant so I can get back to my guests."

All conversation around them stopped. Mrs. Rose was pale as she spoke, but Mila thought she detected a certain amount of satisfaction in the housekeeper's voice. "The caterer says you only paid for enough food to feed thirty people, and there are over a hundred guests in attendance tonight. She claims that the last time you underestimated the number of guests, you refused to pay the difference, so unless you give her cash now, she's leaving."

Raquel shrugged contemptuously. "Tell the caterer that I will pay for the extra guests later, but if she leaves before this party is over I will see to it that she is out of business by the end of the week." Turning sharply away from Mrs. Rose, Raquel said to Mila, "Come this way please."

As they walked away, Mila glanced back and saw Mrs. Rose standing where they had left her—a look of pure hatred on her face.

"Help yourself," Raquel encouraged when they reached the buffet table. "While I go make sure Quin meets all the right people!"

After Raquel left, Mila put some food on her plate and searched the room for her friends from Haggerty. Finally she found them at a table near a window with an incredible view of the ocean. "Mind if I join you?" she asked as she approached their table.

"Mind?" Miss Polly said in surprise. "We've been saving you a seat!"

The ladies all scooted down to make room for Mila. Then Miss Eugenia said, "Where's Quin?"

"I left him talking to Cade and some hotel owner," Mila explained.

"Well, he's not talking to Cade anymore. Our host is over there," Miss Eugenia pointed to balcony a few feet away.

Mila followed the direction of her finger, and sure enough, Cade was standing there talking to Raquel's personal secretary, Leilani Fiero.

"Who is that beautiful young woman with him?" Miss Polly asked, squinting to see into the deep shadows.

"That's Leilani Fiero," Mila said. "She's a native girl who works for Raquel."

"What does she do for Raquel?"

"She's her secretary—sets up appointments, things like that."

"She looks awfully cozy with Raquel's handsome husband," Miss Eugenia observed.

"Eugenia! You promised!" Annabelle objected.

Mila looked between the sisters, bewildered. "Promised what?"

Annabelle sighed. "Eugenia is completely incapable of minding her own business, but she promised to keep her observations to herself."

"Sorry," Miss Eugenia apologized.

Mila pushed the fruit around on her plate. "What observations?"

"She has a theory that Raquel got this estate by disreputable means."

"I said I didn't think she *bought* it," Miss Eugenia corrected her sister. "I figure she married a man with one foot in the grave and inherited it."

"See what I mean?" Annabelle demanded. "She's incorrigible."

Mila frowned. "Actually, Raquel did get the estate from her first husband—but not because he died. It was part of the divorce settlement."

Miss Eugenia gave her sister an "I-told-you-so" look.

Annabelle rolled her eyes. "You weren't *exactly* right."

Miss Eugenia ignored this comment and asked, "How long have Cade and Raquel been married?"

"Please," Annabelle begged. "Stop prying."

"Just a couple of years, I think," Mila answered with a smile at Annabelle.

"And as far as you know, they are happy together?" Miss Eugenia pressed.

"As far as I know," Mila confirmed.

"They seemed very much in love this afternoon," George Ann pointed out.

"Eugenia thinks the passionate kiss and the flower behind the ear were just for show," Annabelle informed them.

"I'm not saying he doesn't love Raquel," Miss Eugenia said, qualifying her opinion.

Miss George Ann leaned forward and asked, "You think he's unfaithful to Raquel?"

Miss Eugenia nodded. "Definitely."

"Oh, my," Miss Polly said in obvious distress.

"You have absolutely no proof," Annabelle tried again.

Miss Eugenia raised an eyebrow. "If he's so in love with his wife, why is he out on the balcony with her secretary?"

Mila considered this then said, "She has a point."

"Last spring I read an unauthorized biography about Lucille Ball and Desi Arnez," Miss George Ann contributed. "The author claimed that Desi really loved Lucy, but the Hollywood starlets wouldn't leave him alone. Finally he succumbed to temptation and broke Lucy's heart."

Miss Polly pulled out her handkerchief and dabbed at her eyes. "If that isn't the saddest thing. They seemed so happy on *I Love Lucy.*"

Miss George Ann raised her chin a notch. "I always knew their marriage was doomed, since Lucy was determined to be in show business and Ricky was adamantly opposed."

Miss Polly dabbed fresh tears. "Poor Little Ricky."

Annabelle shook her head. "Heaven help us."

Mila laughed and whispered, "We'll blame it on jetlag."

Annabelle nodded. "That's better than considering other possibilities."

* * *

While the others discussed the *I Love Lucy Show,* Eugenia checked her watch. It was seven thirty HST, but her body was still on Haggerty time—where it was already Tuesday. Tired and ready for a good night's sleep, Eugenia was trying to think of a polite way to decline Mila's invitation to the sushi restaurant when there was a disturbance at the front entrance.

Eugenia looked over to see a young man with shaggy, blonde hair burst into the room. His knee-length shorts were frayed along the hemline and he was wearing a T-shirt advertising an oyster bar. Raquel was right behind him.

"If you don't leave at once, I will call the police!" she threatened.

Eugenia heard several gasps from the old ladies behind her, but the young man didn't seem concerned. He searched the crowd. "I'll leave as soon as I speak to Leilani."

Eugenia's eyes moved to the balcony where Cade and the secretary seemed to be frozen in place.

"Leilani is not here," Raquel told him.

The boy shook his head. "I don't believe you. She said she'd be here at seven o'clock."

"She was *supposed* to be here at seven," Raquel acknowledged, her tone changing from angry to aggrieved. "But she hasn't shown up, and I don't know where she is."

Eugenia looked back to the balcony as the girl stepped out. "I'm here," she said simply.

The boy glanced over his shoulder at Raquel. "I knew you were lying," he said before he addressed Leilani. "We need to talk."

The secretary nodded and moved toward him. Eugenia noticed that Cade stayed out of sight on the balcony—leaving the girl to face the awkward situation alone.

When Leilani reached the doorway, Raquel grabbed her arm. "Where were you?" she demanded.

"I just got here," the girl offered as an explanation.

"I told you to be here at seven," Raquel hissed. "Have you forgotten that you work for *me*?"

Leilani shook her head, causing her silky black hair to sway becomingly. "No. I haven't forgotten."

"Then you should have also remembered that I told you I didn't want this . . ." Raquel paused in her description of the young man, apparently searching for a sufficiently derogatory word, "*trash* on my property."

Leilani shot her visitor an apologetic look. "We're leaving," she said.

"No, he is leaving," Raquel corrected. "You are staying."

"Raquel," the girl began, but her employer cut her off.

"If you leave with him now—you're fired."

Leilani's eyes dropped to the floor for a few seconds. Then she squared her shoulders and nodded. "Okay." She pulled away from Raquel's grip, and as she left with the young man, Eugenia saw tears shining on her cheeks.

"Dear me," Polly whispered.

"What a horrible display," George Ann concurred.

Eugenia kept one eye on Raquel and the other on Cade, who was still hiding on the balcony.

"Well," Raquel said to her guests with a forced smile. "I'm sorry that you had to witness that little bit of unpleasantness. But it's over now—so please go back to enjoying yourself."

A short silence followed this announcement, then general murmuring as the crowd discussed what they had just seen. Eugenia watched Cade slip out of his hiding spot and approach his wife. Raquel spoke to him quietly, and he gave her a comforting hug.

Eugenia was staring at Raquel's lips, trying to figure out what she was saying, when Quin joined them. "I think that was our cue to leave," he told them.

Mila nodded. "Sounds good to me."

"Just let me make some plates for Kate and Mark," Eugenia requested.

"I'll help," Annabelle volunteered. "To speed the process."

Once the to-go plates were made, they all stood and walked to the entryway, where Raquel and Cade were still involved in a deep discussion. Mila cleared her throat, and when the startled couple looked up, she said, "I'm sorry to interrupt, but we need to go."

Raquel stepped forward. "I hope you're not leaving because of that nasty little scene with Leilani. I assure you that there won't be any further disturbance."

"No," Mila replied. "We just have other plans for the rest of the evening."

"Thanks for inviting us," Quin added. "Mr. Lehman could turn out to be a good business contact."

Raquel seemed relieved. "Well, good."

"Are you really going to fire that girl?" Miss Polly asked.

Raquel gave them a nervous laugh. "No, and I'm sorry if it seemed like I overreacted just now, but my secretary has been neglecting many of her duties lately and arriving late tonight was the last straw."

Eugenia waited for Cade to defend the girl or at least explain that she had arrived earlier than Raquel realized, but he didn't say a word.

"Besides, I've told her that I don't want that boyfriend of hers on my property. He's got a bad reputation, and I'm afraid he'll steal something." Raquel stopped, seeming to realize that she was going on too much. "Anyway, again, please accept my apologies."

"No apologies necessary," Polly said graciously.

"And the food was wonderful," Annabelle added.

"I did notice that the cheesecake wasn't on the buffet table," Polly pointed out.

"Polly!" Eugenia cried for the whole horrified group.

George Ann nodded. "How rude, Polly!"

Polly looked crushed. "Oh, I'm sorry, Raquel. I just thought you'd like to know that the caterer forgot."

"I'm not offended in the least," Raquel told them. "But I am annoyed. I gave the cake to Mrs. Rose and told her to have the caterer serve it, so one or the other disobeyed my instructions." Raquel turned to Cade. "Will you find Mrs. Rose for me please?"

"Maybe we could handle this later," he suggested, but Raquel shook her head.

"No, I want this settled now," Raquel insisted. "And tell the caterer I want a word with her as well."

Cade nodded and hurried off in search of the unfortunate housekeeper.

The last thing Mila wanted was to be involved in another scene. "We've all had plenty to eat and certainly don't need any cheesecake."

"It's the principle," Raquel replied.

Eugenia took Polly by the arm and pulled her toward the door. "Are you trying to get someone else fired?"

"Oh, my," Polly whimpered. "I didn't mean to cause trouble."

Before Raquel could respond, Mrs. Rose walked into the entryway, followed closely by a young woman dressed in white— presumably the caterer. Eugenia noticed that Cade did not return for the showdown.

Mrs. Rose addressed her employer. "You wanted to see us?"

"Why wasn't that cheesecake I gave you this afternoon served tonight?" Raquel demanded.

Mrs. Rose looked surprised by the question. "I don't know. I took it to the kitchen and put it in the refrigerator. The caterer hadn't arrived yet so I left a note on the counter instructing that it be added to the dessert selections."

All eyes turned to the woman in white. "There was no cheesecake in the refrigerator when we arrived," she said without hesitation. "And there wasn't a note on the counter."

Both women seemed completely sincere, but since one of them had to be lying, Eugenia braced herself for Raquel to explode with anger. Instead, their hostess sighed. "I'll bet I know what happened. Leilani probably took it."

"Leilani?" Mila repeated.

"The secretary?" Eugenia added.

Raquel nodded with a tolerant smile. "She has a terrible sweet tooth and is always pilfering things from the kitchen. I don't really mind, but it drives Mrs. Rose crazy."

The housekeeper stood a little straighter. "I just wish she would ask me first."

"Leilani probably opened the refrigerator and saw the cake but didn't notice the note on the counter. Mystery solved." Raquel seemed okay with the situation now, and Eugenia heaved a sigh of relief.

"Well, it's good that we've got that settled," she said, pulling Polly toward the door. "I guess we'll be going now."

"I'm sorry you didn't get to try any of the cake," Raquel told Polly. "I'll order another one tomorrow."

"Oh, that's not necessary," Eugenia answered as they descended the front steps.

"I hope you enjoy the rest of your evening," Raquel called after them.

They gathered in a little group at the bottom of the steps. "Do you think the secretary really steals food?" Polly asked.

Mila shrugged. "Both Raquel and Mrs. Rose claim she does."

"Maybe Raquel doesn't pay her enough to buy food so she has to resort to thievery," George Ann suggested.

"She did look awfully thin," Polly pointed out in apparent agreement with this theory.

"Maybe she's a kleptomaniac," Eugenia proposed.

Mila said, "Maybe she considers the food in the refrigerator a perk of her job."

"And goodness knows she needs a perk or two—working for Raquel," Annabelle murmured.

"It would take more than a few sweets to keep me," Eugenia agreed.

Mila addressed Quin. "So, what did you think about Mr. Lehman's offer to let you sell surfboards to his hotel guests?"

He smiled. "It's not what I always dreamed of doing with my life, but it will help to pay the bills until the Surf Shop gets enough business."

"You're going to do it then?" Mila asked.

He nodded. "I think so, although the proposal was pretty vague. He actually seemed more interested in Makai and how many guests Raquel could sleep comfortably than in my boards."

Mila frowned. "That's odd. Why would he care about Makai?"

"Maybe Raquel and Cade are thinking of selling it," Eugenia suggested.

Mila looked around for a few seconds, then shook her head. "Who in their right mind would sell this?"

Quin laughed. "No one. Now let's head to Aloha Sushi."

Eugenia cleared her throat. "I hate to be a party pooper, but I think I'm going to have to pass as on the sushi tonight."

"I don't think I could eat another bite," Polly agreed.

Then George Ann said, "And my feet are killing me."

"It's not that we don't like sushi," Annabelle was quick to explain.

Polly nodded. "Or that we don't want to see more of this beautiful island."

Eugenia put an arm around Mila's shoulders. "We're all just so tired."

Mila smiled. "Maybe we can work in a sushi trip later during your stay."

"Thank you for understanding," Annabelle said for the Haggerty ladies. "I guess we'll go on up to bed and see you in the morning."

Mila pointed at the plates of food Eugenia was carrying. "Quin is going to walk me home. Would you like us to drop those off by the Iversons' bungalow on the way?"

Eugenia frowned. "I wanted to tell the children good night."

"I'm sure they have been asleep for hours by now," Annabelle said.

Eugenia relinquished the plates. "I guess you're right."

"Breakfast will be at my bungalow tomorrow morning at nine," Mila announced. "Unless that's too early."

"We're all still on Haggerty time so we'll probably be up by three A.M.," Annabelle predicted.

"Are you cooking?" Eugenia asked Mila.

Mila shook her head. "No, I love you all too much for that. I bought muffins and orange juice."

Eugenia laughed. "Good, then we'll see you at nine."

CHAPTER 3

On Tuesday Eugenia woke up with the sun after only a few hours of restless sleep. Although she had two suitcases full of new clothes, she dressed in the same green outfit she'd worn on the plane. Then she walked over to Annabelle's room to borrow her sister's cell phone. Annabelle was still asleep, so she surrendered the phone without argument.

Eugenia took the phone into her room and called Whit at his office. His secretary, Idella Babcox, answered. "Oh, Eugenia, Whit has been trying to reach you. He called your hotel, and they said you had canceled your reservation."

Eugenia could have kicked herself. "There was a last-minute change of plans, and we're not staying at the hotel," she told Idella. "Why, is something wrong with Lady?"

"Oh, no," Idella replied. "The little mutt is just fine. But Whit's oldest daughter had to have emergency heart surgery so he went to North Carolina."

"That's terrible!" Then an awful thought occurred to her. "So where is Lady?" Eugenia asked, praying that Whit hadn't left her sweet little dog with the crabby and allergic Idella.

"Why, he took the dog with him," Idella replied. "I offered to find one of those dog kennels to put her in until you got back, but Whit said you'd entrusted Lady to his care, and he couldn't let her out of his sight, or some such nonsense."

Eugenia felt tears sting her eyes. Dear Whit. "Is his daughter okay?"

"He said the surgery went fine," Idella reported. "He told me to give you his cell number and said he didn't care if he gets a brain tumor the size of Baltimore—you're to call him on it the minute you get this message. Whatever that means."

Eugenia found herself smiling through her tears. "Give me the number, and I'll call him."

After disconnecting the call with Idella, Eugenia dialed Whit's cell number. When he answered, she said, "Your voice is like hot coffee on a cold winter afternoon—back when I used to drink coffee, that is."

He laughed. "It's so good to hear from you. I was afraid you'd met some handsome Hawaiian and had run off to live with him in his hut on the beach."

"Well, I have met a handsome Hawaiian, and I'm living in one of his guestrooms, but he's not my type."

"Then I'll try not to be jealous."

"Jealous!" Eugenia scoffed. "The very idea."

"Here, Lady wants to talk to you," Whit said.

A few seconds later Lady barked into the phone. Eugenia talked to the little dog, thankful there was no one else in the room to hear such nonsense. When Whit returned to the line, Eugenia said, "Idella told me about your daughter's surgery and that she's doing fine."

"Yes, the doctors expect she'll be ready to leave the hospital on Friday. If all goes well, I should be able to fly home on Saturday."

"Thank you for taking Lady with you," Eugenia said. "And I hope she's not being a nuisance."

"Oh, no," Whit assured her. "She's helped to keep the great-grandchildren occupied. In fact, I may have a hard time getting her away from them when it's time to leave."

"Don't you come back to Haggerty without my dog, Whit Owens," Eugenia told him, only half kidding. "Lady is a part of my family now. I even had her name changed on her American Kennel Club registration forms to Lady von Beanie Weenie *Atkins*!"

She heard Whit laugh again and was surprised by how much she enjoyed the sound. "I know. I'll take good care of Lady, and—like me—she will be waiting for you when you return home."

Now that was a heartwarming thought. "Well, I guess I'd better let you go," Eugenia said reluctantly. "But I might call you back tomorrow if that's okay."

"It will give Lady and me something to look forward to."

Eugenia ended the call and walked back to Annabelle's room. She knocked once in fair warning and then pushed open the door. Annabelle was dressed and applying her makeup. "Well, I'm glad to see that you finally decided to get up," Eugenia greeted.

Annabelle shot her sister an irritated look. "Good morning to you too."

Eugenia ignored Annabelle's ill humor. "I spoke to Whit and Lady. They're both fine but are missing me. Whit's daughter had to have emergency heart surgery so they are in North Carolina. His daughter is recovering well, and Whit plans to be back in Haggerty by the time we arrive on Sunday." Eugenia paused. "Annabelle, turn up your hearing aid."

"I don't have a hearing aid," Annabelle returned.

"Then maybe you need one. Have you heard a single word I've said?"

"I heard you," Annabelle confirmed. "I just couldn't find a way to squeeze in a comment." She closed her makeup bag. "What are you doing here so early? We're not supposed to be at Mila's for another hour."

"I wanted to stop by the bungalow where Kate and Mark are staying and see if the children would like to take a walk on the beach before breakfast," Eugenia explained. "If you're ready, I'll let Polly and George Ann know we'll meet them at Mila's."

Annabelle nodded. "I'm as ready as I'll ever be."

When Mark opened the door of the bungalow, he was wearing a white button-down shirt, open at the neck, and a pair of dark pants.

"I can see that the islands have already had an effect on your dress habits," Annabelle teased him.

Eugenia frowned. "He looks just like he does at home."

"He left off the tie," Annabelle pointed out. "And maybe he's planning to wear the lei Mila gave him yesterday."

Before Mark could defend himself, Kate called to them from the bedroom. "Come see *my* vacation clothes!"

They found Kate unpacking suitcases. Her long, light brown hair was pulled back in a ponytail, and she was wearing a pair of turquoise Capri pants with a coordinating blouse. Emily and little Charles were sitting on the bed, still in their pajamas, watching cartoons on a small television set.

Kate struck a pose, showing off her new clothes. "Well, what do you think?"

"I declare, I don't know what to think," Eugenia replied as she leaned down to kiss each child in turn. "I hope you didn't spend your entire vacation clothing budget on yourself so that the whole time you're in Hawaii the kids have to wear their pajamas and Mark has to wear his work suits."

Emily glanced up. "Mama bought everybody new stuff. Even Daddy."

"He has pink shorts with flowers," Charles reported.

"But he says he's not going to wear them," Emily added.

Eugenia leveled a narrow look at Mark, who was now standing in the bedroom doorway. "I'm sure he'll wear them since I know he doesn't want to hurt your mama's feelings."

Kate laughed. "The shorts were a joke. Mark can wear whatever he feels most comfortable in."

"Humph," Eugenia said. "If he goes around like that, people will think he's your bodyguard."

"I do love your outfit, Kate," Annabelle said in an obvious attempt to divert attention from Mark.

Kate looked down at her colorful clothes. "You don't think it's touristy, do you?"

Annabelle smiled. "Maybe a little—but it's okay to look like a tourist if that's what you are."

"I can hardly wait to get the kids dressed and see how they look," Kate said as she approached the bed carrying two small stacks of clothes. "Would you like to help me?" She extended Emily's outfit toward Eugenia.

"I'd be delighted."

Once the children were dressed and had been admired at length, Eugenia returned her attention to Mark. "Why don't you be a good sport and put on your pink, flowery shorts?" she suggested. "You might be fooling everyone else, but I know you're not as opposed to looking touristy as you pretend."

Mark seemed annoyed by this remark. "What do you mean?" He walked over to the dresser and started collecting the plates and soft drink cans that Eugenia had sent them from Raquel's party the night before.

Eugenia pointed a no-nonsense finger at him. "I've noticed that you've let your hair grow out, and you've been working on a tan."

Eugenia expected Mark to be embarrassed, but she was surprised to see him turn pale. "I don't know what you're talking about."

"I'm talking about the fact that your hair is hanging over your ears and touching your collar in the back," Eugenia told him. "And about Miriam Woods seeing you at a tanning salon over in Tifton last week."

Mark's knuckles turned white as his hand clenched around a Sprite can. Some of the liquid spilled out onto the floor, and he stared at it in surprise.

"What in the world is the matter with you?" Eugenia demanded as she grabbed a towel from the bathroom and wiped up the mess.

"Sorry, I just had a clumsy moment," Mark said.

Eugenia had never known Mark to be clumsy. "Did I say something wrong? About your hair and tan I mean?"

"For heaven's sake, Eugenia," Annabelle interrupted. "It was probably a surprise for Kate. Why else would he have gone to all the trouble to tan in Tifton when there are plenty of tanning salons in Albany?"

Eugenia was instantly contrite. "I'm sorry."

"It's too late now," Annabelle said. "You've already spoiled the surprise."

Mark looked positively ill, and Eugenia felt a twinge of alarm. "It's okay," he said.

"Mark." Kate's eyes were riveted on her husband. "Did you grow your hair out on purpose?"

"Yes," he answered—his tone as solemn as someone on a witness stand.

"And you've been going to a tanning salon in Tifton?"

He nodded.

"Did you do these things because we were going on vacation and you wanted to surprise me?" Kate continued her inquiry.

He crossed the room to stand beside his wife. "No."

"Mark," Kate whispered. "What's going on?"

Mark sighed. "I got a memo a few weeks ago telling me to get a full-body tan and to let my hair grow out."

"If that's not the silliest thing I've ever heard!" Eugenia exclaimed. "Why in the world would the FBI tell you to do that?"

"Eugenia," Annabelle said in a warning tone.

Mark seemed oblivious to everyone but Kate. "There's been some terrorist activity in South America. They probably won't use me," he prefaced his next remark, "but Atlanta has put all of their Spanish-speaking agents on alert."

Kate reached out and clutched his hands in hers. "Oh, Mark."

"Please don't worry," he pleaded. "My field experience is so limited I'm sure I would be their last resort. I wasn't even going to mention it, but . . ."

"But Eugenia took care of that for you," Annabelle inserted with an annoyed look at her sister.

"I had no idea there was an ulterior reason for Mark's long hair," Eugenia said in defense. "And besides, Kate needs to know if there's a possibility that he'll be leaving on a field assignment."

Mark smiled at his wife. "I'm sure it's nothing to worry about."

Kate didn't look reassured and continued to hold her husband's hands.

Annabelle stood. "Well, now that we've cheered everyone up, I guess we should go."

"I was thinking that the kids might like to take an early morning walk on the beach," Eugenia said, feeling terrible that her keen sense of observation had upset Kate.

Mark nodded. "That would be fine. We'll join you in a few minutes."

Annabelle held out her hands to the children and led them to the door.

Eugenia lagged behind. "We'll be waiting for you on the beach," she said. "And Mark, when you come out I expect you to be wearing those pink, flowery shorts," she added, hoping to tease Kate into a better mood.

Mark gave her a wan smile for her effort, but Kate's eyes filled with tears. "Please don't let the kids get in the water," Mark requested.

Accepting defeat, Eugenia followed Annabelle outside. As they walked to the beach, Annabelle fussed at Eugenia for upsetting Kate.

"How was I supposed to know that the FBI was making Mark grow his hair out?" Eugenia demanded.

"You couldn't have known that," Annabelle admitted. "But you could mind your own business for once in your life."

Eugenia shrugged. "I'm too old to change my ways now."

* * *

By nine o'clock on Tuesday morning, Mila had the boxes of pastries she had purchased for her guests arranged on the small table in her kitchen. Once all was ready, she called Quin. "Are you coming for breakfast?" she asked.

"Did you get some of those apple and raisin muffin things?"

"Of course."

"Then I'm on my way."

"Will Daniel open the shop this morning?" She referred to Quin's only employee, a college student who worked part-time as needed.

"Yeah, he's planning to work every day for the next two weeks, but I'd like to go by the shop sometime today and come up with a proposal for Mr. Lehman."

"Choosing which surfboards you are going to sacrifice as souvenirs so that we can buy groceries?"

"Right," Quin confirmed.

"Well, hurry and come over. I'll try to save you a muffin, but if you're late I won't make any promises."

They ended their conversation, and Mila was about to put away her phone when it rang. She didn't recognize the number and almost ignored the call, but something made her decide to take it.

"Edwards," she said into the receiver.

"Detective?" a tentative voice asked. "It's me, Spike."

Mila sighed. "What can I do for you?"

"You can find out who killed my friend the Gent."

"You should call my partner, Detective Hirasuna . . ." Mila began, but Spike cut her off.

"I been calling him. He don't care about the Gent."

"Spike," Mila tried again. "We can't do anything until the toxicology report comes back."

"Then what?"

"If there is compelling evidence that a crime has been committed, we'll investigate."

"I'm telling you that the Gent was killed," Spike insisted. "If you don't find *compelling evidence,* it'll be because you ain't looked hard enough."

"I'm sorry," Mila said, and she was. "But I'm on vacation for the next two weeks and . . ."

"And nobody cares about a dead wino."

The dial tone sounded in Mila's ear as the doorbell rang. Mila stared at her phone for a few seconds, then closed it and crossed the room to admit her guests.

"Good morning!" Miss Eugenia greeted cheerfully. "The children have already been for a walk on the beach and collected some beautiful seashells."

Emily and Charles Iverson held out sand-covered hands as evidence of this. "Do you want to see?" Emily asked.

Mila glanced at the small shells and smiled. "They are very nice. Would you like a plastic bag to keep them in?"

Kate stepped forward. "Yes, please."

Kate's eyes looked a little red, and Mila asked if she was feeling okay.

"I'm fine," Kate replied.

"She's probably just allergic to the Hawaiian flora and fauna," Annabelle added a little too quickly, making Mila wonder if there was something going on that she didn't know about.

"Can we use your bathroom to wash up?" Kate requested. "I didn't realize that beach-combing was such dirty work."

Mila produced two ziplock bags then pointed Kate and her children toward the bathroom while the others filed in and took positions around the small living room. "Did everyone sleep well?" Mila asked politely.

"I slept like a rock," Miss Polly replied.

"I slept pretty well considering that I'm away from my husband," Annabelle said.

"I didn't sleep a wink." Miss George Ann rubbed the small of her back. "It's impossible for me to get comfortable in a strange bed."

Miss Eugenia rolled her eyes. "Then who was that I could hear snoring all the way across the hall?"

"Snoring!" Miss George Ann repeated in horror. "Well, I never!"

Kate returned from the bathroom with the children and asked, "You never what?"

"Snored a day in my life!" Miss George Ann said defensively. "Eugenia is making things up."

"I don't know how you can be sure you don't snore since it's something you'd do when you're *asleep*," Miss Eugenia pointed out.

Before a full-fledged war could develop, Mila stepped forward and suggested that Mark give the blessing on the food so everyone could eat. This kept Miss George Ann from making further comment. Everyone bowed their heads, and after the prayer, Mila gestured for everyone to come to the table. "Please help yourselves. There is plenty more juice in the refrigerator."

Once everyone was served, Miss Eugenia asked Mila why she wasn't eating. "I just had a rather upsetting phone call," Mila admitted. "And I lost my appetite."

"What kind of phone call?" Miss Polly wanted to know.

"I won't go into the unpleasant details during breakfast, but basically a homeless man died on Monday, and his friend thinks he was murdered."

"What do you think?"

Mila grimaced. "I think the man was probably murdered, but since I'm on vacation, my partner gets to make the call. The murdered man's friend just basically accused me of not caring since the dead man was, well, not an asset to society."

"And you feel guilty?"

Mila shrugged. "I guess."

Kate frowned. "You shouldn't. If your partner decides not to investigate, it's not your fault."

"You're getting *married*," Miss Polly added. "You should be thinking only about that."

Mila knew they were right, but it didn't change how she felt. "This phrase keeps running through my mind."

"What phrase, Mila?" Kate asked, her green eyes full of concern.

Mila exhaled deeply. "If not me, then who?" She glanced up and saw Mark Iverson watching her with perfect understanding. Realizing that she was neglecting her hostess duties, Mila smiled and said, "But enough of that. Everyone just enjoy your meal."

While the others were eating, Mark walked over and stood beside Mila.

"What should I do?" she asked him.

"I can't tell you that," he answered. "But the way I see it, you basically have two choices. You can cancel your vacation and concentrate on the case."

Mila looked around at her guests. "I don't see how I could do that."

"Or you can accept your partner's decision not to investigate."

Mila stared at the boxes of pastries on the table. "I don't see how I can do that either."

"If you can't choose between your options—then you'll have to juggle them both."

Mila nodded. "Then that's what I'll do."

* * *

Quin arrived, and after he'd filled his plate with apple and cinnamon muffins, Annabelle asked, "So, what are the plans for today?"

"Well," Quin said, "first we want go to Poli Lookout."

"That's where King Kamehameha ran a whole army of his enemies off a cliff," Annabelle provided knowledgeably. "And the wind blows so hard you think it's going to rip your clothes off."

Eugenia rolled her eyes. "Yes, Annabelle, we all know you've been to Hawaii before."

"I hope the wind won't whip my clothes off," Polly said with concern.

"I just hope we don't have to walk far," George Ann added. "My doctor says it's not good for my bunions."

"What's a bunion?" Mila asked as she closed the pastry containers on the table.

Much to Eugenia's displeasure, George Ann was only too happy to explain.

When the medical discourse was over, Kate asked, "Do they hurt?"

"Only when I'm on my feet too long," George Ann reported.

Mila came up behind Quin and wrapped an arm around his waist. "Assuming we don't blow off the Poli Lookout, we'll go by the Surf Shop so you can see how creative Quin is."

"The shop isn't nearly what I hope it will be someday," he said.

"The shop may not be all we want it to be, but he makes the best boards in the world," Mila bragged in his behalf.

"Well, some of the best," he admitted.

"We'll have lunch at Sam Choy's, and then most of you are going out to Sand Island for the afternoon," Mila informed them. "There is a lot for the kids to do, but there are also plenty of places to sit and just watch," she added with a look in George Ann's direction. "In case your bunions are hurting."

"Most of us?" Quin repeated.

"I've got to wrap up a few loose ends on a case Jerry and I started yesterday."

"The wino?" Quin guessed.

She nodded. "But I'll be finished in time to meet all of you at Café Sistina for dinner," she informed the group. "It's the best Italian restaurant on the island."

"And since Mila doesn't even like food—this place must be great," Eugenia said with a smile.

"I like food," Mila objected. "It's just that my appetite is sensitive to stress."

Polly laughed. "Stress makes me want to eat more!"

"Don't we all know that," Eugenia muttered.

Quin spoke quickly. "After we eat, we thought we could drive along Waikiki and show you some of the beachfront hotels."

"That all sounds wonderful," Miss Polly enthused as a knock sounded on the door.

With a glance at Mila, Quin said, "I'll get it." A few seconds later he ushered Raquel into the room.

Greetings were exchanged, then Mila offered Raquel some breakfast. "Thanks, but I never eat before noon," their hostess declined. "I'm on my way to the studio to film today's cooking segment but wanted to drop off these autographed pictures." Raquel distributed the pictures of her much younger self, and the guests thanked her enthusiastically.

"I love to cook," Polly divulged. "In fact I'm collecting recipes for a new Haggerty Baptist Church cookbook called *Dishes from Sea to Shining Sea*. We're trying to get recipes from every state. Maybe you could contribute one from Hawaii?"

Raquel seemed mildly impressed. "Well, I'd be glad to. In fact I'll have to find a spectacular recipe for such a worthy cause."

Not for the first time Eugenia was afraid that Polly might burst—this time with joy. "Oh, I'm so thrilled that we'll have a recipe in our cookbook from a famous person."

Raquel smiled, and Eugenia realized that the "famous person" remark had worked magic. "In fact," Raquel continued, "why don't you all come watch me do my segment this morning, and if there's time at the end, you can give your cookbook a little plug."

Polly put a hand to her chest. "You mean I'll be on television?"

Raquel nodded as she pulled her cell phone out and dialed. "I'll have my secretary arrange things." After a few seconds Raquel frowned then turned off the phone. "Leilani's not answering her cell phone. I guess she's pouting because I yelled at her last night."

"You were pretty hard on her," Mila said.

"Maybe you could apologize," Polly suggested.

Raquel nodded. "I will if I can ever get her to answer the phone. She probably went home with that horrible boyfriend of hers. I've got his number written down in my office. I'll try there later. And in the meantime, I'll make the arrangements with the television studio myself."

Tears were back in Polly's eyes as she cried, "How can I ever thank you enough for giving me the opportunity to share the ministry of our cookbook with your millions of viewers?"

"Well, millions would be an overstatement," Raquel said modestly.

Belatedly, Polly realized that she should get this schedule change approved by Mila. "Will it be okay for us to go to Raquel's studio this morning and Poli Lookout later?"

Mila didn't seem thrilled, but she nodded. "I'm sure we can work a trip to the television station in, since it's for such a good cause."

Raquel smiled. "Wonderful."

"Okay, well we've got a busy day," Mila said, and Eugenia could tell she was hoping to encourage Raquel's departure.

"I'm sorry that I threw you off schedule again." Raquel looked anything but repentant.

"No problem," Mila said politely.

"I'll see you soon, then." With a wave, Raquel hurried out the front door.

"Is it just my imagination, or does Raquel seem determined to monopolize our company?" Mila murmured to Quin once their landlady was gone.

He smiled. "We have plenty to go around, so let's be generous."

"Maybe she doesn't have much company of her own," Annabelle suggested.

Mila frowned. "Well, I'm getting tired of sharing mine." She checked her watch. "Everyone who wants to go to the television studio needs to be ready in about thirty minutes."

"We'll probably just stay here and let the kids play on the beach," Mark said.

"I don't blame you," Mila told him. Then she turned to Quin. "I'll call you when we leave the station, and we can all meet at Poli Lookout."

He nodded. "It looks like I'll get some work done at the Surf Shop after all."

* * *

Mila loaded Miss Eugenia and the other Haggerty ladies in her car and left Makai headed for the television station. While they drove, she called Jerry Hirasuna on her cell phone.

"The toxicology report shows traces of arsenic in both the wine bottle and the dead man's body," Jerry told her. "But there was rat poison, which contained arsenic, in the dumpster and the alley. So, it's impossible to tell if the stuff was put in the wine or if our victim ate it by mistake while pilfering food from the dumpster."

"It was put in the wine," Mila said with certainty.

"Unfortunately we'll need proof if we're going to take this to court," Jerry pointed out. "We'll also need a suspect with a motive."

"It's your job to find one," Mila reminded him.

She disconnected the call and put away her cell phone as they arrived at the television station. While parking the car, Mila couldn't help feeling frustrated. She could be working on the wino case or enjoying Poli Lookout, but thanks to Raquel's gigantic ego, she was wasting time watching today's broadcast of the *Morning Show.*

* * *

Once inside the Channel One television studio, Mila and her group of ladies from Haggerty were assigned to a harried associate producer who led them to their seats and gave them a list of instructions.

"When that red light is on, the set has to be completely silent," she told them. "And under no circumstances are you to get out of your seats."

"Oh, dear," Polly said. "In that case I'd better go to the restroom now."

"Me too," George Ann chimed in.

Annabelle sighed. "We might as well all go."

The producer looked annoyed. "I have a thousand things to do before the program starts and can't keep an eye on you. Just make sure you're in your seats at eleven." The producer pointed to the rest rooms and then rushed off.

When they reached the ladies' room, Eugenia said, "I don't need to make use of the facilities, but I would like to look around the studio a little."

Mila turned to Annabelle. "If you'll make sure Miss Polly and Miss George Ann get back to our seats, I'll stay with Miss Eugenia."

Annabelle nodded, accepting her assignment. "Remember, we only have thirty minutes."

"I'll remember," Mila promised. "I don't want that producer mad at me."

While Annabelle led her charges into the rest room, Mila followed Eugenia into the kitchen area. "It's not as large as I expected," Eugenia commented.

"It is pretty small," Mila agreed.

A woman appeared suddenly from the shadows created by the spotlight, startling them both. Eugenia put a hand to her mouth. "I declare, you nearly scared me to death," she told the woman. Then she extended a hand. "My name is Eugenia Atkins, and I'm here visiting from Georgia."

The woman removed a cake from the oven and put it on the counter. Then she clasped Eugenia's hand in her own. "I can tell you're not from around here. And I'm Darlene Moore."

"Nice to meet you, Darlene. This is a friend of mine, Mila Edwards."

Mila exchanged nods with the other woman.

Eugenia leaned forward and looked into the pan. "Is that the recipe that Raquel is featuring today?"

"Yes. It's strawberry sponge cake." Darlene transferred the cake to a cooling rack underneath the counter.

"I guess you help Raquel with the cooking for her show?" Eugenia continued in a conversational tone.

Darlene laughed. "Raquel never touches more than a designer pot holder. I do *all* the cooking, and Raquel shows up just in time to step in front of the camera."

Eugenia raised both eyebrows. "Well, that doesn't seem quite fair."

Darlene tucked a clump of curly blonde hair behind her ear. "Oh, I don't mind. Raquel loves to be a star, and I love to cook—so our partnership works out perfectly."

"And what delicacy do you have for us today?" a male voice asked from behind them.

Eugenia turned around to see a man about her own age looking at the cake that Darlene had placed under the counter.

Darlene blushed with pleasure. "Oh, Mr. Baldwin, it's just a strawberry sponge cake."

"It smells divine," the elderly man said. "Please save me a piece, and I'll want a copy of the recipe for my collection."

Darlene giggled. "You know I will."

Mr. Baldwin transferred his attention to Mila and Eugenia. Mila extended a hand. "Hello, Mr. Baldwin. We met briefly at Raquel's party last night, but you probably don't remember. My name is Mila Edwards. I rent a bungalow from Raquel."

Mr. Baldwin smiled. "How could I forget such a lovely face? You're the bride-to-be if I remember correctly."

Mila nodded. "Yes, sir. And this is my friend Eugenia Atkins. We're here to watch the *Morning Show.*"

"We're very glad to have you as our guests," Mr. Baldwin said graciously. "And the cooking segment is always the best part of the show—thanks to Darlene."

Darlene blushed at the compliment. "Mr. Baldwin is an excellent cook himself."

"Well, that just makes his opinion even more valuable," Eugenia told the woman.

Mr. Baldwin checked the time. "You still have a while before airtime. Would you like me to give you a quick tour of the studio?"

Eugenia knew that if they returned to their seats, she'd have to listen to George Ann complain until the program began. So she smiled at Mr. Baldwin and said, "I'd love that."

"Then come right this way. The best view is from above." Mr. Baldwin led them to an elevator and they rode it up one floor. "This level consists mostly of uninteresting offices," he told them. "But I want you to see the sound booth. The installation was just completed a couple of weeks ago. It's completely soundproof, and all the equipment is state of the art."

He pushed open the door of a small room. One wall was made entirely of tinted glass, and the other three were covered with monitors, computer consoles, and flashing lights. An unkempt young man with a scraggly ponytail was sitting in a rolling chair in the center of the room.

"This is our sound technician, Mike Royer," Mr. Baldwin introduced. "Mike, these ladies are here to watch this morning's program."

"Nice to meet you," Eugenia told the technician.

The young man nodded without much interest. "Ditto."

Eugenia walked to the window and looked down at the studio below. She could see the kitchen set, where Darlene was still preparing for Raquel's food segment, and a little living room area that was unoccupied. By squinting she could even see the chairs where Annabelle and Polly and George Ann were sitting.

Eugenia turned and studied the wall of monitors—all flashing varied angles of the sets below. "You must be incredibly smart to manage all this," she told Mike.

He smiled. "Actually, the equipment is so intelligent that I'm not really necessary."

"I'll remember that the next time we discuss your salary," Mr. Baldwin said.

"I take that back," Mike said, quickly withdrawing his statement.

"Why don't you show Ms. Atkins how it works?" Mr. Baldwin suggested.

Mike swung around in his computer chair and moved the switch labeled "lights" into the *on* position. Immediately the area below was illuminated, and garbled sounds filled the room. "When the lights of any set are turned on—whether from up here or down at the set itself—the computer starts recording. Right now I'm picking up sounds from all over the studio," Mike explained. "I can limit the intake area with these buttons here." He pointed at a panel that was neatly marked, identifying various sets. "But the only way to stop the recording is to turn off the lights on the set."

"That's a security measure that eliminates the possibility of error," Mr. Baldwin explained. "Without a feature like this, a show could run and not be recorded."

"Like if I'm taking a nap when one of our shows starts," Mike added with a smile at Mr. Baldwin.

"You'd better not be taking a nap up here!" Mr. Baldwin said.

Mike held up both hands like he was surrendering. "Just kidding."

"Why do you need to record your shows? Aren't they televised live?" Eugenia asked.

"Some of them are," Mr. Baldwin responded. "But some are prerecorded for broadcast at a later date."

"And we use clips from old shows for advertising," Mike contributed.

Eugenia frowned. "What if someone is on the set and needs the lights but doesn't want their conversation recorded?"

Mr. Baldwin smiled. "That's a very good question. Explain how that works, Mike."

"There's an override button on each set that kills the sound," Mike told her. "So, if you don't want something recorded you hit the button. But as another security feature, it only lasts for two minutes. Then they have to hit the button again or the computer will start recording."

Eugenia was impressed. "Very efficient."

"I'm glad you approve." Mr. Baldwin really did seem pleased. "Well, I guess we should continue our tour and let Mike get back to work." He waved at the technician then led Eugenia into the hallway, and Mila followed. "Now I'll show you around downstairs."

"I'd like that," Eugenia said. "But we need to be in our seats before the *Morning Show* starts."

Mr. Baldwin looked disappointed but nodded. "Well, maybe we can finish our tour another time." He walked them to the elevator and, with a little salute, sent Mila and Eugenia on their way.

* * *

Mila and Miss Eugenia returned to their seats with two minutes to spare. The co-hosts, a painfully thin young woman and a fatherly man, took their places on the couch in the living room set. The red light came on and the co-hosts beamed at the camera.

"Aloha!" they chorused, then laughed together in what was probably intended to be a warm moment. Mila clenched her teeth in frustration. This was such an incredible waste of time.

The anchor people discussed the weather, health tips, and an earthquake in India with the same cheerful expressions. Then they broke for a commercial, and the instant the red light went off, the smiles disappeared.

"Where's my coffee?" the woman demanded.

"That light is right in my eyes," the man complained.

"They seemed so happy a few minutes ago," Miss Polly remarked.

Mila shrugged. "That's show business."

After the commercial break, the co-hosts exchanged more friendly banter and introduced the daily segment of the Dream Weaver, and all attention switched to the next set, where a small man sat at a desk and faced the camera.

"Good morning," he said politely.

"That's Mr. Miyagi!" Miss Eugenia whispered loudly, earning herself a murderous look from the associate producer.

"Who?" Annabelle whispered back, more quietly.

"Mr. Miyagi from *The Karate Kid.* Don't you remember?"

Annabelle shook her head. "I don't even know what you're talking about."

The associate producer was motioning wildly, and Mila reminded her guests to be quiet as Mr. Miyagi discussed dreams.

"Our letter today is from a young woman named Anna on the Big Island," he informed the audience. "She says that she has had several dreams lately that involve dogs. Anna, the presence of dogs in your dreams probably means . . ."

Mila stifled a yawn as she checked her watch. Time was crawling.

Finally the dream segment was over, and they moved on to the "What happened a hundred years ago today" bit. Just as Mila thought she would lose her mind, they introduced Raquel. The lights came up on the kitchen set, and there stood Raquel, resplendent in a lacy peasant dress and a cute little apron that was obviously just for show since it didn't provide more than a foot of protection. Raquel glided gracefully around the kitchen, opening cupboards and mixing ingredients in various bowls. She put a pan into the oven and then, with a conspiratorial smile at the audience, pulled the finished cake from under the counter, where Darlene had left it.

Raquel cut a piece and arranged it artfully on a china plate, then offered some to the co-hosts. The camera cut briefly to the anchor woman who looked thrilled by the prospect of cake. "We'll have a piece later," she promised Raquel with a face-splitting smile.

During this off-camera moment Raquel motioned for Miss Polly to join her on the kitchen set. Miss Polly scurried up to stand beside Raquel—her recipe collection for the new Haggerty Baptist Church's cookbook clutched in one plump hand. She reached Raquel's side moments before the camera returned.

"Friends, I'd like to introduce Polly Kirby from Georgia," Raquel said, putting a hand on Miss Polly's arm. "She's a guest at my lovely estate, Makai—which was built in 1904 by Harold Solomon. Next week we are opening our estate up for public tours. Just a small donation affords you the opportunity to see a piece of Hawaiian history. If you'd like to learn more about Makai and the tour schedule, you can visit my website at www.recipesfromraquel.com." Raquel flashed a quick smile at Miss Polly before returning her attention to her viewers. "You can also find my delicious strawberry sponge cake recipe on the website, along with several personal tips to help make your baking experience successful." Raquel paused to throw a kiss at the camera. "So, until tomorrow, aloha!"

The lights went out in the kitchen set as the camera switched to the anchor people. Raquel removed her apron and laid it on the counter beside the piece of cake that the anchor people would never try, then walked toward the area where her guests were seated.

"What about the cookbook?" Miss Polly whispered.

"Shhhhhh!" the associate producer pleaded.

Raquel waved for Miss Polly to join her then said very quietly, "I'm sorry, but the production people underestimated the length of today's project, and I didn't have air space for you to mention your cookbook."

Mila wanted to point out that Raquel could have let Miss Polly describe *Dishes from Sea to Shining Sea* instead of giving her mini-commercial for Makai and her website. But she was afraid that further conversation might cause the poor associate producer to have a stroke.

"I'll see you later," Raquel mouthed. Then she hurried off the set.

"Well," Miss Eugenia said, obviously miffed.

The red light went out, and the associate producer approached them with purpose. "I told you that we had to have complete silence on the set," she reminded them. "I'm afraid you will all have to leave."

This was good news as far as Mila was concerned, so she stood.

Miss Eugenia said, "I was hoping to speak to Mr. Miyagi."

"Who?" the woman asked in obvious irritation.

"The man who did the dream segment," Annabelle translated for her sister.

The producer nodded. "Oh, the Dream Weaver. He's probably in the lounge. Second door to the left after you get into the hall."

"Thanks," Mila spoke for everyone, leading the group into the hallway.

"I need to use the ladies' room again," Miss Polly announced.

"And I'd like to speak to the dream man," Miss Eugenia added. "Why don't we all meet in the lobby in a few minutes?"

Mila checked her watch. "In a very few minutes," she agreed conditionally before following Miss Polly toward the rest rooms.

* * *

Eugenia waved for Annabelle to accompany her, then walked down the hall and opened the second door on the left. The Dream Weaver was standing by the vending machine drinking a Diet Coke.

Eugenia introduced herself and Annabelle, then asked, "Were you by any chance in the movie *The Karate Kid*?"

The man smiled. "No, but a lot of people ask me that. My name is Tony Booth."

Eugenia was mildly disappointed that he wasn't a movie star but was still interested in him since he interpreted dreams. "Are you a psychic?"

He shook his head. "I'm a professor of ancient history at the University of Hawaii. I just do this on the side to earn a few bucks."

"Was your mother a holy woman? Is that how you got your powers?"

Tony laughed. "I don't have any powers, and I don't really interpret dreams. What I do is analyze the various components of dreams using a scientifically accepted method."

Annabelle frowned. "What method is that?"

"I look them up in books."

This made Annabelle smile, but Eugenia remained serious. "How much would you charge to analyze a dream for me?"

Tony sighed. "I'll give you a quick evaluation for free. What was your dream?"

Eugenia related the dream she had on the plane about the maggots crawling out of her birthday cake. "I've had several people give suggestions about what it means," Eugenia told him, "ranging from the need to go on a diet to imminent death."

Mr. Booth smiled. "Do you remember having any feelings of fear or uneasiness during or immediately after the dream?"

Eugenia considered this. "Well, I was mildly disturbed by the dream when I had it, and now I'm not afraid, but I just can't seem to forget it. I'm beginning to think it might be a premonition of some kind."

"Premonitions are way out of my league," Tony told them. "But dreams about maggots probably mean you were feeling anxious about something. Are you afraid of flying?"

Eugenia nodded. "In fact, I had taken some motion sickness pills that put me to sleep for over five hours."

"Drugs often exaggerate our dreams and make them more intense."

"So, there's your answer," Annabelle said. "You dreamed about maggots in your birthday cake because you were afraid of flying and you took motion sickness pills. Now let's go."

Eugenia wasn't anxious to leave the Dream Weaver. "We're staying with Raquel Simon. I guess you know her?"

"I know her all right," Tony said grimly.

"It doesn't sound like you like her very much."

"I don't think anyone really likes Raquel," Tony replied. "But I absolutely detest her."

Eugenia couldn't help herself. "Why?"

"A few months ago I got a chance to put the Dream Weaver into syndication—which means it would have been available to stations worldwide."

"I'll bet that would have earned you a lot of extra bucks," Annabelle remarked.

Tony nodded. "And more than that, it would have given me exposure that could have developed into a major career change. But Raquel found out about it and put a stop to the deal."

"How did she do that?" Eugenia asked.

"I don't know, but she did. The deal was canceled, and the part that really gets me about it is that there was no advantage for Raquel. It wasn't like they were either going to take her sappy little cooking segment or my Dream Weaver bit. They only wanted me, and when my deal was canceled, she was no better off."

Eugenia frowned. "Why do you think she did it?"

"All I can figure is she can't stand to see anyone else more successful than she is."

Eugenia wasn't sure what to say. She had no defense for Raquel's actions, but since they were staying at Makai thanks to Raquel's generosity, she didn't feel comfortable gossiping about the woman. So, she thanked Tony for his free interpretation of her dream and moved to the door with Annabelle right behind her. They had only taken a few steps when Tony's voice stopped them.

"Even if your dream wasn't a premonition, I suggest that you ladies be careful. Association with Raquel can be dangerous."

"We'll be careful," Eugenia promised. Then she opened the door and walked into the hallway.

"I was afraid you were going to ask him to read your palms," Annabelle hissed as they walked toward the lobby.

"Ridiculous," Eugenia said with disdain. "I don't believe in that silly sort of thing."

They found the others waiting for them by the front entrance. Eugenia waited until they were settled in the rental car before telling them about Tony Booth.

"Where are we going now?" George Ann asked.

"I hope somewhere to eat," Polly added. "I'm starving."

"Imagine that," Eugenia muttered.

Polly leaned forward. "I'm sorry, Eugenia, what did you say?"

"I was just thinking what a shame it was that you didn't get to talk about your cookbook on Raquel's show."

"I'm so disappointed," Polly agreed. "The publicity would have been wonderful for our cause."

"I had prepared a little speech about the history of Haggerty," George Ann chimed in. "But Raquel didn't even let me come up on the set."

"Raquel apologized," Annabelle reminded them. "And she said it was the production staff's fault."

"Miss Polly, you should ask Raquel to put some information about your cookbook on her website," Mila suggested as she pulled out her cell phone.

Miss Polly's face brightened. "Do you think she would?"

"It can't hurt to ask," Mila replied. "I'll call Quin and tell him to collect the Iversons and meet us at Poli Lookout. We'll look around there for a while then go to lunch."

"Don't worry, Polly," Miss Eugenia said. "I've got some crackers in my purse."

* * *

They rushed through their visit to Poli Lookout so they could savor their lunch at Sam Choy's. By the time Mila regretfully separated herself from Quin and the others, she was comfortably full of duck breast and spinach salad with ginger-soy vinaigrette. Her mood was mellow as she headed toward the seedier side of Honolulu to the alley where they had found the Gent's body. On the way she called Jerry Hirasuna.

"Have you heard anything about our victim?" she asked when Jerry answered.

"Hold on a second," Jerry requested. Mila could hear paper rustling, and then Jerry spoke into the phone again. "The prints they took off the body belong to one Philip Carson, a stockbroker who disappeared back in 1995 before he could be arrested for embezzling several hundred thousand dollars from his employer."

"I wonder what happened to the money," Mila mused.

"I can't tell you that, but he sure didn't have any by the time he died. He was living in an abandoned warehouse, and his possessions were meager, even for a homeless person."

"Any family?" Mila asked.

"Apparently the scandal was too much for his wife, because she committed suicide right after he disappeared. He had a couple of daughters, both just kids at the time. An aunt came and got them and took them to the mainland."

"Any idea where they are now?"

"Nope, but I guess you want me to find out."

"While you're at it, see what you can come up with on the company Carson stole money from."

She heard Jerry sigh. "Okay, although for the life of me I can't see why you care."

"Morbid curiosity," Mila told him. "Have you heard from Spike lately?"

"Only about every fifteen minutes."

Mila laughed. "Well, the next time he calls, tell him to meet me at the entrance to the alley where we found Carson's body. I want to see where the victim did his panhandling."

"You want me to come along?" Jerry asked with an obvious lack of enthusiasm.

"No, I can handle this alone."

Mila closed her phone and pulled into a gas station. After filling up her car, she purchased a bag of potato chips and a can of Sprite. Then she eased back into the heavy traffic. By the time she reached the entrance to the alley, Spike was already there waiting. She rolled down her passenger side window, and he leaned into the car, giving her a large, crooked-toothed grin. "I knew you weren't like the others," he said approvingly.

"I'm exactly like the others," Mila corrected him. "I just happen to be on vacation, so I don't have twenty more pressing cases to claim my attention."

"Naw." He refused to accept this. "You're different."

Mila decided that argument was useless. "Show me the Gent's territory." She leaned across the seat and opened the passenger door.

Spike slid in and closed the door. "Go up to North Bethel and turn left," he instructed. "Then it's about six blocks."

She pointed at the chips and soft drink. "I brought you a snack."

Spike opened the drink and took a long sip. "Thanks."

Mila kept her eyes on the traffic. "Did the Gent walk this far from the warehouse every day?"

"Yep."

"His name was Philip Carson," Mila told him. "Did you know that?"

Spike shook his head. "No, we never tell each other our real names. It's safer that way—for everyone."

"He stole money years ago," Mila continued, watching Spike surreptitiously in hopes of catching a reaction. "His wife killed herself because of it, leaving two daughters basically orphaned."

Spike nodded. "I knew something bad had happened. The Gent was always preaching to me about making good decisions and how no man is an island and that children inherit the sins of their fathers. Stuff like that. At first I thought he was just a crazy." Spike glanced over at Mila. "But once I got to know him, I knew he was trying to help me."

"He didn't want you to make the same mistakes he did?"

"Right." Spike pulled a battered pack of cigarettes from his pocket. "Mind if I smoke?"

"I certainly do," Mila returned.

Spike laughed. "The Gent was always fussing at me for smoking, and he freaked if I ever drank a beer. He told me that if I took drugs, he wouldn't help me anymore, and I believed him."

Mila frowned. "Didn't that seem odd to you—that he got drunk all the time, but he wouldn't let you drink?"

"Yeah, at first he made me mad. But then he explained. He said it was too late for him—he was already hooked on the stuff, and he wasn't never getting off the street. For me it was different." Spike stared at his dirty hands for a few seconds, then cut his eyes over in Mila's direction. "You got parents?"

Mila's heart pounded, and she had to struggle to keep her voice even as she replied, "I have a mother. My father is dead."

"I don't claim no parents except the Gent." Spike's voice broke, and he turned away. "I really miss him."

"If you remember the things he taught you, he won't ever leave you completely," Mila told him.

Spike glanced at Mila. "Is that how it is with your father?"

She nodded. After a few minutes, she asked, "Are we there yet?"

Spike peered through the windshield. "Yeah, just a couple more blocks. The Gent worked the business district."

Mila parked the car in front of a branch of the Hawaii National Bank, and they climbed out. As they walked down the busy sidewalks past the modern office buildings, she asked, "So, how did you and the Gent meet?"

"At the old warehouse, where a bunch of homeless folks live. I was beat up pretty bad by my last foster parents, and he took care of me. He taught me about literature and poetry and music. He taught me manners and how to look out for guys weaker than me." Spike paused for a few seconds. "He taught me that life wasn't all bad, and it's not right that somebody killed him."

"Are you still living in the warehouse?"

Spike nodded. "It's the only home I got."

"I could help you sign up for some classes, maybe get you a real job. Then you could afford an apartment—live a normal life."

Spike laughed. "Normal means different things to different folks."

"My father was very important in my life," Mila told him. "And after he died, I spent a lot of time trying to live his life. But finally I realized that I had my own life to live and I had to let go. It's still hard, and sometimes I find myself slipping back."

"*The familiar is very seductive,*" Spike told her. "That's what the Gent used to say."

"I can't argue with that."

"I never understood it before, but I guess if he used to work here, maybe that's why the Gent came here everyday, even if he didn't make no money. Because he felt comfortable here."

Mila nodded. "Like he said—the familiar is very seductive."

They continued around the Gent's normal route on both the sidewalks and the alleys but didn't see anything significant. "I'm sorry you wasted your time," Spike said when they came to a stop beside her car.

"I wasn't really expecting to find evidence," Mila told him. "I just wanted to get a feel for the area." She noticed the Channel One studios a block north and made a mental note to ask Raquel if she'd ever seen the Gent. Raquel was so self-absorbed it was unlikely, but it wouldn't hurt to ask. "Would you like me to give you a ride back to your territory?" Mila asked.

"Naw," Spike declined as she opened the door of her car. "I'll walk." He flashed her a grin. "Who knows? Some of these rich folks might feel sorry for me and give me a dollar."

"Call me if you think of something important," Mila told him, "but only if you think of something important." He waved and headed down the street.

Mila drove back to the police station and dropped the Sprite can off at the lab. "Pull as many prints off of this as you can get and run them through the computer," she requested of a lab technician named Marko. "As soon as you have a name, call me on my cell phone." She handed him one of her business cards.

Marko frowned. "I thought you were on vacation."

"I am," Mila said. When she got upstairs, she found Jerry in his cubicle. "Have you found out any more about Carson?" she asked.

Jerry shook his head. "The company he worked for went bankrupt, and his daughters were adopted."

"Did the aunt adopt them?"

Jerry shrugged. "I don't know. The files are sealed." He leaned forward. "It's a dead end, Mila. Forget Carson and concentrate on being a bride. The world is no worse off without one wino."

Mila sighed. "Tell that to Spike."

* * *

Mila met up with Quin and the others at Café Sistina. After they placed their orders, she asked for a report on Sand Island.

"Quin let me and Charles ride on a little surfboard," Emily was pleased to report.

Mila raised an eyebrow in Quin's direction.

"I was with them every second," he assured her. "They were completely safe."

"Mark was the one we had to worry about," Kate said with a smile at her husband. "I was afraid that watching the lesson was going to give him a nervous breakdown."

"I prefer for my children to keep their feet firmly on solid ground," Mark admitted.

"Then we got to go to a playground that had a train," Emily continued.

"I rode the train," Charles said proudly.

"We *all* rode the train," Annabelle told Mila. "In fact, I didn't think we were going to be able to get Eugenia off the thing."

Miss Eugenia dismissed this with a wave of her hand. "The very idea! I was just playing along to help entertain the children."

Miss Polly diverted everyone's attention by announcing, "I collected several recipes for *Dishes from Sea to Shining Sea*. I got one from California and one from Rhode Island."

Kate patted Miss Polly's plump hand. "So, you've covered the *seas* at least!"

Mila turned to Annabelle. "Did you have fun?"

Annabelle rolled her eyes. "As much fun as I could have holding a video camera. Eugenia wanted me to catch every second on film."

"This is a once-in-a-lifetime experience," Miss Eugenia reminded her sister. "And I will enjoy watching that surfing lesson for many years to come. Emily and Charles are both so well coordinated, and they love water. Either one of them could end up being a famous surfer."

"Over my dead body," Mark murmured.

Mila laughed. Then she turned to Miss George Ann and forced herself to ask, "What did you do on Sand Island?"

"I soaked my feet in the saltwater," she replied. "Not that it helped much. They are still killing me."

"I tried to convince Miss Polly to give surfing a try," Quin said with a discreet wink at Mila. "But she didn't think I knew enough about surfing to give her lessons."

"Oh, Quin!" Miss Polly cried. "That's not true. I just forgot my swimsuit is all."

"Heaven help us," Annabelle whispered.

Further conversation became impossible when a mariachi band arrived at their table and played enthusiastically. Mila's head was hurting by the time they left, and she suggested that they drive to Waikiki Beach.

They drove by some of the more spectacular hotels then parked and walked down to the public beach.

"So, did you find out who your dead guy was?" Quin asked as he sat beside Mila.

"We found out who he is and that he might have been poisoned, but that's it. There are no other leads, and Jerry wants to drop it. I don't have the time to pursue it, so if he's not willing to, our victim will end up as just another unsolved case."

"I think I told you that I'm working for Kate's sister, Kelsey," Miss Eugenia said. "She runs an Internet investigation service, and I'd be glad to ask her to check on your dead man."

Mila smiled. "Thank you, but we don't have enough evidence to justify the expense of a private investigator. It's mostly just curiosity on my part and a gut feeling that the victim was killed."

"Didn't you say he was a drunkard?" Miss George Ann asked.

"Yes, he was a homeless alcoholic."

Miss George Ann lifted her chin in disdain. "I'll bet hundreds of people like that die everyday. It would cost a fortune to investigate them all."

"He may not have been the best person, but he was important in the life of a boy, and I'd like to repay him for that." Mila looked up and shrugged. "I'm hoping that I can get the boy into better living conditions—maybe help him finish high school. That might be the best I can do."

* * *

It was well after dark by the time the group returned to Makai that evening. Mila dropped the Haggerty ladies off at the main house and followed Quin and the Iversons around to the bungalows. Mila got out of her car and waited until the Iversons were inside their own bungalow, then she climbed into Quin's car and pulled him into a tight embrace.

"This is the first time I've had you to myself all day," she whispered. "Maybe we should have just gotten married without telling anyone."

Quin laughed. "Is it too late for us to give our company to Raquel?"

"Don't tempt me," Mila grumbled.

Quin pressed a gentle kiss on her cheek.

"Come on, you can do better than that," she encouraged him.

His lips were moving toward hers when Raquel knocked on the driver's side window. Quin and Mila exchanged a startled look. Then he rolled down the window.

"Sorry to interrupt again," Raquel said a little breathlessly. "But I still haven't been able to get in touch with Leilani, and I wondered if Mila would help me."

Assuming Raquel was referring to police resources, Mila said, "I can call the station and ask someone to check into it tomorrow. But it's too late now, unless you think Leilani is in imminent danger—then you should call 9-1-1."

Raquel laughed. "I didn't mean for you to involve the police. I just want you to call her boyfriend and ask if Leilani is there."

Mila was confused. "Why can't you call him?"

"I'm afraid if I call, he won't tell me the truth," Raquel admitted. "We don't have what you'd call a *friendly* relationship."

Mila thought about the encounter she'd witnessed at the party the night before and nodded. "Okay." She pulled out her cell phone. "What's the number?"

Raquel ran her fingers through her curls in a gesture of frustration. "Oh, I forgot to bring it with me. It's in the rolodex on my desk. Would you mind coming with me to my office?"

Mila hated to sacrifice any of her limited private time with Quin, but cooperating was probably the quickest way to get rid of Raquel, so she nodded. Turning to Quin, she said, "I'll be back soon."

He leaned forward and kissed her forehead. "I'd better go. It's late, and we both need some sleep."

Annoyed that her agreement to help Raquel had come at a higher price than she had anticipated, Mila told Quin good night. Then she followed Raquel up to the main house. When they walked inside, they met Miss Eugenia in the entryway.

"I declare, you nearly scared the life out of me," the elderly woman cried, clutching her chest.

Mila had to work hard to control a laugh as Raquel apologized profusely. "I'm so sorry, but I didn't expect anyone to be up this late."

"I'm having a little indigestion and was heading to the kitchen to see if I might be able to find something to settle my stomach," Miss Eugenia explained.

"Come with us to my office," Raquel commanded. "I'll have Mrs. Rose bring you some milk."

Miss Eugenia nodded. "I'd appreciate that, unless you think Mrs. Rose has already gone to bed."

"Nonsense," Raquel dismissed as they continued down the hall. "Mrs. Rose never sleeps." They entered the office, and Raquel flipped on the light, then crossed the room to her desk. She called Mrs. Rose and asked her to bring the milk. That task completed, she opened her rolodex. "Leilani is still missing, and I've asked Mila to try and get in touch with that horrible boyfriend of hers," she explained for Miss Eugenia's benefit. Then she read the boyfriend's number aloud.

Mila entered it into her cell phone and asked, "What's his name?"

"Blake," Raquel provided.

Mila pressed "send" and a male voice answered promptly. "Hello."

"Blake?"

"Yes," the young man answered with a trace of hesitation.

"My name is Mila Edwards and I'm renting one of the bungalows at Makai. Leilani isn't answering Raquel's phone calls, and she's getting worried. Is Leilani there with you?"

"No." Blake sounded surprised by the question. "Why would she be here?"

"Well, you're her boyfriend, aren't you?"

Blake laughed, but it wasn't a happy sound. "I was never Leilani's boyfriend, and I haven't even seen her in a couple of months."

"Except for last night at the party."

She heard him sigh. "Yeah, except for then. I talked to her for like two minutes before I split."

"Can you tell me what you and Leilani talked about?"

"I could, but I don't want to. It's personal."

Since Leilani was not yet listed as a missing person, Mila didn't want to use her police authority and felt that she couldn't press him on the subject otherwise. So instead she asked, "But when you left last night, Leilani stayed here?"

"Yeah, she was standing on the driveway when I drove away."

"Well, if you hear from her, would you ask her to give Raquel a call?"

"Yeah, sure," Blake said. Then he disconnected.

Mila looked over at Raquel. "He doesn't know where she is."

"Maybe you could try Leilani's apartment number and her cell phone," Raquel suggested. "If the call is coming from someone besides me, she might answer."

"I guess that's worth a try," Mila agreed. Raquel provided the numbers, and Mila dialed. Finally she turned off the phone and shook her head. "She's not answering."

Raquel sat in the chair behind her desk. "I'm beginning to wonder if the girl packed up and quit without giving notice."

"Have you checked her apartment?" Mila asked.

Raquel nodded. "She's not there. Mrs. Rose has knocked several times but says she gets no response."

"Mrs. Rose?" Miss Eugenia repeated. "Are you saying that Leilani lives here on the estate?"

"Yes," Raquel confirmed.

"Then why don't you just open her apartment door and see if all her things are gone?" Miss Eugenia suggested.

Raquel made a face. "I thought of that, but Mrs. Rose seems to have misplaced the extra set of keys to Leilani's apartment."

The housekeeper walked in as if on cue and handed the milk to Miss Eugenia. "Is there anything else you need?" she asked Raquel. There was an edge to her voice, and Mila was sure she had heard Raquel's remark about losing the keys.

"Not unless you've found the keys," Raquel replied.

Mrs. Rose shook her head. "No, the keys are still missing. We'll probably have to call a locksmith."

"It might be time to report Leilani's absence to the police," Miss Eugenia remarked.

"Do you count as the police?" Raquel asked Mila.

"No, I'm on vacation," Mila said as she checked her watch. Every minute that she spent with Raquel was one she couldn't spend talking to Quin on the phone.

Raquel bit her lip. "Do you think something has happened to Leilani? Is that why you want me to notify the police?"

"Terrible things happen to young women these days," Miss Eugenia pointed out ruthlessly. "She may have been abducted or murdered or . . ."

Mila interrupted at this point. "Leilani is probably fine, but if you notify the police that she's missing, they can be on the lookout for her car—just in case."

"But Leilani doesn't own a car," Raquel said. "She drives Cade's old Honda."

Mila frowned. "Is the Honda accounted for?"

Raquel nodded. "It's in the garage."

Mila glanced at Miss Eugenia and saw the concern she felt mirrored in the old woman's eyes. "I think Mrs. Rose should call a locksmith and ask him to come right away."

"Now? In the middle of the night?" Raquel asked in surprise.

"Leilani hasn't been seen in over twenty-four hours," Mila said gently. "You haven't been able to reach her by phone. No one saw her leave the estate, and she doesn't answer at her apartment, but the car she drives is in the garage. I think that justifies the cost of an emergency visit from a locksmith."

Raquel's expression remained calm, but Mila noticed that her hand was trembling as she turned to Mrs. Rose. "Will you take care of that at once?" she requested.

The housekeeper nodded and hurried from the room. Then Raquel addressed Miss Eugenia. "It looks like you need more milk. Why don't we go to the kitchen and get you a refill?"

Miss Eugenia stood. "That sounds like a good idea."

Mila sighed. Obviously she wasn't going to get home anytime soon. On the way to the kitchen, Mila called Quin and explained the situation.

"I'm walking in the apartment now," he said. "Would you like for me to come back?"

"There's no need for you to do that," Mila replied. "Leilani is probably mad at Raquel and staying away on purpose to worry her, but I'll feel better once we make sure that her apartment is empty. You get some sleep."

She heard Quin yawn. "What's on our tourism schedule for tomorrow?"

"I'm too tired to remember," she told him honestly. "Just come to the bungalow for breakfast, and we'll figure it out."

* * *

By the time the locksmith finally arrived, Eugenia had consumed three glasses of milk. But her stomach was still churning. She was about to ask Raquel for an antacid, but Mila spoke first.

"How many entrances are there to Leilani's apartment?"

Raquel twisted her hands nervously. "There's one that goes directly outside and there's one here." She pointed to a little hallway that branched off from the kitchen.

"Let's try the inside one first," the locksmith suggested.

Eugenia left her empty milk glass on the kitchen table and followed the others down the hall and into a small vestibule. "This used to be the quarters for the family's governess," Raquel explained to no one in particular. "The fact that it's near the kitchen indicates servant status, but the extra privacy of a separate suite shows that education was respected in the household."

Eugenia understood that Raquel was chattering to cover her anxiety and tried to help. "That's very interesting," she said, and Raquel gave her a grateful smile.

When they reached the door, the locksmith put his toolbox on the ground and kneeled to examine the lock. "It's old and not very sophisticated," he told them. "I'll have it open in a jiffy."

While he worked, Raquel wrinkled her nose. "What is that smell?"

The housekeeper, who had accompanied them, replied, "I noticed the odor earlier today. I think the sewer lines are backing up again so I've called the plumber, and he promised to come first thing in the morning."

Instead of commending Mrs. Rose for handling the situation so efficiently, Raquel said, "You should have insisted that he come immediately. By tomorrow morning we may be floating in sewage."

Eugenia was trying to rid her mind of this horrifying mental picture when the locksmith announced, "Got it." Then the door to Leilani's apartment swung open. The bad smell intensified.

"The blockage in the sewer must be right under this apartment," Eugenia said, trying to breathe through her mouth.

"Whew!" the locksmith said. "Unless you need me to unlock something else, I'll go home."

"That's all," Raquel told him with a strained smile. "Mrs. Rose will handle your fee."

"I can send you a bill," he offered, packing up his tools quickly.

Raquel nodded. "That will be very convenient. Thank you for coming to our rescue, and now Mrs. Rose will show you out."

Mila waited until Mrs. Rose and the locksmith were in the kitchen before she stepped across the threshold into the apartment.

Raquel put a finger under her nose. "I think I'll wait out here while you look around."

Mila nodded as she walked into the small living room with Eugenia in her wake. "Leilani?" she called, but there was no answer.

The room was furnished with a little couch and a matching chair—both of which were aimed toward a modest-sized television. A floor lamp in the corner had been left on and provided the only light. The room was basically neat with just a few personal items scattered around. Eugenia could picture Leilani coming in after the unpleasant scene at the party, throwing her purse on the chair, and kicking her shoes into the corner. Mila circled around the furniture and walked to the bedroom door.

Eugenia followed, but when she reached the bedroom door, Mila held up a hand. "Stay back," she instructed.

Eugenia looked into the dark room and saw Leilani lying on the bed. She would have thought the girl was asleep if it hadn't been for the smell.

"She's dead?" Eugenia asked, although she already knew the answer.

"Yes," Mila confirmed. "I'm sure she is."

"Is *she* what smells so bad?"

Mila frowned. "I don't think the body would have had time to decompose much even in this hot, moist climate."

Mila used the fabric of her jacket to cover her hand as she flipped on the light. Then the source of the smell became clear. Obviously Leilani had been very sick before she died and had thrown up several times. Mila crossed the room and checked the body for a pulse. "Nothing," she said. "She's probably been dead for hours."

"Bless her heart," Eugenia spoke in a quiet tone, wanting to be respectful of the recently dead. Then she noticed a plate on the table by the bed. "Is that cheesecake?"

Mila followed the direction of her finger and nodded. "I think so. In fact, it looks like *chocolate chip* cheesecake."

Eugenia controlled a gasp. "The cheesecake that was supposed to be served at the party but was stolen from the refrigerator?"

"That would be my guess. Let's get out of here." Mila turned, pulling out her cell phone as they walked. With the phone to her ear, Mila led the way into the small kitchen. On the counter was the cheesecake that had been in Raquel's office the day before, and a space equivalent to about three pieces was missing. Eugenia watched as Mila checked the refrigerator and sink while reporting the situation to the police and requesting that a patrol car be sent over.

"We'll also need the coroner," she added before disconnecting the call.

When Mila and Eugenia returned to the vestibule, they found Mrs. Rose waiting with Raquel. "She's dead, isn't she." Raquel's voice was full of dread.

Mila nodded. "Yes."

Mrs. Rose looked too stunned to speak, but Raquel managed to ask, "How?"

"It looks like she got sick and then just . . . died," Mila explained. "We might know more after the coroner has a chance to examine the body."

"I need to call Cade," Raquel whispered.

Eugenia checked her watch. It was almost ten o'clock. "Isn't he home?"

"No," Raquel answered. "He had to work late."

Very late, Eugenia thought to herself.

Mila extended her cell phone toward Raquel. "Here, use this to call him." Mila didn't make eye contact with Raquel, and Eugenia wondered if Mila had suspicions about Cade's absence as well.

Raquel shook her head. "You might need your phone. I'll call from the extension in the kitchen." Then she walked down the little hallway. Mrs. Rose followed behind her, still looking dazed.

"I guess I'd better call Quin and give him the bad news." Mila dialed a number on her cell phone. When Quin answered, she succinctly detailed what they had found in Leilani's room. Quin offered to come back, but Mila told him there was nothing he could do at Makai, then encouraged him to go to sleep and said she'd see him in the morning.

After Mila closed her phone, Eugenia said, "So I guess Leilani *did* steal the cheesecake. She ate it, and it killed her."

"We won't know for sure until they do an autopsy and check her stomach contents," Mila replied with caution. "But if her death was caused by something she ate, it probably was the cheesecake. The only other thing in the kitchen was bottles of Evian water."

"I wonder why she didn't call anyone to help her when she got so violently sick."

Mila shook her head. "I don't know. Maybe she didn't have anyone to call."

Eugenia detested doctors and hated asking for help, but even she found this unfathomable. "She didn't have to call anyone in particular. She could have called 9-1-1!"

"Leilani probably didn't realize just how sick she was until she was too weak to call for help."

"I doubt if it was a food allergy, but you'll need to contact the Cheesecake Company and get a list of ingredients so you can check with Leilani's doctor."

Mila gave Eugenia a grim smile. "I agree that someone should do that, but it won't be me. I'm *not* here officially, and I *am* getting married in four days."

Eugenia frowned. "Well, you can suggest that to the detectives assigned to the case."

Mila shook her head. "It may never become a case with detectives assigned. If it's ruled death by accidental or natural causes, it won't warrant many man hours."

Eugenia remembered the dream she'd had on the plane and a chill ran down her spine. Maybe it had been a premonition after all. "What if the cake was poisoned?"

"Then I'll be happy to pass along any suggestions you have to the detectives in charge."

They saw red flashing lights through the kitchen window as Raquel rushed in. "The police are here," she announced unnecessarily.

"I'll go out and meet them," Mila volunteered. "And Miss Eugenia, you should probably go tell Annabelle and the others what's happened. If they see the police cars, they might panic."

Eugenia nodded and went upstairs. She knocked on each occupied guest room's door and waited for her fellow travelers to meet her in the hallway.

Annabelle spoke first. "I hate to ask this, but why did you wake us up in the middle of the night?"

Eugenia quickly outlined all that had happened since she left her room in search of a glass of milk. When she finished, Polly dabbed her eyes with her ever-present handkerchief.

"It's very sad," Polly whimpered. "She was such a lovely young woman."

"You didn't even know her," George Ann pointed out, more irritable than usual since she was sleepy. "And did you say that the sewer lines are backed up?"

Eugenia shook her head. "No, you weren't paying close attention to my story. They *thought* the sewer lines were backed up because of the smell, but the odor was actually caused by the dead girl."

"Oh, my," Polly said. The handkerchief was now pressed to her nose.

"Well, that's a relief," George Ann went on, drawing astonished looks from her companions.

"You're glad that Leilani is dead?" Eugenia was shocked into asking.

George Ann gave her an impatient look. "No, of course not! I'm just glad that they aren't having sewage problems. My sense of smell is very sensitive, and bad odors are agony for me."

Eugenia stared at the woman for a few seconds, astounded that even George Ann could consider a dead person preferable to a stopped-up sewer. Finally she said, "The sewer is fine. As long as murder doesn't bother you, you can stay here in complete comfort."

"How will we be able to go back to sleep?" Polly sniffled into her handkerchief. "I'll be afraid to close my eyes."

Eugenia took pity on her longtime friend. "If you don't think you can sleep, get dressed and we'll go downstairs. Mrs. Rose just made fresh coffee."

"That sounds good to me," Annabelle said wearily.

George Ann sighed. "Me too."

"We'll meet back here in a few minutes," Eugenia told them. "I've got to call Kate and Mark."

Annabelle looked at Eugenia. "I guess you want to borrow my cell phone?"

Eugenia nodded. "I'm about to decide the convenience of cell phones outweighs their health risks."

Annabelle smiled. "Welcome to the new millennium."

Eugenia followed Annabelle to her room and got the cell phone. Then she walked to her own room to make her call. Mark answered on the second ring.

"Were you asleep?" Eugenia asked by way of greeting.

He cleared his throat. "I usually am at this time of night."

"Well, I thought the arrival of the police cars might have awakened you."

Now she had his attention.

"Police cars?"

"I'm afraid I have some disturbing news."

"What's the matter?" Mark asked in obvious concern.

"Raquel's secretary is dead. She ate some of Raquel's missing cheesecake, which was probably poisoned. Mila and I just found her body in her little apartment off the kitchen."

After a brief pause Mark said, "You're kidding."

Eugenia was appalled. "Why in the world would I kid about something like that?"

"I guess it was just wishful thinking." Eugenia heard the sound of bedcovers rustling and assumed that Mark was moving to a location away from his wife and children. "So, where are you now?"

"I'm in the hallway, waiting for Annabelle and Polly and George Ann. Once they're dressed, we're going to the kitchen."

"Why?"

"Well, I figure the police will want to question us since we're staying here at the house and since we attended the party. Why, we even saw Cade on the balcony with Leilani just before she died."

Mark's voice took on a warning tone. "You need to let the police handle this."

"Oh, I am," Eugenia assured him. "But we have to get this wrapped up so Mila can get married on Saturday."

"The *police* have to get it wrapped up," Mark corrected. "But I'm glad you let me know."

Eugenia smiled. "So you can come over and help too?"

"No," Mark replied. "So I can reserve us a hotel room."

"You don't need to do that," Eugenia was quick to say. "Raquel didn't say she wants us to leave."

"Well I don't *want* to stay any place where people are dying—possibly even being murdered."

Eugenia was put out with him. "It seems like you'd *want* to help solve the crime."

"Why?" Mark sounded truly mystified.

"Because you're an FBI agent," she reminded him. "Aren't you sworn to uphold the law?"

"I'm required as a citizen of the United States to uphold the law," Mark replied, and she could tell he was amused. "But as far as the FBI is concerned—I'm on vacation and have no jurisdiction here."

Eugenia couldn't think of a sufficiently scathing reply, so she just said, "Humph." Then she added, "Well, I'm sure the police will need to talk to you,. too."

"We won't move to a hotel until morning. Tell the police they are welcome to come by and speak to us there."

"Just try to get someplace close," Eugenia said when she realized she wasn't going to be able to change his mind. "I hate being away from the children."

After disconnecting the call, Eugenia hurried out into the hall, where the others were waiting. They walked into the kitchen just as Mila reentered with two uniformed policemen.

"This is Officer Wong and Officer Gates," Mila introduced. "They need to take a statement from everyone."

"Do I have to make a statement?" Polly asked in alarm. "I don't know anything!"

"Then that's your statement," Officer Gates said, making some notes on a wrinkled pad of forms that looked like it had been in the officer's back pocket for weeks. "I'll just need your name and address."

Eugenia studied the policeman, who had the look of an overgrown beach bum. He was flabby—like an athlete who had stopped exercising. His hair was too long—like someone who didn't make a point to get regular haircuts. The uniform Officer Gates was wearing was too tight in some places and wrinkled in others—which Eugenia considered a particularly bad combination. As if his slovenly appearance wasn't bad enough, Officer Gates was also smacking gum in a manner that seemed inappropriate for the occasion.

Based on her quick character evaluation, Eugenia determined that she could not work with Officer Gates. So she turned her gaze to his partner, Officer Wong. The young man was neat in appearance and had a solemn attitude. Eugenia liked him instantly.

While George Ann explained at length to Officer Gates that she also knew nothing, Eugenia walked over to Officer Wong. "Excuse me," she said. "Would you like to take my statement?"

Officer Wong seemed surprised, but nodded. "I can if you'd like me to."

"I believe I would," Eugenia confirmed.

Officer Wong opened his clipboard and removed a pristine incident report form. He asked for Eugenia's personal information, and she gave it to him concisely. Then she described the events of the evening and was pleased that he took careful notes. When they finished, she looked up to see that Officer Gates had taken statements from everyone else in the same time it had taken for Officer Wong to obtain hers.

"Are you done finally?" Officer Gates looked a little impatient.

"Well, I've given my statement," Eugenia confirmed. "But now I have a few questions."

Both officers seemed startled. Officer Gates turned to Mila and asked, "Who is this?"

"Her name is Eugenia Atkins," Mila replied with a quick glance at Eugenia. "She's a friend of mine visiting from Haggerty, Georgia, and she does have some experience in crime solving."

If possible, the officers seemed even more amazed.

Eugenia smiled. "I'm glad to be of help. First, you should preserve the apartment like a crime scene—just in case."

"Just in case what?" Officer Gates demanded.

"Just in case Leilani's death is eventually classified as murder," Eugenia elaborated in the same tone she used with the mentally infirm patients at the nursing home near Haggerty.

It took a few seconds for this to sink in, then Officer Gates leaned his head back and shouted with laughter. Once his laughing fit had passed, he leveled a stern look at Eugenia. "That's not going to happen."

"Don't speak too soon," Annabelle said from the kitchen table. "Eugenia loves drama, and if you don't watch out, she'll find a way to turn this into a murder, regardless of the facts."

Eugenia scowled at her sister as Officer Gates said, "There's no way she's turning this into a murder."

Officer Wong stepped forward and spoke in a diplomatic tone. "The most likely cause of death was a virus."

Eugenia was determined not to go down without a fight. "Viruses usually kill only weak, sickly people and even then only slowly through dehydration—not quickly like Leilani apparently died."

"There are some aggressive viruses that kill young, healthy people," Mila remarked. "But they are rare."

"Then perhaps it was a food allergy. Some things like peanuts cause fatal reactions," Officer Wong proposed.

Eugenia had considered and discarded this idea. "It's highly unlikely that Leilani had an allergy she wasn't aware of and even more improbable that she purposely ate something she was allergic to."

"Maybe she was lactose intolerant," Officer Gates contributed, and Eugenia gave him a scornful look.

"Then why did she eat three pieces of cheesecake?" Eugenia wanted to know. "And besides, lactose intolerance is not fatal."

Annabelle stood. "Are you finished with us?"

"Yes, you ladies are free to go." Officer Gates made a point of including Eugenia in his statement, but she ignored him.

As the other guests from Haggerty were leaving, Cade rushed into the room. He collected Raquel into the comfort of his arms then said to the policemen, "This has all been very upsetting for my wife. How much longer are you going to be here, officers?"

Officer Gates stood a little taller and replied, "We're waiting for the coroner, then we'll clear out."

Eugenia took a step closer to the policemen, reclaiming their attention. "You should consider the possibility that the cake was poisoned."

"Poisoned!" Raquel shrieked. "You mean someone *killed* Leilani?"

"Even if she was poisoned, it was probably unintentional," Officer Gates claimed.

Mila looked skeptical. "How can you poison someone accidentally?"

"Maybe the cake was spoiled," Officer Gates said.

"The Hawaiian climate might accelerate spoilage," Mila agreed.

Eugenia rejected this with a wave of her hand. "The climate here is not much different from the one I live in. In fact, if anything, the climate here is milder. A cake made with preservatives would not have spoiled in an air-conditioned room in the few hours between its delivery and its being opened."

"Maybe the cake wasn't given the proper amount of preservatives during the preparation process," Officer Wong contributed.

"Or maybe it was left out in the heat during transport," Mila added.

"A million things could have happened to it," Officer Gates summarized. "From what you've been able to tell us, the girl had no known enemies. There are no signs of forced entry at either door to Miss Fiero's apartment. There is no bruising on the body to indicate that the girl was restrained in any way. So, it's silly to assume that she was killed."

Mila was frowning. "Besides, if the cake was poisoned, then Leilani wasn't the intended victim."

The room was silent until Officer Gates said, "Huh?"

"Leilani stole the cake from the refrigerator," Mila reminded them. "It was originally given as a gift to Raquel."

"Someone is trying to kill *me*?" Raquel whispered.

Cade's arms tightened around his wife. "Are you saying that Raquel is in danger?"

"No," Officer Gates replied.

"It's a possibility," Mila disagreed.

"Hey!" Officer Gates objected. "We're running this investigation."

"The poison theory *is* very premature," Officer Wong aligned himself loosely with his partner.

"Well, I want you to find out how Leilani died immediately!" Cade demanded. His anger seemed a little exaggerated, and Eugenia couldn't help but wonder if it was meant to distract everyone from the fact that he wasn't home when the body was discovered.

"The medical examiner will run toxicology tests," Mila assured him.

Officer Wong cleared his throat. "If there is any poison in Miss Fiero's system, we should know within a few hours."

"There are a lot of poisons that don't show up on toxicology reports," Eugenia was pleased to inform them. "We had a case in Georgia a few years ago where a woman was poisoning people with an overdose of heart medication, and it looked like they died of natural causes."

"That does it," Raquel said. "Until this is resolved, I want round-the-clock police protection."

"Ma'am," Officer Gates began in a conciliatory tone. "First of all, we haven't even classified this as a homicide; and if we do, it will be up to the chief to decide whether you need police protection."

"I happen to know the chief personally," Raquel informed him. "I'll be giving him a call."

"If I were you, I'd make that call tonight," Eugenia advised.

Officer Gates gave Mila a look that Eugenia interpreted as *will you get her out of here?* Apparently Mila translated it the same way, because she stepped forward and addressed Eugenia directly. "It's been quite a night and you probably don't want to be here when the coroner arrives, so why don't I walk you to your room?"

On the way upstairs, Eugenia said to Mila, "Those officers seemed a little resistant to suggestion and were, at times, downright condescending."

Mila smiled. "They just aren't accustomed to dealing with people who obviously know so much more than they do."

* * *

After depositing Miss Eugenia safely in her room, Mila headed back toward the kitchen. She knew she would have to tread carefully if she didn't want to alienate Gates and Wong any further, but she had learned from past experience that Miss Eugenia had good instincts. If Miss Eugenia thought that the cheesecake was poisoned, it probably was.

When she entered the kitchen she heard Cade talking to the officers. "It's easy for you to say 'be calm,'" he nearly shouted. "But what if someone *is* trying to kill my wife and makes another attempt in the meantime?"

"She needs to be careful what she eats," Gates advised.

"Are you making light of this situation?" Cade demanded.

Gates took a step backward. "No, sir. I meant that she should only eat food prepared by people she trusts and nothing delivered anonymously—at least until the toxicology reports are in."

Mila walked up behind Gates and suggested quietly, "I hate to agree with Miss Eugenia, but you should probably secure the apartment as a potential crime scene—just in case."

Gates gave Mila a sour look, but before he could respond, Raquel walked in. "I've been on the phone with the chief, and he said he would take the steps necessary to ensure my safety," she told them with a satisfied smile. Then she addressed Cade. "Let's go upstairs. Mrs. Rose is here to get them anything they need."

Mila watched Cade put his arm around her shoulders and lead his wife out of the kitchen. Then she was about to repeat her warning about the need to protect possible evidence in the apartment when Mrs. Rose walked in—followed closely by Detective Jerry Hirasuna.

"Are you working the night shift now, Jerry?" Mila asked.

Her partner gave her a sour look. "No, but we're short staffed because several folks are on vacation."

Mila was immediately contrite. "I'm sorry."

Jerry winked. "Just kidding. The chief said this case has the potential to be a PR nightmare, so he wanted me to come personally. What's the situation here? Murder, mayhem?"

Mila shook her head. "We do have a body . . ."

"But unless you believe an old woman from Georgia who's here for Mila's wedding—it ain't no murder," Officer Gates interrupted Mila to say.

Mila shot the policeman an irritated glance. "We also have a hysterical prima donna. I'm not sure which the chief is more concerned about," Mila said.

Jerry frowned. "Since dead bodies can't complain to the commissioner—I'm guessing the prima donna. Where are they?"

"The prima donna's upstairs, and the body's in here." Officer Gates gestured toward the hallway that led to Leilani's apartment.

Jerry raised an eyebrow in Mila's direction but didn't ask any questions. "Take me to see the body," he requested. Gates pushed away from the counter, intending to provide this service, but Jerry pointed at Mila. "If you can spare a few minutes from your vacation, maybe you can do the honors?"

"This way." Mila avoided eye contact with Gates as she led the way down the hall, but she could almost feel his malevolent stare.

"Why hasn't the area been secured?" Jerry asked when they reached the door to Leilani's apartment.

"Since it hasn't been established that any crime has been committed, Gates felt like treating the area as a crime scene would be premature."

Jerry gave her an incredulous look as he pulled on a pair of latex gloves. "If you wait to protect the scene until *after* it's established that a crime has been committed, all the evidence will be destroyed."

Mila was reluctant to say more since the officer wasn't there to defend himself, so she just shrugged. "There are two entrances to the apartment, and the extra set of keys that is supposed to be in the kitchen is missing."

"How did you get in?"

"The housekeeper called a locksmith at my suggestion, since the victim hadn't been seen or heard from in over twenty-four hours." Mila stepped across the threshold and into the room. When they reached the kitchen, she pointed at the counter. "This is the cheesecake that probably killed her, one way or another." Mila proceeded into the living room. "The lamp was left on."

Mila waited while the detective did a thorough visual examination. "Okay, let's see the body."

Mila circled around the couch and walked into the bedroom. The smell was overpowering, but Jerry didn't flinch. "I checked her for a pulse, but otherwise the room is undisturbed."

"Good." Jerry pointed to a towel on the bed beside Leilani. "It looks like she made an attempt to clean up, but finally got too weak."

Mila nodded, agreeing with his assessment.

Jerry studied the room and the position of the body for several minutes then waved for Mila to follow him out. As they walked, he pulled out his cell phone and called the station. He requested that a photographer and an evidence collection team be sent immediately. "The chief is personally interested in this case," he said into the phone, giving Mila a wink. "So, you'd better get them here fast."

"Something you should know before you talk to Raquel," Mila said.

"The prima donna?" Jerry confirmed.

Mila nodded. "The cake that presumably killed Leilani was delivered to Raquel, anonymously, yesterday."

"I guess that explains the hysterics." When they reached the kitchen they found two men from the coroner's office waiting to collect the body. Jerry gave them the bad news that they were going to have to wait until after photographs had been taken and evidence collected. Then he led Mila to a couple of chairs across the room where they could talk in relative privacy.

"Okay," he said once they were seated. "Start at the top and run through the whole thing."

Mila took a deep breath and began with the party on Monday night. She told Jerry about seeing Leilani on the balcony with Cade Simon, the arrival of Leilani's friend, Blake, and the nasty scene with Raquel that followed. She told him about the missing cheesecake and about how the conclusion had been reached that Leilani took it from the refrigerator.

"So, the cake was sent to Mrs. Simon as a gift?" Jerry interrupted to confirm.

Mila nodded. "Yes. Apparently the girl had a habit of taking food from the refrigerator without asking."

"That bad habit may have prevented this from being much worse," Jerry mused. "If the cake had been served at the party, many more people might have died."

"Yes."

"So, when did Mrs. Simon realize that the girl was missing?"

Mila told him about Raquel's numerous attempts to reach Leilani and how she finally enlisted her help late that evening. She related her phone conversation with Blake and his claims that he and Leilani did not have a romantic relationship and that he had spoken to her only briefly and about a private matter on Monday night. "Blake said that when he left Makai, Leilani remained on the estate. I tried Leilani's numbers on my cell phone, but she still didn't answer, so Raquel had her housekeeper call the locksmith at my request," Mila concluded as the photographer and evidence team arrived.

Jerry went to supervise the documentation of the scene, and Mila remained where she was, trying to ignore the murderous looks she was getting from Gates. Yawning, she checked her watch. It was after midnight. Mila sent a text message to Quin in case he was asleep. Her phone rang immediately, and she smiled at the comforting sound of his voice. They talked until Jerry Hirasuna returned to the kitchen— at which point Mila ended her call and put away the phone.

"You guys can get the body now," he told the men from the coroner's office. "We'll need an extended toxicology report—ASAP."

"Don't you always," one of the men said as they wearily wheeled their gurney down the hallway.

Jerry waved Mila over and once she had joined the group of fellow policemen, he said, "Okay, here's how we're going to handle this. Gates, you're assigned to stay here tonight and keep an eye on things just in case Mrs. Simon's life really is in danger."

"Thanks a lot," he said to Mila. "My babysitting duty is your fault."

Jerry spoke before Mila could. "That assignment came straight from the chief. Mrs. Simon is a local celebrity and could bring a lot of negative press our way if we don't handle this right, so the chief wants someone here he can trust."

Gates seemed to feel better immediately. "Oh, yeah, well I can see that."

"Wong, since my partner is on vacation," Jerry cut his eyes briefly at Mila, "you're working with me. I want you to follow the body down to the morgue and rush up those tests. You know the squeakiest wheel gets the most grease. I'll get a guest list from the party on Monday night, and when you get back from the morgue we can start interviewing them. Everyone who was in the house the night of the party is a potential suspect."

Officer Wong looked alarmed. "It will take quite a while to inter-view a hundred guests."

"We'll whittle the list of suspects down by eliminating people with no motive along with those who had alibis—like Mila here. I'd like for one of us to talk to each guest by phone—just in case they saw something useful—but we'll only personally interview people who have a motive." Jerry turned to Mila. "Which is where you come in. I need you to make a list of people who might want Raquel Simon dead."

"Jerry, I'm on vacation."

"Come on, Mila," Jerry begged. "A few minutes at a computer is all I'm asking."

"Jerry," she tried again. "I'm getting married on Saturday."

This didn't seem to faze the young detective. "So, this is one A.M. on Wednesday morning—you got time to make a little list for me, don't you?"

Mila sighed. "Sure."

Jerry gave her a smile. "Good. Try and have it ready by mid-morning. With Wong," Jerry gestured toward the policeman, "and the chief both putting pressure on the coroner's office, we should have at least preliminary toxicology results by then. Let's meet in my office at noon. I'd like to interview the Simons personally, and I'll probably do it here to avoid upsetting them more than necessary. Then we can compare notes."

Mila and Officer Wong both agreed to this plan with varying degrees of enthusiasm. For Elliot Wong, the chance to work with Jerry on this case was a huge career opportunity. For Mila, it was a complication she could do without.

"Great." Jerry seemed full of energy despite the late hour. "Let's get to work."

As Mila trudged to her bungalow, she tried to think of people who might want to kill Raquel Simon. Mrs. Rose and Leilani herself had reason to dislike, perhaps even hate, Raquel, but that was a long way from murder. Mila made a mental note to check into Raquel's ex-husband, and although she hated to, she knew she'd have to find out whether Cade had any extramarital relationships. A girlfriend might want Raquel out of the way so she could have Cade to herself.

She opened the door to the bungalow, then she settled in front of the computer and went to work.

CHAPTER 4

On Wednesday morning, Eugenia found Mrs. Rose drinking coffee at the kitchen table. She took a seat beside her and said, "What a terrible night."

"I still haven't been to bed," the housekeeper confided. "The police detective that's investigating the case is coming by in a few minutes to pick up a list of all the guests from Monday night's party, and I just finished it a little while ago."

Eugenia controlled a smile at the news that Leilani's death was now a *case* with a detective assigned to investigate it. "You poor thing," she said.

Mrs. Rose shook her head. "I can't believe that Leilani is really dead."

"Were you friends?" Eugenia asked.

Mrs. Rose stirred her coffee listlessly. "Not really. She'd only been working for Raquel for a few months, but before that she was an employee at Cade's firm, so I've kind of known her for almost a year."

Now this was interesting news. "Really?" Eugenia tried not to sound too curious. "What did she do for Cade?"

"She worked in the mailroom, I think."

"And what made her decide to work for Raquel instead?" Eugenia knew if she were choosing a boss, she'd take the handsome, easygoing husband over the temperamental wife any day.

The perpetual frown on Mrs. Rose's face deepened. "I'm not sure. I think it had something to do with the fact that Raquel used to be a television star, and Leilani had dreams of becoming an actress."

"She thought Raquel could help her?"

The housekeeper shrugged. "Leilani said Raquel was going to get her a role in a sitcom, but I don't know if that's true. Maybe it was just that working for Raquel was so much easier than a *real* job in the mailroom at Cade's firm."

"I noticed that every time Raquel needs something, she calls you no matter what time of the day or night."

Mrs. Rose nodded. "She loves to boss me around."

"Why is that?"

Mrs. Rose sighed. "I worked for her ex-husband, and he made my continued employment a stipulation in the divorce settlement."

"You seem like an excellent housekeeper," Eugenia said with sincerity. "Why wouldn't Raquel be glad to keep you?"

"I don't think Raquel has any complaints about my management of the house. It's just that I know everything about the estate and its history, and I think Raquel would prefer to be the resident authority."

Eugenia's eyes narrowed shrewdly. "I'll bet you also know a great deal about Raquel herself."

Mrs. Rose acknowledged this with a tip of her head.

"Tell me about Raquel's first husband."

Mrs. Rose smiled. "Rodney Dennison. He was such a dear man."

"He's dead, then?"

"Yes. He died shortly after the divorce. She simply broke his heart."

"Raquel?" Eugenia confirmed, and Mrs. Rose nodded. "By divorcing him, you mean?"

"Oh, no!" the housekeeper seemed appalled by this thought. "She broke his heart by taking his *house*."

Eugenia realized that she had tapped into a motherlode of bad feelings, but she didn't want to awaken any sense of employer loyalty in Mrs. Rose, so she proceeded with caution. "Then Raquel married Cade?"

"Yes, almost immediately," Mrs. Rose said, her distaste obvious. "They had been involved before the divorce, of course."

"Raquel and Mr. Dennison weren't happy in their marriage?" Eugenia guessed.

"I think they were reasonably happy together until Raquel met Cade," Mrs. Rose said. "Raquel was completely fascinated by Cade.

She just had to have him—no matter who got hurt. She was the same way about this house."

"She just had to have it?"

Mrs. Rose nodded. "And Raquel always gets her way."

"Good morning, ladies," Mila said from behind, startling them both.

"Well, good morning," Eugenia greeted. Then, after a closer examination added, "It doesn't look like you got much sleep last night either."

Mila shook her head and took a seat beside them. "I didn't. I was up trying to compile a list of people who hate Raquel. That's why I'm here. I'm hoping that Mrs. Rose can help me with it."

"Did you put that Dream Weaver man from Channel One on the list of people who hate Raquel?" Eugenia asked. "The one who looks like Mr. Miyagi from *The Karate Kid*?"

Mila shook her head. "No, but I can add him. Why does he hate Raquel?"

"He told us it was because she kept his Dream Weaver segment from going into syndication, but there could be more to it than that." Eugenia watched as Mila made some notes on the computer printout she was holding. "And what about Darlene, the cooking assistant?"

Mila frowned. "Darlene is the only person I've talked to who doesn't seem to hate Raquel."

"Darlene worships Raquel." Mrs. Rose covered her mouth to hide a yawn. "I don't know why."

"Maybe she just acts that way to keep her job," Eugenia contributed.

"I doubt that," Mrs. Rose disagreed. "Darlene has complete job security. There would be no *Morning Show* cooking segment if it weren't for Darlene. Raquel can't make a decent piece of toast."

"Since you and Mrs. Rose were both up all night preparing lists," Eugenia said. "I presume that the police are taking Leilani's death seriously now?"

"Yes," Mila confirmed. "After Raquel called the police chief demanding protection, my partner was assigned to investigate, and Officer Gates was told to be Raquel's bodyguard until further notice." Mila looked around. "Speaking of Officer Gates—where is he?"

"Raquel sent him home to get a little rest and clean up," Mrs. Rose replied. "She said if he's going to follow her all day, he's going to have to be presentable."

"I don't blame her for that," Eugenia concurred.

Mrs. Rose seemed to suddenly remember her manners. "Would either of you like coffee?"

Mila and Eugenia shook their heads, but a voice from the doorway said, "I'll take some."

Eugenia turned to see a dark-haired young man wearing dress pants, a white shirt, and a flower-print tie. He had a friendly, intelligent look about him, and Eugenia's initial impression was favorable.

"I thought we weren't meeting until noon," Mila said.

"We're meeting at noon in my office to compare notes at noon," the young man said. "Right now I'm still in the process of collecting information—which is why I came to get my list from Mrs. Rose."

Mila seemed to remember her manners. "Miss Eugenia, this is my partner, Detective Hirasuna. Jerry, I'd like to introduce a friend of mine, Miss Eugenia Atkins from Haggerty, Georgia."

Detective Hirasuna shook the hand that Eugenia extended. "Aloha," he said with a smile.

"Well, aloha to you, too," Eugenia replied.

Mrs. Rose pushed a sheet of paper toward Detective Hirasuna. "This lists all the guests who were invited to the party on Monday night. I put asterisks beside the names of the people who actually attended."

The detective took the list from her. "Thanks. That was very efficient of you."

"I'm hoping Mrs. Rose can help me as well," Mila said. "I've done a background check on Raquel and found several people who might wish her harm, but most of them live on the mainland."

"Planes take off and land here all the time," Jerry pointed out.

"That's true," Mila said with a trace of sarcasm. "But I thought I should include at least a couple of *local* suspects."

Detective Hirasuna sighed in apparent resignation. "If you have to."

"He kids around a lot," Mila told Eugenia before asking Mrs. Rose, "Can you think of anyone who would hate Raquel enough to want to kill her?"

Mrs. Rose gave them one of her grimacing smiles. "How about everyone who knows her?"

Mila raised her eyebrows. "Raquel had that many enemies?"

The housekeeper shrugged. "Well, most of the folks at the television station hate her, from the owner, Mr. Baldwin, all the way down to the janitors. She tortures them with constant demands and complaints. Then she's used that cooking segment of hers on the *Morning Show* to offend half the island."

"How does she offend them with her cooking segment?" Detective Hirasuna asked.

"She spreads gossip—that's the real reason people watch it. Goodness knows Raquel has no cooking skills."

"Raquel tells what she knows about people's personal lives?" Mila confirmed, and Mrs. Rose nodded.

"Oh, yes. She's ruined many marriages and a couple of corporations with her vicious gossip. When she's in a generous mood she'll just criticize a society matron's appearance or the way they decorated their house—which in some social circles can be just as fatal."

"She didn't mention any gossip on the show we watched yesterday," Eugenia reminded Mila.

This caused Mrs. Rose to smirk again. "That's because she used her leftover air time to do a commercial for Makai."

Mila looked up from her notes. "What was all that about?"

Mrs. Rose pressed her lips into a firm, unhappy line. "You'll have to ask Raquel about that."

For a few seconds Eugenia thought Mila might press the housekeeper, but instead she turned to a fresh page in her notebook and titled it "Raquel Hate List."

"Okay," Mila said. "It sounds like you can definitely give me a few candidates. But remember, we're looking for people who hate Raquel enough to *kill* her."

Mrs. Rose rattled off an impressive list of names. When she was finished she said, "That's a start."

Eugenia glanced at Mila's notes. There were more than twenty names on the "start" list.

"I got a call from the owner of the Cheesecake Company a little while ago," Detective Hirasuna reported.

Mila glanced at the clock. "This early?"

"Yeah, he's furious that his company's name was used in the report of Leilani's death in the morning paper."

"Today?"

Mila's partner nodded. "The article has a picture of the Cheesecake Company at Ala Moana Mall and says that Leilani had died from eating a 'tainted' cake made by their company."

Mila frowned. "We don't have proof of that yet. How would the newspaper know anything about it?"

"I don't know," Detective Hirasuna said with a shrug. "Either a reporter lucked onto the story or someone called in a tip. The newspaper is printing a clarification tonight—saying that the cause of Leilani's death has not been established," Jerry said, "but the cheesecake guy thinks it's too little too late and that his company will pay the price in future sales."

"He's probably right," Mila agreed. "How soon will the lab guys have something for us on the cake?"

"The chief called me while I was driving over here. The preliminary tests are back and," the detective glanced at Eugenia, "both the body and the cheesecake were full of arsenic."

"Rat poison?" Mila confirmed.

Jerry nodded. "Yep, our killer didn't even try to be subtle."

"Poor Leilani," Eugenia said.

Detective Hirasuna seemed to step out of police mode for just a second as he nodded. "Yes, she was too young to die."

"And for such a silly reason," Eugenia continued. "She paid a high price for the habit of pilfering food."

Mila looked at Mrs. Rose. "Are you sure that Leilani was the person stealing your food?"

"Yes," Mrs. Rose answered. "I've always found the remnants in her apartment when I cleaned."

"So, she didn't even try to hide her guilt from you?"

Mrs. Rose shook her head. "No."

Eugenia noticed that Mrs. Rose's hands were clenched together in apparent anxiety.

"I don't want you to think I reported her for making a sandwich or eating leftovers," Mrs. Rose explained. "I wouldn't begrudge her that. But once a week or so Leilani would take a whole cake I had made for a party or a pie from the bakery or a new carton of specialty ice cream—things I had purchased or made for a special reason."

"And she always did so without asking?"

The perpetual frown on Mrs. Rose's face deepened. "Always."

"Did you confront her about it?"

"No, I didn't feel that it was my place to do so, but I had to replace the stolen items, which increased my household expenses, so I had to report the behavior to Raquel."

"How did she react?" Mila asked.

"Sometimes she just laughed it off, and sometimes she seemed irritated. She always told me not to worry—that she would talk to the girl."

"But the food continued to disappear?"

Mrs. Rose nodded. "Yes."

Mila turned to Jerry Hirasuna. "You saw Leilani's refrigerator. It was completely empty. Since she didn't keep food on hand, if she had a visitor . . ."

"She stole food when she was entertaining?" Detective Hirasuna seemed to like this train of thought.

"I think it's a reasonable possibility," Mila confirmed.

"Who was she entertaining?" Eugenia asked. "That boyfriend, Blake?"

"She only stole good stuff for her guests," Mila mused. "I'm thinking it must have been someone she wanted to impress."

"Not Blake, then," Eugenia concluded.

Mila shook her head. "I think we can safely assume her guest was someone other than the oyster bar guy."

"So Leilani was expecting a visitor on Monday night either during or after the party," Detective Hirasuna hypothesized. "And when she checked the refrigerator for something to serve—the poisoned cake was there waiting."

Eugenia put a hand to her mouth. "I just realized that if Raquel had cut that cheesecake on Monday afternoon when Polly so rudely suggested it—we might all be dead."

"The killer had to know that innocent people might be killed along with the intended victim," Mila added.

"Apparently he or she didn't care," the detective remarked. "However, on the plus side, the killer didn't have to bring the weapon to the party and risk being caught with it—since it was already here."

"Raquel came home early on Monday to meet my guests," Mila said thoughtfully. "If she'd been following her normal routine, she probably wouldn't have even seen the cheesecake before the party began."

Detective Hirasuna considered this. "Maybe the killer planned to convince Raquel to go somewhere for a private conversation during the party."

"Like her office?" Mila proposed.

"Yes," the detective agreed. "The killer would ask, 'Did you get that cheesecake I sent you today?' Mrs. Simon would laugh and say she wondered who it was from. Then the killer would suggest they have a piece and . . ."

Mrs. Rose cleared her throat, interrupting the conversation. "If the cheesecake was poisoned, and if the killer knows Raquel, then they would also know that she never eats sweets. She's very concerned about staying thin and doesn't eat much of anything, but never, ever, sweets. No exceptions."

Mila raised an eyebrow. "None?"

Mrs. Rose shook her head. "Never."

"Then maybe it didn't matter who got killed," Mila searched for another explanation, "just as long as someone died here and Raquel suffered from the fallout."

"Suffered how?" the detective asked.

Mila shrugged. "Mental anguish, police investigations, bad publicity."

"If several guests had died from eating poisoned cheesecake, people would have thought twice about attending another one of her parties," Eugenia pointed out.

"A murder is not the kind of press coverage she would want," Mila said. "Especially now that she's opening Makai to the public for tours."

Jerry Hirasuna chewed his lip. "You've heard the old saying that there is no such thing as *bad* publicity."

Mila frowned. "I think we have to consider it a possibility. And if that's the case, it will reduce the number of suspects from the guest list. Raquel told me that she had invited everyone from the station and a few other colleagues that day. So, at least some of the guests at the party didn't know in advance."

"In time to poison a cheesecake," Detective Hirasuna finished the thought for Mila before turning to the housekeeper. "Mrs. Rose, would there be any way to narrow this list down to just the people who were invited originally?"

"I should be able to tell you everyone that received an official invitation," the housekeeper replied. "But Raquel was constantly issuing *casual* invitations to her parties, so there's a chance that I'll miss someone that she included at the last minute."

"Right now we just need those invited early," Detective Hirasuna said. "But later if you think of anyone who came whose name is not on the guest list, please let us know."

Before Mila could respond, they were interrupted by the arrival of Annabelle, Polly, and George Ann. Detective Hirasuna stood as he was introduced to all the ladies. Then he excused himself to get back to work. "I'll see you at noon," he told Mila, and she nodded.

Mrs. Rose sprang into motion, providing coffee, fresh fruit, and a variety of sweet rolls for the guests.

"You should call Quin and invite him to join us," Eugenia suggested to Mila.

Mila pulled out her cell phone, and after a brief conversation, reported, "Quin says he's already eaten several of the pastries left over from yesterday, so he'll pass on breakfast. But there's a surfing demonstration this morning, sponsored by the Surf Shop, and he wants you to see it. As soon as you finish eating, we'll walk to the bungalow to meet him."

"Will there be real live surfers there?" Polly asked.

"Yes," Mila confirmed. "Some of the best surfers in Hawaii."

Polly smiled. "That sounds thrilling."

"Could we stop by a drugstore on the way?" George Ann wanted to know.

"I'm sure Quin will be glad to take you to a drugstore," Mila said.

"Good." George Ann lifted her chin. "I've got a toe fungus and need to get some foot powder."

Eugenia controlled a shudder and made a mental note never to put her bare feet where George Ann's had been.

While they ate, everyone questioned Mila about Leilani's death. Eugenia put in her opinions from time to time, and finally Polly held up her hand.

"Please, no more," she begged.

"You're the ones who asked," Eugenia reminded her.

"I know," Polly acknowledged. "But all this talk of death and murder is making me sad, and Hawaii is supposed to be a happy place."

"Eugenia can't help herself," Annabelle said. "Every conversation with her is destined to end up as a discussion of crime, and she has a particular penchant for murder."

Eugenia frowned. "What is that supposed to mean?"

"It means that wherever you go, trouble follows," Annabelle elaborated.

George Ann nodded sadly. "Even here in paradise."

"Miss Eugenia certainly didn't cause Leilani's death!" Mila jumped to Eugenia's defense. "She's just trying to help me solve the case so I can enjoy my wedding."

"I don't see how any of us are going to be able to enjoy the wedding now," George Ann predicted. "The murder has spoiled everything."

"It does seem that way," Polly agreed.

As if further proof was needed, Annabelle added, "I called and talked to Kate this morning. She said they're moving to a hotel."

Eugenia had been hoping Mark would change his mind, and this announcement was not good news. "The very idea of renting a hotel room when you have free accommodations available to you is ridiculous. Why, that sounds like something Annabelle would do!"

Annabelle looked up from her coffee, but before she could comment, Polly said, "Mark just wants to be sure his family is safe."

"Humph," Eugenia replied. "I'm sure they won't be able to find a decent room on the entire island without an advance reservation."

"Actually the hotel where they'll be staying sounds very nice," Polly said. "It's the Honolulu Hilton Village, and Mark said they have five pools and ninety shops and even exotic wildlife."

"Exotic wildlife sounds interesting," Polly said. "Did he say how much a room costs there?"

"He didn't give me an exact price, but he said it was fairly reasonable," Annabelle reported. "And they got a room with a view of the village garden."

"Why don't we call and see if they have more rooms?" Polly suggested.

"I agree," George Ann concurred. "We should all leave immediately before our vacation is completely ruined."

Polly used her ever-present handkerchief to dab some perspiration from her top lip. "It seems impolite of us to remain here as guests when Raquel has this terrible situation to deal with."

Eugenia was determined to stay in the thick of things and searched for a good excuse. "I doubt if the police will let us leave yet," she told them.

"Why ever not?" Polly asked.

"Well, they might have more questions for us," Eugenia said.

Annabelle dismissed this. "They can come and talk to us at the Honolulu Hilton if they need to ask anything else."

Desperate, Eugenia said, "If we leave, it might make us look guilty."

George Ann frowned. "Of what?"

"Why, the murder, of course!" Eugenia clarified.

"Murder!" George Ann cried.

Polly pressed the handkerchief to her temple. "I think I'm going to swoon."

"Should I call my attorney in Albany?" George Ann asked.

Eugenia shrugged. "Not unless you killed Leilani."

"Heaven help us," Annabelle muttered.

"None of you are suspects," Mila intervened with a stern look at Eugenia. "You didn't know Leilani, had no motive to kill her, and since you were all together at the party last night, you provide each other with alibis. If you'd feel more comfortable at a hotel, then you should to leave. But I don't think your presence here is a problem."

As this moment, their hostess walked into the kitchen, looking amazingly refreshed considering the events of the previous evenings.

"Good morning all," she said. "I trust you slept better than I did."

Mrs. Rose poured Raquel a cup of black coffee without being asked. Eugenia noticed that Raquel did not thank the housekeeper for her thoughtfulness.

"It's terrible about your secretary getting poisoned," George Ann blurted out.

"We're so sorry for your trouble," Polly added.

"Thank you," Raquel said.

"In fact, we were wondering if we should get a hotel room to reduce your stress," Annabelle added.

Raquel looked horrified. "Oh, please don't do that. I feel much safer with lots of people around."

"But once you finish with the police, you'll still have the funeral to contend with," Annabelle persisted.

"There won't be a funeral here," Raquel informed them. "I spoke with Leilani's aunt this morning. They are having the body sent to Molokai, the island where they live, and the funeral will be held there."

"But won't you want to go?" Polly asked.

Raquel shook her head. "I'm sorry that Leilani died, and I feel a certain amount of responsibility since I was her employer and her landlord. But we weren't *friends,* and I don't feel obligated to attend the funeral. I've already ordered a spectacular flower arrangement for the cemetery, and I think that's enough." She flashed them a smile. "And it's nice having company to distract me from sad thoughts."

"Well, now, see how rude it would be for us to leave Raquel in her time of need," Eugenia said. "I guess that's settled. We'll be glad to stay."

Annabelle gave her an annoyed look. "I'm not sure it *is* settled."

"If our presence here makes Raquel feel safer, how ungrateful would it be for us to pack up and leave?" Eugenia asked them. "After the way she's opened her home to us."

Annabelle was still scowling, but Polly nodded. "I guess we should stay if you're sure we won't be in the way."

"I'm sure," Raquel confirmed as she checked her watch. "Now, I've got to get to the studio."

"You're going to do your cooking program today?" Annabelle asked. "After, well, what happened last night?"

Raquel nodded firmly. "There is no one who can fill in for me, so if I don't do my segment, the station is left with ten minutes of dead time. Besides, I want to show whoever is trying to kill me that they did not succeed."

"That might just make them try again," Mila pointed out.

"Now that I'm alerted to the danger, I'll be prepared," Raquel said as Officer Gates walked into the kitchen, looking much neater than he had the night before, and informed Raquel that he was ready to escort her to the television station.

"I'm off then." Raquel started toward the door but paused and spoke to Polly. "Be sure and watch my show this morning. I'll try to mention your cookbook."

"Oh, that would be so nice!" Polly gushed.

With a wave over her shoulder, Raquel left the room with her bodyguard.

Her departure was followed by a few seconds of silence before Eugenia asked, "Well, what's on our agenda for this morning?"

"I was supposed to be at the church in twenty minutes to meet with Sister Kaneohe and go over final plans for the reception," Mila told them. "But now I have a list of people who hate Raquel to contact."

"Annabelle and I will meet with Sister Kaneohe so you can get your suspects contacted by noon," Eugenia offered. "Just write down very specific driving directions. Annabelle has a tendency to get lost."

Annabelle scowled. "Annabelle also has a tendency to get roped into things."

Mila gave them a smile. "I can reschedule the meeting with Sister Kaneohe if you want to see the surfing demonstration."

Annabelle sighed. "It's okay. Surfing scares me anyway."

"I really appreciate it," Mila said. "And Sister Kaneohe is very organized, so it's really just a touching-base kind of meeting." She checked her watch before addressing the others. "Quin's ready whenever you are."

Eugenia took one last bite of her nectarine as she stood. "I'll run upstairs and get my purse while you give Annabelle the directions." She turned to her sister. "Then I'll meet you in front by our rental car."

When Eugenia got to her room, she saw Annabelle's cell phone sitting on the dresser, where she had left it earlier. She picked it up and dialed the Iverson's cell number. Mark answered on the second ring. "Have you eaten breakfast?" she asked by way of greeting.

"Not yet," he replied.

"Quin's at their bungalow eating pastries from yesterday, and Mrs. Rose has fresh things here at the main house if you're hungry."

"We're not coming anywhere near the crime scene," Mark replied. "Kate packed some Pop-Tarts, and they'll get us through breakfast today. Tomorrow we'll be eating at the Honolulu Hilton."

"Polly's already told me all about it." Eugenia tried not to sound exasperated. "With the excitement over moving, have you forgotten that Quin's taking you all to see a surfing demonstration this morning?"

"I haven't forgotten," Mark said. "Aren't you going?"

"No, Annabelle and I are meeting with Mila's wedding coordinator to make final plans for Saturday."

"Well, have fun, and we'll miss you."

Eugenia felt a little better as she closed Annabelle's phone.

CHAPTER 5

Annabelle followed Mila's directions with precision, and they arrived at the meetinghouse five minutes early. Inside the cultural hall they found Kaula Kaneohe, who was undoubtedly the largest human being Eugenia had ever seen. She was over six feet tall, and Eugenia conservatively estimated her weight at five hundred pounds. She was also probably the most enthusiastic hugger—with the possible exception of Cornelia Blackwood, the Baptist preacher's wife back home. Sister Kaneohe had hugged them both twice before Eugenia was able to make introductions.

"I'm Eugenia Atkins, a friend of Mila's," she finally managed breathlessly. "And this is my sister Annabelle."

"Aloha!" Sister Kaneohe welcomed them. Then she gave them another hug, and Eugenia began to fear for her seventy-six-year-old ribs. "And you can call me Kaula," she offered. "It means *prophet* in Hawaiian," she added with a proud smile.

"I've noticed that many names here in the islands have a meaning," Eugenia said. "I wonder if my name means something."

Kaula laughed. "A meaning. Oh, you haoles are funny." She patted Eugenia's back so hard that she took several involuntary steps forward. "I don't know about that, but I will surely find out."

"Mila had something come up at work, so she asked us to go over the final arrangements for the reception with you," Eugenia explained.

Kaula nodded. "Oh, I see. Sit and we'll talk."

Eugenia wasn't sure what to expect from the enormous wedding planner, but Kaula was very organized. After listening to the plans for flowers and refreshments and entertainment, Eugenia shook her head. "Kaula, this may be the first time I've ever said this—but I can't think of a single suggestion that would improve the wedding."

"That is good news!" Kaula spread her arms, and Eugenia braced herself for another bone-crushing hug.

As they left the chapel, Eugenia asked Annabelle, "Do you know what *haole* means?"

"I think it's the Hawaiian word for *foreigner* or *stranger.*"

Eugenia considered this then shrugged. "I've been called worse."

* * *

After the others left for the surfing demonstration, Mila returned to her bungalow and went to work contacting people from the Raquel Hate List. While she was talking to the caterer from the party, who was only too happy to discuss her grievances against Raquel, Mila got a call on her cell phone from the police lab. She didn't want to interrupt the caterer, so she waited until she completed that interview, and then she called the lab back. Once she had the information from the lab technician, she called Jerry Hirasuna.

"Spike's real name is Henry Gosslinger, and he's only sixteen years old," Mila said when Jerry answered his phone.

"Yeah, the lab guys called me, too. I don't blame Spike for choosing a nickname."

Mila ignored the joke. "So, what are we going to do?"

"No choice," Jerry returned. "We'll have to give what we've got on him in to DHR."

"If they put him in another foster home, he'll just run away again."

"Probably."

"And he'll hate the police more and trust them less," Mila added.

"Almost certainly," Jerry agreed. "But that's not our problem."

"Can you give me some time?" Mila asked.

There was a pause before Jerry asked, "How much?"

"Just a couple of days. I want to try and find a situation for Spike that will suit him better."

"Are you going to convince Quin to let you adopt the kid?"

"No," Mila replied, although the thought had crossed her mind. "But there must be someplace where Spike could be fairly independent while getting an education."

"I think you're living in a dream world," Jerry said. "But I'll give you until Friday. Then I'm passing what we know on to DHR."

Mila knew he was being generous. "Thank you."

"You're welcome. Now get to work on that Raquel Hate List."

Mila smiled. "So far that's been easy. All I have to do is call people, and the list writes itself."

"Great," Jerry replied. "Too many suspects is worse than none at all."

Mila took a deep breath and asked, "Do you think it's significant that both the Gent and Leilani were poisoned with arsenic?"

"At the most, it's a coincidence," Jerry told her. "Arsenic is cheap and easy to obtain, so it's always been the preferred choice for murder by poison."

"I just thought it might be a good idea to look and see if there's a connection between our two victims."

"You're trying to make this case harder than it has to be," Jerry accused her mildly. "I'm beginning to wonder if you're looking for an excuse not to get married on Saturday."

Mila couldn't think of an appropriate response, so she just disconnected the call.

* * *

Annabelle took the long way back to Makai so the trip home lasted almost an hour. Annabelle claimed that she was not lost, but Eugenia felt certain that her sister made a wrong turn while trying to follow Mila's directions backwards. In any case, the scenery was spectacular, so Eugenia kept her complaints to a minimum.

When they arrived at Mila's bungalow, they found her still working on her suspect list. She invited them in, but Eugenia knew they would distract her, so she and Annabelle took a walk along the beach.

The others returned from the surfing demonstration just in time to watch Raquel's cooking segment on the *Morning Show*. They gathered around the television in Mila's bungalow and focused all their attention on Raquel. Today she showed her viewers how to make perfect shish kebabs utilizing fruits and vegetables native to the islands.

"Darlene did a good job on those," Eugenia whispered to Annabelle as Raquel displayed the finished product. "Lots of color and very appetizing."

"I wish you could smell this!" Raquel told her viewers.

"Oh, that looks delicious," Polly said with a sigh.

Then Mr. Baldwin stepped into view right behind Raquel. "Can I have a taste?" he asked.

Raquel acted flustered, but she was smiling, so Eugenia doubted that the station owner's presence was a surprise. Mr. Baldwin got his own plate and silverware while Raquel made a comment to her audience about how good it was for a man to know his way around the kitchen. Then he tested the shish kebab and deemed it "divine."

The music that ended the segment started to play, and the camera zoomed in on Mr. Baldwin feeding Raquel a piece of grilled guava. Then the cooking portion of the show ended, and they were looking at the solemn face of Mr. Miyagi (a.k.a., Tony Booth). "Welcome to the Dream Weaver," he said.

"Well," Polly huffed as Mark turned off the television. "Raquel didn't mention the Haggerty Baptist Church cookbook again!"

"I wonder whose fault it was this time?" Annabelle mused. "Mr. Baldwin's?"

"It does always seem to be someone else's fault when anything around Raquel goes wrong," Mila admitted.

"That's probably part of what makes her so popular," Eugenia said sarcastically.

"And why your Raquel Hate List is so long," Annabelle added.

"Exactly," Mila agreed.

"Can we go swimming at the beach?" Emily asked her mother.

Kate shook her head. "No, let's wait until this afternoon when we're at our hotel."

Emily walked over to stand beside Eugenia. "We're going to a hotel with five pools."

Charles joined them and held up his hand with all the fingers splayed. "Five." He flexed his fingers for emphasis.

Eugenia drew the children into a quick hug. "That's what I heard, although I don't know why in the world you need a hotel with five pools. That's more than one a piece."

Emily giggled. "You could come with us and use the other one."

"I will certainly visit you," Eugenia promised. "But I'm going to stay here."

"Are you all packed up and ready to go?" Annabelle asked Mark and Kate.

"We just need to load the car," Mark replied.

"And clean up a little," Kate added.

"Don't bother about cleaning," Quin told them. "I don't like the idea of Mila being out here alone, so I'm going to sleep in that bungalow until our parents get here on Friday." Quin smiled at Mila. "I'm sure my friend won't mind having his couch back a few days sooner than we had originally planned."

Mila walked over and put an arm around Quin's waist. "That sounds like a wonderful idea." Then she addressed the others. "I've got a meeting with the detective assigned to Leilani's case at noon, so I've got to go downtown. The Iversons are moving to their hotel, so the rest of you have a little time to relax here or on the beach before Quin takes you to the Teriyaki Grill for lunch." Mila glanced at Mark. "Quin can give you directions."

Mark nodded as George Ann said, "I hope they serve regular American food. I have a very sensitive stomach, and all this foreign cuisine is playing havoc with my digestion."

"They serve American dishes in addition to traditional Hawaiian foods," Mila assured her. "After lunch, Quin will take you to the Ala Moana Mall to shop. Then you're signed up for a bus tour this afternoon. We decided that would be the easiest way to make sure you see all the local landmarks without having to walk very far."

"I am so glad to hear that," George Ann said. "The drugstore Quin took me to didn't have my brand of foot powder, and the kind I got doesn't stop my toes from itching."

"You can soak them when you get home tonight," Polly suggested. "That might help."

"Or you can scratch them," Eugenia proposed. "Just please quit talking about them."

Kate interrupted this exchange to say, "We may skip the bus tour and take the kids back to the hotel so they can swim and take a nap."

Mila nodded. "You do whatever is best for you. Then tonight we have reservations at the Polynesian Cultural Center."

"Oh, I've heard that is something you cannot miss during a trip to Hawaii," Polly said.

"It is probably my favorite place on Oahu," Annabelle agreed. "Although I'm partial to the island of Maui."

"She just wants you to know she's been to Hawaii before," Eugenia informed the others. "To keep Annabelle from having to continually remind us—I'll just make an announcement." In a loud voice, Eugenia continued, "In case anyone here doesn't already know it—Annabelle has been to Hawaii before."

"Quit acting childish," Annabelle remonstrated.

"Anyway," Mila said with a reproachful look at the sisters, "I'm sure you'll all enjoy your afternoon, and I'll see you tonight."

* * *

Mila collected the information she had compiled for Jerry Hirasuna, then Quin walked her to her car. Once they were alone he pulled her close.

"I can't thank you enough for assuming my hostess responsibilities," she murmured against his neck.

"It's my wedding too," he reminded her. "I don't mind showing our guests around."

She reached up to stroke his cheek. "But I mind not being with you. I thought I had everything arranged so that I could be free for the next few days."

"You couldn't have predicted a murder happening right under your nose."

Mila shrugged. "I guess that's true."

He used a finger to tilt her face toward him. "But on Saturday you're mine—no matter who dies."

She gave him a tremulous smile. "I love you so much."

He kissed her. "I know. Now go solve this crime so you can concentrate on our wedding."

When Mila walked into Jerry's cubicle at the district police station, Detective Hirasuna and Elliot Wong were already there waiting for her.

"I thought you'd never get here," Jerry said.

Mila pointed at the clock as they took seats at the table. "I'm five minutes early."

Jerry waved this aside. "Let's get busy."

Mila didn't know if it was lack of sleep or their disagreement over how to handle Spike that was causing his uncharacteristic grouchiness, but she decided to ignore it.

"What's this?" Elliot asked, pointing to a filing cabinet in the corner of Jerry's small office. Mila turned and saw the empty wine bottle Spike had retrieved from the dumpster in the alley where the Gent's body was found. The bottle was balanced precariously on a pile of computer printouts.

"It's trash," Jerry told Elliot.

"It's evidence from another case," Mila corrected with a reproving look at her partner.

Jerry ignored this.

"Okay, let's start at the top. We've confirmed that we're dealing with a murder—even if the wrong person died," Jerry said. "Now, show me what you've got."

Mila handed him her list. "This is my list of some of the many people who hate Raquel, and Mrs. Rose wasn't exaggerating last night. Apparently to know Raquel is to despise her."

"But how many of those people hated her enough to want her dead?" Elliot asked.

"To want her dead is one thing," Jerry pointed out. "To kill her is another."

"I don't know the answer to that," Mila replied. "I've talked to all of these people. Some had big reasons to hate Raquel—others had smaller grudges. I've noted all their whereabouts on Monday night, but because of the way the cake was delivered, an alibi for the time of the murder doesn't mean much."

"That's true," Jerry acknowledged. "If the murderer didn't care who died—just wanted Raquel to suffer the fallout—then they may not have even been at the party."

Mila turned to Jerry. "I'm hoping that you were able to get some information from the Cheesecake Company that will help us pin down when and how the cake was ordered. Then maybe we can trace the murderer."

Jerry shook his head. "Can't help you there. The Cheesecake Company has no record of anyone purchasing a cake for Raquel. Since much of their business is handled on a cash basis, this doesn't surprise me. They also have no record of a cake being delivered to Makai—which was a little surprising. The killer took a big risk if they delivered it personally."

"Unless the murderer frequently brought food into the house—like Mrs. Rose," Elliot suggested.

"You think the housekeeper is our killer?" Mila asked.

Elliot shrugged. "I think she's a valid suspect."

"Or the murderer could have hired someone to deliver the cake," Jerry proposed. "If he used a one-man errand service and paid in cash—telling the delivery person the cake was a surprise . . ."

Mila was disturbed by this thought. "Don't you think the delivery person would have come forward when they saw that Leilani died from eating the cake?"

"The delivery person may not have seen the news yet," Elliot pointed out. "Or maybe they didn't make the connection since the victim was different from the recipient."

Jerry Hirasuna ran his fingers through his dark hair. "Okay, so since the records from the cheesecake stores won't help us identify the killer—is there any other way to pare down your list to a manageable size?"

Mila considered this. "All of these people had access to Raquel and the cheesecake since they were all at the party on Monday night. All of them had reasons to hate Raquel. None of them have convictions for violent crimes in the past."

"Let's separate out the people who have little grudges and keep only the ones who have big reasons to hate Raquel," Jerry suggested.

"That could be dangerous," Mila warned him. "What may seem small to us may seem huge to the killer."

"I know, but we've got to concentrate our efforts somewhere."

"I agree with Jerry," Elliot said, obviously campaigning for a promotion. "If we're checking into the wrong people, at least we can remove them from consideration. By trying to look at too many people at once, we'll just dilute our efforts."

Jerry raised an eyebrow in Mila's direction. "Well, then. My motion has been seconded."

Mila shrugged. "As long as we're all clear on who made the motion," she looked at Elliot. "And who provided the second."

Jerry ignored this comment and addressed Officer Wong. "Good job on getting the toxicology reports so fast."

Elliot blushed at the praise. "Thank you."

"Did you talk to everyone on your half of the guest list?"

"All except two people," Elliot confirmed. "Mrs. Simon's dentist is out of town, and her hairdresser is recovering from surgery and couldn't be questioned."

"Follow up with them later," Jerry instructed. "Did any of the guests you talked to see anything suspicious?"

"Several saw the victim talking with Mr. Simon on the balcony," Elliot reported. "And all but one heard the argument between the victim and Mrs. Simon. But no one saw a cheesecake, no one heard Miss Fiero complain about feeling sick, and no one saw her leave the estate."

Jerry nodded. "That matches what I got—nothing. My half said the food was great, and for the most part, they thought Mrs. Simon's little spat with her secretary was entertaining. Only one person defended Raquel Simon's actions—the cooking assistant from Channel One named Darlene. She said the secretary was often undependable, and she didn't blame Mrs. Simon for yelling at her."

"Mrs. Rose said Darlene likes Raquel for some reason. Miss Eugenia thinks she's just nervous about losing her job, so she's careful never to be critical of Raquel," Mila told him.

Jerry nodded. "I guess that explains away Mrs. Simon's one friend. Now, summarize the caterer's complaints for me."

"Apparently Raquel told the caterer to prepare for thirty people," Mila began. "She told Quin and me that she had invited some local businessmen to meet him so we were expecting a small dinner party when we arrived."

"Just like the caterer," Jerry interjected, and Mila nodded.

"But there were over a hundred people in attendance at the party. Raquel invited everyone from her television station, colleagues she saw at lunch, and even her dentist and hairdresser. It's like she invited everyone she knew." Mila shook her head. "Raquel has a pretty big ego, so I guess she might have overinvited so that there would be a big crowd."

"What would be another possibility?" Jerry asked.

Mila shrugged. "A lot of people create a lot of confusion."

"Perfect for covering murder," Jerry added.

"Maybe someone else invited people without Raquel's knowledge," Elliot proposed.

"I doubt that," Mila rejected this. "No one would dare. Mrs. Rose confirmed the caterer's statement that Raquel had a habit of underestimating the number of guests she would have at various occasions. I assumed it was a cost-cutting maneuver, since Mrs. Rose said Raquel also refused to pay for the additional guests later. But maybe the murderer knew that Raquel would invite more people than she originally planned and counted on that to help mask the murder."

"That's a good theory," Jerry agreed. "But it doesn't help us identify the killer."

"I think we are looking for someone who knows Raquel very well. Someone who is familiar with her eating habits, her work habits, and even her party-giving habits," Mila said. "So we can start by marking off anyone who is only a casual acquaintance."

Jerry nodded. "We've got to start somewhere. Let's do it."

When they were finished they had the list pared down to fifteen names. "We could knock off a couple more of these people who know Raquel well but only have fairly small grievances against her—like the owner of the television station," Elliot said.

"I'm still not comfortable with doing that yet." Mila wanted her objection on the record. "But I'm not officially on the case—so it's your call," she told Jerry.

"We'll keep the list as it is for now," Jerry decided. "I had interviews with the Mister and Missus this morning. Nothing new there either."

"Did Cade say where he was Tuesday night?" Mila asked.

Jerry nodded. "Still claims he was working late. We're checking on that."

"Excuse me," a voice said from the opening in the partitions that formed Jerry's door. Mila looked up and saw Mrs. Rose staring at them in obvious discomfort. She addressed Jerry, "You said you wanted to talk to me."

Jerry stood and pulled an empty chair up to the desk. "Yes. Please have a seat." He glanced at Mila as Mrs. Rose sat down in the chair. "I thought it might be better to talk away from Makai and all the distractions there."

Mila nodded. Mrs. Rose might speak more freely if she didn't have to worry about Raquel or Cade overhearing her remarks.

"Thanks for coming here today," Jerry began in a friendly manner. "I know you are a busy woman."

"I don't mind," she replied.

"We noticed that the guest list for Monday's party was very diverse. Mrs. Simon invited her coworkers, business people she thought could help Quin with his surfboard business, and other random people like her dentist and hairdresser. Does this strike you as unusual?"

Mrs. Rose shook her head. "No, Raquel is always issuing invitations to random people she runs into. We always have more guests than we plan for, and it always infuriates the caterer."

Jerry nodded. "Now, according to my notes, Leilani wanted to be a television actress. Is that true?" Jerry asked.

Mrs. Rose nodded. "That's what she said."

"But most of those jobs are in the states." Jerry frowned. "I don't see how working for Mrs. Simon in Honolulu was going to help Miss Fiero get a television part."

"Leilani said Raquel still had contacts in Los Angeles from her television days. She promised to put in a good word with them for Leilani."

"Mrs. Simon must have been very fond of Leilani," Jerry remarked.

The housekeeper shrugged. "I guess."

Jerry gave Mrs. Rose a look of sympathy. "But she's very hard on you."

Mrs. Rose lowered her eyes without comment.

"It must be difficult to keep a huge estate like Makai running smoothly," Jerry prompted.

Mrs. Rose hesitated briefly then said, "Yes."

"I've heard that Mrs. Simon can be a little . . . harsh."

"Some people might think so," Mrs. Rose replied carefully.

"Was Mrs. Simon nicer to Leilani than she had been to her other secretaries?"

Mrs. Rose looked confused. "Raquel never had a secretary before. Leilani was the first."

Mila saw Jerry's eyes widen with surprise. "So, this was a newly created position?"

Mrs. Rose nodded.

"And it was a very good job," Mila contributed. "She had lots of time off and free run of the house. She even got to use one of the Simons' cars and had a nice private apartment there at Makai."

"With housekeeping services!" Mrs. Rose added. Then she looked as if she regretted her words.

"You didn't like cleaning Leilani's apartment?" Jerry guessed.

"It wasn't fair," Mrs. Rose said in an aggrieved tone. "She was just an employee like me."

Jerry gave the housekeeper an encouraging smile. "Now, I'd like to go over the guest list with you and see what you can tell me about these people."

Jerry did a good job of interrogating Mrs. Rose without her realizing what was happening. He extracted several useful pieces of information, including the fact that the Simons argued the night of the party.

"Did you hear what they fought about?" Jerry asked.

"I didn't actually listen," Mrs. Rose claimed, although Mila doubted this was true. "But from what I could tell, it was mostly about Leilani. Cade objected to the way Raquel yelled at her during the party."

"Do you get along with Mr. Simon?"

Mrs. Rose lifted a shoulder. "He's a very nice man. I get along with him fine."

"What about Mr. Baldwin, the owner of Channel One?"

"He's nice too. I've only met him a few times."

"Is he a regular guest at Raquel's parties?"

"He used to be, but he hasn't attended any lately until the one on Monday night."

"Had he been invited?"

Mrs. Rose considered this. "I'd have to check to be sure, but I don't think so."

Mila and Jerry exchanged another meaningful look. Maybe Raquel and her boss were on worse terms than they had realized.

"What about the cooking assistant, Darlene?"

"She comes around the fairly often. She's more like Raquel's secretary than Leilani ever was, but she rarely attends social occasions."

"She was on the guest list for Monday night," Mila said.

"Yes, well, only because she was an employee of Channel One and because Raquel had invited them all. But Darlene didn't come to the party," Mrs. Rose informed them. "She came by just before the party started to give Raquel something for Tuesday's cooking segment, and I encouraged her to at least get something to eat, but she said she wasn't dressed properly and hurried off."

"What about Mr. Simon?" Jerry changed directions. "When did he arrive at the party?"

"I never saw him arrive," Mrs. Rose replied. "After Raquel had words with Leilani, he just sort of appeared."

"What about the boy, Blake, who came to see Leilani during the party?" Mila asked. "How often did he come to Makai?"

"Never as a guest," Mrs. Rose assured them. "But he served at parties occasionally. I don't remember seeing him recently, though. I don't think they were dating anymore."

"I understand that the caterer was particularly mad at Raquel the night of the party," Jerry continued.

"I've never seen her so upset," Mrs. Rose confirmed. "She said Raquel had abused not only their professional relationship, but also their friendship and that even if it ruined her business, she wouldn't work for Raquel again."

Mila raised her eyebrows. "I didn't realize she was that angry."

"She packed up and left before the party was even over," Mrs. Rose said.

Jerry stood at this point. "Thanks so much for coming, Mrs. Rose. You've been very helpful." He escorted the housekeeper to the elevator, and when he returned, he was rubbing his hands together. "Okay, we've got our short list. We'll divide it up and see what . . ." he was interrupted by the ringing of the phone. He reached across the desk and grabbed the receiver. Once he had it to his ear he said, "Hirasuna."

Mila watched Jerry's expression as he listened and already knew it wasn't good news before he had hung up the phone. "There's been a new development," he told them. "Three other local television celebrities received the delivery of a cheesecake this morning."

Mila couldn't control a gasp. "Were they from the Cheesecake Company?"

"Were they poisoned?" Officer Wong asked.

"Yes, and I don't know yet," Jerry answered each of his coworkers respectively. "But we'll go with the worst case scenario and assume that they are."

"Did anyone eat the cakes?" Mila asked.

Jerry shook his head. "No. Thanks to the press, the recipients were forewarned."

Mila sighed with frustration. "We've just gotten our suspect list down to a manageable size and now we're going to have to expand our search beyond people who hated Raquel."

"Yes," Jerry agreed. "We need to be looking at a bigger scheme."

"Someone who had a grudge against all four of the potential victims?" Elliot murmured.

"Or against people on TV in general," Mila suggested.

"I don't see that we have any choice but to abandon this course for the time being anyway," Jerry said. "We'll each take one of the new victims and go interview them. At the same time we can check out the circumstances to be sure they're similar. If you can, get copies of any reports, crime scene photographs, etc."

Mila stacked her list and notes. "The cakes were delivered anonymously?"

Jerry nodded.

"Did anyone see who delivered them?" Elliot asked.

"That's one of the things we're about to find out. Wong, you take Philip Murphee, the sportscaster over at Channel Six. Mila, you take Allison Hammer, the meteorologist at Channel One. I'll take Hugh Dobbs, the anchor for the evening news at Channel Six. We'll meet back here and compare notes at," Jerry checked his watch, "three thirty. That gives us two hours."

* * *

Lunch at the Teriyaki Grill was the best meal Eugenia had eaten since she'd arrived in the Hawaiian Islands, and she was in a good mood when they left. Her mood was dampened slightly when she watched Kate and Mark put the children in their rental car and drive off to their fancy resort hotel for swimming and naps.

But Quin didn't give her time to mope. He loaded the rest of his touring group into his car and drove them to the mall at Ala Moana. A live band was playing in the center of the mall, and there were several comfortable-looking benches available for weary shoppers to relax and enjoy the music.

At the mall entrance Quin checked his watch and said, "The bus tour will pick us up outside in about an hour. Until then you can either listen to the music or shop."

Eugenia was tempted to take the easier, musical option, but George Ann immediately claimed a seat, and there was no way Eugenia was going to be trapped listening to complaints about feet and fungus. So she waved to Annabelle and Polly. "Let's go shopping, girls."

"I guess I'll stay here with Miss George Ann," Quin offered without enthusiasm, and Eugenia gave him an approving smile.

Eugenia was absently window shopping until she saw the sign for the Cheesecake Company. "I need to go in there," she told Annabelle and Polly. The others followed the direction of her finger with their eyes.

"I wouldn't really care for a cheesecake anymore," Polly said. "That's nice of you to offer, though."

Eugenia resisted the urge to roll her eyes. "I'm not planning to buy a cheesecake, but I'd like to ask a few questions for Mila."

"Heaven help us," Annabelle muttered.

"It will just take a minute," Eugenia promised. "And I know you both want Mila to solve her case before the wedding."

Annabelle shook her head in disgust. "Do what you want. I'm just going to stand here and call Derrick."

"I'll come with you," Polly said like a true friend. "I'll enjoy looking at all those nice cakes even if I'm afraid to eat them."

Satisfied with this, Eugenia led the way into the deserted store. She left Polly browsing through the Gifts for All Occasions section and walked to the back, where a woman was standing at a register. Behind her were several rows of cheesecakes

"Business seems slow," Eugenia said. "I guess it's because of that article in the newspaper about the poisoned cheesecake?"

The woman nodded. "We haven't sold a single cake since then, and it's so unfair. I'm sure that a cake made by our factory was not tainted or spoiled as the article suggested. Our company goes to great lengths to provide quality products for our customers."

"I've never tried any of your cakes, but I did see one recently," Eugenia told the woman. "But the one I saw was at least an inch taller than those behind you, and the crust came all the way up to the top of the cake instead of stopping halfway."

The woman glanced over her shoulder. Then she shook her head. "The only cake we have that isn't standard sized is the heart-shaped one we sell for Valentine's Day, and all of our cakes have our signature half-crust. You must have seen a cake made by another company."

Eugenia frowned. "No, it was from the Cheesecake Company. I remember the name very distinctly because it was printed in gold on a black label in the middle of the red foil-embossed box."

The saleswoman gave her a confused look. "That sounds like our Christmas box, but we haven't sold any cheesecakes in red boxes since December. You must be mistaken about the color."

Eugenia shook her head. "How could I be mistaken about that?"

"I don't know," the woman said. "The UPC number from the botttom of the box can be traced. That will tell you where the cake was purchased."

Eugenia smiled. "Well, thanks for being so helpful, and I hope people get an appetite for cheesecake soon."

Eugenia headed out of the cheesecake store, calling for Polly as she went.

"Why are you in such a rush?" Polly asked as they rejoined Annabelle and headed for the center of the mall, where the concert was being held. "I was trying to work up the courage to give the marbled chocolate cheesecake a try."

"If you're going to work up courage, invest it somewhere else," Eugenia suggested. "The woman at the cheesecake store gave me an idea about Mila's case, and I need to call her right away."

Annabelle scowled at her sister. "I presume you want my cell phone."

"Just for a minute," Eugenia returned. "And only to make a call that could save Mila's marriage."

"I don't know where you get this dramatic streak," Annabelle said as she surrendered her phone.

Eugenia ignored the insult and found a quiet corner. Then she placed a call to Mila's cell phone. Mila didn't answer, so she left a detailed message before joining the others on the bus trip of Oahu.

* * *

On the way to the Channel One studios, Mila's cell phone rang. She answered it, but no one returned her salutation. "Spike, is that you?" Mila asked, fervently regretting her decision to trust the boy with her cell number. "Calling and then refusing to speak is a waste of my time and yours." She tried again. Still no answer. Finally, she disconnected the call and turned off her phone. She wasn't going to be intimidated by a sixteen year old.

This time when Mila pulled into the parking lot of Channel One, she saw several police cars parked near the entrance. She pulled into the first available space and crossed the hot asphalt to the flower-lined sidewalk. The receptionist she had met the previous day was at the information desk, flanked by two uniformed police officers.

The receptionist focused red, puffy eyes on Mila. "May I help you?"

Mila displayed her police credentials with practiced ease. "I'm Detective Mila Edwards with the Honolulu Police Department, and I'm here to see Allison Hammer."

"Do you mind if I look at your badge?" one of the policemen requested. "Since I don't know you."

Mila handed him the badge. "I don't mind at all. My partner is Detective Jerry Hirasuna. You may know him."

The policeman returned her badge and gave her a smile. "Oh, yeah, I met him a few times. Pretty good guy."

Mila put her badge back into the pocket of her jacket and addressed the receptionist. "I'd like to ask you a few questions first."

The woman's expression was full of dread as she nodded.

"Was the cheesecake delivered to your desk?"

"Yes," the woman said, her lips trembling as she spoke. "I didn't see anyone, though. We had several school groups here this morning, and the cake was put on my desk while I was giving a tour."

"I guess you had read the newspaper article about Leilani Fiero eating a poisoned cheesecake, and that's why you alerted the police?"

"I did hear about Miss Fiero's death," the receptionist was nearly whispering, so Mila took a step closer. "But the reason I was upset by the cheesecake is because of the note. I knew when I saw it that the cake wasn't a nice gift."

Mila cleared her throat and hoped that she didn't sound surprised when she asked, "What note?"

"It was taped to the top of the box," the woman said.

"What did it say?" Mila prompted.

Tears sprang into the receptionist's eyes. "The card had Ms. Hammer's name typed in bold letters. Then underneath her name it said, *You're a murderer and deserve to die.* The name Mary Zelinski was typed on the very bottom with a date and *Sylacauga, Alabama.*"

"Did you touch the box?"

"Yes," the receptionist said with obvious regret. "I'm sorry, but I picked it up before I read the note."

Mila nodded. "I understand. Then what happened?"

"I kind of screamed and attracted a pretty big crowd," the receptionist related. "There was a photographer here taking pictures of the school kids for the newspaper, and he took several shots of the box."

"So much for containment," Mila muttered. "Well, thanks for the information. Now I'd like to speak to Ms. Hammer."

The officer who had checked Mila's badge waved her through. "She's in Mr. Baldwin's office on the second floor. You can't miss it. Just look for the huge one at the end of the hall."

"Thanks," Mila told him, then she moved toward the elevator.

Mila found Mr. Baldwin's office, as the policeman had predicted, without any trouble. There were several uniformed policemen at the doorway, and while Mila waited for her identification to be checked, she looked into the room. It was large and impressive—as was to be expected for the owner of a television station. She could see a small woman sitting on a couch. The streaks of mascara on her face indicated that she had been crying, and the enthusiasm with which she was chewing her nails was further evidence of anxiety. Mila assumed this was the intended victim, Ms. Allison Hammer.

When the policeman waved her inside, Mila walked over to Mr. Baldwin, who was standing beside his desk looking pale and worried.

"First Leilani and now this," she said quietly.

He seemed startled to find anyone near him but recovered quickly. "Yes, what a terrible thing. I can't believe Miss Fiero is dead. And who would want to harm Allison? It makes no sense."

"Did you know Leilani?" Mila asked.

"Just in passing," he replied. "She was at the station often with Raquel."

"I'm helping with the investigation to determine who killed Leilani, and I was sent over here to interview Allison Hammer about the cake that was delivered earlier," Mila told him. "Is there any way that I can talk to her privately?"

Mr. Baldwin nodded. "I'll arrange for everyone else to leave my office. I'm sure that an officer will have to stand at the door . . ."

"That's fine," Mila assured him. "I just don't want to ask Ms. Hammer sensitive questions in a roomful of strangers."

Mr. Baldwin nodded. "That is very kind of you." Then he moved forward and asked everyone to step out into the hallway except the officer guarding the door.

Once the room was empty, Mila approached the small woman sitting on the couch. "Ms. Hammer?"

The other woman looked up with dull, hopeless eyes. "Yes," she returned.

"I'm Mila Edwards, and I need to ask you some questions."

Ms. Hammer nodded.

"Will you tell me what the note on the cheesecake box referred to?"

With a sigh, Allison Hammer began, "Almost ten years ago, long before I even dreamed about a career in television, I was just plain Mary Zelinski, living in Sylacauga, Alabama. I had a boyfriend who was not a contender for man of the year, and one night while we were out on the town, he told me to stop at a liquor store so he could buy more alcohol. I waited in the car while he went in."

"He robbed the store," Mila guessed.

Ms. Hammer nodded. "He not only robbed the store, but he also killed a cashier in the process of stealing about two hundred dollars. Because I was driving the car, I was charged with murder as well. I served three years of a fifteen-year sentence, and when I was released, I decided to put the past behind me. I changed my name, moved to California, and went to college. Eventually I came to Hawaii and built a successful television career." The weather woman laughed, but it sounded more like a sob. "Well, it used to be successful. Now I'm finished."

Mila's sense of fair play was offended. "A youthful mistake made so many years ago shouldn't be held against you. Surely once you explain . . ."

Ms. Hammer shook her head. "When you're in television, you aren't tried by a jury of your peers. You're tried by the press. I will be convicted and sentenced to life without parole before the end of the ten o'clock news tonight."

"Because you lied and falsified your employment forms in order to get your job in the first place?"

"That and the fact that Channel One requires us to do a lot of community service. I speak to schools and church youth groups—and my platform has always been *Violence is never the answer*. Once it's widely known that I was convicted and incarcerated for a violent crime . . ."

Mila sighed. "No one will take you seriously."

"I've lost my credibility, and in a cutthroat business like television—that's fatal."

"Do you think there's a chance that you could get an anchor job in another market?"

"Siberia maybe," Ms. Hammer replied. "My reputation will precede me wherever I go, and besides, I'm almost thirty. My only hope of staying on the air was being established in a market and having loyal viewers. I've given my last televised weather forecast."

Mila knew nothing she said could comfort the woman, so she used her most professional tone when she asked, "Who do you think sent the cake to you and why?"

Allison Hammer looked up with bewilderment in her eyes. "I have no idea."

CHAPTER 6

Mila listened to her cell phone messages on the way back to the police station after interviewing Allison Hammer. In addition to a hang-up call, Mila had a message from Miss Eugenia. She replayed it several times, trying to make out the last few sentences, but the words were garbled. As she walked into Jerry's cubicle, she wondered if the phone might be malfunctioning.

Reaching across his desk, she said, "I need to borrow your phone."

"So I see," her partner responded.

She dialed the number for the research department, and when a clerk answered, she read a number from the caller ID feature of her cell phone. "Please find me an address to match this number," she requested, "as quickly as possible. I'm in Detective Hirasuna's office."

When she ended the call, Jerry asked, "What was that about?"

"I've gotten a couple of hang-up calls. I presume they're from Spike, but I want to be sure."

Mila expected Jerry to say *I told you so* and possibly even to lecture her about giving out her cell number. Instead he frowned and said, "Spike isn't the type to make nuisance phone calls. He likes to talk too much."

"But if Spike didn't make the calls, who did?"

Jerry shrugged. "You've been interviewing people from Raquel's Hate List. Maybe you've hit a nerve."

"The murderer?"

"It's possible," Jerry acknowledged. "From now on you need to be extremely careful. No walking out to your car at night alone—things like that."

"I'm always careful," Mila said as she sat down in a chair by his desk.

The phone on Jerry's desk rang, and he picked it up. "Hirasuna," he said. After a brief pause, he thanked the caller and replaced the receiver. "That was research," he told Mila. "The number is from a pay phone on Bishop Street."

"The business district downtown," Mila murmured. "The Gent's territory."

Jerry hit his desk with the palm of his hand. "Just wait until that kid calls me again." He checked his watch. "Which should be in about five minutes. I'm going to give him a piece of my mind."

Mila smiled. "Don't give him too much—you're going to need all your brain power to solve Leilani's case. Speaking of which, I also got a call from Miss Eugenia. She visited the Cheesecake Company at Ala Moana and says that the cake she saw in Raquel's office is the wrong size or something. She thinks that means that the murderer made the cake and put it in a box leftover from Christmas."

Jerry smiled. "She's a smart old woman. That's exactly what our lab guys just told me. They were suspicious since the arsenic was distributed pretty evenly throughout the cake—which would not be the case if you were trying to inject it after the cake was cooked."

"And if you tried to poison a cake that had already been baked it would be almost impossible to add the poison without leaving evidence of tampering," Elliot Wong pointed out. "But if you add the poison during the mixing process . . ."

"So, does knowing that help us?" Mila asked.

"Not really," Jerry wasn't encouraging. "We had reached a dead end at the cheesecake store anyway." He lifted some files off a chair and pointed to it. "Sit down and give us your report."

Mila sat down and told them about the unfortunate weather woman at Channel One, the circumstances surrounding the cheesecake's delivery and the effect on her career.

"The anchor man at Channel Six is an illegal alien," Jerry told them. "A cake was delivered with a note taped on it saying as much and now he's not only out of a job—he's going to be deported." He turned to Elliot. "How about the sportscaster over at Channel Six?"

"I didn't get to actually talk to him," Officer Wong told them. "But the card taped to his cake accused him of being a drug addict."

"Is he?" Jerry asked.

"Apparently," Elliot answered. "He resigned from his position at the television station and was unavailable for comment."

"Boy," Jerry said. "Those notes were almost as lethal as the cakes."

Mila looked up. "The lab has already determined that these other cakes were poisoned too?"

The detective nodded. "Yes, since they knew what they were looking for this time it didn't take long. They were full of arsenic just like the one sent to Raquel Simon."

"At least the notes alerted the victims and kept anyone from actually eating the cakes," Mila said.

"It's odd that Mrs. Simon's cake didn't have a note on it," Elliot remarked.

Jerry frowned. "Yes, that is odd."

"Maybe Raquel's cake did have a note on it, and Raquel just failed to mention it," Mila suggested.

Jerry considered this for a few seconds before he pulled out his cell phone. "I'm going to call Gates and tell him to get Mrs. Simon over here right now so we can ask her," he said as he dialed. After a short conversation with Officer Gates, he closed the phone and faced them with an incredulous expression. "Gates says Mrs. Simon is just finishing up a satellite interview for the *CBS Evening News.*"

Mila was astounded. "You're kidding?"

"Nope, and he says she's already taped segments for the *Today Show, Good Morning America,* and *Access Hollywood.*"

"About the poisoned cheesecakes, I presume?" Mila confirmed.

"Oh, yeah," Jerry answered.

After a short silence, Mila said, "It sounds like Raquel has found a way to take lemons and make lemonade."

* * *

After several failed attempts to reach Mila on her cell phone, Eugenia appealed to Quin. He tried, but didn't get through either. "Her battery might be dead," he suggested. "If you need to tell her something important, we can call the police station."

Eugenia nodded. "Let's do that."

Quin placed the call and then reported, "Mila's in a meeting and can't be disturbed. Do you want to leave a message?"

Eugenia considered this and then shook her head. "Could you just drop me off there? I'd like to talk to her as soon as she gets out of her meeting, and I can ride back to Makai with her."

Quin smiled. "I just hope you don't mind waiting. Sometimes those police meetings can go on forever."

Eugenia didn't return his smile. Her old joints were aching, and all she wanted was to soak in a tub of warm water. But she felt the information she had for Mila was vital—so she nodded. "I can wait if I need to."

* * *

While waiting for Raquel to arrive, the detectives and Officer Wong went over the evidence: handwriting comparisons, fingerprints, and trace DNA. Mila's mind kept wandering to Quin and their plans to attend the Polynesian Cultural Center that night. Finally she excused herself to call him. She turned on her phone but found that the battery was low. So she walked out into the reception area and found Miss Eugenia sitting on a worn leather couch.

"What are you doing here?" Mila asked in amazement.

"Quin dropped me off. I wanted to be sure you got my message," the old woman replied, rising slowly.

Mila smiled. "You were right about the cakes. The murderer made them and put them in boxes from the Cheesecake Company."

"Boxes?" Miss Eugenia repeated. "There's more than one poisoned cheesecake?"

"Come into Jerry's office," Mila invited. "I have a lot to tell you."

* * *

Eugenia received a warm welcome from Detective Hirasuna and Officer Wong. Then they took turns filling her in on the day's events.

"So, now we're looking for someone who wanted to kill four people—not just Raquel Simon," Detective Hirasuna summed up. "The FBI is even interested—thinking we might have a serial killer."

"I declare, it sounds as if you consider that good news," Eugenia said when they had finished.

"Not good news, exactly," Mila's partner backpedaled.

"Solving a case involving a serial killer is a good way to advance your career in law enforcement," Mila explained with a smile.

Before further comment could be made, Raquel arrived with her escort, Officer Gates.

"What a day!" Raquel exclaimed as she rushed in. "First, I had all those interviews," she glanced at her audience and smiled, "which was exhausting, but kind of fun. And then I heard from a Hollywood director who might be interested in doing a movie about this case, so . . ." She tossed back her curls. "My life is going to get even more hectic."

"We're sorry to interrupt your busy life, Mrs. Simon," Detective Hirasuna said. "But I guess you heard that three other local television personalities received poisoned cakes today?"

Raquel checked her manicure. "Oh, yes, I heard. Terrible," she said, not sounding at all upset.

"We've got to catch this person before someone else gets killed." There was an edge to the detective's voice, and Raquel looked up from her fingernails. "I have a question to ask you and I want you to be perfectly honest."

Raquel's expression became guarded. "Okay."

"All three of the other people who received poisoned cheesecakes today also got a nasty note. Did you get a note with your cheesecake that you forgot to mention to us?"

"I didn't forget," Raquel said. "I just hoped that no one would ever have to know."

"I'm sorry," Detective Hirasuna apologized in advance. "Based on what the other notes said, yours must have been very malicious. But you're going to have to tell us."

Raquel took a deep breath. "It said 'Your husband is unfaithful.'"

There was a short, respectful silence before Detective Hirasuna asked, "Do you think that's true?"

As Raquel shook her head, Eugenia saw tears glittering in her eyes. "I refuse to consider the possibility," she told them. "Some people might say that is naïve or foolish, but I believe that what you don't know can't hurt you."

Eugenia glanced around the room and saw the same sympathy she felt reflected on the faces of the others.

"I need to see the note," Detective Hirasuna requested.

"I burned it," Raquel replied.

"Where?" he asked.

"Why do you want to know?" Raquel looked irritated by the question.

"Because we may be able to obtain a handwriting sample from a burned fragment."

"I burned it and flushed the ashes down the toilet," she said. "Now, if that's all your questions, my cooking assistant is waiting for me at Makai. We have to go over the recipe we're featuring on my *Morning Show* segment tomorrow."

The detective nodded. "We're done for now."

Raquel took a step toward the door then turned and asked, "Is it okay for me to have Leilani's apartment cleaned? The longer we wait, the harder it's going to be to get the vomit stains out of the carpet."

Detective Hirasuna considered this briefly before nodding. "I think that would be fine."

"Thank you." With a wave for Officer Gates to follow, Raquel exited the room.

Eugenia pushed herself up into a standing position. "If you'll point me toward the ladies' room, I believe I'll go take some of my arthritis medication."

Mila gave her directions, and Eugenia walked as quickly as her old legs would carry her down the hall. In the police station lobby she found Raquel, repairing her makeup, and Officer Gates, who gave Eugenia a scowl. Ignoring the policeman, Eugenia approached Raquel.

"I'm so sorry about this new development—a possible serial killer on the loose in Honolulu—threatening to kill television personalities," Eugenia said. "You must be terrified."

Raquel expertly reapplied eyeliner using the mirror in her compact. "Thanks for your concern, but I'm not scared at all. I've got Officer Gates to protect me."

"We need to go," Officer Gates said, and Raquel took a step toward the door.

"I met Mr. Baldwin yesterday," Eugenia went on in a conversational tone. "He seems nice."

Raquel stared at Eugenia for a few seconds then nodded. "Yes, I suppose."

"I guess he is very upset about the poisoned cakes."

"I'm sure he is," Raquel said. "Since two of his employees have received one."

"It's almost as if the murderer has singled out Channels One and Six," Eugenia remarked.

Raquel shrugged.

"Is he good to work for?" Eugenia asked.

"Who?"

"Mr. Baldwin," she clarified.

"Oh, yes," Raquel answered. "His approach is basically hands off. Unless there's a problem, he doesn't get involved." Raquel seemed to be warming to her subject. "And he never complains about the cost of more modern equipment. I love that about him."

"Has he been in the business long?"

Raquel considered this. "Yes. He built the station from nothing back in the seventies, I think."

"Is he married?"

Raquel put away her compact. "Why, are you interested?"

Eugenia laughed. "No, just curious."

"He does have a wife, but nobody ever sees her. I think she has Alzheimer's or something. Well, it was nice talking to you, but I've got to go. I just got word that there are reporters waiting to talk to me at Makai." Raquel turned to Officer Gates. "Let's go."

The officer gave Eugenia another scowl. Then he followed Raquel outside.

Eugenia went into the rest room and took two arthritis pills. Then she returned to Detective Hirasuna's office. As soon as there was a pause in the conversation, she reported the presence of reporters at Makai.

"I figured it wouldn't take long for the press to arrive in full force," Detective Hirasuna replied. "I'll request more men to secure the area."

When the detective finished his phone call, he said, "Okay, now I think what we're going to have to do is look deeper into the background of our victims. We need to find a common denominator—which will hopefully lead us to a common enemy. Mila's Raquel Hate List will be a good reference point. If you find out that anyone on that list had a grudge against one of the other victims, make a note and we'll take a closer look."

"Will we keep the same victim assignments as before?" Mila asked.

"Yeah," the detective confirmed. "But Wong, I'll need you to double up and look into Raquel too. Do you think you can handle that?"

"I'll do my best," Officer Wong promised.

"I want everything on these folks," the detective told them. "Check their financial records and work histories, etc. We're looking for any other little scandals in their past that we don't know about. You've got two hours. We'll meet back here at seven and compare notes. Any questions?"

"Jerry, I have plans for tonight," Mila said.

The detective gave her an incredulous look. "Mila, we've got attempted murder times four here! Your vacation will have to wait."

Eugenia saw the anguish on Mila's face. "Why don't you call Quin and discuss it with him?" she suggested. "If you're needed here, they can go on without us."

"I don't want you to miss it on my account."

"I'm not really in the mood for sightseeing anyway," Eugenia told her. "Now you call Quin, and show me a phone I can use to call Annabelle."

"There is a television van parked in front of the estate!" Annabelle informed her sister instead of saying "hello" when she answered the call.

"Yes, we know," Eugenia replied. "There have been some new developments in our case."

"*Our* case?" Annabelle cried. "Eugenia, you really are the very last word."

Eugenia didn't let this ridicule bother her. "I'm serious. Three more people received poisoned cakes today, but thankfully nobody ate any of them."

"Well, thank goodness for that," Annabelle said in a more subdued tone. "But where are you? It's almost time for us to go to dinner at the Polynesian Cultural Center."

"I might not be able to come." Eugenia was careful to keep the regret from her voice.

"But the children are coming!" Annabelle reminded her sister. "Kate said she bought them little matching outfits. Emily's is a sundress, and Charles has a little aloha shirt made out of the same material. I just know they'll be adorable."

Eugenia took a deep breath and prayed for courage. "I'll have to see them later. Mila needs me here."

"Eugenia, for once you've left me speechless," Annabelle replied.

Eugenia had to smile. "Thank the Lord for small mercies," she said and ended the call.

* * *

When Quin answered his phone, Mila apologized for not having hers sufficiently charged. "I guess I forgot, since I never really went to bed last night. I've borrowed one from the station so you'll be able to reach me until I get mine charged." Mila read Quin the number then told him about the poisoned cakes that had been delivered during the day.

"So this case just got big," Quin commented.

"Unfortunately it did," Mila agreed. "If it will just get a little bigger, the FBI will come in and take it away from us. But in the meantime, we've got to try to keep anyone else from dying." Mila paused briefly, then said, "I can't go out to dinner tonight, Quin. Jerry has given me an assignment, and I have to do it right away."

"Can't you come eat, and then I'll help you do your assignment?" Quin suggested as an alternative.

Mila was tempted. "I'd love to," she said, "but if I'm out having fun and someone on my list turns out to be the murderer and kills again . . ."

"It was a bad idea." Quin withdrew his suggestion. "Don't worry about dinner. It's okay."

"It's not okay," she said in frustration. "I know it's not fair of me to desert you at a time like this."

"Can someone else take over for you?"

She frowned. "Someone could, but I wouldn't be able to stop thinking and worrying about the case—so I might as well be doing the work."

Quin was quiet for several seconds, and finally Mila said, "But if you really want me to remove myself from the case, I will." Mila waited for his response. She heard him sigh.

"There's no point in that. Like you said, until the murderer is caught, you won't be able to think about anything else." There was something in his tone that made her feel an unmistakable sense of impending doom. "Maybe we should consider postponing the wedding."

"Quin!" she cried out as tears sprang into her eyes. "You don't want to get married on Saturday?"

She could hear the emotion in his voice when he answered, "Of course I do. But when we get married I want your undivided attention, and if the murderer is still at large—you won't be able to concentrate on us."

Mila felt her tears slip onto her cheeks, but she couldn't argue. "I hate myself for being that way."

"Your tenacity is one of the things I love about you," he said.

"Can we wait to decide about postponing the wedding?" she asked. "The case could be solved at any minute."

"It seems inconsiderate for the people at the temple to be gearing up for a wedding that might not happen."

"We could call the temple and warn them that there's a possibility we'll have to cancel," Mila proposed. "And since our parents don't fly in until Friday afternoon—we still have some time. I can't bear to cancel it yet."

"We can't wait much longer," he warned. "Tomorrow afternoon at the latest."

She was grateful for the temporary reprieve. "Okay, by tomorrow afternoon we'll make a decision."

"Well, you'd better get back to work."

She clutched the phone, reluctant to let him go. "There's nothing I want more than to be your wife," she whispered emphatically.

She expected him to acknowledge this, but instead he said. "I'll call you when we get back tonight."

When Mila heard the dial tone, she hung up the receiver.

Mila and Miss Eugenia both returned to Jerry's office at the same time. The men were both standing—apparently ready to leave. "Everyone has their assignments?" Jerry clarified.

Mila and Elliot nodded.

"Okay, then, we'll meet back here at seven."

* * *

Eugenia slipped into Mila's car and arranged her old bones gently. Mila was quiet as they drove, and Eugenia thought she saw the girl wipe away an occasional tear. She was still trying to think of something comforting to say when they pulled into the gates of Makai.

"What are we doing back here?" Eugenia asked. "I thought you were doing research for the case."

"I am," Mila acknowledged. "But I can use my computer at home as easily as I can use the one at work. And this way I get to see Quin for a few minutes." Mila glanced at Eugenia as she parked her car in front of the main house. "And you don't have to miss the Polynesian Cultural Center."

Eugenia thought about Emily and Charles in their little matching clothes and thought she might burst into tears herself. "I hate to desert you."

Mila gave her a wan smile. "I work faster alone. You have a good time, and thanks for your help."

Eugenia got out of the car and walked into the house. No one was in the entryway, so she proceeded up the stairs. Anxious to check in on Whit and Lady, she knocked on the door to Annabelle's room intending to borrow her sister's cell phone. Annabelle answered a minute later, looking sleepy.

"Are you taking a nap?" Eugenia demanded. "We're supposed to be leaving for dinner in less than thirty minutes!"

"Well, I was trying to spend my valuable free time resting," Annabelle replied. "Now, I guess I'm going to spend it listening to you carry on like you're a private detective or an undercover agent for the Honolulu police."

Eugenia had been planning to tell Annabelle the most recent developments in the case, but her sister's flippant attitude hurt her feelings. "I certainly don't want to bore you, so if you'll loan me your cell phone, I'll leave."

Annabelle sighed and pulled the door open wide. "I'm sorry," she said. "I'm just upset because I talked to Derrick a little while ago."

"Is something wrong with Derrick?"

"Oh, no," Annabelle dispelled the notion. "He's having such a wonderful time on his fishing trip that he said he'll probably go again next year."

Eugenia studied her sister. "You're unhappy that Derrick is having *fun?*"

"Without me!" Annabelle wailed. "What wife would be happy about that?"

Now Eugenia understood. Annabelle was feeling a little insecure. "Derrick is the most devoted husband I've ever seen," she said reassuringly. "The fact that he wants to do 'men things' every once in a while doesn't mean he loves you less."

"I guess," Annabelle agreed reluctantly.

"When you go places with me and Polly and George Ann, do you forget about Derrick?"

"Of course not," Annabelle returned. "Being with all of you makes me even more anxious to get home."

Eugenia frowned. "That was a bad analogy then. Think of people you enjoy being with—if you spend time with them, it doesn't mean you don't love Derrick. No matter how much fun you have, you'll still be glad to see him again."

Annabelle smiled. "I was kidding about not having fun with you."

Eugenia nodded. "I know."

Annabelle sat on the edge of her bed and patted the space beside her for Eugenia. "Since you're here, you might as well tell me about your case."

"You really want to know?" Eugenia confirmed.

"I know you really want to tell me," Annabelle replied. "So, go ahead."

Eugenia decided that was encouragement enough. She started with the news that three poisoned cheesecakes had now been delivered to television personalities around Honolulu, the possibility that they were dealing with a crazed serial killer, and the chance that the FBI might soon take over the case. She informed Annabelle that the police were very impressed with her discovery that the cheesecakes were made by an individual—presumably the killer—and not by the Cheesecake Company. Then she described the notes sent to each local celebrity and how they essentially destroyed the careers of the recipients.

Finally she added, "Raquel has been doing national television interviews all day about the case and says she's working on a deal to do a mini-series. And I was right about Cade—Raquel's note said that he is unfaithful."

"An anonymous note is not really proof that Cade is unfaithful," Annabelle pointed out.

"All the other notes were accurate," Eugenia defended. "And Raquel didn't exactly deny the charge. She just said she refused to consider the possibility."

Annabelle was frowning, which Eugenia took as more criticism. "What? You still believe that Cade is a perfect husband?"

Annabelle shook her head. "No, you've convinced me that he's the devil. I was just thinking that Raquel's note, while unquestionably cruel, seems a bit tame compared to the other notes."

Eugenia didn't like it that Annabelle was trying to assume her role as sleuth. "You call having the whole world know you're husband is unfaithful just a *little cruel*?"

"You had that figured out the minute you saw them together," Annabelle reminded her. "And it won't cost Raquel her job. In fact, she's doing interviews on national television; it might actually help her."

Eugenia sat down on the bed beside Annabelle. It was rare for her sister to get the best of her, but it did happen occasionally. "That's all true," Eugenia admitted. "Although my observation skills are well-honed, I'm sure that other people who see Raquel and Cade together often had already reached the same conclusion. So, what do you think it means? Why would Raquel's note be mild compared to the others?"

"Did anyone actually see the note from Raquel's cheesecake?" Annabelle asked.

Eugenia shook her head. "No, she said she burned it and flushed it down the toilet."

Annabelle smiled. "Ahhh. I'd be willing to bet that her note really said something else much worse, and she chose a replacement 'scandalous statement' since there was no evidence to the contrary."

Eugenia gasped. "You think she used an unsubstantiated rumor that most people probably already knew to protect herself from something worse?" Eugenia repeated to get the feel of the new idea.

Annabelle nodded. "That's what I think. The cake was delivered before Raquel returned home from work, but she saw it before anyone else did and was able to remove the card. She never would have mentioned it if the other cakes hadn't been delivered with their libelous cards."

"Maybe that's why the killer delivered the others more publicly," Eugenia mused. "Because the note to Raquel never saw the light of day." She looked at her sister with respect. "I believe that you inherited some investigative tendencies too."

"Oh, I hope not," Annabelle responded. "One amateur detective in the family is more than enough."

Eugenia laughed and stood slowly, rubbing her aching back. "Okay, well I'm going over to Mila's bungalow to tell her our new theory."

Annabelle pointed at her phone on the dresser. "I thought you wanted to call Whit."

Eugenia picked up the phone. "I'll call while I'm walking."

* * *

Mila took the time to make a quick call to a contact she had in Child Services, hoping to come up with a housing solution for Henry Gosslinger, a.k.a. Spike. The only possibility that sounded attractive to Mila was a mentor program sponsored by local businesses. Teenagers accepted into the plan were housed in a dormitory and trained to do a useful trade. The school offered a variety of employment options and even helped graduates find a job. Spike would not have complete freedom, but he would be less restricted than in most other available programs. Mila asked that the paperwork be started for Spike; when and if he was accepted, she'd figure out how to convince the boy to go.

Once she had done all she could for Spike, she settled in front of the computer and began delving into the history of Allison Hammer/Mary Zelinski. She e-mailed the chief of police in Sylacauga, Alabama, and put out a few feelers before Miss Eugenia arrived.

"I hope I'm not interrupting," Miss Eugenia said.

"I am a little busy," Mila replied. "I'm trying to find a connection between Allison Hammer and our other three victims before my meeting with Jerry."

"I promise I won't keep you long, but I was just talking to Annabelle about the notes and the poisoned cheesecakes, and she had an idea that I think you should look into."

"What's the idea?" Mila rubbed her temples and tried to keep a pleading tone from her voice.

"Annabelle said it was strange that the information written on the notes taped to the other three cheesecakes was much more damaging than Raquel's note."

"More damaging?" Mila repeated.

"I know that on the surface Raquel's note seems pretty bad, but realistically—Cade's lack of fidelity is not much of a secret, and announcing it didn't hurt Raquel's career. In fact, the whole situation seems to be helping it."

"So?"

"Well, Annabelle thinks Raquel was lying about what was written on her note. She thinks that the real message was something much worse—like on the others."

Mila considered this for a few seconds, and then she smiled. "I think Annabelle's right. That's something we do need to look into. I'll call Jerry and suggest that he question Raquel again."

* * *

Quin arrived at Makai to pick up the guests for their trip to the Polynesian Cultural Center just as Mila was leaving for the police station. Mila gave him a kiss before they joined the Iversons by their bungalow and admired the children in their Hawaiian clothes.

"Mama says we're twins," Emily told Mila. "Except I'm a girl and Charles is a boy."

"I'm a boy," Charles repeated in case there was any doubt.

"Well, I think you're both very cute," Mila said.

"We're going to see hula dancers," Emily added. "But Mama thinks Charles will fall asleep because he didn't take a nap."

"I hate naps," Charles informed her.

Mila smiled. "I hope you both stay awake long enough to enjoy the show."

Then Miss Eugenia arrived along with the other Haggerty ladies, and they all took turns making a fuss over the children.

"I'm glad Mark is coming with me tonight," Quin confided to Mila and Mark as they watched the old women admire Emily and Charles. "I don't think I can handle them all by myself again."

"I won't let them eat you alive," Mark promised.

Quin smiled. "I'm not worried about my life. I just don't want to have to think up a sensible response when Miss George Ann mentions bunions and fungi."

"And he doesn't want to have to referee fights between Annabelle and Miss Eugenia," Mila teased.

"Really, the worst thing is the way Miss Polly bursts into tears for no reason," Quin admitted. "That's very unnerving for a guy."

"Take care of him, won't you, Mark?" Mila asked as she pressed a kiss to Quin's cheek.

"Don't worry about him," Mark instructed. "You just solve this murder case."

Mila thought her heart would break as she watched them leave without her. But she waved good-bye bravely then got in her car and drove downtown. She was pleased that she arrived before Jerry or Elliot, and she made a point of looking at the clock when they walked in.

"I thought we said seven," she teased.

"We figured you'd be late, and we didn't want to make you look bad," Jerry returned with a smile. "Did you find anything?"

"Not much," she admitted. "Have you had a chance to talk to Raquel yet about her note?"

"She's sticking with her original story, and there's no way I can see to prove it if she's lying."

"When Miss Eugenia came over today and told me her theory about the notes, it gave me another idea."

Jerry spread his hands. "We're certainly open to suggestions. Let's hear it."

"Well, there are several differences between the three cakes that were delivered today and the one that was delivered to Raquel on

Monday." Mila used her fingers to itemize each point. "First, no one died from eating today's cakes. Second, they were delivered in a much more public way. And third, they had career-destroying notes attached to them."

"That's all true," Jerry agreed, making a hurry-up gesture with his hands.

"Just for the sake of argument," Mila said, "let's suppose that the last three cakes were sent by a completely different person."

Jerry frowned. "A copycat killer?"

Mila shook her head. "No, I don't think they ever meant for anyone to die. They just used the situation to their advantage."

"By 'advantage' I presume you mean they wanted to destroy the careers of these three other people who were—what—competition, enemies from the past?" Jerry guessed aloud.

"Anything like that," Mila confirmed. "By putting the notes on the boxes and having them delivered in a very public way—they virtually guaranteed that no one would actually *eat* the cakes."

"Not anyone who had watched the news that morning," Elliot agreed.

"Or read a newspaper," Mila added.

"One little murder and nobody's in the mood for cheesecake," Jerry said sarcastically.

"But even if they hadn't seen a news report—no one would eat a cake with a vicious note taped on top," Mila continued. "And the delivery of three cakes, all to local celebrities, turned the murder case of a secretary into a sensational serial crime."

Jerry frowned in concentration. "Someone did it to get press coverage?"

"And to destroy the recipients professionally," Mila explained.

Jerry leaned back in his chair, rubbing his eyes. "That's a valid theory. I'll call the lab and ask them to check all four cakes to see if the ingredients were the same. That should tell us if we have more than one poisonous cook."

"I can't imagine someone sending out poisoned cheesecakes just to eliminate competition." Elliot seemed mystified. "Even if no one ate them, it's still a felony."

"They weren't planning to get caught," Mila said. "They expected Leilani's murderer to be accused of sending all four cakes."

"I presume you have a suspect for these extra cakes?"

Mila nodded. "The only person who had something to gain was Raquel Simon."

Jerry considered this. "She had insider information through the chief and Officer Gates."

"What kind of information?" Elliot asked.

"Things that haven't been released to the public," Jerry explained. "Like the fact that arsenic was the poison used by the murderer."

Mila massaged her forehead. "The question is would Raquel really go that far and risk that much? Like Elliot said—it's a felony."

"After we see what the lab can come up with, we'll talk to Mrs. Simon again," Jerry promised as he pulled out his cell phone, "just in case. Wong, you call Gates and tell him to get the Simons over here. I'll call the lab and ask for additional tests on the cheesecakes."

When Jerry completed his call he said, "The technician promised to run the necessary tests immediately and call me back."

"And Gates said the Simons have a dinner engagement, but he'll bring them here afterward so we can question them," Elliot reported.

Jerry leaned his chair back against the wall. "Well, we've rattled some cages. Now, let's see what crawls out."

CHAPTER 7

The team took a break then reassembled to go over the results of their research. Jerry took a sip of coffee and made a face. "Man, this stuff is bad."

"I told you this coffee isn't good for you," Mila reprimanded mildly.

"I'm not sure that even qualifies as coffee." Jerry put the cup on the far corner of his desk. "Did you find out anything else about Ms. Hammer?"

"I've confirmed that the information on the card was correct," Mila told her partner.

"That's pretty much all I got on the sportscaster," Elliot volunteered.

"Let's make a chart combining what we know about our cheese-cake victims," Jerry suggested. "That will make it easier to see if their lives intersect."

Elliot produced a large piece of poster board, and Mila found markers. They used a different color for each victim, and soon they had a readable map of the four lives.

"They have several things in common," Jerry said, pointing at the intersecting lines.

"Which is not unusual since they worked in the same industry," Officer Wong remarked.

"True," Mila agreed.

"All our victims were employed at one time or another by Channel One," Elliot said.

"And the owner of Channel One, Albert Baldwin, was a guest at the party on Monday night," Mila told them. "And he's on the

Raquel Hate List, although I never was able to come up with any specific reason except that she's demanding."

"All the potential victims were also members of a professional society called the Hawaiian Media Guild." Jerry picked up the conversation. "All were members of the Honolulu Chamber of Commerce, and all were nominated as 'Most Popular Television Personality in Honolulu' last year—but none of them won."

Elliot checked his notes before saying, "All the other potential victims were invited to Mrs. Simon's party on Monday night according to the list the housekeeper compiled. But only the sportscaster from Channel Six actually attended."

Jerry nodded. "That might be significant. Highlight it."

"Then we have several partial matches." Mila pointed at her list with a pen. "Raquel and Allison use the same hairdresser, the anchor man and the sportscaster belong to the same gym."

"Would the hairdresser or anyone at the gym have access to sensitive personal information?" Jerry asked.

"Hairdressers hear all kinds of things," Mila replied. "And they would have had to fill out applications to join the gym. Someone intent on digging up dirt could probably use their social security number or an old address to begin a search."

"They must have done some checking into backgrounds for the Favorite Personality award thing," Jerry remarked. "Wong, will you talk to someone there and see who did the research? And Channel One would have employment records. We need to see who has access to those."

"The Chamber and Media Guild probably have applications too," Mila suggested. "It would be nice if there were one firm who handled the background checks for them all."

Jerry smiled. "That would be really nice—but not likely."

Then the phone rang and Jerry answered it. He listened for a few minutes, then thanked the caller and hung up. "That was the lab," he announced. "All of the cakes had the same ingredients in basically the same proportions—the variances were what you'd expect from an amateur cook preparing four different cakes under non-industrial conditions."

Mila was disappointed. "I was so sure about that."

"It was a good hypothesis," Elliot commiserated.

"Is it possible that two different cooks used the same recipe?" Mila asked.

Jerry shook his head. "It was a good idea, Mila, but it was wrong. We have to move on with the investigation. But don't get too discouraged! We'll find the answer."

Mila turned the page in her notebook and picked up a pen. "Okay, let's make a new suspect list using the matches on our chart." Before she could go any further, the cell phone she had borrowed from the station rang.

"Edwards," she said into the small receiver.

"Mila?" It was Miss Eugenia. "I just thought of something and wanted to mention it before I forgot. When are you going to need me to come in and give you samples of my fingerprints?"

Mila was confused. "Why would we need your fingerprints?"

"Why, for elimination purposes, of course. I touched the box that had Raquel's poisoned cake in it and I'm sure that expensive foil paper picked up my prints very clearly."

Mila repeated Miss Eugenia's question, and Jerry Hirasuna frowned. "I don't think I've seen a fingerprint report yet. Where's the stuff we got from the evidence collection team?"

Elliot dug through the file and finally shrugged. "It's not here."

Jerry cursed under his breath. "Tell Miss Eugenia to come in first thing in the morning. We'll have to call the lab and have them do another fingerprint test on the cake box since we've apparently lost the first one."

"I didn't lose it," Elliot responded defensively.

"Of course you didn't," Mila said with a stern look at Jerry. "We're all tired and frustrated." Then she turned her attention back to the cell phone. "Miss Eugenia, Detective Hirasuna wants you to come in first thing tomorrow morning." Mila finished her conversation, and then she closed the phone. "She'll be here."

"Okay, once we have a new suspect list we'll split it between us. When Raquel Simon gets here, we can talk to her and call it a day."

"Two days," Elliot corrected. "Maybe three."

Jerry ignored this. "So, who do we keep from our old list? Cade Simon?"

"We don't have any connection between him and the other victims," Mila pointed out.

"Whoever has him should look into that," Jerry said. "They moved in the same social circles, they were invited to parties at the Simons' home. Cade Simon may have had an involvement we don't know about."

"One was a woman, and the other two had wives," Elliot provided. "Since Cade Simon is apparently a philanderer—that could be the connection."

Jerry chewed his lip for a second. "If that's the motive, it makes more sense for someone to try and kill Cade Simon."

Mila shrugged. "Maybe he was the intended victim and Leilani took the cake before the murderer could arrange any time alone with *him* at the party."

"Okay, keep Cade Simon on the suspect list and look for connections with the other victims. Keep the Baldwin guy since they all worked for him. We'll want to look into the hairdresser and ask around at the gym that the television guys use."

"The caterer might have handled parties for the other victims," Mila suggested.

"Good," Jerry approved. "We'll keep her on the active list."

Mila hated to ask but felt she had to. "What about Raquel herself?"

"Let's add her. I'd rather have too many people than miss someone obvious." Jerry stood and stretched. The phone rang, and he reached to answer it. "Hirasuna." After a brief pause he asked, "You're absolutely sure about that?" Apparently the person on the other end of the line confirmed their certainty, and Jerry hung up the phone. He sat down in his chair and faced them. "I'm afraid we've got a problem."

Mila groaned inwardly. "What?"

"That was the gal from evidence collection assigned to our case. She said the reason we can't find a fingerprint report on the cheesecake box is because they didn't send us one. And the reason they didn't send us one is because there were no prints on the box that Raquel's cake was delivered in."

"No prints!" Elliot repeated. "That's impossible."

"Miss Eugenia said she held it for a good two minutes, so she should have had several sets on the box," Mila agreed. "Raquel's prints should have been on it and Miss Polly's and Mrs. Rose's and Leilani's." Mila shook her head. "Think of all the people who touched that box."

"So, what does that mean?" Elliot asked. "No prints on the box?"

Mila shook her head. "Maybe someone switched the boxes?"

"Why? How?" the detective demanded.

Mila shrugged.

"It's the same box," Jerry pointed to the color photo on the table. I remember that crease in the corner."

"Then someone wiped the box clean," Mila said with a stricken expression.

"Who would do that?" Elliot asked.

"The murderer," Mila answered grimly.

"Elliot, call them and see if they've checked the boxes delivered today for prints," Jerry instructed, and the officer jumped to obey.

They waited in silence until Elliot hung up the phone. "The only prints on the other three boxes are ones from the delivery scene."

Jerry sighed. "So, apparently we have been headed in the wrong direction since the beginning of this investigation. Miss Fiero didn't die by mistake after eating the cake she'd stolen from the refrigerator. The murderer was with her when she died and wiped the box clean before leaving the scene."

Officer Wong nodded morosely. "That's the only explanation for *no* prints."

Jerry slammed his fist against his desk in frustration. "I can't believe all the time we've wasted going in the wrong direction again! The murderer is probably laughing at us."

"The murderer has also had plenty of time to successfully cover their tracks so we may never find them," Elliot added.

"Then Leilani was the intended victim all along?" Mila confirmed.

Jerry nodded. "Yes. The focus of our investigation has to do a U-turn. Now we're looking for someone who wanted to kill Leilani specifically."

"And all the rest is just smoke?" Mila thought out loud. "The other three cakes were decoys?"

"I think so." Jerry thought for a few seconds then said, "The murderer must have been at that party Raquel held on Monday night. He or she *knew* that Miss Fiero would be there and sent the cake in advance, planning to kill her."

"So we're looking at the same basic scenario—just changing our intended victim?" Elliot verified.

"Help me out here," Jerry appealed to his coworkers. "Throw out some ideas, and let's see what works."

"The murderer had the cake delivered to Raquel—knowing she didn't eat sweets and expecting that she wouldn't even see it until the party," Mila proposed.

"Then during the party the murderer lured Leilani to her apartment with the cake and convinced her to eat some," Elliot added.

"Yes," said Detective Hirasuna. "I guess it happened something like that."

"Wasn't that very risky?" Mila asked. "Anyone could have eaten the cheesecake or it could have been discarded or . . ."

"I agree that it was pretty haphazard," Jerry interrupted. "It might mean that the murderer had a backup plan."

"Or that Leilani didn't have to die on that particular night," Mila said. "If things didn't work out at the party on Monday night, the killer would have other opportunities in the future."

"I like that," Jerry agreed.

"This theory assumes that the murderer knows the household situation," Officer Wong said.

"Oh, I think our murderer knows a great deal about the household," Jerry predicted. "We can't be sure whether Miss Fiero stole the cake in advance or whether the murderer arranged for her to see it and suggested that she take it. But either way, they ended up in her apartment, where Miss Fiero ate a lethal dose of poisoned cheesecake."

"The party itself provided the perfect cover," Mila remarked. "All the confusion—people everywhere—nobody would notice when Leilani and the murderer slipped away."

"So, they went to her apartment." Jerry tried to sequence the events. "The murderer fed Miss Fiero some cake then sat there and watched her vomit until she died."

The room was silent for a few seconds. Finally Mila whispered, "The murderer must be very cold-blooded."

Elliot nodded in agreement. "And must have truly hated Leilani Fiero."

A shocked look crossed Jerry's face, then he hit himself in the head with the heel of his hand. "I can't believe I told Mrs. Simon she could have Miss Fiero's room cleaned! There's no telling how much evidence was destroyed."

"You had the photographer come," Mila reminded him. "And the evidence collection team got plenty of samples."

"They only take a few specimens here and there," Jerry replied, obviously furious with himself. "I wonder if I'm going to make every rookie mistake on this one case."

"We need to search the apartment again anyway," Mila said gently. "Now that we know Leilani was the intended victim, we might be able to find some kind of clue there."

Jerry still looked devastated as he stood. "We might as well give it a try."

"Do we need a warrant?" Elliot asked.

"Check with legal and find out. If we get permission from the Simons, we might be able to get around it."

"They'd be crazy to let us search their house if either one of them is guilty," Elliot pointed out.

"Then let's hope they are either crazy or innocent." Jerry picked up the phone on his desk and made a quick call to Officer Gates. He told the police officer to interrupt the Simons' dinner and ask for permission to look through Leilani's apartment again. Jerry waited for a minute or so before Officer Gates returned to the line. "Great," he said. "And when they are through eating, just bring them to Makai. We'll talk to them there."

Jerry seemed a little more optimistic when he hung up the phone. "They gave permission for us to search Leilani's apartment?" Mila guessed.

Jerry nodded. "Yep, they're either crazy or innocent."

"I'm hoping for crazy," Mila said as they collected their paperwork and headed outside. "We need to wrap this case up before it ruins my life."

* * *

When Mark pulled his rental car in front of the main house at Makai, Eugenia offered again to go with him to the hotel and help him get the children settled.

"That's not necessary," Mark assured her for at least the tenth time. "Emily can wake up enough to walk to our room, and I'll carry Charles."

"Well, I appreciate you dropping me off here on your way. Dinner was delicious, and I'm sure that the entertainment will be just as nice—but I need to take my arthritis medicine, and I'd like to check on Mila."

Mark nodded. "I understand. See you tomorrow."

Eugenia walked up the stairs and knocked on the front door. Mrs. Rose opened it a few seconds later. "You're home early," she said.

"I'm getting too old for these late-night adventures," Eugenia replied. "Mark had to bring the children home, and I decided to call it a night myself."

Before she could say more, there was another knock on the door. Mrs. Rose opened it to admit Darlene Moore, Raquel's cooking assistant.

"Is Raquel here?" the woman asked.

"No, she and Mr. Simon have gone out to dinner," Mrs. Rose replied.

Darlene stepped inside and headed down the hall. "I'll just put this recipe on Raquel's desk then," she called over her shoulder.

"Poor woman," Mrs. Rose said when Darlene was out of earshot. "She has no life."

"She seems to work very hard," Eugenia agreed and then realized that Mrs. Rose felt a kinship with Darlene. Raquel didn't appreciate her housekeeper, either. Before she could say more, Darlene was back.

"Tell Raquel to call me if she has questions—even if it's late," she told Mrs. Rose. "You know I don't sleep much." With a nod in Eugenia's direction, Darlene opened the door. On the front porch stood Detective Hirasuna. His arm was raised like he was about to knock. Mila and Officer Wong were right behind him.

"Oh, it looks like you have more company," Darlene said as she stepped outside and hurried down the stairs.

Eugenia was pleased to see the police personnel; however, Mrs. Rose didn't seem to share her feelings. "The Simons aren't home," Mrs. Rose informed them stiffly.

"We just need to see Miss Fiero's apartment again," Detective Hirasuna told the housekeeper. "The Simons have given us permission. Could you unlock it, please?"

"I can't unlock it," Mrs. Rose replied. "The key is still missing."

The detective muttered something under his breath, and Eugenia was pretty sure it was a curse word. Then he said, "Does anyone have a key or are we going to have to have the locksmith come back?"

"Leilani's keys were probably in her purse, which means the police have them," Mrs. Rose replied. "But there's no need to call a locksmith. As far as I know Leilani's apartment has been unlocked since the body was taken out."

"Great," Mila said softly. "The entire island has had access to the room."

"Why would anyone want to go into Leilani's apartment?" Eugenia asked, falling into step beside Mila.

"To remove or destroy evidence," Mila told her. Then she filled Eugenia in on the change of direction their investigation had taken. "And mostly thanks to your timely question about fingerprints," Mila added.

"Well," Eugenia smiled. "I'm glad I was able to help."

Officer Wong's cell phone rang, and he stopped to answer it while the others continued on through the kitchen.

"Do you have some new evidence in the case of Leilani's death?" Mrs. Rose asked.

"We're just going to look around again," Detective Hirasuna sidestepped the question. "Is this the way Leilani accessed her apartment?"

Mrs. Rose shook her head. "Usually she came in through the back."

"Leilani used the door that opened to the outside?" the detective confirmed.

"Yes, but the door in the kitchen is more convenient for me," Mrs. Rose explained, "so I always go in this way."

Officer Wong rejoined them and said, "Gates says that the Simons' dinner is lasting longer than they anticipated, and Mrs. Simon said unless you have a warrant for her arrest, your conversation with her will have to wait till morning."

"Well, I certainly wouldn't want to interfere with their social life," Detective Hirasuna said through gritted teeth.

As they entered the hallway that led to Leilani's apartment, Eugenia felt a little anxiety, but she took a few deep breaths and forced herself to keep going.

"Has anything been removed from the apartment?" Detective Hirasuna asked the housekeeper.

"Only the trash and the dishes," Mrs. Rose replied. "But Leilani's aunt is coming tomorrow to collect her things."

The detective closed his eyes briefly. "Sounds like we got here just in time. Thank you, Mrs. Rose. We won't take up any more of your time." He waited until the housekeeper disappeared into the kitchen, then he said, "Wong, Mrs. Rose's comment about Leilani's keys reminded me that I need to see the contents of Leilani's purse. The next time one of us is at the office, we need to go by evidence and get an inventory. They might even have pictures, and if they do, I want to see them."

Officer Wong nodded. "I'll make sure we get the list and any pictures they have."

They proceeded into the little vestibule where the detectives and Officer Wong pulled on pairs of latex gloves, then Detective Hirasuna pushed open the door and they walked inside.

The apartment was immaculate, and if Eugenia hadn't seen the body with her own old eyes, she would never have believed that a murder had taken place there just a couple of days before.

The detective waved for Mila to come with him. "Wong, you look around in here," he instructed. Then he seemed to realize for the first time that Eugenia was with them. She couldn't tell from his expression if it was a good or a bad surprise, but he politely invited, "You can come with us too, Miss Eugenia."

Eugenia followed Mila and the other detective, trying to be observant but at the same time staying out of their way. While they checked the closet, Eugenia walked over to the dresser and sniffed repeatedly. Finally she asked, "Do you smell anything?"

Detective Hirasuna gave her an incredulous look. "You mean besides the industrial-strength air freshener they've used to cover up the scent of death and vomit?"

Eugenia ignored the sarcasm. "Something more subtle. I think it's perfume—I just can't put a name to it."

"We'll watch for a bottle of perfume," Mila said in a diplomatic tone.

While Mila cataloged the clothes in the closet and the detective searched the bathroom, Eugenia moved closer to the dresser. "Is it okay for me to open the drawers?" she asked.

Detective Hirasuna left the bathroom long enough to hand her a pair of latex gloves. "Put these on and then you can open the drawers, but try not to move the contents around much. Their position could be important."

Eugenia slipped on the gloves and gingerly opened the top drawer. It was full of makeup, carelessly heaped in no apparent order. She didn't see any perfume, so Eugenia closed the drawer and opened the next one. It was full of lacy lingerie.

"A lot of these clothes still have the tags on them," Mila commented from the closet.

"Same here," Eugenia said as she examined the underclothing. "Most everything looks brand new."

"And this stuff isn't cheap," Mila added. "I know clothes, and based on what I see here—Leilani spent thousands of dollars on clothes recently. But she wasn't wearing any of them."

Eugenia thought about all the clothes Annabelle had forced her to buy for their trip that she had no intention of keeping. "Maybe she was planning to return them to the stores and get her money back."

"Then why buy them in the first place?" Officer Wong asked as he walked in from the living room. "Clothes are not a good investment."

"Well, maybe she was saving them for her trip to Los Angeles with Raquel," Eugenia offered as an alternative suggestion.

Mila nodded. "Maybe."

Detective Hirasuna walked out of the bathroom and joined Mila by the closet. He examined several price tags before saying, "What I want to know is where did she get the money to buy a closet full of jeans that cost two hundred dollars a pair? Her salary from Raquel was generous but not enough to spend *this* much on clothes. She was getting extra money from somewhere."

"I found it," Eugenia said from her position by the dresser.

"You found out how Leilani was getting extra money for expensive clothes?" Mila asked.

"Oh, no!" Eugenia corrected. "I found the perfume." She pointed to the back of a bottom drawer of the dresser. Turned onto its side was an empty perfume bottle.

Detective Hirasuna walked over and picked up the bottle carefully. "Chanel No. 5. I think I've heard of it."

"It was popular back in the '50s and '60s," Eugenia informed him. "My sister, Annabelle, used to wear it."

Mila nodded. "It seems like I remember a famous quote about it by Marilyn Monroe or someone else from that era," Mila remarked.

"It's a very elegant fragrance." Eugenia stepped closer to the detective and breathed deeply. "But I must say I'm surprised that someone as young as Leilani would wear it. I thought that in this day and age all the girls wore those fruity scents."

"She must have liked it," Officer Wong said, "since she used it all."

Mila was frowning. "Still, it is an odd choice for a girl in her early twenties."

Detective Hirasuna raised his eyebrows. "This particular perfume might indicate that Leilani had an older boyfriend—one who was around in the '50s when the fragrance was popular."

Mila nodded. "Older and rich enough to buy her expensive clothes."

"Or maybe he just gave her money to buy whatever clothes she wanted," Eugenia proposed.

"That's more likely," Mila agreed. "This is trendy stuff that an older man wouldn't choose. And besides, she'd have to try things on to be sure they fit."

"If that's the case, we need to check with these stores," Detective Hirasuna pointed to the closet where the clothes hung. "Miss Fiero was probably paying cash, but some of the sales clerks might remember her."

"Maybe her older boyfriend accompanied her on some of her shopping sprees?" Mila said hopefully.

Her partner smiled. "I wouldn't count on that, but it's worth asking. We've got to find out who the older boyfriend was."

"You think the boyfriend was the murderer?" Officer Wong asked.

"Yes," Detective Hirasuna said. "I think that is most likely."

"But why?"

"We probably won't know that until we figure out who he is," Detective Hirasuna predicted, "but there are lots of reasons a man kills his young girlfriend. Maybe he's married, and she's pressuring him to divorce his wife."

"Maybe she was pregnant," Eugenia suggested.

Mila shook her head. "The autopsy report would have mentioned that."

"Well," Eugenia said, not quite ready to abandon this possibility. "Maybe she just told her boyfriend she was pregnant. If you believe the movies, people do that all the time."

"I guess that's possible," Officer Wong admitted.

"Or she could have been blackmailing her boyfriend. That might be where all the money for clothes was coming from," Mila suggested. "And that would also be motive for murder."

Detective Hirasuna sighed. "We've got some good scenarios. Now we just have to find the older boyfriend."

"The older boyfriend could be Cade," Eugenia said reluctantly. "After all, she did work for him before she took the job as Raquel's secretary."

"She did?" Mila asked in surprise. "I don't have that in my notes."

"Mrs. Rose told me," Eugenia explained.

"Cade's not what I would call old," Mila added. "Just early thirties I would say."

"Leilani was in her early twenties," Eugenia said. "Cade might have seemed older to her."

"Not old enough to remember Chanel No. 5 from the '60s," Detective Hirasuna agreed.

"Maybe it was the kind of perfume his mother wore," Eugenia said.

Mila nodded. "Or just a fragrance that was recommended to him by a store clerk."

"And he might have acquired mature tastes from being married to Raquel—who was definitely around during the '60s," Eugenia added.

"If Cade was having an affair with Leilani, why would Raquel let her live here?" Mila asked. "That would almost be *encouraging* the relationship."

"Maybe Mr. Simon forced his wife to accept the arrangement," Officer Wong said.

Mila laughed. "Can you imagine Raquel being forced to do anything?"

The young police officer blushed. "You're right. That was a crazy thought."

"What about Blake, the boyfriend who came to the party?" Eugenia asked. "Maybe he gave her the perfume."

Detective Hirasuna considered this. "He's younger than Cade Simon and much less likely to have sophisticated tastes."

"Where would he get the money for all those clothes?" Mila asked. "He couldn't be making much at that oyster bar."

"Maybe he sells drugs on the side," Eugenia suggested.

"That's a lot of maybes." Detective Hirasuna didn't sound convinced. "But I guess we need to check him out." He turned to Mila. "Will you interview him?"

Mila nodded. "Okay."

"Wong, I need you to contact the stores where these clothes came from and see if any of them remember Miss Fiero. Then we'll go back over our suspect list and concentrate on men—particularly any who would seem 'older' for Leilani Fiero."

"The murderer could easily be a woman," Mila pointed out. "Poisoning a cake has a feminine quality to it and would take no strength."

"The killer may be a woman, but I think the boyfriend is the key. Either he killed her or someone else did because of him."

Mila nodded. "That's as good a lead as we've got."

"Okay, Wong, you go see what you can come up with on Leilani's clothes. Mila, you're going to the oyster bar?"

She nodded.

"You want me to go with you?" Detective Hirasuna offered.

"No, that would be a waste of time. You need to be looking for older men who played a significant role in Leilani's life." Mila turned to Eugenia. "And you need to get some rest."

"We all need rest," Detective Hirasuna agreed. "Mila, Wong, work on your assignments for a while, and then try to get a little sleep. We'll meet at the station tomorrow at eight." He saluted Eugenia then hurried down the steps toward his car.

* * *

When Mila got to her bungalow, she went into the bathroom and splashed water onto her face in an effort to revive herself. She looked into the mirror and saw that her skin was pale under her newly acquired tan, her eyes were circled with fatigue, and her hair hung in stringy clumps on her shoulders. "What a radiant bride you are," she told her reflection. Then she turned away in disgust.

She walked into the bedroom and looked longingly at the bed. A few hours of sleep sounded almost intoxicating. But she needed to interview Blake at the oyster bar, and this was probably a good time to do that. So she changed into a pair of jeans and a T-shirt, hoping to fit in more with the oyster bar's crowd.

Mila was climbing into her car when Quin drove through the front gates. Mila watched him drop Miss George Ann, Miss Polly, and Annabelle off at the main house. She walked out to the twisting driveway and waited for him to approach. He brought the car to a stop and rolled down the driver's side window. He smiled, and she felt better instantly.

She leaned down and kissed him through the window. "How was dinner?"

"Great," he murmured against her lips. "You look tired."

"I am," Mila admitted. "But we've had to switch directions on our murder case again."

"Which way are you headed now?"

She had to smile. "We've abandoned the serial killer approach and are looking for someone who wanted Leilani dead."

Quin raised his eyebrows. "So, she was the intended victim after all?"

Mila nodded. "We think so, but by this time tomorrow—who knows?"

"Are you headed out somewhere this late?"

She sighed. "Yes. I've got to go to the oyster bar where Leilani's old boyfriend works and see if I can talk to him.

Quin leaned over and pushed open the passenger door. "Climb in," he offered.

"Oh, Quin," Mila objected. "I know you're tired, and you have to open the Surf Shop early in the morning and . . ."

Quin held up a hand to stop her. "There's no way my wife is going into downtown Honolulu at this hour without an escort."

Mila walked around and got in. "Your wife, huh?"

"Well, almost."

She smiled. "I like the sound of that."

He squeezed her hand briefly. "Me too." Then he returned his hand to the wheel and backed out of the driveway. Mila closed her eyes just for a second, and the next thing she knew they were parking in front of the oyster bar.

"I fell asleep." She stated the obvious. She was overwhelmed with guilt. Quin was doing her a favor, and the least she could have done was stay awake and keep him company. "I'm so sorry."

"You needed the rest," he said simply. "Do you want me to go in with you or wait in the car?"

"Blake might be more cooperative if I'm alone."

He nodded. "Just keep your cell phone on and call me if you need me."

She leaned over and gave him a kiss, then walked in the bar. It was dark inside so she had to stand by the door for a minute until her eyes adjusted. Once she could see, she crossed the room and asked the bartender where she could find Blake.

"I'll get him for you," the man offered. Then he called out to a busboy, "Tell the boss he's got a visitor."

The boss? Mila was surprised and impressed.

"Why don't you have a seat," the bartender invited. "He'll be here soon."

Mila sat on a stool and ordered a bottled water. Blake rushed in a few minutes later. Mila identified herself, and he asked, "Did we have an appointment?"

"No," she said in an apologetic tone. "And I'm sorry to bother you at work, but I had a couple of questions and thought I could get them out of the way."

He nodded, but he still wasn't happy.

Mila studied him and realized that he was older than she had originally thought—probably close to thirty. "I need to ask you again about your relationship with Leilani Fiero. You said it wasn't romantic in nature, but," she paused for effect, "honestly, I find that hard to believe."

"Well, it's true," he insisted.

"How did you meet Leilani?" she asked.

"The first time I saw her was about a year ago when she came by here asking for a job. She had no references or experience. Besides, I didn't need anybody. So, I had to send her away. When I left that night I found her curled up asleep in the back of my car. I woke her up and she said she'd do anything if I'd just give her something to eat."

Mila was too stunned to speak for a few seconds. This did not fit with the image she had of the beautiful, self-possessed Leilani. "You're kidding," she finally managed to say.

Blake shook his head. "No, she had run away from her aunt's house on Molokai. The boat ride here took all her money, and she'd been living on the street—doing who knows what—to survive. So, I took her home with me and let her sleep on my couch for a few weeks."

"That was nice of you," Mila said.

"I'm a pretty nice guy," he said. "And I felt sorry for her."

Mila took a sip of her water. "Working here you must see a lot of people in bad situations. Why did you help Leilani?"

"I'd feed anyone who is hungry," Blake claimed. "But the beggars we usually get are old and hopeless. Leilani was so young and beautiful—I thought if I could just give her a chance, she might make it."

"How else did you help her?"

"I gave her a job at the bar—just washing dishes—but she learned fast and worked hard. Once she saved up enough money, she got her own place."

"But you were never intimate with her?"

He shook his head. "I care too much about my body to expose it to danger, and since I didn't know anything about Leilani's past, I wouldn't have risked it if I'd been tempted. But honestly, I wasn't. She was just a kid."

"How did she get the job at Mr. Simon's tax preparation firm?"

Blake frowned. "I'm not sure."

"Working for the Simons turned out to be a very good career move for her."

"Yeah, I guess," Blake agreed. "Until it got her killed."

Mila couldn't argue with his logic. "You said you hadn't seen Leilani much lately."

"No, at first she'd come around now and then, but for the past several months she'd been too busy."

Mila thought about Mrs. Rose's description of Leilani's job for Raquel. "Doing what?"

"Getting ready to go to Los Angeles to be in some television show."

"So there was an actual deal for Leilani to be in a TV show?"

"Yeah, she said Mrs. Simon set it all up with a producer who was a friend of hers. She was supposed to leave in a few weeks, and that's all Leilani could think or talk about."

"Did you think it was odd that someone like Mrs. Simon was so willing to help Leilani?"

Blake frowned as he considered this. "I guess it was a little strange, but Leilani had a way of attracting people."

"And why did you come to the party on Monday night?"

Blake sighed. "I loaned Leilani three hundred dollars when she moved in with me so she could buy herself some decent clothes. I didn't pressure her to pay me back at first, but she was making plenty of money working for Raquel Simon, and I figured she should pay me. I called and left messages on her cell phone, but she wouldn't call me back. So, I decided to show up in person."

"Did she give you the money?" Mila asked.

He shook his head. "No. And now I guess I can kiss that three hundred dollars good-bye."

Mila thanked Blake for his time and returned to Quin's car. She found him listening to talk radio. "Anything interesting?" she asked.

"Some guy says he thinks his daughter's body has been taken over by aliens and other callers are giving him advice."

Mila laughed. "Does this guy know how teenagers are supposed to act? An alien might be preferable."

Quin turned off the radio and asked about her conversation with Blake.

"Well, he says he took Leilani in when she first came to Oahu. He claims she was homeless and living on the street. Jerry should be able to confirm that if it's true. He gave her money and a job and a place to stay until she got on her feet. Then once she was on her way, she wouldn't return his calls or repay the money she owed him."

"So the girl wasn't very loyal," Quin remarked without taking his eyes off the road.

That was an interesting choice of words, and Mila considered it for a few seconds. It was awful that Leilani had been killed, but so far she hadn't found out much that was good about the dead girl. She allowed Blake to take her in, give her a job, and buy her clothes and then cut him out of her life when her circumstances improved. Raquel also took her in, gave her an even better job, and there was a good possibility that Leilani betrayed her by sleeping with Cade.

With a sigh she looked over at Quin. "Let's talk about something happy. I'm sick of death and murder and poisoned cakes."

Quin smiled at the road. "We could talk about ice cream."

Mila raised an eyebrow. "Now *that's* what I call happy."

Quin laughed as he pulled into a McDonald's that had an all-night drive-through and ordered two hot fudge sundaes. They ate their ice cream while sitting on the private beach at Makai. The stars were glittering, and the waves were crashing, and as Mila watched Quin eat, tears sprang to her eyes.

"This was supposed to be a happy activity," he reminded her.

"I just want this all to be over so we can get on with our lives," she whispered.

He put down his ice cream container and wrapped his arms around his bent knees. When he spoke, he addressed the incoming tide, and she could tell he was choosing his words carefully. "There will always be challenges in life, Mila. Sometimes it will be a big case like the one you're working on now. Sometimes it will be our efforts to promote the Surf Shop or our church callings and eventually kids."

Mila's stomach quivered at the thought of their future children.

"I think the secret to being truly happy is learning to 'get on with life' no matter what our circumstances are."

She studied his profile as the wind ruffled his hair. Quin wasn't a big talker, but when he did speak, what he had to say was usually worthwhile. This time, though, she didn't know how to respond. Was he saying that she should forget about the murder case and concentrate on the rest of her life? Or did he just mean that they had to love and support each other in times of crises? Finally she decided to go with a noncommittal response. "As long as we love each other, things will work out."

He turned to her and smiled. "Well, I guess I'd better let you get inside so you can work through the night." He stood and held out a hand to pull her up.

Once she was on her feet, she brushed the sand from her jeans and yawned again. "I won't make it all night, but I will try to send out some e-mails before I go to bed. Because of the time difference, when I wake up I might have a few responses."

Quin led her to the door of the bungalow, then kissed her and said good night. She waited until he had parked next door and disappeared into the other bungalow. Then she walked inside and called Jerry on his cell phone.

"So, what did you find out?" he asked.

She filled them in on her interview with Blake. "Since he corroborates Mrs. Rose's story that Leilani was planning a trip to Los Angeles, I guess we can assume that's why she was stockpiling clothes."

"A new wardrobe for a new life?" Jerry asked.

"Yes," Mila said. "And he seemed more upset that she didn't pay him the $300 than he was about her leaving."

"So, you don't think this Blake guy is a reasonable suspect?"

"I don't think we can discount him completely," Mila qualified her remarks. "But I don't think he's our man. He dresses sloppy, doesn't look or act like he has any money. I just can't see him appreciating Chanel No. 5."

"Okay, we'll move him to the bottom of our list," Jerry decided. "Wong was able to get in touch with the managers of a couple of the stores where Miss Fiero bought her clothes," he continued. "He faxed them a picture of her, and they've all agreed to check their records and talk to their employees tomorrow."

"Did you find any new names to add to our list of suspects?"

"A few. I've included Cade Simon and this Blake guy and Mr. Baldwin and Leilani's hairdresser—who it turns out is a man. I think the hairdresser is gay, so he's probably not the boyfriend, but he turned out to be a font of knowledge about Leilani and her social life. According to him, she's dated most of the men on the island."

"Great," Mila muttered.

Jerry laughed. "But he was able to give me a few names of men he thought she was serious about, at least for a few weeks. I've added them to the list, and we'll discuss them tomorrow."

Mila yawned. "Sounds good."

"One more thing. We're scheduled to interview the Simons in the morning at ten, but I'd like to talk with Cade Simon alone—without his wife's knowledge. Do you think that's possible?"

"Why?" Mila asked.

"Because if she knows he's coming to talk to us, she'll either coach him or accompany him, and I don't want either one," Jerry explained.

Mila considered this. "Why don't you call Officer Gates and tell him to change the Simons' appointment for sometime tomorrow afternoon. In the morning I'll wait until I see Raquel leave for the television station—then I'll call the main house and ask Cade to come down. You can just happen to be here."

"I'll be there at eight," Jerry promised. "I'll bring Wong with me, and we can work at your place until I get a chance to talk to Simon."

CHAPTER 8

On Thursday morning when Mila opened her eyes at seven o'clock, she could smell bacon cooking in the kitchen of the bungalow. That meant one of two things. Either sleep deprivation had driven her crazy or someone was making breakfast. Mila climbed out of bed and poked her head out of her bedroom door. Miss Eugenia was moving purposefully around the small kitchen—humming to herself.

"Good morning," she said when she saw Mila. "I thought you could use a good meal, so I went by the store and got a few things."

"I'm sorry you had to go to the store as well as cook."

Miss Eugenia laughed. "I looked through your cupboards and refrigerator and, well, I couldn't have made anything with the food you keep on hand."

Mila looked at the array of breakfast foods Miss Eugenia had arranged on the counter. Scrambled eggs, biscuits, bacon, and fruit. "It looks delicious, but I'll never be able to eat this much."

"I hope you don't mind, but I invited Annabelle and Polly and George Ann to come eat with us. They'll be here in a few minutes, so you'd better hurry and get dressed," Miss Eugenia suggested.

"I don't mind at all." Mila picked a strawberry off the plate and ate it as she walked back to her bedroom. She took a quick shower and dressed before returning to the kitchen. Miss Eugenia and the other Haggerty ladies were gathered around the table, waiting for her to begin breakfast.

After greeting her guests, Mila took a seat. George Ann said grace, and then everyone fixed a plate.

"I called Quin and invited him to come to breakfast," Miss Eugenia said as she heaped her plate with bacon. "He said thanks, but he's already at the Surf Shop."

Mila smiled at Miss Eugenia, grateful for her thoughtfulness. "Thanks anyway." Then she turned to the other ladies. "How was your trip to the Polynesian Cultural Center last night?"

"It was wonderful!" Miss Polly exclaimed. "I loved the food, and those hula girls were very talented."

Miss George Ann sniffed. "That dancing was pornographic if you ask me."

"No one did," Miss Eugenia said without looking up from her plate.

"You're dating yourself, Miss George Ann," Annabelle added. "Today, pornography is much worse than women shaking their fully clothed hips."

Miss George Ann lifted her long neck. "Well, I thought it was just awful and kept my eyes closed the whole time."

"You were asleep!" Annabelle accused. "I heard you snoring!"

"I do not snore!" Miss George Ann denied.

"You do, and now I have a witness!" Miss Eugenia was quick to say.

Anxious to avoid more fighting, Mila tried to remember the itinerary that she had planned for her guests. "This morning is the tour of Pearl Harbor, isn't it?" she asked tentatively.

"Yes," Annabelle confirmed. "We're meeting Quin at the Surf Shop in thirty minutes."

The only thing that kept Mila from bursting into tears was her pride. She wanted nothing more than to walk around Pearl Harbor while holding hands with Quin.

"Everybody better finish eating," Miss Eugenia instructed. "We need to leave early. That way we won't miss the tour if Annabelle gets lost."

Annabelle scowled at her sister as Miss Polly pulled her handkerchief from the neckline of her dress and dabbed her eyes. "I know I'm going to cry when I see the *USS Arizona*."

"You're already crying!" Miss Eugenia pointed out.

"I know!" Miss Polly admitted. "Just thinking about all those boys drowning in defense of our country breaks my heart!"

This exchange was interrupted by the arrival of Jerry Hirasuna and Elliot Wong. Miss Eugenia fussed over them and insisted that they sit down and eat breakfast. Once the men were served, Miss Eugenia began clearing the dirty dishes from the table.

"Here's our new suspect list," he said. "And this is the list of contents from Miss Fiero's purse."

Mila took the papers from Jerry and reviewed them. "There's an antique brooch on the list," Mila commented. "It says here that there are pictures in the file."

Jerry shuffled through the folder and finally held out several Polaroids. "Here you go."

Miss Eugenia walked in from the kitchen and studied the pictures over Mila's shoulder. "That big stone in the middle is a ruby," she told them. "If it's real, that brooch is probably valuable."

"But not very attractive," Mila pointed out. "By modern standards anyway."

"It's like the Chanel No. 5 perfume," Miss Eugenia remarked. "Something you wouldn't expect for a young girl to wear."

"So, the brooch points us back toward an older boyfriend," Jerry muttered.

"Or a young man with sophisticated tastes," Elliot added cautiously.

Annabelle stood. "Well, it's time for us to go. Come on, girls." Miss George Ann and Miss Polly immediately gathered at the door, but Miss Eugenia hung back.

"Come on, Eugenia," Annabelle said with impatience. "You're the one who's worried about being late."

Miss Eugenia stepped out of the kitchen and shook her head. "I'm going to stay here and clean up the kitchen," she announced to everyone's amazement.

"You're going to miss the tour of Pearl Harbor?" Miss Polly asked.

"Don't worry about the kitchen," Mila said. "We'll clean it up later."

"If you have a minute to spare, you need to spend it sleeping," Miss Eugenia replied. "I'll clean up my own mess, and I'll see Pearl Harbor another time."

Mila looked at Miss Eugenia's wrinkled face. It was unlikely that she would ever make a trip like this again, but it was even more unlikely that Mila would be able to talk Miss Eugenia out of her plan of action. Therefore, gracious acceptance was called for. "Thank you for your help."

"We're gone, then," Annabelle said with one last exasperated look at her sister.

Once the door closed behind them, Miss Eugenia pointed at the picture Mila was holding. "If that's valuable, it's probably insured. I'd be glad to call around to the insurance agencies and appraisers in town and see if one recognizes it."

Mila knew that once the kitchen was clean, Miss Eugenia would be trying to run the investigation, so she nodded. "I think that would be a very good idea."

Miss Eugenia seemed pleased with her assignment. Mila walked over to the window and looked out just in time to see Raquel's Lexus, followed closely by Officer Gates's patrol car, pass through the gates of Makai.

"Raquel is gone," she told Jerry. "I guess it's time for me to make my call to Cade." She took out her cell phone and dialed the Simons' home number. "Mrs. Rose?" Mila said a few seconds later. "I need to talk to Cade, but first I have a question for you. We're working under the assumption that Leilani had a boyfriend—someone older who probably visited mostly on weekends. Did you ever notice signs of an overnight guest?"

"I can't say for sure," Mrs. Rose replied. "But sometimes the bed looked like two people had slept there."

Mila knew this was as much as she was likely to get. "Thank you, Mrs. Rose. Now could you let me speak to Cade?"

Mila was put on hold for a few seconds before Cade Simon's voice greeted her. "Good morning, Mila."

"Good morning," she returned. "Would it be possible for you to come down to the bungalow now? Detective Hirasuna needs to talk to you."

After a brief pause, Cade replied, "I have a meeting at nine, but I can give him a few minutes."

"I'm sure he'll be very grateful."

Cade either missed or ignored the trace of sarcasm in Mila's voice. "I'll be right down."

Mila closed her phone and said, "Cade Simon is on his way."

Jerry nodded. "Good. Now let's go over this list."

They took each name in turn, and when they had finished, Mila said, "I think they're all viable."

"Then we'll keep digging until we find something."

Mila looked back at the list of names. "Do we care if they know we're investigating them?"

"Try to be discreet, but if they get wind of it . . ." Jerry shrugged.

"Whenever I talk to Mrs. Rose about Blake, I always get the impression that he was with Leilani more than he admits. That's why I don't want to dismiss him completely."

"You think he's lying about no romantic involvement with Leilani?" Jerry asked.

"I'm not sure what he's lying about, but I don't think he's been completely honest with us. And he did come to Makai on the night of the party."

"And we only have his word that he left after the scene with Raquel," Miss Eugenia added from the kitchen. "He could have gone to Leilani's apartment, fed her poisoned cake, and watched her die before returning to his place."

"Did you ever find out if the numbers on the bottom of the cheesecake boxes could tell you anything about who purchased them?" Miss Eugenia asked.

"The numbers on the box?" Jerry asked.

Miss Eugenia looked at Mila. "I told you when I called about the cheesecakes being in the wrong color box that the label on the bottom has a USPC number or something like that."

"UPC," Jerry provided.

"The end of your message was garbled," Mila said. "I only heard the part about the boxes being left over from Christmas."

"Yes. Well, the lady at the Cheesecake Company store said that the number tells what kind of cake it was and which processing plant made it and possibly even who bought it—depending on how the customer paid for the cake."

"The murderer would probably have been smart enough to pay cash, but it's worth a try," Jerry said. "I'll call the evidence folks and get them to give me the numbers. Then I'll call the owner of the Cheesecake Company and get him to run the numbers through the computers for me."

Mila smiled as Cade Simon knocked on the door. Mila let him in and noticed that he was dressed casually in a tropical print shirt and khaki shorts. Cade was a beautiful sight, and Mila thought she heard Miss Eugenia sigh as she seated him on the couch. Jerry pulled a chair from the kitchen and placed it directly in front of their guest.

"I appreciate you coming to talk to me," Jerry said, sounding completely ungrateful.

Cade blinked. "You're welcome."

"Why didn't you mention during our earlier conversation that Leilani Fiero was your employee at the tax preparation firm before she became your wife's personal secretary?"

"I didn't think that was significant."

Jerry pursed his lips as he considered this response. "What did she do for you? At the tax preparation firm," he added as if it were an afterthought.

Cade's gorgeous brown eyes became a little guarded. "She had an entry-level job in the mail room. Raquel met her and felt that she had potential, so she hired her."

"Mrs. Simon recognized Leilani's potential as a secretary or as an actress?" Jerry asked.

"What do you mean?"

"Well, it's our understanding that your wife was helping Leilani to establish herself in television. She said she was moving to Los Angeles and already had a job—thanks to Mrs. Simon and her connections."

Cade laughed. "That's ridiculous."

Mila stepped forward. "Leilani told several people about the arrangement."

"Then she lied. If Raquel had that kind of power in Los Angeles— she'd be there herself."

Mila had to admit that sounded reasonable, and she saw the same uncertainty she felt reflected on Jerry's face. "Did Leilani have a boyfriend?" she asked.

Cade frowned. "You mean besides that guy at the party?"

"He says he wasn't her boyfriend," Mila replied, feeling less sure of herself.

Cade shrugged. "Then I don't know. What Leilani did with her own time was her business."

"But you never saw her with a man?" Jerry pressed. "We think she might have been involved with an older guy."

Cade shook his head. "Nope. I never saw Leilani except in passing and she never had a man with her—old or young."

"Mrs. Rose said Leilani frequently used the outside entrance to her apartment," Jerry said. "So, it would have been easy for someone to slip into the apartment without anyone seeing them."

"Is that a question?" Cade wanted to know.

Jerry narrowed his eyes at Cade. "I was just verifying this with you."

"There is an outside entrance to the apartment," Cade confirmed. "And if Mrs. Rose said Leilani used it most of the time—I'm sure that's right. I didn't keep up with the girl's comings and goings."

"You don't have a security guard to patrol the estate at night?" Jerry asked.

"Never had any reason for one. It's pretty quiet up here."

Finally, Mila decided to cut to the heart of the matter. "I'm sorry if this offends you, Cade, but I have to ask. Did you have an extramarital affair with Leilani?"

Cade looked pained. "No, I did not."

Mila regretted the necessity to press further. "We saw you talking to Leilani Monday night on the balcony during the party. What were you talking about?"

"Oh, that," he said. "Raquel's birthday is in a few weeks, and I was asking Leilani to give me some suggestions about what I could buy her."

All the other occupants in the room stared at him with various degrees of doubt. "You were out on a dark balcony at your wife's party conferring with her personal secretary about a birthday present that you wouldn't need for weeks?" Jerry repeated in a condensed version of Cade's terrible excuse.

"Yes." Cade was sticking with his story.

Before anyone could say more, the birthday girl burst into the room. Raquel looked around with an accusatory expression on her face.

"Raquel!" Mila and Cade said in unison.

"Aren't you supposed to be at the television station?" Cade asked.

"I was on my way there when I called Mrs. Rose to check on dinner for tonight." Raquel turned to address Mila. "Imagine my surprise when she told me that you called for Cade to come over for an interview right after I left. Why wasn't I informed?"

"He's not a minor," Jerry replied. "And you're not his mother. It was up to him to notify you about this interview—if he wanted you to know about it."

Mila smiled to herself. It was at times like this that she knew Jerry had what it took to be a great detective. Officer Gates stepped into the room and took a neutral position by the door.

Cade Simon stood and pulled his wife into a partial embrace. "I didn't want to worry you, honey. It's nothing, just a friendly little chat."

Mila could tell that Raquel wanted to be reassured, but she still seemed agitated when she asked, "What did they want to talk to you about?"

"Just questions about Leilani, like what she used to do at the tax preparation firm, if she had a boyfriend, if she used the outside door to her apartment a lot, and if I was having an affair with her." Cade smiled as he said this last part and Raquel relaxed against him, smiling too.

"I hope you satisfied their morbid curiosity," she said.

Cade's summation of their questions did make them sound a little ridiculous, and Mila felt slightly uncomfortable.

"I told them that Leilani worked in the mailroom, and I barely knew her before she went to work for you. I said I don't know if she had a boyfriend. I don't know what door to her apartment she used, and I *definitely* was not having an affair with her."

Raquel reached up to pat his cheek. "You're such a darling," she said.

"They also have some crazy idea that you were helping Leilani get an acting job in Los Angeles," Cade told his wife.

Raquel included them all in her mystified look. "Why in the world would I do that?"

"That's what I told them," Cade said. "It's silly."

Raquel turned from her husband to the police personnel in the room. "Why are you asking all these questions about Leilani?" she demanded. "I thought you were looking for the person who wants to kill *me*."

"We've changed the focus of our investigation," Jerry admitted. "There have been some new developments that lead us to believe that Leilani was the intended victim after all."

Raquel gave them an incredulous look. "Leilani!" she fairly screeched. "Why would anyone want to kill *her*? She was nothing—a nobody!"

Mila didn't know how to respond to this and apparently no one else did either because the room remained in uncomfortable silence for several seconds. Finally, Cade flashed them all one of his breathtaking smiles and said, "Well, I've got to get to my office for a nine o'clock meeting." He kissed his wife and took a step toward the door. "If you need to ask me any more questions, give me a call."

"If you have any more questions, call our lawyer," Raquel corrected. Then she blew Cade a kiss and watched him walk out the front door. After they heard the engine of his car start, Raquel said, "I don't appreciate you trying to interrogate my husband behind my back."

Jerry acted offended. "I don't understand what you mean. Your husband is a grown man."

"He's very trusting and doesn't realize that cops, desperate to solve a case, might accuse an innocent man just to make their jobs easier."

This was a terrible insult, but Jerry didn't flinch. "I don't need to accuse innocent people. I always find the guilty ones."

Raquel shrugged and walked over to the couch. She sat beside Mila and flicked a stray lock of hair over her shoulder. "You realize that I will have to tell my friend the police chief that you've put me back in danger?"

"I don't see how my changing the direction of our investigation puts you in danger," Jerry objected, gesturing at Officer Gates. "You still have a police escort."

"Officer Gates can't be with me every minute!" Raquel exclaimed. "So, by refusing to look for the person who tried to kill me, you are jeopardizing my life and safety."

Jerry had finally had enough. "All we are jeopardizing is your chance for a television movie."

Before Raquel could respond, Mila backed the detective by saying, "You have to admit that you are getting a lot of free publicity out of Leilani's death."

Raquel turned to Mila and sighed. "I'm not trying to deny that. It's an unfortunate fact of life that any publicity is good publicity."

"So, it's true that you've been offered a movie deal?" Jerry asked.

"Nothing official, but NBC is interested," she replied. "And I'll admit that I've enjoyed the sudden interest. The camera is cruel, and it's hard to get jobs in television if you're, well, older than twenty-nine." Raquel gave them a coquettish smile. "It's been nice to have people beating down my door again."

Mila saw Jerry's hands clench into fists and knew he was about to say something he would later regret. So she leaned forward to claim Raquel's attention. "We don't begrudge you a successful career, Raquel. But it's our job to find out who killed your secretary. We haven't completely abandoned the possibility that you were the intended victim, but we are exploring other scenarios."

Raquel seemed mollified by this. "I guess I can accept that," she said. "But what made you think that Cade might have been having an affair with Leilani?" The tone of her voice left no doubt how absurd she considered this notion.

"Well, you said your note accused your husband of being unfaithful," Mila pointed out. "And all the other notes were one hundred percent correct."

"So based on that—we decided to find out who he was cheating with," Jerry added with a smirk. "And since Miss Fiero was murdered in your home, we decided to start with her."

Raquel shook her head. "If Cade did decide to take a mistress, he'd have to choose one with a great deal of money since he has none of his own."

Jerry frowned. "I thought he owned a tax preparation firm."

"I own the firm," Raquel corrected. "Cade runs it, but he only works a few hours a week. The rest of the time he's on the beach. Mila can confirm this. Cade spends a fortune at her future husband's Surf Shop."

Mila nodded. "He does buy a lot of surfing equipment."

Raquel smiled. "Cade enjoys his luxurious lifestyle, and he wouldn't do anything to jeopardize it. Besides, he has sophisticated tastes. A street rat like Leilani wouldn't have a chance with him. Now, if you'll excuse me, I have a cooking segment to do." Raquel stood and walked to the door.

"I'm still wondering if the note taped to your cheesecake may have said something else, something vicious and career-damaging like the others. Would you care to comment on that?" Jerry asked.

With her hand on the doorknob, Raquel turned and said, "As a matter of fact, I wouldn't. Remember, further questions must be cleared by our lawyer. And if you try to sidestep me again, I'll complain to the press and to the chief—in that order." Then she was gone.

"Well," Mila said after a few seconds. "That was interesting."

"So, does she or doesn't she?" Jerry quipped.

"Does she what?" Elliot asked.

"Lie," Jerry clarified.

"Oh, I think that's definitely a yes," Miss Eugenia contributed from the kitchen, where she had remained discreetly out of sight during the interviews with the Simons.

"The note really said something worse?" Jerry thought out loud.

Miss Eugenia nodded. "Yes, but she'll never tell us what. And she knows her husband is unfaithful."

Elliot frowned. "And she just doesn't care?"

Mila shook her head. "There's just not anything she can do about it."

"I agree," Miss Eugenia said. "Raquel is an aging woman married to an extremely handsome man. She knows she can't have him exclusively, but as long as she can have him—she accepts that."

"How sad," Mila whispered.

"The fact that Leilani Fiero is dead is even more sad," Jerry reminded her. "Do you think Cade Simon is our murderer?"

"No," Mila shook her head. "I really don't. But I think Raquel is worried that he might be."

"If Cade Simon wasn't involved romantically with Miss Fiero, what would be his motive?" Elliot asked.

"I've been thinking about that," Mila told them. "And I wonder if Leilani was blackmailing him."

"What for?"

"Maybe she learned something while she was at the tax preparation firm that could hurt them."

Miss Eugenia was nodding. "Thus the sudden rise from mailroom employee to personal secretary and lots of money to buy clothes."

"Yes," Mila said. "Raquel created a new position for Leilani with no duties."

"She had plenty of perks though," Miss Eugenia reminded them. "Like a free apartment and the use of one of the Simons' vehicles and even housekeeping services."

"If Leilani had something on them, it would also explain why Raquel promised to help Leilani get a job in a television show." Jerry said thoughtfully. "To get her out of Honolulu."

"And out of Cade's reach," Miss Eugenia concurred.

"All to protect her relationship with Cade?" Mila asked.

Miss Eugenia frowned. "You saw how she was with him just now. She'd do anything for him."

Jerry raised an eyebrow. "How about murder?"

"I wouldn't put it past her," Miss Eugenia said softly.

"We'll add Raquel back to the suspect list and dig into her background. Mila, you take that," Jerry instructed. "I'll look into the tax preparation firm and continue to see what I can find out about their finances, etc. Wong, you take the old boyfriend list and check for large, unexplained cash withdrawals."

Mila didn't want Miss Eugenia to feel left out, so she said, "And Miss Eugenia is going to call insurance and appraisal companies to see if anyone recognizes the brooch."

Jerry addressed Elliot. "Did anyone at the stores you contacted recognize Leilani's picture?"

"Yes," Elliot seemed pleased to report. "She was a frequent customer and several of the clerks remembered her. They said she always shopped alone and always paid cash."

Jerry smirked. "I wish we could have gotten a description of the guy, but at least we know that looking for a man who was making large cash withdrawals should give us a hint."

There was a knock on the door, and Miss Eugenia offered to answer it. A few seconds later she ushered in a uniformed policeman. "They sent me from downtown," the young man explained as he held up a large, heavy-duty ziplock bag. "I was told to give this to Detective Hirasuna."

Jerry stood and held out his hand. "That's me."

"It's from Evidence, and you'll have to sign for it." The young policeman presented a form for Jerry's signature. "And you'll have to make sure that the evidence bag isn't opened while it's in your possession."

"I'll make sure," Jerry promised. After the young man left, Jerry took the bag over to the table. "Well, I didn't think they'd let us look at the actual contents, but this is great."

Mila joined him and glanced at the items in the bag. A compact, several lipsticks, some receipts, and the brooch. "There's no money," she pointed out.

Jerry looked up. "Huh?"

"I said she didn't have any money in her purse," Mila repeated.

"We didn't find any money in the apartment either," Elliot said.

"But Leilani was going around buying $200 jeans. So, where is her money?" Mila asked.

Jerry shook his head. "I don't know. Maybe the murderer took it."

"Blake was pretty upset that she didn't pay him the money he owed her," Mila said thoughtfully. "If he's the murderer, it would make sense for him to take any money she had."

"If he's the murderer, then why didn't he take all those expensive clothes?" Elliot asked. "They must be worth something, even on the black market."

Jerry pursed his lips. "It seems like every time I think we're making progress, we come up with another unanswerable question." He thought for a minute then started pacing around the room. "Something has been bothering me, and I just remembered what it is. How did the murderer get the vicious, career-ending dirt on the victims?"

Mila considered this. "It's not the kind of stuff that you'd be likely to just run across."

Jerry nodded. "That's what I think too."

"Maybe we can find a private investigator that was hired to find dark secrets about these four people," Elliot suggested.

"It's worth a try." Jerry addressed Elliot. "Wong, you get looking for unexplained cash withdrawals from any account held by one of the suspects on our list, and call me as soon as you have something. I'll head to the Simons' tax preparation firm and check for creative financing. Mila, you see if you can come up with a PI who worked for our murderer."

Once Jerry and Elliot were gone, Mila settled Miss Eugenia at the computer and showed her how to work the fax machine. "When you call someone who agrees to look at the brooch, just send them a fax of the picture like this." Mila demonstrated by sending a picture of the brooch to her mother in Florida.

"That looks simple enough," Miss Eugenia said.

"And if you don't mind using the Internet Yellow Pages, I'll use the ones in the phone book."

"That's fine with me," Miss Eugenia agreed.

Then Mila took her cell phone and the phone book into the bedroom and started calling private investigators. After an unsuccessful hour, she went out to check on Miss Eugenia.

"Have you had any luck?"

The elderly woman shook her head. "No, but I've talked to some very nice people."

Mila smiled. "That's good at least. Would you like a bottled water?" Mila asked as she took one from the refrigerator.

"No, thank you," Miss Eugenia declined. "But I was thinking . . ."

With a combination of hope and dread, Mila walked over and sat down at the table beside Miss Eugenia. "What were you thinking about?"

"If I were planning to murder people and wanted terrible information about them—I don't believe I'd use a local private investigator."

"But what other option would they have—unless they knew someone in the states?"

"Well, I was thinking that they might have used a service like Kelsey's. The Internet is much more anonymous than having to actually meet with someone, and they might have broader research abilities."

"That's a good idea. I wonder if Kelsey could help us contact some of the major Internet investigation companies?"

Miss Eugenia smiled. "Well, I'm sure she can. Do you mind if I make a long-distance call on this phone?"

Mila stood. "Not at all. Thanks for helping me with my project. I wish there were something I could do to help you find someone who remembers Leilani's brooch."

"I'll keep calling, and maybe I'll get lucky. But right now I'm going to call Kelsey."

Mila went back to making calls and tried not to let her mind wander. A few minutes later Miss Eugenia walked into the bedroom.

"Don't tell me you've already found the private investigator who dug up dirt on our victims."

Miss Eugenia laughed. "No, but I did talk to a gentleman who said the brooch sounded familiar. He's an appraiser and does a lot of estate stuff for insurance companies. He said if you'll bring him the pictures, he'll try to match it up with one he has on file."

Mila closed her phone. "Are you coming with me?"

Miss Eugenia nodded. "Just take me by the main house so I can get my purse."

CHAPTER 9

During the ride to the appraiser's office, Eugenia looked out the car window, fascinated by all the unique plant life. "I wonder if I could take cuttings of some flowers home with me and plant them in my yard," she said to Mila.

"You could try, but don't expect much," Mila warned. "The climate in Hawaii is like a greenhouse—not too hot, not too cold, and moist without being humid. It would be difficult to recreate that atmosphere anywhere else."

Eugenia accepted this with a shrug. "I guess the Lord knew where to put plants where they'd grow best, and I shouldn't try to rearrange things."

Mila smiled. "It wouldn't hurt to transplant a few cuttings. If anyone in the world can get tropical flowers to grow in Georgia—it's you!"

Eugenia was pleased by the compliment. "Well, thank you."

Mila's cell phone started to ring, and she answered it as she pulled off the road and parked in front of a large glass and metal building. Her conversation was brief, and when she hung up, she looked at Eugenia and smiled. "That was Jerry. He said the Cheesecake Company was able to trace the UPC numbers on the four boxes to a large corporate purchase back at the first of December.

"What corporation bought the cakes?"

"Channel One," Mila informed her. "Jerry talked to Mr. Baldwin's secretary. She says they bought a hundred cakes and gave them to their preferred customers and advertisers as a holiday gift. And the best part is that according to her records, four cakes were left over, and she doesn't know what happened to the cakes or their red boxes."

"So, we've narrowed our suspect down to someone who had access to cheesecakes at Channel One."

Mila nodded. "We're getting closer. Now let's go see what Mr. Eden can tell us."

They found Eden Appraisals on the third floor and Mr. Eden himself sitting at the reception desk. He was very old, and his frail appearance made Eugenia feel young and vigorous in comparison. A fringe of wispy white hair circled the sides of his mostly bald head, and he seemed very pleased to see them.

"Welcome! Welcome!" he said, waving them inside.

"I'm Mila Edwards with the Honolulu police," Mila introduced herself. "And this is Eugenia Atkins."

If Mr. Eden thought Eugenia was a little old to be working for the police, he had the good manners not to say so. "You're the ones with the brooch, correct?"

Mila nodded. "Yes." She handed him the Polaroids, and he studied them carefully. Finally he nodded. "I'm pretty sure I appraised this for an estate about ten years ago. If I remember correctly, I encouraged the family to have this ruby reset in something more modern, but the piece had sentimental value."

"Who's the family?" Mila asked.

Mr. Eden shook his head. "My memory isn't that good. I'll have to look through my files."

Eugenia could see the disappointment on Mila's face. "How long will that take?" she asked. "This information might help us catch a murderer."

Mr. Eden smiled. "In the old days it could have taken months, but there are no dusty file cabinets anymore. It's all on computer."

Mila looked encouraged. "So, you can just look through a few computer files . . ."

"Well, I have more than a few files," Mr. Eden informed her. "But I should be able to tell you if this is a piece I appraised, and, if so, who it belongs to within two hours tops."

Mila nodded. "That would be very good."

"The miracle of modern technology," Eugenia said.

Mr. Eden laughed. "Computers truly are a miracle—beyond anything I could have dreamed up as a boy. Better than going to the moon, even."

Eugenia frowned at the man. "I declare, who would want to go to the moon?"

"I wouldn't want to anymore," Mr. Eden said with another little giggle. "But when I was young it was something I thought of all the time. I hoped that by the end of the twentieth century scientists would have come up with a cheap way to get to the moon."

"Well, I'm glad that our scientists invested their time in making computers instead," Eugenia said.

Mr. Eden nodded. "Me too."

"I have a nice new computer at home," Eugenia told him. "I work for an Internet investigation company called For Your Information, and the owner bought a computer for me to use."

Mr. Eden's eyebrows rose. "Well, if I ever need something investigated on the Internet, I'll know whom to call."

"We're the best in the business," Eugenia said confidently.

Mila smiled as she handed Mr. Eden one of her business cards. "She is very good, and we appreciate you taking the time to look for the brooch. Please call my cell number as soon as you have the information we need."

"Why don't you just wait?" Mr. Eden suggested. "I can call down the street and have Chinese takeout delivered, and you can eat lunch while I search."

"We appreciate the offer," Mila said.

"And we love Chinese food," Eugenia added.

"But some friends of ours are supposed to be at the National Cemetery in a few minutes," Mila told Mr. Eden gently. "If we leave now, we might be able to catch up with them."

"Ah." Mr. Eden nodded with understanding. "Have you ever been to the National Cemetery?" he asked Eugenia.

"No," she replied. "I don't live in Hawaii. I'm just here visiting."

"Well, the National Cemetery is my favorite landmark," Mr. Eden confided. "The view is spectacular, and as you look out over the island, you're so impressed with God's handiwork. Then you turn and see the rows and rows of grave markers." Mr. Eden paused to clear his throat. "It's built in an old crater nicknamed the Punchbowl, but the Hawaiian name for it is 'Hill of Sacrifice.' I think that's very appropriate."

"The markers are for service men," Mila explained softly. "Many of them were killed during World War II."

"Some died right here during the attack on Pearl Harbor," Mr. Eden interjected. "There were bodies that couldn't be identified, so several of the markers just say 'Unknown.' It's a sight every American should see at least once."

Mila nodded. "I agree."

"I go there a couple of times a year," Mr. Eden told them. "I think it's a good place to reevaluate your life and focus on what's really important."

Eugenia smiled at the little old man. "Well, you're an appraiser and a philosopher."

Mr. Eden blushed. "My wife used to love for me to go to the National Cemetery. She said after a trip there I was the best husband in the world—for a week or two anyway." He paused as tears filled his eyes. "She passed away last April, and now I wish I'd gone more often, because she really deserved the best husband in the world."

Eugenia reached out and patted Mr. Eden's arm. "I'm sorry about your wife. My husband died five years ago, so I know how you feel."

Mr. Eden wiped his eyes with the sleeve of his shirt. "Well, I'll get to work. You ladies enjoy the cemetery, and I'll call this cell number when I find the brooch." He held up Mila's business card.

"Thank you," Mila said. Then she led the way outside. "I think Mr. Eden was flirting with you," she told Eugenia on the way back to the car.

"Flirting!" Eugenia cried. "The very idea. He's just a sad, lonely old man who wanted some company for lunch."

Mila stopped and glanced back up at the building. "Did you want to stay and eat Chinese with him?"

Eugenia shook her head and opened the passenger door of Mila's car. "Of course not. I just feel sorry for him. Now, hurry and call Quin to see where we should meet them."

Eugenia waited until Mila concluded her conversation with Quin before she said, "I thought Mr. Eden was kind of eloquent, though.

Talking about the cemetery and reevaluating your life. It sounds like a place all of us need to go."

"I wasn't really paying attention," Mila said as she pulled out into the busy traffic. "He was sort of rambling."

Eugenia narrowed her eyes at Mila. "You didn't hear him say that visiting the cemetery helped him focus on what was really important in life?"

Mila kept her eyes on the road as she answered, "I heard him."

"Well?"

Mila glanced at Eugenia. "You think I don't have my priorities straight?"

Eugenia pretended to consider. "Let's see. How much time would you say you've spent with Quin during the last week? Or wait, don't you have time for your own fiancé?"

Mila's cheeks turned pink with anger. "I have time for Quin!"

Eugenia waved this aside. "Most brides spend the days before their wedding thinking of their gown and their veil and their honeymoon. But not you! You're thinking only about murder."

"It's my job," Mila reminded her. "I have to think about it."

"You *want* to think about it," Eugenia said. "And I don't know how you can possibly be ready for a wedding on Saturday."

"I don't know either," Mila admitted, biting her lip. "We may have to postpone the wedding until this case is solved."

Eugenia was shocked by this revelation. "Oh, Mila, I think that would be most unwise."

"Quin understands," Mila responded defensively. "He knows that until this case is over, I won't be able to think about anything else."

Eugenia felt a deep sadness. "If that is true, then maybe you shouldn't marry him at all."

"Why would you say such a thing?"

"Because Quin shouldn't have to play second fiddle, Mila," Eugenia said. "Not even to a murderer."

"But this case will be closed soon . . ."

"There will always be another case," Eugenia pointed out as gently as she could. "You have to decide what's really important in your life. Then you put the important things first and let the less important things take a backseat."

Mila didn't reply, and Eugenia searched her mind for the words that would touch her young friend. "Remember back in Haggerty when I told you about the short story by O. Henry, *The Gift of the Magi*?"

"Of course I remember," Mila muttered.

"That young couple each sacrificed their most prized possession for the other in a show of love."

Mila nodded impatiently. "Yes, I know. That's why I sold my Mustang and came to Hawaii."

"But marriage isn't a short-term commitment," Eugenia pointed out. "You can't make one sacrifice—even a large one—and feel like you're done. It's a lifelong process—one sacrifice after another. But, in the end you'll have something to show for your time on earth."

Mila considered this. "Last night Quin said we had to figure out how to live life no matter what else is going on."

Eugenia smiled. "Yes, because nothing else that's going on is as important as your life together."

"So, you think I should remove myself from the case?"

Eugenia took a deep breath. She wanted very much to be a part of finding the murderer, but Mila and Quin and their happiness was a much higher priority. "I think it's not a decision you should make lightly. Pray about it, and you'll know what to do."

"What do you think I've been doing?" Mila asked as they pulled into the parking lot of the National Cemetery. "Every prayer I've prayed for the past several months has been for the Lord to show me the way to work a personal life into my career."

Eugenia nodded. "Well, if you're praying that hard, the Lord will find a way to get the answer to you."

When they arrived at the Court of Honor they saw their group waiting. George Ann was sitting on a bench, rubbing one of her feet. Annabelle was on her cell phone, presumably talking to Derrick, and Polly was eating an ice cream cone. Quin was seated a little distance away from the others, staring out at the spectacular view. Based on his serious expression, Eugenia wondered if he was thinking about the wedding too.

Mila walked straight to Quin, and they greeted each other with a discreet kiss. Eugenia frowned, thinking that if a couple of people were ever meant for each other, it was these two. She had to find a way to make sure that happened. Then George Ann saw her and said, "My feet are killing me!"

"George Ann, you're either going to have to invest in some more comfortable shoes or rent a wheelchair," Eugenia told the other woman. "I can't listen to your complaints anymore."

"Well!" George Ann replied. "I look for a little sympathy from a friend, and this is what I get."

Polly stepped between them. "Now, girls," she said. "How can you argue at this beautiful place?"

Several responses came to Eugenia's mind, but she controlled them. "How was Pearl Harbor?" she asked instead.

"Oh!" Polly whimpered, reaching for her handkerchief. "It was wonderful."

"Don't get Polly started on that," Annabelle said as she walked up. "She's going to dehydrate if she doesn't stop crying."

"What did Derrick have to say?" Eugenia asked with a pointed look at the cell phone.

Annabelle smiled. "That he's missing me, of course."

Eugenia nodded. "Of course."

"Let's go on up to the lookout," Quin suggested.

They moved as a group to the steps and began their ascent. George Ann was slow, and Quin stayed by her side like the gentleman he was while the rest of them climbed upward at a more normal pace. Along the way they read the touching memorials to various battalions from different wars and even from other countries. By the time they reached the landing, everyone was in a somber mood.

Eugenia walked to the railing and looked out at the ocean. The view was incredible, just as Mr. Eden had promised. She could see Diamond Head and Honolulu and even Magic and Sand Islands. Mila was on the other side of the lookout, so Eugenia moved to stand beside her. This view was also as Mr. Eden had described—rows of marble headstones marking the graves of service men and women who had died for their country.

"I hope Polly doesn't see this," Eugenia said. "She'll cry for sure."

Mila gave her a wan smile. "This might be enough to make even Miss George Ann cry."

"If George Ann cries it will be because her feet hurt," Eugenia predicted. "She doesn't have a heart."

"Isn't the view fabulous?" Polly gushed as she joined them. Then she looked out and saw the grave markers. "Oh, my." She fumbled for her handkerchief and pressed it to her eyes.

Annabelle stood beside her sister and addressed Polly. "Will you try not to cry everywhere we go?"

"I can't help it," Polly defended herself. "I'm just such a patriot."

"It's a touching sight," Eugenia agreed. Then, in an effort to distract Polly, she pointed to the brochure the weeping woman was holding in her hand. "Diamond Head Memorial Gardens," she read out loud. "Is that another tourist attraction?"

Polly sniffled and shook her head. "No, it's a cemetery. I'm thinking about buying myself a plot there."

"Why in the world would you do that?" Eugenia demanded.

"You already have a plot in the Baptist Church's cemetery—right beside your mother and father," Annabelle added.

"I know," Polly replied, raising her chin in rare defiance. "But I can be buried anywhere I want, and I think this would be a wonderful place to be on resurrection day."

Eugenia couldn't argue with that, so she said, "But you'd be too far away for anyone to visit your grave."

Annabelle nodded. "And put flowers on it."

"I don't have any family left to visit my grave," Polly reminded them. "So it doesn't really matter where I'm buried."

"You have us," Annabelle said, patting Polly's plump hand. "We'll visit and put flowers on your grave."

"Until we die ourselves," Eugenia added realistically.

"Why do we have to talk about people dying?" Mila exclaimed in an uncharacteristic burst of bad humor.

"Mila!" Polly gasped in surprise. "Are you okay?"

"I'm sorry," Mila whispered as Quin and George Ann finally made it to the landing. When they joined the group Mila took Quin's hand and said to the others, "Excuse us, please." Then she led him to a quiet corner.

"I wonder what's bothering her?" Annabelle said.

"Maybe it's just pre-wedding jitters," Polly submitted.

Eugenia smiled as she watched Mila pull Quin's head down close to hers. "No, I think that Mila's finally decided to put first things first."

* * *

Mila struggled to keep back tears as she whispered, "Oh, Quin, I'm so sorry."

"Why?" he asked in confusion.

"For making you play second fiddle," Mila told him. "You are the most important thing in my life. I love you more than anything, and I can't imagine living without you."

He nodded. "I know that."

Mila shrugged. "Well, I kept thinking about what you said last night on the beach—about how we have to get on with life no matter what our circumstances are. Then when I took that brooch to the jeweler, he was telling Miss Eugenia about this place and how it makes you realize what your priorities should be. He said coming here made him a better husband, and now his wife is dead and he misses her."

"I'm not sure I'm following you," Quin said.

Mila took a deep breath and continued. "When we got back in the car, Miss Eugenia said I didn't deserve you if I couldn't put you first in my life." She swallowed a sob. "Then we got here and I saw all those grave markers of people who died before they had a chance to really live, and Miss Polly started talking about not having anyone to visit her grave when she dies because she doesn't have a family and . . ."

"Whoa." Quin put a finger on her lips. "So, what are you saying?"

Mila took a deep breath. "I'm saying that the Lord has had to work hard to get me to see the answer to my prayer. As long as I'm with the police department there will always be another case. And when I change to social work there will always be another child in trouble. We need to get on with our lives, and I have to put you and our marriage first. There are other people at the police station that can take over my part of the investigation. I want us to get married on Saturday just like we'd planned."

She saw tears fill his eyes as he pressed his lips to her forehead.

"That's what you were trying to tell me last night, isn't it?" she asked.

"I wasn't trying to tell you anything," he murmured. "You're a strong-minded woman. I wanted you to decide for yourself."

She smiled. "That's one of the things I love about you most—the way you let me figure things out on my own. I just wish it didn't take me so long."

"We've got plenty of time," he reminded her. "We've got eternity."

* * *

After ten minutes on the lookout, George Ann had switched from complaining about her feet to whining about being hot. "At least she's giving us some variety," Annabelle pointed out to Eugenia.

"That's because she's afraid if she mentions her feet again, I'll leave her up here," Eugenia responded. Then she glanced over at the corner where Mila and Quin were still alternately conferring and kissing. "Somebody's going to have to put a stop to that."

Annabelle followed the direction of her gaze. "They're getting married in less than two days. Give them a break."

"Humph," Eugenia said, turning away from the embarrassing display of young love. "I guess we might as well head down. At the rate George Ann moves it will be dark before we get to the bottom of the stairs."

They gathered the group of old women together, but before they actually started down the stairs, Quin and Mila joined them.

"We're going ahead with the wedding," Mila whispered to Eugenia. "And I'd like to apologize to all of you," she said loud enough for the others to hear. "I've been a terrible hostess up to this point, but all of that is going to change. I'm calling Detective Hirasuna to tell him to get someone else to help on the murder case."

"Are you sure about that?" Annabelle asked. "It seems to mean so much to you."

"And you're so good at finding criminals," Polly added.

While Eugenia was trying to figure out how she could kick both Annabelle and Polly at the same time, she saw Mila smile up at Quin.

"Other things mean much more. It was so nice of you all to come to the wedding, and I'm very sorry that I've neglected you. But I promise that for the last few days of your trip—things will be different."

"We have been well taken care of so far," Annabelle assured Mila. "But we'll be glad to see more of you."

Mila turned to Eugenia. "I hope you won't mind being left out of the rest of the investigation."

Actually, Eugenia minded quite a bit, but she knew Mila was making the right decision, so she said, "Of course not. I just hope Detective Hirasuna and Officer Wong can solve it without us."

Mila laughed. "Probably not as quickly or efficiently, but they will figure it out eventually." Mila's cell phone started to ring, and she opened it. "Hello, Jerry," she said into the receiver. "I was just about to call you."

She listened for a few seconds, then answered, "No, I haven't heard from the appraiser." She checked her watch. "He said it could take a couple of hours." She listened again while the others stood around her in polite silence. Finally she said, "I'll call him."

She disconnected the call and addressed the group as a whole. "Jerry and Elliot think they have identified the murderer."

"Who is it?" Eugenia asked as Mila's cell phone rang again.

Mila held up a finger and opened the phone. "Hello." After a brief pause she added, "Thank you, Mr. Eden. If you'll fax that information to the number on my card it will be very helpful." She closed the phone and said, "The brooch belonged to the estate of Harriet Baldwin."

"Is she related to Albert Baldwin at Channel One?" Eugenia asked.

Mila nodded. "She was his mother. Albert inherited the brooch when she died ten years ago."

"So Albert Baldwin was Leilani's boyfriend?" Eugenia clarified.

Mila nodded again as she dialed a number using her cell phone. "And presumably her murderer. Elliot found several large cash withdrawals from Mr. Baldwin's checking account over the past six months."

"Didn't you say that his wife is sick?" Polly asked.

Mila nodded. "I think she has Alzheimer's."

George Ann shook her head. "Scandalous."

"Jerry?" Mila said into her phone. "I just got a call from the appraiser. The brooch belonged to Mr. Baldwin's mother, and he inherited it. The appraiser is faxing you the information." Mila listened for a few seconds, then said, "I'm glad that's enough for a warrant, but I won't be able to meet you at Channel One for the arrest. I'm taking myself off the case."

They could hear Jerry Hirasuna yelling through the phone as Quin reached over and took it from Mila's hand. "She was kidding, Detective Hirasuna," he said into the phone. "She'll be there." He closed the phone and handed it back to Mila.

"Why did you do that?" she asked him.

Quin smiled. "You've worked hard on this and deserve to be there when the guy is arrested. Go on. We'll meet you back at Makai as soon as you're finished."

"Are you sure?" Mila asked.

Quin nodded. "Besides, I think you'd better wean yourself off gradually."

Mila gave him a grateful smile. "I would like to be there when they arrest him." She looked at Eugenia and asked. "Are you coming?"

"Of course," Eugenia replied, moving toward the steps.

"Do birds fly?" Annabelle added sarcastically.

* * *

On the way to the television station, Eugenia tried to imagine Albert Baldwin as a murderer. When she had met him, he seemed so gentle and kind. It was almost impossible for her to conceive that he would make poison cheesecakes and kill Leilani. Finally she said, "Mr. Baldwin doesn't fit all the criteria."

Mila glanced over at her passenger. "He's old, he hated Raquel, he was at the party on Monday night, and he's been a guest on Raquel's cooking segment several times, so he knows his way around the kitchen. What doesn't fit?"

"Well, he had plenty of money. There was no reason for him to take any from Leilani's purse."

"Unless he gave her the money and was afraid it had his finger-prints on it," Mila pointed out.

"You really believe that he fed Leilani poisoned cheesecake and then sat there and watched her die?"

"I'm just going by the evidence—which you helped us to collect," Mila returned. "If he loved her and then found out she was leaving for Los Angeles to be a television actress, he must have gone crazy and killed her."

"Raquel denied that she had arranged anything for Leilani in Los Angeles."

"Raquel lies," Mila responded.

"Well, I think you'd be wise to check with producers in Los Angeles and see if any of them have heard from Raquel recently."

Mila nodded. "I'll tell Jerry."

"And killing someone with poisoned cheesecake isn't a crime of passion. It requires premeditation."

"You've been after me for days to wrap up this case so I can concentrate on Quin and our wedding!" Mila cried in exasperation as they pulled into the Channel One parking lot. "We've finally found the murderer, and now you're trying to talk me out of it?"

"I just want to be sure we have the right person."

"I've done my job," Mila said with finality. "It's up to Jerry and Elliot to tie up the loose ends."

The only response Eugenia could think of was her sister's favorite phrase. "Heaven help us."

Detective Hirasuna and Officer Wong were waiting in an unmarked car by the front entrance to the Channel One studios. "We got the warrant," the detective announced, waving a sheet of paper. He pointed to a patrol car a few feet away. "Those guys are here to search Baldwin's office, and another set of uniforms are searching his house even as we speak. We've also got some lab boys here to do fingerprinting."

Mila squared her shoulders. "Let's get this over with."

Detective Hirasuna led the group into the lobby. The receptionist looked mildly alarmed when he told her that he needed to speak to Mr. Baldwin immediately. She called the station owner's office and after a brief conversation, nodded at the detective. "He said to come right up."

Eugenia gave the receptionist a friendly wave as she hurried to keep up with the others. The woman waved back and watched them all the way to the elevator. When they reached Mr. Baldwin's office they found him sitting at his desk. Eugenia noted that he was a little pale but calm. He nodded politely to Eugenia as Detective Hirasuna put the warrants on the desk.

The detective pointed to the uniformed policemen and technicians. Then he said, "These guys are going to be looking around your office. Is there somewhere else we can talk?"

"Should I ask my lawyer to come over?" Mr. Baldwin asked.

"Yes," Jerry advised. "I think that would be a very good idea."

Mr. Baldwin reached for his phone. Once he had instructed his secretary to contact his lawyer, he stood. "We'll go to the lounge at the end of the hall."

The lounge was small and the seating limited. Mr. Baldwin made a point of getting Eugenia a chair before he sat down and faced the detective.

Detective Hirasuna said, "Mrs. Atkins is not here in an official capacity. She will leave if it would make you more comfortable."

Mr. Baldwin glanced at Eugenia. "I'd like for her to stay."

The detective then asked, "Did you read both of the warrants?"

Mr. Baldwin nodded. "I did."

"Then you know that you're going to be arrested."

Mr. Baldwin nodded again.

The detective handed him a card and explained. "This is the Miranda statement. We're required to have you read it too."

Mr. Baldwin did so. Then he handed the card back to the detective. "I understand my rights. What is this all about?"

"Would you like to wait until your lawyer arrives?" Mila asked.

"No," Mr. Baldwin declined. "I'd like to go ahead and start."

"You were having an affair with Leilani Fiero," Mila said gently.

Mr. Baldwin smiled, but there was no humor in his eyes. "She was the most beautiful girl in the world. I loved her more than," he paused, "well, more than anything."

Detective Hirasuna gave Mila a nod, indicating that he wanted her to continue the questioning. "You gave her a lot of money."

"Yes. Leilani never had nice things when she was young, and little gifts pleased her so much. She particularly loved clothes."

"You gave her the brooch that you inherited from your mother."

"It was part of my great-grandmother's dowry—a treasured family heirloom." Mr. Baldwin seemed a little pained by this admission. "It was foolish to give her that brooch," he said with a self-depreciating smile. "She couldn't begin to understand its value, and it was too old-fashioned for her to wear. But I have always loved it, and, well, I just wanted her to have it."

"How long had you and Leilani been seeing each other?"

"For about three months. I met her at a party Raquel and Cade gave on Memorial Day."

"And why did you kill her?" Mila pressed.

For the first time since their arrival, Mr. Baldwin looked distressed. "I didn't kill Leilani!" he claimed. "I wanted to *marry* her."

Mila frowned. "But you're already married."

He nodded. "I was going to divorce my poor wife, Edith." He looked down at his hands. "I knew it was a despicable thing to do and that it would cost me the respect of the community and possibly the ownership of the station. But I didn't think I could live without Leilani." He glanced over at Eugenia. "I've behaved very poorly, and I'm sure you don't have any respect for me now. But I want you to know that I had every intention of caring for Edith for the remainder of her life."

Eugenia nodded in acknowledgement of this.

"Did you ask Leilani to marry you?" Mila asked.

"Yes."

Mila leaned closer. "Did she accept?"

Mr. Baldwin shook his head. "No, actually, she laughed. She said she had bigger plans for her life than being married to an old man like me."

Eugenia sighed. Mr. Baldwin should not have broken his wedding vows, but she did feel sorry for him.

"That must have made you very angry," Mila said.

He shrugged one thin shoulder. "I guess I was angry, but mostly I was desperate to change her mind. I promised her everything I could think of, but the thing she really wanted was a career in television, and only Raquel Simon could give her that."

Mila glanced over at Eugenia. Raquel *had* lied.

"So, she broke off your relationship?"

"I guess you could say that," Mr. Baldwin acknowledged. "She told me not to call her or come to her apartment again."

"When was this?"

He put a hand to his head as he considered the question. "Saturday night." He looked at Mila earnestly. "So, do you understand?"

Detective Hirasuna leaned forward and said, "We understand that you just gave us a motive for murder. The only question in my mind was which woman you wanted to kill most—Leilani Fiero or Raquel Simon. Or maybe you were planning to kill them both."

Mr. Baldwin moved his head from side to side in a vehement denial as his lawyer and one of the uniformed policemen appeared at the door simultaneously.

"The guys searching his house found pictures of him with the murder victim," the policeman reported. "We found a bottle of arsenic granules hidden in the back of a desk drawer in his office and the techs lifted a couple of prints off it. They faxed them into the station, and we just got a call that they belong to one Mr. Albert Baldwin. There's also a file in his desk drawer with reports from a private investigator on several of his employees and other television people."

Elliot Wong rushed in and extended a bottle of wine toward Detective Hirasuna. "Look what else we found," the officer said breathlessly. "There's a whole case of it in his office. I'll bet if we check the numbers on that bottle you've got . . ."

Detective Hirasuna took the bottle from Officer Wong.

"He killed the Gent, too?" Mila asked, and Jerry nodded.

"Apparently."

"I don't even know who the Gent is," Albert Baldwin said with very convincing bewilderment.

"This conversation is at an end," the lawyer said grimly. "And you can be sure I'll file a formal complaint about this unauthorized questioning."

Detective Hirasuna smiled at the lawyer as he stood. "He knew his rights." He turned to Mr. Baldwin. "We're going to have to ask you to accompany us to the police station. Your lawyer is welcome to come too as long as he keeps his mouth shut."

The policeman stepped forward and pulled out his handcuffs.

"Surely that's not necessary," Eugenia objected.

"Standard procedure," the policeman replied as he snapped the cuffs in place.

Mr. Baldwin was staring at the floor—the picture of dejection. Mila motioned for Eugenia to join her by the door. Frustrated and very sad, Eugenia stood beside Mila and watched the policeman lead Mr. Baldwin from the room.

When the station owner passed Eugenia, his eyes locked with hers. "You've got to help me," he said in quiet desperation. "I would have died myself before I hurt Leilani."

* * *

After Albert Baldwin was gone, Jerry looked at Mila. "So, do you want to tell Spike or shall I do the honors?"

"I'd like to if you don't mind," Mila said. "DHR has arranged for him to take a spot at the technical school I was telling you about."

"He won't stay," Jerry warned.

"He might not," Mila couldn't deny the possibility. "But at least we're giving him a chance. And I think the news that we've found the Gent's killer will help him."

Jerry smiled. "Okay, you tell him, and who knows—maybe he'll beat the odds."

* * *

On the way back to Makai, Eugenia became convinced with an absolute certainty that Albert Baldwin did not kill Leilani. Equally certain was the fact that Eugenia herself had helped to have him arrested. With a sigh she realized that she had a moral obligation to now bring the truth to light.

However, the evidence against him was substantial, and she still hadn't come up with a way to prove his innocence by the time they arrived at Mila's bungalow. They found the others inside, celebrating in Mila's behalf.

"Congratulations on solving the murder!" Polly cried. "We were watching on the news when they took Mr. Baldwin out of the television station in handcuffs!"

"A shocking spectacle," George Ann said, shaking her head in disgust. "You'd think a man his age would know better."

"Thank you," Mila said, walking straight into Quin's arms. "I'm glad it's over."

"I guess that means you're out of the detective business," Annabelle said to Eugenia.

Eugenia shrugged. "I guess."

Annabelle laughed. "Don't look so sad! There are other things to do in Hawaii besides search for murderers." Annabelle reached into a bag beside her chair and pulled out a little T-shirt. "We stopped by the Dole Pineapple Factory on our way home from the National Cemetery, and I got one of these for Emily and one for little Charles."

Eugenia studied the small shirt. It had a pineapple with a smiling face in the middle and the words "Somebody who loves me bought me this in Hawaii."

Annabelle shook the little shirt. "Isn't it cute?"

"It's darling," Eugenia replied—and it was. In fact, she wished she'd been the one to buy it.

"Oh, and the pineapple was delicious!" Polly said. "I've never eaten pineapple so sweet and juicy."

"It was good," George Ann agreed. If anything, the fact that George Ann didn't have a single complaint about the trip made Eugenia feel worse about missing it.

"We were going to walk through the pineapple garden maze," Polly added. "But George Ann said her feet hurt, and besides, she didn't want to pay the five-dollar admission price."

"I certainly wish I could have been there with you," Eugenia finally said. "I love pineapple, and I would have invested $5.00 in the garden maze just to get away from George Ann."

"Well, I never!" George Ann replied.

Annabelle smiled. "I brought you a little sample." She pulled a small box from her bag and extended it toward her sister.

Eugenia opened it to see several long slices of pineapple. "Thank you."

"It was the least I could do since you were off saving the world and all."

Eugenia rolled her eyes as she walked to the kitchen for a fork. The pineapple was juicy and delicious—but only increased her desire to see the factory. "Maybe we could go back tomorrow?" she suggested as she walked back to the living room.

"I'd love to." Polly was in favor of the idea.

"Me too," Mila said. "I haven't had any pineapple for months." She looked up at Quin. "Maybe we could go with them in the morning?"

"Maybe," Quin agreed vaguely. "Could you come out on the porch? I've got something to talk to you about."

"Isn't that sweet?" Polly asked, pointing to the intertwined shadows they could see through the front window. "They seem so in love."

"I say it's about time," Eugenia muttered. Then she tried to enjoy her pineapple, but she couldn't help thinking about Mr. Baldwin. He was probably at the police station by now, wearing an orange jumpsuit and having mug shots taken. She shook her head. "Poor Mr. Baldwin. He's so nice and gentle and . . ."

"Stop thinking about that murderer, and think about Kate and Mark and the children," Annabelle suggested. "We're moving to their hotel tomorrow."

Eugenia wasn't completely displeased by this announcement, but she was surprised by the timing. "Tomorrow?"

"Yes," Annabelle confirmed. "We didn't feel right staying here since Mila's been investigating Raquel for murder. So we got rooms for us and Quin's parents and Mila's mother and stepfather at the Honolulu Hilton."

"We're leaving Quin and Mila here alone?" Eugenia asked.

"I think that they're going to stay in their parents' hotel rooms tomorrow night and then move into the storage room behind the Surf Shop after they are married," Annabelle confided quietly. "That's probably what Quin is telling her now."

"I hate for them to have to stay in cramped, primitive quarters," Eugenia said. "Especially after they put so much time and effort into fixing up this bungalow."

"But I'd hate worse for them to be here, especially if Raquel is mad at them," Polly added.

Eugenia looked at Annabelle in concern. "Are you sure you know your way around Honolulu well enough to find that hotel? You know how I hate to get lost."

Annabelle seemed insulted by this remark. "Of course I can find the hotel. I have a map and a cell phone and I know how to read street signs. I don't know what else I could possibly need to find the hotel."

Eugenia shrugged. "Okay. So when are we leaving?"

"We can't check in until one, but Kate said to come at ten so we can eat the breakfast buffet. She said we can stay in their room until ours are available."

Eugenia considered this. "Then I guess we should leave here about eight thirty."

"But Kate doesn't want us there until ten," Annabelle repeated.

"I know," Eugenia said. "I want to allow plenty of time for you to use your map and your cell phone when we get lost trying to find the hotel." Eugenia crumpled up the box that her pineapple sample had been in. "In fact, Annabelle, why don't you try out your navigational skills by taking me to that pineapple factory?"

Annabelle thought for a few seconds before she said, "I guess we can do that."

"And then I thought we could drive out to Diamond Head."

"Heaven help us," Annabelle exclaimed. "Are you going to make me pack a week's worth of sightseeing into one afternoon?"

Eugenia shook her head. "I wouldn't do that to you. We've got tomorrow as well."

* * *

That night when they returned from their whirlwind tour of Oahu, Eugenia used Annabelle's cell phone to call Mila. "I hope I'm not disturbing you," she said when Mila answered.

"Oh, no," Mila assured her. "Quin and I are just sitting here playing Scrabble."

"Have you heard anything from Detective Hirasuna?"

"He's called several times, but I'm ignoring him."

"Aren't you curious about what's going on with the case?"

"Yes," Mila admitted. "But Jerry's got to learn to depend on someone else besides me. As you so often remind me, I do have a life."

"Maybe I should call him," Eugenia suggested.

"No, you shouldn't," Mila said firmly. "I'm off the case now. I told Jerry not to call me with questions or updates, and I'm doing my best to forget about it. You could help me keep my priorities straight by doing the same."

Eugenia sighed. "I guess you're right."

"I know I am," Mila sounded confident. "Now enjoy what's left of your Hawaiian vacation and let Jerry and Elliot handle Leilani's murder investigation."

"Okay," Eugenia said. "Good night."

She closed Annabelle's phone, but she couldn't stop feeling that she still had a responsibility to help poor Mr. Baldwin, who was in jail thanks to her.

CHAPTER 10

On Friday morning Eugenia woke up grumpy after a restless night full of guilt-ridden dreams. She turned on the small television set in her room and watched the morning news while she got dressed. They devoted a long segment to Mr. Baldwin and his arrest for the murder of Leilani Fiero. They had pictures of him wearing handcuffs as he was taken into the police station. He looked small and sad, and Eugenia was about to turn it off when the reporter began an interview with the police chief.

"A bottle of the same poison used to kill Miss Fiero was found in Mr. Baldwin's office, and traces of it were on the set of the kitchen at the Channel One studio. His fingerprints were on the bottle of poison and on many pans and appliances in the kitchen."

The reporter thrust the microphone closer to the police chief's face. "So, Mr. Baldwin prepared the poisoned cakes at the television station?"

The chief nodded grimly. "Yes. The circumstantial evidence against Mr. Baldwin is impressive, and I feel that we are presenting the district attorney's office with an open and shut case."

Eugenia turned off the television set, shaking her head. The trouble people got themselves into in the name of love.

Mila and Quin came up to the main house at eight thirty and helped the ladies from Haggerty load their suitcases into Eugenia's rental car in preparation for the move to the Hilton Hawaiian Village. Mrs. Rose was standing by the door as they walked out for the final time.

Eugenia was glad that she didn't have to face the Simons personally after all she'd learned about them during the murder investigation. "I hope things work out well for you," Eugenia said to Mrs. Rose. "And please thank the Simons for their hospitality."

"I will," Mrs. Rose agreed.

"Thank you so much for all you did to make our visit pleasant," Annabelle told the housekeeper.

"Yes, thank you for everything," Polly added.

"I noticed that the light fixture in my room has a bulb out," George Ann informed her. "I thought you'd want to know."

Mrs. Rose nodded. "I'll have the bulb replaced."

When all the suitcases were in the trunk of the rental car, Eugenia invited Mila and Quin to join the group for breakfast.

"We've got to start packing and transfer our stuff to the Surf Shop this morning," Quin said.

"We'd like to get everything out of here today if possible," Mila added.

"But you've got to eat," Eugenia pointed out. "Why don't you load up the car and then come have breakfast with us. Afterward you can drop a load by the Surf Shop."

Quin glanced at Mila, who nodded in agreement. "Okay, we'll meet you there as soon as we can get my car loaded."

Eugenia smiled. "Well, I'm glad that's settled." Her expression dimmed. "And I'm sorry that it didn't work out for you to stay here." She looked across the grand old estate to the waves crashing onto the white sand beaches. "It's a beautiful place."

Mila followed the direction of her gaze. "Yes, but some things are too good to be true."

"And some things aren't—like you and Quin."

Mila took Quin's hand and smiled up at him.

Eugenia waved to them and headed toward the car. "Hurry and come to the breakfast buffet before Polly eats everything!"

* * *

The Iversons were still trying to get their children up and dressed when the ladies from Haggerty arrived at the hotel. Eugenia insisted on helping while Annabelle took George Ann and Polly down to the lobby. Once the children were ready, Eugenia filled the Iversons in on the most recent developments in Leilani's murder case.

When she was finished, Mark said, "We saw Mr. Baldwin on the news last night."

"And Mila told us that you were a great help in collecting evidence against him," Kate added.

Eugenia sat down on the edge of one of the room's double beds. "Mr. Baldwin claims he didn't kill Leilani, and the strange thing is that I believe him."

"Why?" Kate asked.

Eugenia shrugged. "I don't know. Mila thinks it's because he's old and looks harmless. Annabelle says I just don't want the investigation to be over. But for some reason that I can't really define—I just feel that he's innocent." She expected Mark to scoff at her silliness, but he didn't.

"I've had that feeling before," he said. "Unfortunately you're not in a position to help Mr. Baldwin. I'm sure he'll have good lawyers, and we'll just have to pray that justice will be done."

Eugenia took a deep breath. There were other people who could help Mr. Baldwin. It wasn't all up to her. "That makes me feel better."

"Good," Kate said as she lifted Charles into her arms. "Now, let's go down for breakfast."

When they reached the lobby, Quin and Mila had joined the others. They walked through the buffet line and then found a large table outside in the courtyard. Once everyone was settled, Miss Polly asked Quin who would run the Surf Shop while he and Mila were on their honeymoon.

"I have a part-time employee who will be there most of the time," Quin replied. "And my parents are going to help him."

"Where will you spend your honeymoon?" Annabelle asked.

"We've rented a hotel room for the weekend, and then we were planning to go back to the bungalow," Mila explained. "It seemed like a waste of money to go anywhere else since we *live* in Hawaii."

"Now after we check out of the hotel, we'll pretend like we're camping out in the storage room until we can get it fixed up," Quin teased with a smile.

"I used to enjoy camping when I was a girl," Polly contributed.

"Of course that was a hundred years ago," Eugenia murmured.

"All you need for a good honeymoon is a little privacy," Annabelle remarked.

"Listen to Annabelle," Eugenia said in a disparaging tone. "She's had two honeymoons, and she thinks she's an expert."

"That's one more than you've had," Annabelle snapped back. "And I don't have to be an expert to give an opinion."

"So," Polly said, stepping into the conversation quickly before it could deteriorate into an argument. "What are the plans for today?"

"Our parents come in this afternoon and then tonight we have dinner at Bon Appetit," Mila said. "But this morning Quin and I will be busy moving our things out of the bungalow."

"I'll be glad to help," Mark offered.

"I couldn't let you do that on your vacation," Quin declined. "I've got a friend with a truck lined up, and it shouldn't take us too long."

"It will take less time if I help," Mark said firmly. "And now Kate's got Miss Eugenia here to help with the kids."

Quin held out a hand. "Thank you."

Mark grasped it. "You're welcome."

"As for the rest of you," Mila continued, "there are lots of shops here at the Hawaiian village that you might want to visit, or you could just relax on the beach."

"That's fine with me," Polly agreed cooperatively.

"I could use a good nap," Kate said with a yawn.

"I hate naps," Emily informed them.

"Me too," Charles agreed.

George Ann, who had complained every step of every tour since they landed on the island of Oahu, was the only fly in the ointment. "There were a few other sites on the island that I was hoping to see," she said with a disappointed look.

"You're always complaining about your feet," Eugenia reminded her. "It seems like you'd be glad to sit on the beach and rest."

George Ann lifted her head, giving them all an unattractive view of her long neck. "I just want to make sure I get the most out of my vacation."

Eugenia narrowed her eyes at the annoying woman. "Then call a cab and have it take you wherever you want to go."

"Why, Eugenia, I can't go around the city of Honolulu alone!" George Ann cried as if Eugenia had suggested something absurd. "A tourist area like this is full of robbers and murderers and rapists."

Eugenia scrutinized George Ann. Then she shook her head. "No one is *that* crazy."

George Ann crossed her arms over her thin chest. "Well! I don't know why I even try to have a normal conversation with you."

"Maybe it's better when Eugenia is pretending to be a detective," Annabelle suggested. "At least it gives her something to do besides criticize us."

Eugenia was shocked that Annabelle was actually choosing George Ann's side and opened her mouth to tell her just what she thought, but Polly spoke first. "Well, I'm sure we'll all have a very nice morning together whatever we decide to do."

In an obvious effort to help Polly change the subject, Kate asked Mila, "Are you nervous about getting married?"

"A little," Mila admitted. "But I talked to Sister Kaneohe this morning, and she said everything is ready for the reception."

"I can hardly wait to see you in your dress," Polly said. "I know you're going to be a beautiful bride."

"I have a new dress too," Emily informed them. "Mama bought it."

"And I'm sure you will be almost as beautiful as the bride," Eugenia predicted.

Mila smiled. "I hope everything goes perfectly tomorrow."

"Well, it won't," Eugenia predicted. "Be prepared for that in advance, and don't let any last-minute glitches upset you."

"Minor glitches I can deal with," Mila said with a smile at Quin. "All I really care about is becoming Mrs. Quincy Barrington Drummond V."

"Such a lovely name," Polly said.

Mila laughed. "It's growing on me."

"It had better grow on you fast since you're only a few hours away from saying 'I do' or whatever it is you Mormons say in the temple ceremony," Eugenia said, and everyone turned to stare at her.

"You are being particularly cranky today," Annabelle remarked, "even for you. Is something the matter?"

Eugenia realized she'd have to give them an excuse and since she didn't want to bring up Albert Baldwin, she used her arthritis. "My joints are aching a little. I guess I've been on my feet too much."

Annabelle leaned closer and whispered, "Please don't tell me you have bunions and a foot fungus too."

Eugenia had to smile at this. "If I did—I'd have enough sense to keep it to myself."

* * *

When everyone was through eating, Mila invited them to come to the Surf Shop. "This time we'll give you a tour of the storage room so you can see the humble circumstances we'll be living in. And I was thinking that you ladies could give me some ideas about how to arrange our furniture in the small space."

"I'd be glad to give you the benefit of my knowledge of interior design," George Ann offered. "I took several courses on proper use of color at the women's college in Albany back when I was a girl."

"Back when there were fewer colors," Eugenia added.

"So, Kate, would you like to come?" Mila asked quickly.

"Sure," Kate agreed. "And I'll try to keep the kids from breaking anything really expensive at the shop."

"How about you?" Mila asked Eugenia.

"I won't be any help on arranging furniture," she said honestly. "Mine has been in the same spot for decades. But I'd be glad to come along. And if there's not room in Quin's car, because of all your things, you can ride with us."

Mila smiled. "Thanks for the offer, but I'll squeeze in with Quin."

Polly giggled. "You'd better spend as much time with Quin as possible today since you can't see him tomorrow before the wedding."

"I'll make good use of my time," Mila promised. "Now, follow Quin so you don't get lost."

When they got to the Surf Shop, Quin insisted on carrying Mila over the threshold, then gave her a long kiss.

"You don't carry the bride over the threshold until *after* you're married," George Ann was quick to inform them.

"This was just a test run," Quin said. He lowered Mila to the ground but kept his arms around her.

"Goodness gracious," Eugenia muttered when she reached them. "I'm glad Quin's first in your life now, but I declare, you're going to have to learn to restrain yourselves in public."

Mila smiled up at Quin. "Don't mind Miss Eugenia. She got up on the wrong side of the bed."

"And her arthritis is bothering her," Polly contributed.

"She should have bunions and see how bad that hurts," George Ann told them.

Mila grabbed Eugenia by the arm and pulled her away from George Ann before she could do bodily harm. "Come on, and let me show you some of my favorite surfboards."

＊ ＊ ＊

When they got back to the hotel, everyone expressed a desire to go to the beach, except George Ann, who was afraid of contracting sand mites.

"I declare, if that woman isn't about to get on my last nerve," Eugenia told the others as they sat down in the hotel's upholstered outdoor furniture.

"Forget about George Ann and enjoy Hawaii," Annabelle advised.

Eugenia positioned her chair so she could see Kate and the children wading in the surf. The view was beautiful, but Eugenia's mind kept drifting to Mr. Baldwin, sitting alone in a dirty jail cell.

"What's the matter?" Mila asked finally.

Eugenia looked over at the bride-to-be. "You don't suppose Mr. Baldwin would try to kill himself, do you?"

"They'll keep a close eye on him to prevent that," Mila replied.

"He must be terribly humiliated."

"Embarrassment is the least of his problems," Mila said. "Now, let's just lie here and enjoy the sun while we can. In an hour Quin's picking me up so we can go to the airport to meet our parents, and after that I have an appointment to get my nails done."

Eugenia stood and dusted the sand from her clothes. "At my age the closest thing I'll get to a tan is age spots, and the last thing I need is skin cancer. So I think I'll offer to take the children to the inside pool so Kate can get that nap she's been wanting."

CHAPTER 11

Late that afternoon Eugenia returned Charles and Emily to their parents, then she tried to convince Annabelle to take her to Pearl Harbor.

"We won't get out of the car," she promised. "I just want to see the *Arizona* Monument with my own old eyes."

"If you'd gone with us yesterday, another trip wouldn't be necessary," Annabelle reminded her.

"I know," Eugenia said. "And if I'd gone with you, maybe they never would have arrested Mr. Baldwin." She looked up at her sister. "Did you see him on the news this morning when they were taking him to court? I believe he has aged ten years in one day."

"That's what jail will do to you."

"I still can't believe he murdered Leilani."

"Well, apparently he did or the police wouldn't have arrested him," Annabelle replied with barely concealed impatience.

"I guess it's conceivable that he killed Leilani in a fit of passion, but there's no way he made those other three cakes. I wish I could think of a way to convince Detective Hirasuna."

"Mila's off the case now," Annabelle reminded her. "And that means you're off the case too. Just try and forget about it."

Eugenia shook her head. "I've tried, but I can't. I'm just sure that someone copied Mr. Baldwin's idea and made those other cakes. Then they sent them to people they hated with those notes taped on the boxes. And I think I know who it was."

Annabelle was mildly interested now. "Who?"

"Raquel Simon."

"Eugenia! That's ridiculous."

"Is it?" Eugenia asked.

"How could you accuse Raquel of doing such a wicked thing? Ruining people's careers like that?"

"I have no reason to think that Raquel is a particularly nice person. Too many people hate her."

"But whoever made those cakes didn't know for sure that no one would eat them," Annabelle reminded her. "Do you honestly think Raquel is that heartless?"

"When trying to solve a crime you have to look to see who benefited from it the most. Raquel is the only person whose life was improved after those cakes were delivered."

"She lost her secretary," Annabelle said.

"And got to give interviews on national television," Eugenia countered. "But you're right about one thing."

"I'm happy to hear that," Annabelle interjected facetiously.

Eugenia chose to ignore the remark. "I do need proof that Raquel's guilty, and since Mila's off the case—it makes it harder for me to point the police in the right direction."

Annabelle gave her sister a doubtful look. "*You're* pointing the police?"

Eugenia sighed. "If you only knew."

Annabelle picked up her purse. "Raquel already has a policeman following her around. So short of putting a hidden camera in her house, I don't see what more anyone can do. If we're going to Pearl Harbor, we need to go now."

Eugenia smiled. "You have just given me a wonderful idea."

"You're going to hide a camera at Raquel's house?" Annabelle asked in despair.

"Of course not," Eugenia replied. "But instead of taking me to Pear Harbor, I need you to take me by the Channel One studios."

"Please, Eugenia," Annabelle begged. "Please leave it alone."

"I just need to check one more thing, and then I'll be finished. Will you take me or am I going to have to call a taxi?"

"I'll take you," Annabelle said with a sigh. "But I can't stay there with you. I promised Polly and George Ann that I'd take them to see a play about Hawaiian history at the Honolulu Academy of Arts before we meet for dinner."

Eugenia considered this. "You drop me off, and I'll see if Mila can pick me up after her manicure appointment."

"You might end up at the television station for a while," Annabelle warned. "Because you'll *have* to wait on Mila. I'm not going to leave the play early to come get you."

Eugenia nodded in agreement to the terms. "This is important, and I don't mind waiting if necessary."

* * *

Annabelle dropped Eugenia off at the Channel One studios right at five o'clock. Eugenia stood on the sidewalk and took a few deep breaths before pushing through the front doors and into the lobby. The same receptionist she had met on her previous visit was standing by the information desk.

"We're closed," the woman said automatically.

"It's terrible about Mr. Baldwin," Eugenia replied. A steady flow of people headed out of the front door, and Eugenia moved closer to the receptionist to get out of the way.

The woman looked like she was about to cry. "It's unbelievable. We're all so worried about Mr. Baldwin and the station and our jobs."

Another group of people crowded into the exit area, and Eugenia waited until they had passed outside before saying, "Where is every-body going in such a hurry?"

"Well, people are always anxious to start their weekend on Fridays ,and since this has been a particularly *bad* week—most of them are probably rushing to the nearest bar."

"Who could blame them?" Eugenia asked with a friendly smile.

"Not me, that's for sure." The receptionist glanced at her watch. "We're all supposed to be out of here by five so the night watchman can lock up."

"What about the people who do the evening news?"

"They're filming it on location tonight so nobody will be in the station."

Eugenia stepped out of the way as another group of people rushed toward the front door. "I've just got to ask Mike in the sound booth a question," she told the receptionist. "I'll be right back down."

The receptionist looked unsure.

"It's something that will help Mr. Baldwin."

This swayed the woman. "Okay, but you'd better hurry or you'll get locked inside, and then you'll have to find the security guard to let you out."

"I won't be long," Eugenia walked to the elevator as fast as her arthritic joints would take her. She reached the sound room just as Mike, the technician, was leaving. "Oh, I'm so glad I caught you," she told him.

She could tell by his expression that the feeling was not mutual. "It's five," he told her. "The guard will lock the doors any minute."

"I just need to ask you a quick question," she said, stepping into the sound room. "The other day you told me that whenever the lights are turned on in one of the sets, the computer automatically starts recording."

He nodded impatiently. "Yeah." Apparently his friendly attitude had been a result of Mr. Baldwin's presence.

"Well, I was just curious about what happens to those tapes—the ones that record things that aren't important."

He sighed audibly to let her know she was a major inconvenience before pointing to a file cabinet in the corner. "We keep all the tapes for thirty days just in case—then we erase and recycle them."

"Oh, that's wonderful," she told him. "Now, could you pull me the tapes from last weekend, starting on Friday night and going through Monday morning?"

"I think you'll have to come back on Monday for that," Mike said. "I've got to get out of here."

She shook her head. "Monday will be too late." She remembered Mr. Baldwin's desperate plea for help as he was being arrested and the receptionist's claim that everyone was worried about their job security. "Mr. Baldwin has asked me to help him," Eugenia told the sound man. "You do want to help Mr. Baldwin, don't you?"

Mike nodded. "If it will help Mr. Baldwin, I'll get you the tapes, but I can't stay. My son's got a football game tonight."

"You don't have to stay if you can show me how to watch them."

Mike pulled out a stack of mini-video tapes, and after checking the dates, he placed two on the desk and waved toward his chair.

"Have a seat." Eugenia sat down and watched as he inserted the first tape. "I'm fast-forwarding to Friday night."

"Show me how to do that," she requested.

"Just push this button," he told her. "The date and time are always along the bottom of the screen."

Eugenia nodded. "Perfect. Thank you."

"When you get through with this tape, hit the eject button. This tape will come out, and you can put in the other one."

"I think I have it," she said.

"Don't touch anything else," Mike now seemed reluctant to leave her there. "This equipment cost over a million dollars."

"I'll be careful," Eugenia promised.

Finally, he turned toward the door. "Good night then."

"Good night," she called over her shoulder. She heard him close the door behind and then concentrated on the computer screen. She saw the lights come on as the crew prepared for the evening news on Friday night. She fast-forwarded through the pre-show footage, the broadcast itself and the after-show wrap-up. Finally the set was empty and the lights went off. The next section of video tape showed the custodian cleaning all the sets.

On Saturday there were tapings of community interest segments, presumably for use on shows during the next week. Eugenia yawned as she fast-forwarded through these. There were several occasions where the lights were turned on for a few minutes and then turned back off for no apparent reason. Then the custodian came back and cleaned all the sets again. Eugenia was about to decide her idea had been a bad one when the lights came on in the kitchen set. She could see someone moving in the shadows, tying on one of the little lacy aprons Raquel wore for her cooking segments.

Eugenia checked the time on the bottom of the screen. The taping took place at two o'clock in the morning on the previous Sunday. She held her breath, waiting for Raquel to step into the light, but she stayed in the shadows as she unloaded several grocery sacks. Through the clear plastic Eugenia could see eggs, heavy cream, chocolate chips, and cream cheese.

"Well, Raquel, what were you doing in the kitchen set in the middle of the night with all the ingredients for chocolate chip cheese-cake?" she whispered to herself. Then the screen went blank.

"She hit the override button," Eugenia muttered to herself. In all the footage she'd examined so far, no one had ever bothered to turn off the computer. "Because until now, no one was doing anything they didn't want to be recorded on tape," she continued quietly to herself.

Eugenia tried not to be disappointed. It made sense that Raquel would know about the override button, and maybe just the little clip of Raquel and her cheesecake ingredients would be enough to convince the police to investigate further. Eugenia reached toward the computer to eject the tape but her hand stopped when the woman's image popped back up on the screen. Now she was mixing ingredients in a large KitchenAid. Apparently Raquel didn't know about the automatic restart feature of the fancy computer.

Eugenia pushed the fast-forward button and watched the shadow zoom around the set, mixing batter, adding poison, then baking cakes and cleaning up the set. As Raquel started putting the cakes into a plastic tub for transport out of the building, Eugenia reached again to eject the tape. Then she stopped as the woman turned her face to the camera. It wasn't Raquel, but Darlene who had made the poisoned cheesecakes. And she didn't make just the three "afterthought" cakes. She had made all four.

Thinking she must be mistaken, Eugenia pushed the rewind button and watched the segment again at regular speed. The cook was Darlene, and Eugenia didn't count wrong. Darlene baked four poisoned cakes in the wee hours of Sunday morning.

Eugenia took a deep breath to still her pounding heart. If Darlene made all four cakes, then she not only destroyed the careers of three television personalities, but she also killed Leilani. With a trembling hand, Eugenia reached out and pushed the eject button. She wasn't sure if the tape would be admissible in court, but it would definitely convince the police to investigate Darlene and possibly win Mr. Baldwin's release. Tucking the tape into her purse, Eugenia hurried out the door and down the hallway. When she got on the elevator and pushed the button for the first floor, she wished for the first time in her life that she owned a cell phone so she could call Mila.

Resting her head against the wall of the elevator she decided her best course of action would be to go to the receptionist's desk at the front of the building. She could call Mila from there and wait by the front entrance until help arrived. The elevator doors opened, and she stepped out absently.

"Well, what a surprise to find you here so late," a woman's voice spoke from the shadows directly to Eugenia's right. "Your name is Eugenia, right?"

After forcing air into her lungs, Eugenia turned to face the person she least wanted to see. Raquel's cooking assistant, Darlene, stood just a few feet away. "Yes, my name is Eugenia Atkins, and I'm just as surprised to see you here at this hour," she replied in what she hoped was a normal tone of voice.

"Raquel wanted to review the recipe we're using on the show Monday," Darlene said. "And of course when Raquel wants something it's my job to stop what I'm doing and get it for her."

Eugenia realized that she was going to have to come up with some sort of explanation for her own presence. "My sister and her friends were going to see a play about Hawaiian history, but I didn't want to go so they dropped me off here," was the best she could do. "Mila Edwards, the *police detective* I was with the other day, is coming by after her manicure to pick me up."

The mention of Mila's police status didn't have the desired effect. "Oh, yes, I know Mila," Darlene replied. "She lives at Makai with Raquel. Since I'm here, there's no need for her to come here. I'm headed to Makai with this recipe and you can ride with me."

The thought of being in a car with this murderess was almost more than Eugenia could stand. "That's very nice of you," she said. "But I'm not staying at Makai anymore. I've moved to a hotel."

"That's no problem. I'll be glad to take you wherever you need to go."

"If Mila gets here and I'm gone, she'll be worried."

Darlene pulled a cell phone from her pocket. "We'll call her."

"I don't know Mila's cell number," Eugenia tried. "So I guess I'll just have to wait."

"I know her number," Darlene said. "I keep all the numbers from Raquel's rolodex entered into my phone in case she needs one of them."

"How efficient," Eugenia murmured. Then she watched as Darlene looked up the number in her cell phone. Finally she put the phone to her ear.

Then she watched with dread as Darlene waited for an answer. "Mila Edwards?" Darlene spoke into the little receiver. "Darlene Moore from Channel One. I'm Raquel's assistant . . ."

Darlene paused, then smiled. "Yes, well I'm glad you remember me. No, there's nothing wrong, but I'm here at the station with your friend Eugenia, and I'm going to drop her off at her hotel, so there's no need for you to come by."

Eugenia's mind was racing, trying to think of a way to alert Mila that she was in possible danger. "Tell her not to forget that book she promised to loan me," she blurted, composing a plan as she spoke.

"A book?" Darlene repeated.

"It's a novel she's been reading, and she's supposed to give it to me—something to read on the plane. I get nervous when I fly, but the motion sickness pills put me straight to sleep. So on the way home I'm going to try reading." Eugenia gave Darlene what she hoped was a doddering look. "She said it was real interesting, about a murder at a grist mill."

Darlene repeated the information to Mila then shook her head. "She says she's never heard of a book like that."

Eugenia laughed. "Oh, well at my age it's easy to get confused. Maybe it was my sister who had the book. Ask Mila to check with her for me please."

After Darlene relayed this request, she closed her phone. "Come on to the set with me and let me get the recipe for Raquel, then I'll take you to your hotel."

Eugenia looked around, but there wasn't another soul in sight. "Where's the security guard?"

"Oh, by now he's probably asleep in his car," Darlene said with a smile over her shoulder. "That man is absolutely worthless. Let's get the recipe so we can get out of here. This place gives me the creeps at night."

Being there with Darlene was giving Eugenia more than just the creeps, but she couldn't think of a way to get out of it without alerting the other woman. So, with deep trepidation, she followed Darlene. "Yes, we certainly need to hurry," she said as loud as she dared, hoping to attract the missing security man. "We're all going out to dinner tonight, and I don't want to miss that."

"Why are you shouting?" Darlene asked as they reached the kitchen set.

"Oh, I didn't mean to." Eugenia forced a laugh. "It's just that I'm hard of hearing."

Darlene frowned. "I didn't notice you talking loud when we met before."

Eugenia shrugged. "It comes and goes."

Darlene gave her a dubious look as she flipped on the lights. Eugenia instantly felt safer knowing that the computer was recording. "Come over here and let me show you the recipe we'll be doing on Monday," Darlene requested from the counter by the sink.

Eugenia complied, clutching her purse. She arrived at the sink just in time to see Darlene push a red button marked "computer override." "No need to waste video tape," she said, watching Eugenia closely.

"No," Eugenia agreed, trying to ignore the fact that terror was making her heart beat wildly. "So, where's the recipe?"

Without warning Darlene grabbed Eugenia by the arm. "All right, old woman, stop with the games. What were you *really* doing here?" Darlene glanced up at the sound booth, and Eugenia saw that in her haste to leave she had forgotten to turn off the lights. "I see. You were in the sound room. And I'll bet that means you were looking through the old tapes."

"I don't know what you mean." Eugenia pulled free of Darlene's grasp and took a step backward.

"There couldn't be more than a few seconds of me here on Saturday night," Darlene continued as if Eugenia hadn't spoken. "I pushed the override button as soon as I walked on the set."

Eugenia knew that playing dumb was hopeless. There was no guarantee that Mila would understand the amateurishly disguised plea for help she had sent. So with surprising calm Eugenia accepted the possibility that Darlene might kill her. But if that were the case, she was determined to save Mr. Baldwin in the process. She owed him that much for helping to send him to jail. However, to do that she would have to get Darlene's confession on tape. And that meant she had to stall until the automatic restart feature of the computer kicked in.

"Yes, I was in the sound room watching the tapes. It was actually early on Sunday morning when I saw you arrive with grocery bags full of what looked suspiciously like the ingredients for chocolate chip cheesecakes," Eugenia told her. "Several chocolate chip cheesecakes."

"What's so strange about me coming here to try out a recipe?"

"It's strange that you chose to do your cooking in the middle of the night," Eugenia pointed out.

"Since the detectives assigned to the case are kindergarten cops," Darlene smiled at her own wittiness, "I doubt that I'll ever be questioned about it. But if the detectives find their brains—I have an excuse ready. I'll tell them that we were going to make the cheesecakes on our show, and I wanted to make sure we had all the necessary utensils. What better way to do that than to make the cakes here? And as far as the time of night, I'll just say I have insomnia—which is true."

"Even kindergarten cops will think it quite a coincidence that you decided to make chocolate chip cheesecakes days before poisoned ones were delivered to four local television personalities."

Darlene nodded. "Yes, that is a sad coincidence—but then life's full of them. For instance, the fact that you stopped by here to speak with your friend Mr. Baldwin, who was released on bond just a couple of hours ago. And apparently what you had to tell him sent him into another murderous rage, and he killed *you*." Darlene held up an ugly butcher knife. "Mr. Baldwin will take the fall for your murder as well as Leilani's murder."

Eugenia took another step back and then realized her mistake. Darlene had maneuvered her into a corner. Trying not to panic, she asked, "Why did you hate Leilani so much?"

"For ten years I was Raquel's protégée. She *depended* on me. Whatever she needed, I provided. No amount of effort or inconvenience was too much. We became the perfect team. Raquel has such stage presence, and I'm an excellent cook." Darlene's face became a mask of hate. "Then that little tramp showed up."

"Leilani?" Eugenia verified.

"Leilani," Darlene sneered. "She was a horrible, selfish person." Darlene lowered her voice. "She was supposed to be Raquel's friend, but she slept with Cade."

"How do you know?"

"I saw them," Darlene said. "More than once."

"Did you tell Raquel?"

"I tried, but she wouldn't believe me. Then I found out Leilani was sleeping with Mr. Baldwin, too, but I didn't say anything. What was the point?"

"When did you find out that Raquel was going to take Leilani to Los Angeles?"

"Last week," Darlene said. "I knew that Leilani was only using Raquel to get started in show business. Once her career was established, I knew she'd dump Raquel."

"Raquel didn't believe you about that either?"

"No," Darlene nearly whispered. "But I had to do something to keep Raquel from giving up our partnership for *nothing!*"

"So you killed Leilani?"

Pride shone on Darlene's face. "Yes."

Eugenia swallowed, concentrating on her task. "How did you get Leilani to eat the poisoned cheesecake?"

"I told her it was a gift from Raquel. She didn't want to share with me, but I kind of insisted. Then you should have seen the look on her face when she realized what I had done! It was priceless."

Eugenia wasn't amused. Leilani was not the innocent victim she had thought, but no one deserved to die like that.

"I watched until I was sure she was gone."

"Then you wiped all the prints off the cake box."

Darlene clutched the knife tighter in obvious frustration. "That was the only mistake I made! I should have realized that by removing all the prints I was raising a red flag. But I had to be certain that my own prints weren't on it anywhere."

Eugenia didn't know how much longer she could last and prayed that Mila would hurry. "And why did you take Leilani's money out of her purse?"

Darlene's eyes narrowed. "You're not such a stupid old woman after all. Okay, so I took her money. It was just a few hundred dollars, but I figured I deserved it for my trouble."

"Actually, leaving the money might have pointed the police toward Mr. Baldwin sooner." Eugenia couldn't resist the opportunity to needle the other woman, "since they probably had his fingerprints on them."

Darlene smirked. "Oh well, so I made two mistakes."

"And why did you frame Mr. Baldwin for the murder?"

"Because he was handy," Darlene said.

"How did you get his fingerprints on the bottle of arsenic?"

"I made sure he touched the right pans and utensils while he was on the cooking set, including the bottle of arsenic."

Eugenia resisted the urge to look up at the sound room. "And the cake boxes?"

"I saw Mr. Baldwin put the leftover cakes on the table in the staff lounge during the holidays. He stacked the boxes by the garbage can, and I figured that I could use them somehow." Darlene gave her an evil grin. "And how right I was!"

"You knew that the boxes would be traced back to Channel One and Mr. Baldwin?"

"No, that was just another lucky coincidence."

Eugenia nodded. "So, you've been planning this for a very long time."

"Months," Darlene acknowledged.

"It was very clever. I presume you found the folder in Mr. Baldwin's office with the damaging information you used for your notes."

"Yes."

"And again that tied Mr. Baldwin to the crimes. I wonder why he hired someone to investigate the people who worked for him?"

Darlene shrugged. "I don't know—maybe it helped during salary negotiations."

"Did you choose your other victims at random?"

"Actually all of them were rude to me," Darlene said petulantly. "I'll bet they're sorry now."

Eugenia had to admit a grudging respect for Darlene. The plan was complicated and brilliant in an insane way. "So, you sent the additional three cheesecakes to divert attention from Leilani and her murder?"

"Partly," Darlene acknowledged. "I also wanted to sensationalize the murder so that Raquel would get the publicity she wanted. But I didn't want to kill anyone else. Killing people for no reason is wrong."

Eugenia realized that Darlene's sense of right and wrong was skewed. "Who delivered the cheesecakes for you?"

Darlene laughed. "I did it myself! To most people I'm completely invisible." A frown formed on her face. "The only person who saw me was an old wino begging money in the street when I was loading the cheesecakes into my car. But I took care of him by giving him a bottle of Mr. Baldwin's personal wine stock that I had tainted with arsenic." She took another step forward, and Eugenia pressed her back against the wall.

"So, Leilani wasn't your only victim."

"Nobody cares about an old wino," Darlene dismissed. "Now, we've wasted enough time. I've got to get this recipe to Raquel at Makai. Maybe I'll even be there to comfort her when she gets the tragic news of your death."

"Wait!" Eugenia cried. "I have one more question."

Darlene looked annoyed. "I'm not really required to satisfy your curiosity." She raised the knife and moved forward. Eugenia screamed for help, and this seemed to aggravate Darlene—as if she had expected Eugenia to die quietly. "Shut up!" she hissed.

Keeping her eye on the knife, Eugenia waited until Darlene leaned closer. Then she kicked Darlene in the knee as hard as she could. Darlene's eyes opened wide in surprise and pain as she staggered backward, dropping the knife. Eugenia used the opportunity to run from the set into the surrounding shadows. Her progress was slowed by age and countless electrical cords, but finally she made it into the lobby.

"Help!" she cried again, searching for the security guard, but there was no response. She ran to the door and pushed, but it resisted her.

"You're locked in with me," Darlene's voice said from behind her. "I'm going to have a bruise on my leg where you kicked me, and for that I am going to make you pay."

"Please," Eugenia tried as Darlene advanced with menace. "You don't want to kill me."

Darlene smiled. "That's where you're wrong. I've wanted to squeeze the life out of you ever since I met you. Without your fumbling, bumbling meddling, there probably never would have been an investigation."

Darlene lunged, and Eugenia ducked as the door burst open and Mila rushed in, followed closely by a startled security guard. "What the—" he began as Darlene knocked him over.

"Be careful!" Eugenia warned. "She has a knife!"

And then everything went black.

* * *

Eugenia was terribly afraid and felt hands on her arms. Wondering if she was having a recurrence of her dream on the plane, she began to struggle against the pressure on her arms.

"Miss Eugenia!" a voice called from what seemed like a great distance.

Eugenia's eyes flew open. Her heart was pounding, and she couldn't seem to get enough air into her lungs. Mila was hovering over her in obvious concern.

"Darlene?" she gasped.

"She's been taken down to the police station," Mila assured her.

Eugenia looked around, trying to get her bearings. She was lying on a couch in the lobby of the Channel One Studio. She looked down but didn't see any injuries. "What happened?" she asked. "Did Darlene stab me?"

Mila shook her head. "No, you fainted."

Eugenia put a hand to her head. "I declare, I've never fainted before in my life. Not even when Charles died."

Mila shrugged. "Well, you fainted today. But not until after you managed to get Darlene to confess to murder on tape."

Eugenia smiled weakly. "You know about the tapes in the sound room?"

"Yes. We found the one in your purse and called the sound guy. He explained about the old tapes you had asked to see and the one that would have recorded everything that happened on the set tonight. He's on his way back to help us make copies of everything."

"Darlene is crazy," Eugenia told Mila with a small shudder. "I mean truly insane."

"I figured that out the minute I saw her lunge at you with that knife," Mila said grimly.

"Thank goodness you got here when you did."

"Thank goodness you gave me that clever hint that you were in trouble."

Eugenia smiled weakly. "I was so afraid you wouldn't understand."

"I can see why you think I'm slow, after the way Darlene has been able to fool me. And I'll admit that I was confused at first. But when I asked Annabelle about the book, and she said she'd never heard of it, I started thinking about murder and a grist mill."

"You found Quin's sister-in-law who had been kidnapped in that abandoned grist mill near Haggerty," Eugenia prompted.

"But there wasn't a murder there, so I realized it had to be a coded message. And then I was scared to death."

Eugenia nodded. "I was too, believe me."

Mila held up her right hand. Only three of the fingers were painted a pale pink. "I jumped out of the manicurist's chair and ran for my car."

Eugenia stared at the half-painted nails in horror. "Your mother is going to kill me."

Mila laughed. "I'll go back and let them finish up tomorrow." Then her expression became serious. "It was very brave of you to confront Darlene, but also very dangerous."

"I didn't confront Darlene!" Eugenia exclaimed. "I was on my way out of here with the tape when she caught me."

"I'm not sure whether to consider that good luck or bad," Mila said.

Eugenia patted her hand. "Since everything turned out well, let's consider it good luck."

Mila checked her watch. "Well, we're already late for dinner, so I guess I'll run you to the station and let you give Jerry your statement now. Maybe Quin will bring us a take-out plate."

Eugenia shook her head. "I'm starving to death, so you tell Detective Hirasuna if he wants a statement from me, he can come to the restaurant and get it."

Mila considered this for a few seconds then nodded. "You've got a deal."

* * *

When they arrived at Bon Appetit, the hostess led them to the private room where their family and friends were gathered. Mila took the empty seat beside Quin, and Eugenia walked down and sat in between Kate and Mark.

Eugenia exchanged a few polite remarks with Quin's parents before turning to Kate. "Where are the children?"

"They're finished eating so Mila's parents offered to take them on a tour of the gardens," Kate replied. "Are you okay? Mila said you *fainted*!"

"I think fainted might be too strong a word," Eugenia amended. "I just closed my eyes for a few minutes to collect myself after the harrowing experience I'd been through."

"Oh, please, tell us everything that happened!" Polly begged.

"Why don't you order some food first," Kate suggested. "I'm sure you're both starving."

Annabelle found a waiter, and he took orders for Eugenia and Mila.

"Okay," Kate said to Eugenia after the waiter left. "So this Darlene person tried to stab you with a knife?"

"I really have to start at the beginning for you to understand the full extent of what happened," Eugenia told her.

"Heaven help us," Annabelle muttered.

Eugenia ignored her sister and for the next ten minutes regaled her dinner companions with her adventures at the television station. When she finished, Polly pulled out her handkerchief.

"Eugenia, I believe you are the bravest person I've ever known."

Eugenia couldn't help but be pleased, but she modestly waved this aside. "I didn't do anything that all of you wouldn't have done in the same situation."

"In the same situation Polly would have been nothing but a puddle of tears," Annabelle predicted.

Polly laughed good-naturedly. "You're probably right."

The food was delivered, and Eugenia and Mila both ate with enthusiasm. "I didn't realize how hungry I was," Mila said with a mouthful of shrimp.

"Even if I wasn't starving, this flounder would be delicious," Eugenia added.

"I can hardly wait to tell Kelsey about your latest adventure." Kate referred to her sister and Eugenia's employer. "She called, by the way, and said she had the names of some companies that might be what you were looking for."

"We've already found out what we needed to know, but please thank Kelsey for looking," Eugenia said.

"Maybe Kelsey can add your exploits to her already impressive résumé," Kate suggested. "Then *For Your Information* will have more customers than you can handle."

Eugenia shook her head. "Kelsey needs to keep her client load light and concentrate on her husband for a while."

Kate nodded. "I agree." Then she added, "They seem to be doing fine."

"That's good," Eugenia said with a smile.

"So," Mark asked from Eugenia's other side. "When Darlene attacked you with the knife did your life flash before your eyes?"

Eugenia considered this. "You know, I think it did. It wasn't a blow by blow, moment by moment reenactment, but more of a summary. I thought about my life as a whole and what I've accomplished."

"I know they were good thoughts, then," Kate said, her eyes a little moist. "Because you've done so much for so many people."

Eugenia smiled at her. "Thank you for saying that."

"Oh, Eugenia!" Polly cried. "I just realized something. Your dream on the plane was a premonition."

"What dream?" Quin asked.

"During our flight from Atlanta, Eugenia dreamed that her birthday cake was full of maggots," Polly explained. "Annabelle thought it meant that Eugenia was afraid of being old, and George Ann thought it was because Eugenia is overweight, but now I think it was warning you about the murder!"

"I guess that's possible," Eugenia said, deciding to ignore the overweight remark.

Annabelle rolled her eyes. "Great, now Eugenia's going to think she's a soothsayer as well as a private investigator."

Before Eugenia could defend herself, Detective Hirasuna was ushered into the room. The minute she saw him Eugenia stood and said, "I'm sorry but you'll have to excuse Mila and me. We have to take care of official business."

"Correction," Annabelle muttered. "She thinks she's a soothsayer, a private investigator, *and* a policewoman!"

"Don't get up." Detective Hirasuna waved for Eugenia to sit back down. Then he smiled at Annabelle. "And while your sister is not a policewoman, she is one of the best detectives I've ever met."

Eugenia blushed with pleasure. "I declare, you're embarrassing me."

Detective Hirasuna laughed as he pulled a chair over close to Eugenia's.

"Would you like something to eat?" Mila offered. "I'd be glad to find the waiter."

He shook his head. "Oh, no thanks."

"Where is Officer Wong?" Eugenia asked.

"He's with Gates handling the arrest proceedings for Darlene," the detective replied.

Eugenia controlled a shudder. "I hope I never see her again. Will I have to testify at her trial?"

"I'm not sure about that yet," Detective Hirasuna said. "But look on the bright side. If you do have to testify, at least you'll get to come back to Hawaii."

Eugenia tried to consider that a good thing. "Well, go ahead and ask me questions."

The detective smiled. "I don't really need much from you. I watched the film, and it's all there except the action in the lobby."

"That's where Darlene tried to stab me for the *second* time," Eugenia reminded them all.

"Thank goodness Mila's parents took the children away," George Ann remarked. "All this talk of murder and stabbing would have scared them to death."

The detective shook his head. "That Darlene is one piece of work. But you don't have to worry about her anymore. She'll be in jail for a long time." He turned to Eugenia. "My main reason for coming by tonight was to thank you." The detective cleared his throat. "When I started, Mila tried to get me to investigate the Gent's death more thoroughly, and if I had, we might have found the connection to Mr. Baldwin and solved Leilani's case sooner. Next time I'll be less arrogant and more willing to hear what other people have to say."

"That's a good way to approach life in general, young man," Eugenia said. "If you learn from all your experiences in life—then you're on your way to being an excellent detective."

Detective Hirasuna smiled.

Then Polly said, "I heard on television that the Simons are moving to Los Angeles for Raquel to star in a television program. The reporter said that they are going to sell Makai to some man that owns a lot of hotels on the island, and he's going to turn it into an exclusive bed and breakfast."

Mila looked at Quin. "Do you suppose the hotel man is Mr. Lehman?"

Quin nodded. "Probably. He never has called me back about putting surfboards into the gift shops in his hotels."

Mila frowned. "So his presence at Raquel's party wasn't just to help the surf shop?"

"I guess not."

"I told you Raquel had an ulterior motive for throwing that last-minute party." Mila put down her fork. "In fact, I'll bet that the reason she invited all our guests to stay at the estate was just to show Mr. Lehman how easily Makai could be converted into a bed and breakfast."

"You're probably right," Eugenia agreed. "My mother always taught me to be suspicious of excessive generosity."

"If Raquel and Cade sell Makai, what will happen to Mrs. Rose?" Polly asked.

The detective shrugged. "I don't know."

"I'm just glad we've moved to a hotel. I wouldn't have been able to close my eyes in that house," Eugenia said. "Even though Darlene is in jail—I don't completely trust Raquel or Cade."

"You don't *completely* trust anyone," Annabelle remarked.

"Humph," Eugenia responded. "Don't be jealous just because I'm a good judge of character."

Before Annabelle could reply, Mila pulled Quin's hand to her lips and kissed it. "And a good matchmaker."

After the laughter died down, the detective turned to Mila. "I guess you heard that it was Darlene, not Mr. Baldwin, who killed Phillip Carson?"

Mila nodded. "Yes, I heard."

"You still want to be the one to tell Spike?"

"Yes, I'll work the time in to do that somehow."

The detective stood. "Well then, I guess I'm done here. Thanks, Miss Eugenia, and you too, Mila. If I have more questions, I'll be in touch."

Mila shook her head. "Don't call me, Jerry. I'm getting married and going on my honeymoon, and when I'm ready to think about cases again, I'll call you."

Eugenia took pity on the poor man. "Detective, if you need anything while Mila's out on vacation, you call me."

The detective looked unsure how to respond, but after a few seconds he nodded. "I might just do that."

As the detective left, Mila's mother and stepfather returned with Emily and little Charles.

"Daphne!" Eugenia cried when she saw the mother of the bride. "You've lost weight!"

"Thirty pounds," Daphne confirmed.

"Have you been on a diet?" Polly wanted to know.

"Not really," Daphne replied. She glanced fondly at her husband. "Terry and I just watch what we eat and walk two miles every day."

"Thank goodness obesity doesn't run in my family," George Ann remarked. "With my foot problems, walking is torture."

"Don't get George Ann started on her many ailments," Eugenia advised Daphne.

"Well, how do you like Hawaii so far?" Mila asked her mother.

"It's beautiful," Daphne replied. "But the things I've been hearing about your job are very disturbing."

"We'll talk about that later," Mila suggested with a pointed look at the children.

Eugenia pulled Charles into her lap and put an arm around Emily, asking her, "And how do you two like Hawaii?"

"We love it!" Emily replied. "And tomorrow we get to go to the zoo!"

"And see an elephant!" little Charles added.

"Well, then I'm definitely going with you," Eugenia told them with a smile.

"Maybe you should wait to be invited," Annabelle suggested. "Kate and Mark might want some time alone with their children."

Eugenia dismissed this with a wave. "They get them at night. Besides, they need my help."

"Miss Eugenia is welcome to come to the zoo with us," Kate said. "We're leaving at nine o'clock in the morning."

Eugenia nodded. "I'll be ready."

Daphne flagged down the waiter and asked for the check. "Oh, it's all been paid for," the young man informed them.

"Paid for?" Annabelle repeated in surprise. "By whom?"

The waiter pulled a folded piece of paper from his coat pocket. "I was told to give this to a Eugenia Atkins when your party was ready to leave."

Eugenia raised her hand. "That's me."

The young man gave her the paper and she opened it. Inside was written, "Forever in your debt." It was signed by Albert Baldwin.

"Well, I declare.'" Eugenia whispered as she handed the note to Kate.

Kate read the note, then passed it around the table. "How sad."

"It is sad," Eugenia agreed.

"Mr. Baldwin made some terrible mistakes," Mila pointed out. "And now he has to live with them."

Eugenia nodded. "We might not always be able to control our hearts, but we can control our actions." She glanced down at Albert Baldwin's note. "And we can always pay our debts."

CHAPTER 12

When Mila woke up on Saturday morning she looked out the hotel window and smiled. By the end of this day she would be a married woman. She turned over to share the excitement of the moment with her mother, but neither Mila's mother nor stepfather were in the room's other bed. Surprised, Mila stood and looked in the bathroom, but it, too, was empty. Then she saw a piece of hotel stationery taped on the bathroom mirror.

> *Mila,*
> *Gone to help Kaula. Quin's with me. We've got your dress. Remember your appointment at the hairdresser at noon. They'll paint the rest of your nails while you get your hair done. We'll meet you at the temple at two.*
> *Love,*
> *Mother*

Mila frowned at the bold scrawl. She knew she should be grateful that her mother was helping Sister Kaneohe, but instead she felt deserted. She dug her cell phone out of her purse and called Quin's cell number. She got his answering machine and left a message.

Determined not to allow anything to ruin her wedding day, she took a shower and dressed in sweat pants and a T-shirt before going down to take advantage of the hotel's continental breakfast. She fixed herself a bagel with low-fat cream cheese and carried it outside to eat it by the pool. She found Annabelle sitting under a huge umbrella, sipping coffee.

"Good morning," Annabelle greeted. "How's the beautiful bride?"

Mila smiled. "I don't know about the beautiful part, but I'm very happy." She sat down and took a bite of her bagel. "Where is everyone else?"

"Well, Eugenia's with the Iversons at the Honolulu Zoo—so be praying that she doesn't find so much as a dead bug, or she'll be trying to start another murder investigation."

Mila smiled. "I predict that if she does find a dead bug, she'll also figure out who killed it! Miss Eugenia's an excellent detective."

"Please, don't tell her that again," Annabelle requested. "The last thing she needs is more encouragement."

Mila laughed. "Where are Miss Polly and Miss George Ann?"

"They walked down the street to that muumuu outlet."

"Miss George Ann *walked* down the street?" Mila verified.

Annabelle nodded. "Polly bribed her by promising they would get pedicures at the salon in the hotel afterward. Then, let's see, your mother and the Drummonds are with Kaula, who's doing your reception."

Mila nodded. "I called Quin's cell phone but didn't get an answer."

"Maybe he thinks it's bad luck to even *talk* to the bride before the wedding."

"Quin's not superstitious. I'm sure he's just busy." Mila took a bite of bagel. "Mother left me a note saying she'd meet me at the temple. I can't believe she's not going to come back and help me get ready."

Annabelle raised an eyebrow. "If you need help, I'll be glad to give you a hand."

"Well, I guess I don't really need any help, I just," she floundered, "I guess I just want my mother."

"We all feel that way sometimes. Be glad your mother is still alive and that you'll be seeing her in a few hours. She's just trying to make sure your day is perfect."

Mila stood, feeling better. "Well, I guess if I plan to accomplish everything on my mother's list and be at the temple by two, I'd better get busy."

Mila left a little early for her appointment at the hairdresser so she could make a detour through the seedier part of Honolulu. She parked her car at the entrance to the alley where the Gent's body had been found. She ran into Tarzan a few blocks down, and he took her to find Spike. The boy looked genuinely pleased to see her.

"Heard you nabbed the guy who killed the Gent!" he said with youthful enthusiasm.

"Actually, the guilty party turned out to be a woman," Mila corrected. "But we do have a suspect in custody."

"I knew you'd do it," he told her with pride shining in his eyes. "I could tell from the start that you were different."

She started to demure, but then decided to use his admiration to his own advantage. "I did a little checking on you and found out that you're only sixteen years old."

"Hey! I'll be seventeen in two months!" Spike told her.

"Seventeen is still too young to be living on your own."

"Oh, man! You're going to turn me in, ain't you?"

"The law requires me to," Mila said gently. "But, I've worked out a deal for you."

"They're gonna let me stay in the warehouse?"

Mila laughed. "Not that good a deal. I've arranged for you to live in a dormitory at a school that teaches trades. You'll learn basic skills like reading and math . . ."

Spike rolled his eyes. "You trying to kill me?"

"And then practical skills in a career field of your choice," Mila continued as if she hadn't been interrupted. "Then when you're through, they help you find a place to live and a job."

"But I get to live at the school?" Spike verified. "I don't have to stay with no foster family?"

Mila nodded. "But if you don't behave, they'll kick you out. And then you'll have me to answer to."

Spike laughed. "I ain't scared of no lady cop."

Mila raised an eyebrow. "Then you're not as smart as I thought you were."

* * *

Mila was late for her hair appointment, but the stylist worked wonders with her hair and even got Mila's remaining fingernails painted in a short time. Then Mila drove back to the hotel and found a gorgeous new dress spread out on her bed.

Reverently Mila removed the protective plastic and saw that the dress was made by designer Rebecca Taylor. The fabric was soft, rose-colored cotton voile. There was some delicate embroidered lace along the V-neckline, and the skirt was tiered—giving the dress a romantic, feminine look. Mila saw a new note from her mother on the bed beside the dress. *Wanted you to look your best when you arrive at the temple.*

As Mila pressed the dress against her, tears stung her eyes. She didn't regret her decision to help Quin start the Surf Shop or to make any of the sacrifices she had made. But she did love clothes, and it had been a long time since she'd had a new dress—especially one as fabulous as this. She put it on, careful not to disturb her hair and stood in front of the full-length mirror. She barely recognized the glamorous woman who smiled back.

When Mila left the hotel a few minutes later she felt truly beautiful for the first time in months. On the way to her car she called Quin again, and this time he answered.

"I was hoping you'd come to the hotel so we could ride to the temple together," she said.

"I was hoping the same thing," he replied. "But Sister Kaneohe has worked me to death, and I've barely got time to change. So, I'll have to meet you there."

"Is my mother and her husband with you?"

"Yes, they're changing in the rest rooms here at the church, and then we're headed to the temple."

"Well, when you see my mother, tell her I love the dress."

"I will," Quin promised.

"Okay, I guess I'll see you there."

When Mila passed through the hotel lobby, Mila saw Miss Eugenia and the other Haggerty folks standing by the door.

"You look gorgeous!" Annabelle said.

Miss Polly immediately pulled a handkerchief from the neckline of her floral print Sunday dress. "I always cry at weddings!"

"You always cry. Period," Miss Eugenia pointed out. "Now let's get going or Mila's going to be late." She herded them toward the parking deck. "Kate and Mark are waiting for us in their rental car. I'll ride with them to help with the children. Mila, do you want to ride in my rental car with Annabelle?"

Mila knew that riding with Annabelle would mean listening to Miss George Ann complain about her feet all the way to the temple, so she shook her head. "Thank you, but no. I need to get my car to the temple so Mother can take it from there to the Surf Shop."

"I understand completely," Annabelle whispered. Then she raised her voice and said to the others, "Okay, Mila will lead, and the rest of us will follow."

* * *

The Hawaiian temple grounds were spectacular beyond Eugenia's wildest dreams. She settled Polly and George Ann with Annabelle in the visitors' center, then toured the gardens with the children until Mila and Quin emerged through the temple doors.

"Look," Eugenia said, pointing for the children's benefit. "There's the bride and groom!"

Emily stopped smelling flowers and came over to stand beside Eugenia. "I want to be a bride."

Eugenia's eyes filled with tears as she looked down at the child she loved as much as she ever could one of her own. "Someday you will be," she assured Emily.

"Will you come to my wedding?" Emily asked.

"Wild horses couldn't keep me away," Eugenia promised.

Charles broke the poignancy of the moment by announcing, "I want to be a bride too."

Emily shook her head with almost-four-year-old wisdom. "You can't be a bride, Charles. That's only for girls."

"But you can be a handsome groom like Quin," Eugenia told him. "There's your Mama and Daddy," she pointed to the temple doors as Kate and Mark stepped out into the Hawaiian sunshine. "Let's go see them."

Eugenia had to struggle to keep up with the children and arrived at the temple doors a few steps behind them. Members of Mila and Quin's ward along with family and friends had surrounded the couple, giving them best wishes, hugs, and leis. After pictures were taken, Daphne sent Mila and Quin inside to change and told everyone else to meet them at the church.

Since Eugenia had ridden to the temple with the Iversons, she assumed she would be riding to the reception with them as well. But when the group met in the parking lot, Kate announced that they were going to have to go back to the hotel.

"We'll probably be a few minutes late for the reception so you'd better ride with Annabelle," Kate suggested to Eugenia.

Then, without giving Eugenia a chance to argue, the Iversons climbed into their rental car and drove away.

"I wonder why Kate and Mark needed to go back to the hotel?" Eugenia mused as Annabelle drove them to the church.

"Emily said they had to pick up a gift," Annabelle replied. "And that it was a secret."

"A secret gift," Polly said from the back seat. "How exciting."

"It must be a wedding gift for Mila and Quin," Eugenia murmured, trying not to have her feelings hurt that the Iversons hadn't included her in the secret.

"Probably," Annabelle agreed. "And don't sulk. They'll be at the reception soon enough."

Eugenia didn't want to dignify Annabelle's remark by commenting, so she just stared out the window at the spectacular Hawaiian foliage.

When they reached the church, Eugenia led the way inside, and Kaula Kaneohe greeted them at the door. "My haole friends!"

"Kaula!" Eugenia said, bracing herself for the inevitable hug.

After Kaula released Eugenia, she hugged Annabelle, George Ann, and Polly in turn. Then she said to Eugenia, "I researched your name, and now I know that it is a Greek name that means noble and wellborn."

Eugenia glanced over at Annabelle. "Don't feel bad, Annabelle. At least you're *related* to royalty!"

Annabelle rolled her eyes as Kaula led them into the cultural hall where the reception was set up. "This is lovely," Annabelle complimented. "I've never seen so many flowers in one place."

"Or so many waiters," Polly added.

"They are my nieces and nephews," Kaula informed them. "If you think they aren't doing their jobs, you tell me and I'll hit them."

Annabelle raised an eyebrow as she whispered to Eugenia, "And I thought you were hard to work with."

The bride and groom arrived with great fanfare a few minutes later and were installed at the front of the room to cut cake and then receive guests. Eugenia spoke to the guests of honor, stopped by the impressive buffet table, and finally sat in a chair with a good view of the front door.

"Isn't this food fabulous?" Polly asked as she passed by on her third trip to the buffet table.

"It is good," Eugenia agreed.

"Would you like to come with me to get a little more?" Polly invited.

"No, I believe I'll just stay right here and watch for Emily and little Charles," she replied.

Polly giggled. "Eugenia, if I didn't know better, I'd think you were their grandmother."

Eugenia thought to herself that no grandmother could love them more, but she said, "They are the lights of my life. And Lady, too, of course."

"Of course you can't leave out your little dog," Polly agreed. "Well, I hope they'll get here soon so you can start enjoying the party." Polly stepped a little closer. "Do you think it would be rude of me to ask Kaula for some of her recipes to put in the church cookbook?"

Eugenia smiled. "I don't think it would be rude at all. I'm sure Kaula would be glad to help provide Bibles for the people of India."

Polly pressed her napkin to her lips and blinked back tears. "It is such a good cause. I'm going to talk to her right now."

After Polly left in search of recipes, Eugenia returned her gaze to the door. Finally it swung open, and the Iversons stepped through. Eugenia knew she should wait and let them speak to Mila and Quin, but she couldn't help herself. She rushed forward and caught the children in a hug.

"We brought you a surprise," Emily said, her eyes shining with excitement.

"Me?" Eugenia asked. "The surprise is for me?"

Emily pointed to the door behind her. Eugenia's eyes followed the small finger, and to her utter amazement, she saw Whit Owens standing in the doorway. And in his arms was Lady von Beanie Weenie Atkins, wearing a little white bow in honor of the occasion.

Eugenia pressed a hand to her mouth, very afraid that for the first time in her life she was going to dissolve into uncontrollable tears in public. "Whit," she finally managed. "You're here."

He stepped forward and handed Eugenia the little dog. Lady licked her master and barked with happiness. "I was in the airport in Raleigh, buying my ticket to fly back to Albany, and the thought occurred to me—why not just go on to Hawaii and surprise Eugenia. So, I called Mark and Kate, and, well, here we are."

Eugenia pressed her face against Lady's wiry coat. "And I don't know when I've been so glad to see anyone!"

By this time Annabelle and Polly and George Ann had noticed Whit's arrival and came over to greet him.

"Why, Whit, what a surprise to see you here," George Ann said.

"It was a secret," Emily informed her. "We didn't tell Charles because he's too little."

"I'm not little," Charles objected.

"It's nice to see you, George Ann," Whit said politely. "You too, Polly, Annabelle." He nodded to each woman in turn.

"Whit has a room at the Honolulu Hilton with the rest of us and is planning to stay through next week," Kate told everyone.

"I'm hoping I can convince Eugenia to change her ticket and stay as well," Whit said. "I was thinking that we could visit all the sights you missed while helping Mila solve her crime."

"I never did get to see Pearl Harbor," Eugenia said thoughtfully. "And I wouldn't mind visiting that pineapple factory again."

"But we're all leaving tomorrow," George Ann pointed out. "And since Mila and Quin will be on their honeymoon . . ."

Eugenia frowned. "I don't see a problem."

George Ann blushed an unbecoming shade of mottled-red. "Well, who will chaperone you?"

Eugenia hooted with laughter. "For heaven's sake, George Ann, Whit and I are too old to need a chaperone."

George Ann lifted her neck. "I'm just trying to protect your reputation," she said to Eugenia. "People back home will talk."

"I'll be glad to provide the gossips in Haggerty with something new to whisper about," Eugenia replied. Then she addressed Whit. "How do we go about getting my ticket changed?"

"I'll handle that," he promised. "Now, let's go and speak to the bride and groom."

* * *

When it was time for Mila and Quin to leave the reception, Kaula Kaneohe lined the guests up along the sidewalk outside. Then the bride and groom had to run a gauntlet of flower petals and good wishes to get to their car.

Eugenia and Annabelle offered to help clean up, but Kaula wouldn't hear of it. "You go enjoy your last hours on our beautiful island," she suggested.

"You can try to disagree with her if you want," Annabelle whispered. "But I'm going to do exactly what she said."

Eugenia decided to surrender without a fight. She accepted one last hug from Kaula and then waved good-bye. "You haoles come back to Hawaii again soon," Kaula invited.

"We will," Eugenia promised.

* * *

When they got back to the hotel, the Iversons went up to put their children to bed, and George Ann retired to her room to soak her feet. The rest of the wedding guests went out to sit around one of the Hilton Hawaiian Village's five pools.

Once Eugenia was seated and Lady was comfortably arranged in her lap, Annabelle asked Whit, "How did you get permission to bring Lady into the hotel? Did you use Eugenia's old excuse about her being a seeing-eye dog?"

Whit smiled. "No, I considered it, but I decided to stick closer to the truth. I told them Lady was Eugenia's therapy dog and that without her, Eugenia was prone to violent mood swings. The hotel management was happy to make an exception."

Annabelle shook her head. "Too bad we didn't bring Lady along originally." She looked around at the others. "Think of the mood swings we could have avoided."

Before Eugenia could respond, Daphne started to cry.

"I can't believe my baby is married," she said. Her husband, Terry, patted her hand, and she smiled at him gratefully.

"I can't believe it either," Polly wailed, reaching for her handkerchief.

"Don't look at it like you've lost a daughter," Annabelle advised. "Remember that you've gained Quin as a son."

"And now you'll have grandchildren to look forward to," Eugenia added.

"Heaven help us," Annabelle said. "They've only been married a couple of hours, and Eugenia's already making parents out of them."

Before Eugenia could reply, Daphne said, "I hope they like the way we fixed up the little room behind the Surf Shop."

"It's going to be a wonderful surprise for Mila," Annabelle predicted. "The Drummonds told me you managed to get the storage room completely converted into a nice little apartment."

Daphne nodded. "We never could have done it without Sister Kaneohe and her family."

"That woman has an amazing number of nieces and nephews and cousins," Polly remarked.

"She's just amazing all the way around," Eugenia said. "If only I could figure out a way to stop her from hugging me."

Daphne smiled. "She is amazing, and thank goodness she has such a big family. We needed every one of them today!"

"I wish I could have seen the storage room after you finished with it," Eugenia mused. "But I had fun at the zoo." She looked at Whit. "That's someplace we'll have to go next week. Lady will love it."

Whit nodded. "I'll leave our touring schedule in your hands."

"Is the little apartment you made for Mila and Quin behind the Surf Shop as cute as the bungalow?" Polly asked.

"No," Daphne said. "But it's much nicer than it was before we started."

They were quiet for a few minutes, lost in their own thoughts, then Polly said, "Our vacation is over."

"Please don't cry, Polly," Annabelle anticipated. "We'll be coming back in a few months for Eugenia to testify against Darlene."

Polly sniffled, but didn't break into tears. "I guess that *is* something to look forward to."

Annabelle stood. "Well, I don't know about the rest of you, but I've had a long day and am ready for bed."

"Me too," Polly agreed. "Although I would like to go get some of that ice cream at the little shop near the lobby."

"That sounds delicious," Daphne said, pulling her husband to his feet. "Come on, Terry. Buy me some ice cream."

Eugenia looked down at Lady, who was still sleeping in her lap. "I'm not hungry, and I don't want to wake Lady," she said. "You all go on, and we'll be up later."

Once they were gone, Whit said, "Do you think they were trying to give us time alone?"

Eugenia rolled her eyes. "Probably. If they aren't the silliest bunch. Don't they understand the term friendship?"

Whit laughed. "I guess not."

"That's what you are," Eugenia told him earnestly. "The best friend I could have. I can't believe you brought Lady here to see me."

"We've missed you, Eugenia," he told her frankly. "In a friendly way, of course."

"Of course," she agreed.

They were quiet for a few minutes, then Whit asked, "So, are you going to be as sad as Polly when it's time to leave paradise?"

Eugenia smiled. "Paradise to me is an old white house surrounded by flowers in the town of Haggerty, Georgia, with my little dog in my lap and all my friends nearby." She cut her eyes over at Whit. "Although sitting beside a pool in Hawaii with the same dog and the same friends is almost as good. The only thing I'm worried about is the flight home."

Whit seemed surprised by this. "Why?"

"Well, I've only flown twice in my life. The first time was with Winston, and he said I was hysterical the whole time. Honestly, I don't remember much about it."

Whit was smiling. "And the second time was coming here to Hawaii?"

Eugenia nodded. "To avoid the risk of hysterics I took motion sickness pills that put me to sleep for the entire flight, and Annabelle says I drooled. So you have a choice to make."

Whit raised an eyebrow. "Which is?"

"When we're flying home would you rather listen to me scream or wipe my slobber?"

Whit laughed. "I'll take the screaming. That sounds much more entertaining."

"Okay, screaming it is," Eugenia agreed. "But don't say I didn't warn you."

* * *

Before Quin would carry Mila across the threshold into the storage room at the back of the Surf Shop he insisted that she close her eyes.

She complied. Then she said, "My eyes are closed. Now hurry and put me down before you break your back."

She heard him laugh as he stepped inside. "Okay, you can look."

She expected to see a banner saying just married or something on that order. But she was totally unprepared for the transformation that had taken place in the storage room since the last time she'd seen it. The cinderblock walls were now covered by sheetrock and painted a soothing off-white.

"It's French Vanilla, just like the walls at the bungalow," Quin told her.

The concrete floors were hidden by carpet, and curtains hung at the windows. All their furniture had been transferred from the bungalow and arranged with an eye for efficiency and space-economy. The bed was in one corner, blocked partially from view by a folding screen, and the living room furniture was placed to create a sitting area on the other side of the room. The employee lounge—which had formerly consisted of a sink and a card table—had been expanded into a small kitchen, and the employees' rest room had been transformed into a remarkably nice bathroom complete with a shower.

Mila was speechless. "Oh, Quin," she managed finally. "We won't have to eat peanut butter sandwiches for every meal or take spit baths!"

"No," he agreed, as he lowered her gently to her feet. "We now have all the comforts of a real home."

Mila walked over and examined the kitchen. "How did all this happen in such a short time?"

"I had the help of a legion of angels," he explained.

"Angels?"

"Your mother and stepfather, my parents, and about a hundred of Sister Kaneohe's relatives."

It was too much to bear. Mila walked back to Quin and buried her face in the hollow of his neck.

"Hey, don't cry," he pleaded. "Everyone worked hard to make you *happy*."

"I am happy." She lifted her head so she could look into his eyes. "In fact, I'm probably the happiest woman in the world."

Quin gave her a quick kiss and then said, "We should be getting to the hotel so we can start our honeymoon."

She looked around the little apartment. "It's so cute, I hate to leave."

"Then we'll stay."

"We don't have any food," Mila pointed out.

"You can't cook anyway," Quin teased.

"I'm glad to see that you're going into this marriage with your eyes wide open," Mila said approvingly.

"My eyes are wide open, all right," Quin whispered. "And you are the most beautiful sight I've ever seen."

Feeling that mere words were not enough, Mila closed her eyes and pressed her lips against his.

HAGGERTY HOSPITALITY

CHOCOLATE CHIP CHEESECAKE**

Heat oven to 450°F.

3 (8-oz.) pkg. cream cheese
3/4 cup sugar
3 eggs
1 tsp. vanilla
2 cups mini chocolate chips
2 Tbs. whipping cream
1 extra serving graham cracker crust

Beat cream cheese and sugar, add eggs and vanilla. Stir in 13/4 cups of chocolate chips. Pour into crust and bake for 10 minutes. Without opening oven reduce temperature to 250°F and continue baking an additional 30 minutes. Cool completely, cover, and refrigerate until thoroughly chilled.

Topping—Place remaining 1/4 cup chocolate chips and whipping cream in microwave for 20–30 seconds on high until smooth. Let it cool for a few minutes, then stir and spread over cheesecake. Chill until topping sets (about 30 minutes). Serve.

**Arsenic Optional

MISS EUGENIA'S BREAKFAST BISCUITS

2 cups White Lily self-rising flour
    (substitute another brand of self-rising flour if necessary)
3/4 cup Crisco shortening
Buttermilk
Butter

Preheat oven to 450°F. Put 2 Tbs. of butter on a cookie sheet and allow it to melt in the oven. Remove before butter burns. In a bowl, cut shortening into the flour until it reaches a meal-like consistency. Add buttermilk a little at a time, mixing well (you'll probably have to use your hands). When dough reaches proper consistency, roll out onto floured surface until dough is about 11/2 inches thick. Cut biscuits into circles (you can use a glass if you don't have a round cookie cutter) and arrange on the cookie sheet. Bake for 10–12 minutes until light brown.

MISS EUGENIA'S BREAKFAST GRAVY

1/4 cup melted shortening or bacon grease
1 tsp. salt
2 Tbs. self-rising flour
2 cups milk

Heat shortening or bacon grease in a large skillet on medium heat. Add flour and salt, stir until lightly brown. Add milk slowly, stirring constantly. Cook until gravy thickens. Serve over biscuits.

MISS EUGENIA'S BREAKFAST CASSEROLE

2 lbs. Jimmy Dean's sausage (mild)
12 slices white bread (toasted, no crusts)
3 cups cheddar cheese, grated
3 cups milk
1 tsp. Worcestershire sauce
2 tsp. mustard
6 large eggs (beaten)
Salt and pepper

Brown sausage and drain well. Stir in mustard. Grease bottom of a large casserole pan, then line it with 6 slices of bread. Top with half of the sausage and half of the cheese. Combine milk, eggs, and remaining ingredients and pour half of it on top of the first layer. Then put another layer of bread and repeat—ending with the last of the milk/egg mixture. Cover and refrigerate overnight. Bake at 350°F for 50 minutes.

MISS POLLY'S HOMEMADE BUTTERFINGER ICE CREAM

11/2 cups sugar
3 eggs
2 tsp vanilla
1 quart half-and-half
Pinch of salt
Whole milk (approximately 3 quarts)
1 can sweetened condensed milk
4 Butterfingers, crushed

Mix sugar, eggs, and 1 quart of whole milk with mixer. Heat in a sauce pan on low for about 10 minutes. Cool. Pour mixture into ice cream freezer. Add remaining ingredients ending with whole milk (add just enough to get the mixture to the fill line of the ice cream freezer). Freeze according to directions on your freezer.

KAULA'S HAWAIIAN SPARERIBS

2 to 3 lb. pork ribs cut lengthwise
4 cloves garlic (chopped)
1 small (thumb-size) piece of ginger, crushed
1/2 cup vinegar
3/4 cup brown sugar
1/4 cup soy sauce
Hawaiian salt to taste (use Kosher salt if Hawaiian isn't available)
1 can pineapple chunks (save the juice)

Boil ribs in water for 15 minutes. Drain and cut into riblets and put into a skillet. Mix sauce ingredients, then pour over meat and simmer until cooked (about 45 minutes). Thicken the pineapple juice with flour or cornstarch and add to the ribs.

ABOUT THE AUTHOR

Although born in Salt Lake City, Betsy Green spent her formative years in the South. She says she was significantly influenced by the gracious gentility that is an inherent part of southern life. Her most popular character, Miss Eugenia Atkins, is a composite of many remarkable women she has known. And the town of Haggerty was inspired by her father's hometown of Headland, Alabama—the best place on earth.

Betsy currently lives in a suburb of Birmingham, Alabama (Bessemer), with her husband, Robert (Butch). They have been married for twenty-six years and have eight children, one grand-daughter, and one son-in-law. She's the primary chorister for the Bessemer Ward and works in the Family History Center. She loves to read—when she can find the time—and watch sporting events, especially if they involve her children.

Betsy's first novel, *Hearts in Hiding,* was published in 2001. It was followed by *Never Look Back* (2002), *Until Proven Guilty* (2002), *Don't Close Your Eyes* (2003), *Above Suspicion* (2003), *Foul Play* (2004), *Silenced* (2004), and *Copycat* (2005).

Betsy enjoys hearing from her readers, who can write to her in care of Covenant Communications, P.O. Box 416, American Fork, UT 84003-0416, or via e-mail at **info@covenant-lds.com.**